Sophie King is the author of
The School Run

'A lovely debut – warm and engaging' Catherine Alliott

'There is a lot for women to relate to here' Katie Fforde

'A great read (when you're not on the school run, that is!)'
Family Circle

'A funny new novel' *Mail on Sunday*

'Very entertaining' *Prima*

and
Mums @ Home

'Fascinating reading' *My Weekly*

'Entertaining' *Closer*

'Funny and moving . . . captures the love, pain, humour and
guilt of being a parent' *Bella*

By the same author in Hodder paperbacks

The School Run
Mums@Home

About the author

Sophie King is a pseudonym for journalist Jane Bidder, who contributes regularly to national newspapers and women's magazines. She also writes short stories for *Woman's Weekly* and *My Weekly*. She was runner-up for the Harry Bowling Award in 2002 and the winner of the Romantic Novelists' Association's Elizabeth Goudge Award in 2004. She grew up in Harrow and now lives in Hertfordshire with her three children.

SOPHIE KING

Second Time Lucky

HODDER

Copyright © 2007 by Jane Bidder

First published in Great Britain in 2007 by Hodder & Stoughton
A division of Hodder Headline

The right of Jane Bidder to be identified as the Author of the Work
has been asserted by her in accordance with the
Copyright, Designs and Patents Act 1988.

A Hodder paperback

1

All rights reserved. No part of this publication may be reproduced,
stored in a retrieval system, or transmitted, in any form
or by any means without the prior written permission
of the publisher, nor be otherwise circulated in any form
of binding or cover other than that in which it is published
and without a similar condition being imposed
on the subsequent purchaser.

All characters in this publication are fictitious and any resemblance
to real persons, living or dead, is purely coincidental.

A CIP catalogue record for this title is available from the British Library

ISBN 978 0 340 92267 5

Typeset in Plantin by Palimpsest Book Production Limited,
Grangemouth, Stirlingshire

Printed and bound by
Mackays of Chatham Ltd, Chatham, Kent

Hodder Headline's policy is to use papers that are natural, renewable and
recyclable products and made from wood grown in sustainable forests.
The logging and manufacturing processes are expected to conform
to the environmental regulations of the country of origin.

Hodder & Stoughton Ltd
A division of Hodder Headline
338 Euston Road
London NW1 3BH

This book is dedicated to
William, Lucy and Giles who are my foundations
My father and our first house in Harrow Weald.
(Always remembering Doris)
My mother, whose green fingers I dismally failed to inherit
My sister, who got them instead. (Sibling rivalry? Me?)
My friends: better than any double glazing
Friday mornings with Jane
My cousins and their tricks with sticky windows
and drum sticks. (Don't even ask)
My kindly neighbours. (Bet you wish you didn't have
that spare key.)

This book is *not* dedicated to
The boiler that broke down while writing this book/the
boiler company which promised to arrive between
12pm and 6pm but cancelled at 5.55pm/the £3000
that I had to find for a new boiler

Children who walk on clean kitchen floors/use the last
square of loo paper/omit to shut the freezer door/leave
phone messages saying 'someone rang'

Special thanks to:

Phil Patterson from Marjacq Scripts
for believing in my building plans
Carolyn Caughey for getting planning approval
Isobel Akenhead for general housekeeping
Betty Schwartz for handing me my first brick

One

UNUSUAL OPPORTUNITY TO BUY AN ELEGANT
THREE-BEDROOM APARTMENT IN BRIDGEWATER HOUSE,
ORIGINALLY DESIGNED BY SIR CHRISTOPHER WREN FOR A
WELL-KNOWN LOCAL FAMILY.

Features include: large drawing room, kitchen/breakfast room with
French windows out on to the terrace. Private garden and access to
communal grounds with lake and fishing rights.

Shared freehold. Price on application.

'We're all loaded up now, Mrs Howard. Ready to go?'

The removal man had seen it before. Louise knew that from his eyes. The soon-to-be-single mother with three kids, two of whom were old enough to know exactly what was going on. The detached five-bedroom house in the tree-lined road, on the right side of town. The Shaker kitchen with the shiny black and white granite worktops. The long mahogany dining-room table – once capable of seating the dinner parties for sixteen that she used to hold – that wouldn't fit in the new house and which had to be left behind for their buyers who had paid a fraction of its worth for it. The squashy deep sofa in faded William Morris fabric – inherited from her grandmother – that was going to take up the entire floorspace of the new sitting room but which she was damned if she was leaving too.

I've never moved house on my own before. Jonathan, where are you?

'Mum, Mum.' Tim was running up to her, eyes bright with fear. He'd been all right until now, or so she'd thought. 'You've left the trampoline behind. You *said* we could take it.'

She tried to swallow the lump in her throat that was getting bigger by the second. 'Tim, I thought we could but the garden is so small and the neighbours might complain . . .'

'The trampoline?' Justine had got out of the car to see what was going on. For the last half-hour, she'd been sitting in the front seat, staring out of the window. At sixteen, almost seventeen, she'd listened in to too many of the arguments, witnessed too many cold silences. No teenager should have to go through what she had, thought Louise. And she only had herself – and Jonathan – to blame for that. 'You're not leaving the trampoline behind?'

'I can't help it.'

In desperation, Louise turned to the removal man for support. 'It won't fit, will it?'

He shrugged. 'We could come back for it.'

'But it will take up the whole garden.' She glanced pleadingly at her children. 'And besides, aren't you all getting too old for it?'

She recognised her mistake as soon as the words came out of her mouth. At twelve, nearly thirteen, Tim was at that awkward age where he could act like a child when he wanted to and a teenager at other times. Justine might wear make-up and go out with boys but she still liked jumping around on a trampoline. And Nick, at eighteen, would sit on the dark blue shiny material in the evenings, under the guise of revising for his A-levels, while musing into the sunset.

'I don't know.' She hesitated. This wasn't meant to be happening to her. It shouldn't happen to anyone. For God's sake, how did people manage?

Justine's dark brown-almost-black eyes – inherited from her father's side, as was her hair, so different from Louise's blonde looks – sizzled. 'I hate you, Mum.' She flounced off towards the car. 'No wonder Dad went off with someone else,' she yelled before slamming the door shut.

Louise's eyes stung. How could she have said that? How *could* she?

'It's ok,' said the removal man awkwardly. 'They all say things they don't mean.'

She turned so he wouldn't see the tears gushing down her cheeks. 'How much extra will it cost,' she managed to say shakily, 'to come back for the trampoline?'

'I could probably do it for about £50.'

What the hell? She'd spent so much already. The solicitor, the apartment, the move, all the other expenses which she'd never needed to worry about before when she'd been with her husband.

'Ok,' she said, giving up. 'We'll take it. Thanks.'

Wistfully, she looked back at the house. It was so beautiful with its large, airy Edwardian windows and slate roof. The grapelike purple wisteria was just coming out into bloom, resting its trusses on the shutters. In a few weeks, the heady smell would have filled her head when she weeded the lavender beds below the kitchen window. But she wouldn't be doing that this year. Mrs Evans, with her two well-behaved daughters and a husband who would never look at another woman, would be in her place.

Louise shivered. She'd never considered herself to be a materialistic person before and, in comparison with losing her marriage, the house seemed almost irrelevant. During the last few weeks, it had been like living in an empty husk without the security of Jonathan coming home every night. But the garden . . . how she would miss the garden! Even now, as they stood by the topiary bush with its majestic ball of privet, it seemed impossible that they actually had to go and not come back.

There was a cough beside her. The removal man was shifting in his boots from one foot to the other, looking at his watch. Besides, if they didn't get going, it was just conceivable that Jonathan might turn up and then . . . Too late.

'Daddy!'

Over the brick wall, Louise could see Justine running towards her father as the silver Audi TT purred to a stop. This time last year it would have been a treat if Jonathan had come back from the office at 4 o'clock in the afternoon. The kids would have swarmed up to him and she might have suggested that, as he was early, they could all go out to the cinema, followed maybe by dinner at the Italian bistro. What she would never have expected was that while they were waiting for their order at the bistro and he had casually slipped off 'to the Gents', he'd have been ringing *her* from his mobile.

Why oh why hadn't she guessed before it was too late?

Jonathan was already coming in through the gate as though nothing was wrong. He looked at her briefly and then grinned at the children, ruffling Tim's hair.

'Hi, you lot.'

Tim stepped back, clearly furious at the touch. Nick ignored him.

Silently, she thanked the boys, knowing at the same time that she shouldn't.

Jonathan nodded at her. 'Louise.' He said her name clearly, as if it was new to him, as though he hadn't said it every day for the past twenty-odd years. 'Are you all right?'

She could hardly hear him speaking, the way her ears were pulsing with fear. Was this it? Was this really it? The end of shared Christmases and supermarket trips; of evenings spent cosily, or so she'd thought, snuggled up on the sofa; of delivery beds in the hospital and Jonathan urging her on excitedly ('I can see the head, Louise, I can see the head!'); of waking up together on Sunday mornings and reading the papers before one of them, usually her, got up to make tea.

'What are you doing here?'

Her voice came out strangely, as though it belonged to someone else.

'It's my house as well as yours, you know.' He stared at her coldly. 'At least, it was.' He cast an eye at the lorry with Steven Stevens Removals written on the side. 'Got everything in, then, did you?'

'Well, clearly not everything. There isn't room in the flat.' Then she realised. 'So is that why you're here? To check I haven't taken any of your stuff?'

They'd been through the contents in the previous weeks, in painful silence. At his suggestion, she'd put green stickers on the things she wanted and he'd put blue stickers on his.

'You think I came to check up on you?' He laughed dryly. 'No, Louise, I wanted to see the children.'

He glanced towards the Audi and Louise's heart quickened in fear. 'She's not there, is she?'

'What do you take me for, Lou?'

The sound of his old name for her – honed through the years – filled her with unfathomable sadness. She glanced at the boys who were awkwardly kicking stones at each other on the drive, pretending not to listen.

'I don't know. Look, Jonathan, we've got to go. I said I'd leave the keys at the estate agents.'

He stepped towards her. 'Actually, there's something I need to run past you.'

Her heart lurched. He wanted her back! It had all been a huge mistake. It didn't matter about the house. They could buy somewhere else together. Somewhere that would give them a fresh start . . . somewhere that would . . .

His eyes were pleading. 'I know I shouldn't really ask you this in view of everything. But I was just wondering. The dining-room table. Have you definitely agreed to sell it to the Evans? Because I think it would fit into Gemma's house after all.'

'Fuck off.'

The words shocked her as they hurtled out of her mouth. She had never, as far as she could recall, said anything as foul as that before, although she had stopped Justine's allowance for less. Suddenly, she was aware of Nick's protective presence next to her; towering over her with the height of a teenager who had recently shot up fast, both physically and emotionally.

'Yeah, fuck off, Dad. Go be with your girlfriend. We don't need you.'

Tim began to cry. Hastily, she put an arm around him. 'Shh, it's all right.' She glared at her husband. 'Now look what you've done.'

'Ok, ok.' He put his hands up. 'I didn't mean to upset anyone. I'll talk to the Evans myself.'

'Mum!' Justine was standing outside her father's car, yelling. Oblivious of the neighbours who were, no doubt, craning through their upstairs windows. 'Can I go back with Dad while you unpack? He said I could.'

'You did?'

Jonathan shrugged. 'I thought it might help. We could have a pizza or something. Coming, boys?'

'Forget it,' said Nick gruffly.

'You can if you want,' said Louise tiredly.

'I'm staying to help Mum.'

'Me too,' added Tim.

Louise felt a tidal wave of thankfulness.

'We've got to share a room,' added Tim. 'Me and Nick.'

'It will be fun,' said Louise quickly.

Jonathan frowned. 'I hadn't realised. How's Nick going to be able to revise for his A-levels in peace?'

'What's that to do with you?' said Nick tersely. 'You're the one that got us in this mess. Just go, can you?'

Jonathan glanced at the van. 'Sure you'll be all right?'

'I have to be, don't I?'

Louise's eyes swam with tears of self-pity. It was all right for Jonathan. He wasn't going into a strange home. He was going to *her*. It was she who had to cope – for the very first time – with removal men, boxes, strange water systems, unknown heating arrangements, an electric cooker when she'd been used to an Aga for years and a tiny garden that rubbed fences with a neighbour whom she'd never even met.

Through the tears, she watched the Audi TT weave its way down the road. Justine hadn't even said goodbye. It wasn't fair. It had been Jonathan who had wrought the havoc on their lives and yet her daughter – always a daddy's girl – had accepted

her father's misdemeanours and, if anything, sided with him
rather than her. The pain was almost as deep as that night when
she'd discovered . . .

No, she wouldn't go down that road now. She had to stay
sane for the children. And besides, she'd kept this poor man
waiting for long enough.

'Shall I follow you?' she asked.

'Best if we make our own way. I know where it is. Interesting
place. Moved someone there last month, as a matter of fact.'

'Really?' she said, picking off the top of a stalk of lavender
by the path, rolling it in her hand and breathing in its smell for
comfort. 'Who?'

'An American woman and her husband. Seemed quite nice.'
He glanced at the lavender. 'I know it's nothing to do with
me but you can make another garden, you know. Size isn't
everything.'

She nodded. How embarrassing that this total stranger should
see her in such a state of vulnerability and feel the need to
comfort her!

'I'll be fine,' she said stiffly. 'Come on, you lot.'

'Have we got to go?' asked Tim quietly.

Louise put an arm around him. 'Let me tell you something
Granny always used to say. Don't look back because you're not
going that way. Going forward is much more exciting.'

She looked back all the same. Goodbye windows. Goodbye
wisteria. Goodbye garden. Goodbye marriage. How many other
women were doing the same, at this very time, in different parts
of the country?

As they got in the car, she promised herself, like Lot's wife,
not to look back. But just as they rounded the corner of Acacia
Grove, she couldn't resist. A glimpse of white brick. A flash of
wisteria.

And then it was gone.

Two

UNUSUAL OPPORTUNITY TO BUY AN ELEGANT
THREE-BEDROOM APARTMENT IN BRIDGEWATER HOUSE . . .

Mollie tried not to think of the newspaper cutting, carefully folded into four within her skirt pocket. She would deal with that one later. If Nigel thought he could try selling her apartment over her head, he was very much mistaken. Concentrate, she told herself fiercely, despite the heady smell of the lilies adorning the altar which made her feel slightly giddy. Concentrate on the words that are coming out of the vicar's thin mouth. Gideon had always loathed him and he'd hate what he was saying now. So manufactured. So communal garden. So confectionery-laden.

'I am only in another room . . .'

Bollocks. That's what Gideon would say if he was next to her now. Bollocks. I'm not even in this bloody coffin which is a pale ash wood instead of the mahogany that Mollie ordered but which Nigel (never trust an accountant even if he is your own son) overturned as being too expensive. I may not be able to breathe but I can see everything that's going on. And if you think you're putting my wife in a home, you're very much mistaken. She's perfectly capable of looking after herself.

'I am not far away . . .'

If it wasn't for Gideon's comforting presence, she would have gone mad. Mind you, there were a couple of people who might argue that she'd done that already. Mollie smoothed down her slightly tattered pink skirt with the swirling tea roses; the one Gideon had chosen when she had been twenty after they had fucked for the first time. She liked using shocking words every now and then. The good thing about growing old was it gave you the confidence to say what you liked.

That had been the wonderful thing about being an actress. You could jettison the dull, ordinary pebbledash of life and become someone else in another world. And no one would think it strange at all. On the contrary, they feted you. And then, after you retired, they forgot you.

It was then that her husband nudged her sharply in the ribs. 'You should have carried on working.'

She jumped, although not as much as the first time when he'd come back. 'There you are. About bloody time. Shut up, Gideon. Of course I couldn't have.'

'Yes,' he persisted. 'You could. You could have got someone in to look after me.'

'Stupid bastard. I couldn't do that. I love you.'

Gideon brushed her cheek with his lips. 'I love you too. And that's why I'm right.'

'I'd do it all again. Every bit of it.'

Dear me. Had she said that out loud?

'I am only in another room . . .'

That idiot vicar had said that before, hadn't he? Or was it her imagination? Sometimes she imagined life was a giant electric circuit board. You went round and round until you got it right. There were all kinds of combinations that you could plug into along the way. Different words. Different order. Different people. Different choices. Different paths. You chose one lot during one life, another during another. If she got a move on, she could make another path with Gideon.

'Nonsense, you've plenty of time left,' he said, slinging his arm around her on the pew. Hungrily, she devoured his smell. It was on his handkerchief, too, which she always carried around with her. A sort of pine smell, a fragrance that reminded her of bed when he penetrated her, sometimes roughly, sometimes gently, before writhing and pulsating in sweaty passion.

'Look,' he said, running his finger along the inside of her blouse and round her right breast. Her nipples sprang to attention, poking through her blouse; her pink blouse that she had chosen especially to remind him of the fuchsia bush in the garden. 'Look, I'm going.'

His voice was fading.

'No!' Mollie leapt up in alarm. The coffin moved slowly, ridiculously slowly along a grotesque velvet conveyor belt not unlike the plastic one at the supermarket. 'Gideon, come back!'

Nigel got to her first but she shook him off, vaguely aware of the organ playing the final hymn. 'It's all right,' said Gideon. She could swear she felt his lips running over her hair.

'Are you ok, Granny?' asked Flora, slipping her hand into hers while everyone else, including Nigel, was muttering the last prayer.

'Yes.' She made a huge effort to compose herself. 'Say hello to Grandad, darling.'

Flora frowned. 'Don't you mean goodbye?'

'No, hello. Can't you see him? He's right here.' Mollie could have laughed at the expression on her son's face. Purposefully, she slid her hand into her skirt pocket and drew out the newspaper cutting, waggling it in front of his face. 'And by the way, Nigel, don't think I'm moving. Because I'm not.'

'Mother, what are you talking about?'

'You know perfectly well!'

Her voice rose like a stage whisper; she was aware in a rather satisfying way that other guests (such a stupid word for funeral panderers) were staring now the service had finally finished. Nigel flushed a rather unattractive deep red, just as he used to as a child when caught out lying.

'You're advertising my home.' She waved the paper in front of him again. 'Thought you could sell it without telling me, didn't you?'

'Dad, you didn't?' Flora tugged at her father's arm. 'Let

me see. But Gran, this says it's a three-bedroom apartment. You've only got two bedrooms, haven't you?'

'Bloody hell,' said Gideon, drawing on his cigar. 'We got that wrong, didn't we, Mollie?'

'Let me look.' She pulled the cutting out of her granddaughter's hand. Elegant three-bedroom apartment . . . Whoops!

'It's all right, Mother.' Nigel was patting her shoulder. 'You're upset. It's understandable. Mistakes like this happen, especially with everything you've had to go through. Clearly, one of the other apartments in your block is for sale. Although – and I wasn't going to talk about this until later – perhaps you should think about moving. Meanwhile, everyone's waiting for us. Shall I tell them you're not feeling up to it?'

Mollie pulled herself up to her full height. Think Lady Macbeth for courage, she told herself. The reviews some thirty years ago had been astounding. She still had the curled, yellow cuttings. 'I'm perfectly up to it, thank you. Gideon expects it of me. And we most certainly are *not* going to discuss moving later on. There is nothing to discuss.'

Nigel patted her hand. 'Of course I can't sell your apartment over your head – it doesn't belong to me. But you must admit that you can't go on living in that place for ever on your own. You could have a fall. Anything could happen. You need people around you.'

'But I do. I have your father. Don't I, Gideon?'

'Most certainly,' said Gideon in her ear.

It was so good to hear his voice! 'What's it like on the other side?' She'd asked him before but never got a satisfactory answer. Gideon had always been good at that; lots of description but a clever knack of getting out of the practicalities of life. 'Not that different really. I'll tell you later.'

'Gideon? Gideon? Where have you gone?'

She looked around wildly. Gideon had indeed disappeared. In fact, the entire church had emptied now, apart from Nigel and Flora, who were both regarding her with concern, and the bloody vicar hovering by the hymn books. Botheration. He was coming up now, his chin bobbing above his cassock. She couldn't stand men who pretended that a few straggling hairs on the chin constituted a beard.

Whipping out the little gold compact case which Olivier had once given her, she pretended to attend to her face.

'How are you feeling, Miss de May?' The vicar's face was twisted with sickly sympathy. 'I do hope my sermon gave you a little crumb of comfort?'

'Flora.' She snapped the compact shut and turned to her granddaughter. Another advantage of being old was that you really could be extraordinarily rude and no one sent you to bed without supper. 'Will you come with me to the hotel, dear? I'm absolutely gasping for a stiff G and T!'

Three

UNUSUAL OPPORTUNITY TO BUY AN ELEGANT
THREE-BEDROOM APARTMENT IN BRIDGEWATER HOUSE,
ORIGINALLY DESIGNED BY SIR CHRISTOPHER WREN FOR A
WELL-KNOWN LOCAL FAMILY.

'Cool or what? Yes, it's true. Your little sister really is living in a piece of old England just like we used to dream about. David says I might not like it so much in the winter when it's cold and wet, but at the moment, it's perfect. Well, almost.'

Marcie flicked back her shoulder-length auburn hair, adjusted her glasses – she usually wore contacts but today her eyes were feeling sore – and examined the picture from the glossy brochure that she had kept from the purchase of number 2. They had been *so* lucky! David almost hadn't gone to see it because he didn't like the idea of buying an apartment. He had wanted a house with a name, not a number. But right now, it was perfect. His ideas were always bigger than his budget. It was one of the things she loved about him but which also, in a weird way, scared her at times – a bit like their age gap. Virginia hadn't hidden her surprise when Marcie had declared she was marrying a man of forty-two. 'But you're only twenty-five,' her sister had gasped. Marcie had brushed that aside at the time but now occasionally it worried her when he was fussy about things like apartments or houses.

She, on the other hand, had been hooked on their future home from the moment they had driven up the long wide drive, just like Fanny in Mansfield Park. Bridgewater House had stood

out like a bride at the end, waiting for her. Calling out to her.
Telling her that yes, part of this amazing white-plastered mansion
with terraces and statues in the garden really could be hers. It
was everything that she'd always thought of as English. And
there was no comparison with the row houses in Fulham where
they'd been renting, each a clone of the other.

She picked up her pen. *'Sometimes, I can hardly believe we're
here. Of course, it helped being what the English call "first-time
buyers".'*

Marcie stared out of the window. Their own small garden
was bordered with a low beech hedge and beyond that the
communal gardens stretched down to the river. Roses were
everywhere! Pink, red, scarlet, sunset-coloured. She loved to
bury her face in them, especially in the morning when they
were still heavy with dew, and breathe in their scent. If only
her sister was here now to appreciate it with her.

She and Virginia were very different but also similar, perhaps
because they'd both been weaned on the same reading matter
by their professor parents who had specialised in Victorian
English literature. Consequently, both were good at Creative
Writing, as their private letters indicated. But even words
couldn't do justice to this amazing place.

*'You've got to come over as soon as you can. The ceilings are so
high that you could build another room in the space. And there are
fantastic old bits all over the place, including – get this – an old
bread oven in the wall and sash windows! The bathroom is a bit
tacky; why can't the English build a real shower? But the kitchen
is kind of cute. Whoops, there I go again. I'm trying really hard not
to use phrases like that. If I'm going to be English, David says I
need to think like them too.'*

Marcie took a sip of Earl Grey. She was still getting used to
the taste but in her excitement to embrace all things English,
she was determined to persevere. Wow, what was that? A moving
van was coming up the drive. She picked up her pen.

*'How exciting! As I'm writing, it looks as though someone else
is moving in. There are two kids jumping out of the car behind and*

a woman – older than me, I'd guess. They must be moving into the apartment next to us. I heard it had just been sold.'

She put down her pen and stared at the children. One looked quite young – ten or eleven maybe? It was hard to tell their age. He was looking up at the house and then down towards the river. David had said something about fishing rights when they'd moved in. She could imagine him taking their future kids fishing one day. They could wear those cute green boots with frogs' faces on them that she'd seen in the shops. And they could . . .

Stop right there.

The tea cup shook in her hand. Thinking about babies always did that to her. Think of something else, she told herself firmly. Concentrate on the scene in front. The children were following their mother now into the house. Maybe the husband was following later. Perhaps, tomorrow, when they'd had a chance to settle, she'd take them some cookies.

Sighing wistfully, Marcie returned to her letter. *'I don't seem to be getting very far with my thesis. The British Library is an inspirational place – lots of red brick on the outside and very spacious inside – although people say it doesn't have the character of the old one. But it takes about an hour to get there which is a lot longer than it was from Fulham. Besides, I still can't stop thinking about you know what, at the moment. And before you ask, no, nothing has happened yet.'*

Marcie placed a hand on her stomach. Very occasionally, at this time of the month, she felt a sharp ache down one side which, said the consultant, meant she was capable of ovulating. If she could do that, there was hope, given David's fertile history, that she could get pregnant. She sighed, remembering how it had been a whole year now since they had started to try.

'A year is nothing, the consultant says. But it is. It is. It's like playing this awful game where you're sure you're going to win and then right at the end, you find out that you've lost. But you try again because you're sure that this time you're going to strike lucky but when you don't, you just hope it will be the next time. Oh,

Virginia, I wish you were here! I know David is disappointed but he can't show it. And it's so difficult every time the kids come over . . .'

That reminded her. She had to do what David called 'a shop'. As usual, Katy and Robert were coming over for the weekend and it was even more difficult to cope with them now they were on this crazy gluten-and-dairy-free diet their mother had put them on to help Katy concentrate. Because she didn't like the stuff (Marcie could sympathise with her on that one), Robert had to eat the same to encourage her. And it was difficult for her – the stores in Fulham had been far more gluten-and-dairy-free-aware than the local supermarket.

'Well, I'd better go now. Need to make David's dinner and that kind of stuff. Just listen to me! I sound like a regular married lady, as Mrs Bennet might have said.'

Carefully, Marcie folded the letter, placing it in the blue airmail envelope. She could have emailed but both she and Virginia had agreed, before she'd left New York, that they could savour letters. Emailing, as Virginia said, just didn't smell the same.

Marcie stood up. She was sure she could feel a twinge down one side. Or was it her imagination? No. There it was again. That meant that, ideally, she and David should have made love last night or the night before, when her husband had been too tired. But it wasn't too late now, providing it was real soon.

Marcie's finger hovered over the digit '1' on the phone which would take her straight through to David's office. He was in a meeting. She knew that. But when wasn't he? If he came back now, he'd be here in an hour and a half – two, max – and they could get going. On the other hand, it was an important meeting. A partners' one where they would be crunching numbers. Marcie hadn't realised, before she'd married David, how much time solicitors spent crunching numbers as well as doing all the other stuff.

What the hell? She picked up the phone. 'David, it's me.

Yes, I know. It's just that I'm ovulating and if you could be here now – well, not now but you know what I mean – it might work.'

David's voice was tight; deeper than normal; the way it was when he was at work. As soon as she heard it, she knew she shouldn't have rung.

'I'm afraid I will have to call you back.'

No darling. Not even a Marcie. Call you back. Code for I'm-pretending-you're-a-client. Code for how-the-hell-do-you-expect-me-to-come-home-at-this-time?

'Sure.' Her voice sounded flat, even to her. 'Forget it.' Numbly, she let the phone drop back into its groove. Forget it? She'd almost said sorry. But why should she apologise? He wanted a baby as much as she did and one of the reasons – she was certain of it – why they hadn't conceived was that, because of his crazy workload, he either wasn't there or wasn't able to get it up when she was ready.

Moving out hadn't helped him either. The estate agent had assured them that the train service was good, but day after day, David would come back with stories about signal failure or trains that stopped just outside Marylebone and stayed still for ten minutes without an explanation.

Someone ought to schedule that into one of those I'm-ovulating-so-come-and-fuck-me revolving charts that she'd bought from Boots that were meant to indicate her optimum fertile period.

'Hello. Anyone in?'

Marcie jumped. Maybe that was why the English had those weird letter-boxes so they could call through instead of using the knocker.

'Helloooo!'

For two pins – as David's mother was always saying – she'd ignore it but something told her the voice wasn't going to go away. Besides, it was an interesting voice. Not richly and evenly modulated like David's. Not flat and dull either, like the woman from number 6 with whom she'd exchanged remarks about the weather. This voice was sort of bright and bouncy and sassy. Kind of Elizabeth Bennet mixed with Becky Sharp.

'Coming!'

Marcie slipped on her shoes from where they'd been lying under the desk. The ache down her right side was intensifying. Such a *waste*.

'Hi!'

A pretty woman, a bit older than her – mid to late thirties at a guess – grinned at her. Marcie smiled back. It was hard not to. She had what Virginia would have called an infectious face. Sparkly eyes, fresh face without much make-up, hair in a blonde bouncy pony-tail and canary-yellow jogging bottoms. The only thing that spoilt it was her dirty trainers. Why did the British live in these awful things?

'I'm Sally. I've been meaning to call for ages.'

'Come on in.' Marcie's good manners instinctively made her hold the door open wide, despite those trainers. To her relief, the woman kicked them off, placing them neatly on the mat.

'You don't have to . . .' she began.

'No, I always do. Wow, you've got one of the bigger places. They're all different, you know.' She looked around eagerly. 'Blimey, it's fantastic! And I love the rug.'

'Thanks.' Marcie was pleased she'd noticed. 'David – my husband – and I got it from some warehouse in a place called Wembley.'

'Must have cost a bomb.'

'Well . . .' Marcie floundered around for the right words. Sometimes the English could be more direct than her plain-spoken countrymen. 'Which apartment are you in?'

Sally laughed. 'Oh, I don't live here. Cripes, wish I did. No, I clean here. I do most of the flats. That's why I called in. Lydia Parsons – you know, she's at number 6 and is always talking about the weather – said you were looking for help. I've got a couple of vacancies now Sam's at school so I thought I'd come round.'

Looking for some help? Marcie couldn't rightly remember

mentioning it to anyone, although David had been saying for a while they ought to get some help. She'd taken it as a criticism – it was true she preferred to be working rather than tidying up – and after a slightly uncomfortable discussion, they had let the subject drop. Or so she'd thought.

'Well,' she began doubtfully. 'I'm not sure if it's really worth your while. There's only the two of us so I probably just need someone for a couple of hours a week.'

Sally was admiring the watercolour over the mantelpiece. 'Suits me. Say, I like this. I did a module in fine art as part of my degree.'

'You did?' Marcie tried to keep the surprise about the degree out of her voice. Meanwhile, Sally was picking up a small bronze sculpture from David's desk and examining it. Marcie felt she ought to restrain her but wasn't sure how. Besides, she was handling it with such gentleness and genuine admiration that it would have seemed horribly unfriendly to say something.

'Yeah, it's an Open University degree,' continued Sally. 'I'm doing my psychology module at the moment which is really fascinating.'

'Must be hard for you to fit that in with your son.'

'Sons, you mean.' Sally had put down the sculpture now, slightly to Marcie's relief, and was grinning again. 'I've got three. The oldest two are grown-up.'

'Gosh. You don't look old enough. Sorry, I don't mean to be rude but you look kind of youthful.'

'It's my genes.' Sally glanced in the mirror; a beautiful nineteenth-century gilt French mirror that David had had before Marcie met him. 'My mother looks young, too. And my nan. 'Sides, I had my first kid when I was seventeen. So how about it? Do you want me? I can provide references. I'm a hard worker.' She looked at Marcie straight in the eyes. 'And I don't steal.'

'Goodness me, I wouldn't think that!' Marcie felt her neck flush hotly.

'Well some people do and that's when problems start.' Sally ran her finger along the bottom of the mirror. There was a fine line of dust on her finger. Both women looked at it, saying nothing.

'I can do Tuesdays from 10 am to 1 pm if that suits you. Eight quid an hour. And I prefer cash. How do you feel about that?'

'I think it's ok.'

She should run it past David tonight but he *had* said she should get a cleaner. Besides, it would be nice for someone else to do the boring jobs so she could get on with her work.

'There's only one thing.'

Sally's face tightened. 'Yeah?'

'I'm doing some research. Some writing. So, without wanting to sound rude, I need peace. I won't be able to . . .'

'You don't want someone to keep talking.' Sally grinned. 'Suits me. 'Sides, three hours isn't long. I won't have time for nattering if I'm going to sort this place out.'

Marcie's skin prickled. This place, as she'd put it, didn't need *that* much sorting out.

'I've got something I need to mention too.'

Goodness, she'd only met this woman a few minutes ago and already they were negotiating! 'I'll need to bring Sam in the holidays. He won't be any trouble, not if I bring some videos. That ok with you?'

She hesitated. Was this normal for the English to take their kids to work with them? She didn't really like the idea of a kid fingering their stuff – and she knew for certain David wouldn't either – but it seemed rude to refuse. 'Sure.'

'Great.' Sally flicked back her pony-tail. 'Shall I bring my references with me on Tuesday or do you want them before?'

If she went for the latter, it looked like she didn't trust her. On the other hand, the pain down her side was really hurting now and she needed to sit down or go to the loo . . .

'Tuesday will be fine.'

'See you then.' Sally beamed. 'Ta ra.'

She walked past but Marcie could see her eye catching the fertility disc from Boots that she had stupidly left on the hall table.

'New house, new baby? That's what happened to me. Not that Sam was actually planned, between you and me. But the best ones never are.'

Marcie made what she hoped was a non-committal noise. Within a few minutes this woman knew more about her than she felt comfortable with. And she certainly seemed to know more about Sally than seemed decent.

'See you Tuesday then.'

'Yeah. Ta ra. Oh, and pulsatilla.'

'Pulsa what?'

'Pulsatilla. You can get it from good chemists. It's a homeopathic drug. Tablets. Might help your fertility bits and pieces to work. Worth a try. Bye.'

Marcie was too astounded to say anything. For a few seconds, after Sally had shut the door behind her, she stared at it disbelievingly, almost waiting for the woman to come back and apologise for her forward manner. She'd thought the English sat on their feelings! She ought, she felt as she cleared up the living room in preparation for David's return, to feel cross and intruded upon. Instead, she found herself picking up a pen. 'Pulsatilla,' she wrote in loopy handwriting on the Things To Do List that she kept by the phone.

David got back just after the evening news. She was in her dressing-gown by then and those awful plum-coloured slippers that his mother had got her last Christmas but which she felt honour-bound to wear every now and then, especially during these cool summer evenings.

He brushed her cheek, kissing her softly. He smelt of the office and trains. Nevertheless, something inside her melted. 'I'm sorry for ringing,' she began.

He put down his heavy briefcase. 'It's all right. But I can't just drop everything in my position, you know. Come on, let's get cracking now.'

She smiled sadly. 'Too late. The pain's gone.'

'That doesn't mean . . .'

'Probably does.' She stood on tiptoes to smooth back his hair, which was beginning to show grey flecks. She loved doing that; loved stroking it back, even though it revealed deep lines on his forehead. Gently she kissed his eyebrows, running her tongue over them. 'Besides, supper's ready.'

He made an embarrassed face. 'Don't kill me but I grabbed a pie at Marylebone. I was starving but now I'm not sure I could manage anything else. Come on. Let's go to bed. It might still be all right. One of the little devils might just catch your egg.'

She couldn't help smiling at that. But later, as she lay in his arms, looking up at the stuccoed ceiling, Sally swam into her mind. Three boys. At least one unplanned. Then the new family who'd just moved in. Two kids there, too. Everyone else with kids. Everyone except her.

Four

UNUSUAL OPPORTUNITY TO BUY AN ELEGANT
THREE-BEDROOM APARTMENT IN BRIDGEWATER HOUSE,
ORIGINALLY DESIGNED BY SIR CHRISTOPHER WREN FOR A
WELL-KNOWN LOCAL FAMILY.

Features include: large drawing room, kitchen/breakfast room with
French windows out on to the terrace. Private garden and access to
communal grounds with lake and fishing rights.

Shared freehold. Price on application.

'Fuck me. Fuck, fuck me.'

'Sorry, Roddy, mate, you're not my type. Otherwise, believe me, I would. I'm absolutely desperate to get my leg over. In fact, I could just be tempted.'

'Look at this.'

Roddy thrust the copy of *Country Life* into Kevin's hands.

'Very posh.' He passed it back, making a low whistling sound of appreciation. 'Thinking of buying it, are you, on the two quid a week pocket money they give us here?'

Roddy ran his hands through his hair. Every time he did that, he forgot it had been cut to fit in with the regulations. 'It's my home. It's my bloody home.'

'C'mon, mate.' Kevin scratched the stubble on his chin. 'You might be a lord, if you say so, but you rent a one-bed in Battersea, provided it's still there when you get out. Don't tell me you're starting to get delusions of grandeur again. You're meant to have kicked that stuff. And if you haven't, you'd better tell me where you're getting it from cos then I can shop you and get a few extra points myself.'

He would, too, the common little bastard. Roddy began to regret showing the ad to Kevin at all. How could someone like him possibly understand? 'It's where I was brought up,' he said sulkily. 'My bloody stepfather sold it after he married my mother. Sold it to developers. There was a terrible fuss but none of us could do anything, thanks to the papers that he had somehow persuaded my mother to sign. I heard it had been converted but then the shit hit the fan with Annabelle and I had more important things to think about.'

'Like getting stoned and losing your kids and ending up in an expensive dry-out clinic that your stepfather is paying for with the proceeds of the home.' Kevin shook his head. 'You know what they said, Roddy. You've got to stop being mad at people.'

'You can talk.'

'I know, I know. But someone's got to tell you. Let's have a look. Bloody hell, no wonder your stepdaddy's so filthy rich. If each apartment is POA, that means they cost a fortune. He would have got a good price for the lot.'

Roddy hoisted up his jeans which were slipping over his hips. He'd lost weight in this place and it wasn't surprising with the food they served. Such a bloody cheek when the clinic cost a fortune. *His* fortune. The money he should have been given instead of its being diverted through his stepfather. 'He should never have sold it, the bastard. It was my inheritance. The kids should have had that.'

Kevin yawned and Roddy winced; he could smell his stale breath from here. 'Well perhaps he's planning to give them some money directly, rather than through you, just in case you lose it on the way.'

Roddy turned away from him on the bed. That was another thing about this bloody place. How could a man function properly if he had to share a room with someone he'd never met before or who hadn't gone to a school with a recognisable name? Kevin and he had nothing, absolutely nothing, in common. And it irked him – really irked him – that somehow Kevin's fees at this place were being paid for by his local council but that he had to rely on his bloody stepfather to fork out. Where was the justice in that? No wonder he had to pay such high taxes.

Sometimes Roddy wondered if the people who ran the clinic teamed up unsuitable inmates on purpose. Kevin was always pointing out the other side of the story, rather like a parent with infinite patience but an annoying I-know-best manner. Then, at other times, he tried to emulate Roddy's mannerisms or pretend that he came from a similar background, even though he held his knife and fork the wrong way. He'd much rather have shared with Tarquin who was also in here for the same kind of thing. But Tarquin had been roomed up with some comprehensive product who was almost as annoying as Kevin.

'Where did you get this posh magazine from anyway?'

Roddy reluctantly rolled over. 'Annabelle sent it to me.'

Kevin raised his eyebrows. 'Trying to rub it in, is she?'

'Probably.' The shock had brought back the old familiar urge to have a drink – any kind of drink.

The door swung open and he groaned out loud. There was no privacy in this bloody place. Christ, he couldn't wait to get out.

'Phone call time.' Genevieve – pretty girl if you ignored the pockmarks, which he couldn't – stood there, challenging him with her green eyes. She'd made it plain he could have her if he wanted. At times he did but he wanted a drink more. 'Who's going first?'

Kevin was already up, fiddling in his pocket for his phone card. He rang his mother religiously every night; too religiously in Roddy's view. Sometimes he wondered how someone as boring as Kevin could ever have started drinking at all.

'Mind if I do?' Roddy rolled off the bed, swaggering towards Genevieve, his hand in his jeans pocket meaningfully. He picked up the *Country Life* and tucked it under his arm. 'It's rather urgent.'

He brushed past Genevieve, allowing his hips to rub gently but almost imperceptibly against hers. 'Want to meet up afterwards in the drawing room?'

Most of the others called it a lounge but he was buggered if he was going to allow them to infect his vocabulary. Genevieve's green eyes glowed. 'That would be lovely.'

The pay phone was waiting for him. Dryout Hall, as he called it, had very strict rules about that kind of thing. Five minutes' worth every night in complete privacy. If – when – you went over, the Telephone Monitor (this week it was Genevieve) would come in and tell you to stop. Everyone had to buy their own pay card out of their earnings; Roddy's current job was in the laundry and he hated it. The mess on the sheets and underwear was something which no one should ever have to put up with. He wore the plastic gloves provided but God knew what he was in danger of picking up.

But he wasn't going to think about that now. The telephone booth – which afforded very little privacy with its plastic half-cap hood – reeked of disinfectant, which meant someone had relieved himself here in the not too distant past. Roddy shuddered as he dialled his old home number.

'Daniel? It's me.'

The sound of his son's voice almost made his heart stop.

'Hello?'

'It's *me*. Dad.'

For God's sake, didn't he recognise the sound of his own father's voice? He'd told Annabelle this would happen. Told her that if she stopped him seeing them, they'd lose one of the most precious relationships in the world; that of father and son.

'Dad!'

Daniel's voice, which sounded deeper than last time they'd spoken, burst through the pain barrier. He was pleased to hear his father. Roddy could tell that. Yes. *Yes!*

'How are things?'

'Ok.'

God, he hated stilted conversations like this. The counsellor had said that most kids found it hard to have meaningful talks on the phone but sometimes he wondered if it was worth it. There was the initial euphoria at hearing him and then the terrible depression when there was nothing to say.

'School all right?'

'Yes.'

'On an exeat, are you?'

'Dad, we don't have exeats. But half term's next week.'

No exeats? What kind of school was that? He and Annabelle had rowed about that one, too. He personally hated the school she had insisted on sending the kids to. It might pretend to be independent but it didn't have the traditions or mentality of the kind of establishment he would have chosen.

'Been to any good concerts recently?'

Daniel was a keen bass guitarist; just as he had been at that age. He should be around, helping him.

'Yeah.' To his relief, his son sounded more animated. 'We went to Chemical Romance last week. It was naked.'

'Naked?'

For a minute, Roddy had a vision of his sixteen-year-old son cavorting round the Hammersmith Apollo, wearing nothing but a gaggle of schoolgirls.

'Yeah, naked. It means cool, Dad. Didn't you know that?'

Roddy roared with laughter. This was better. Much better. 'That's great. I must remember that. So what's the opposite? What do you call something that's not cool.'

'Clothed.'

'Clothed?' Roddy thought about it for a minute. 'Not as snappy, is it? What else do you kids say nowadays?'

Christ, he was sounding like his own father.

'Well . . .' Daniel seemed to be considering the question. 'There's "Scratch your hairy crutch".'

'*What?*'

'Chill out, Dad. It means "Thanks very much".'

'I hope you lot don't talk to the masters that way.'

'Masters?'

'You know, your teachers.' For a minute there Roddy had felt he'd reached out and touched his son. Now the gulf was widening up again just because he'd used a word which was probably unpolitically correct nowadays. He tried again. 'When I'm out . . . when I'm able to, I'll take you to the next Chemical whatever, if you like.'

'Ok.'

There was an awkward silence again, during which Roddy wondered if he should tell Daniel exactly where he was and why he couldn't see him. He and Annabelle had agreed to tell the children that he was working away from London. He couldn't bear the idea of them knowing that he was in a clinic and that, even when he got out, he wasn't allowed to see them until, or even if, his access appeal worked out. On the other hand, he wouldn't put it past his ex-wife to tell the children the precise circumstances so they never wanted to see him again.

'Well, it was great talking to you. Can I have a word with Helena now?'

'She's watching television.'

Two minutes left. 'Look, Dan, I haven't got much time. Can you get her for me, fast?'

There was a silence during which he could hear the sound of footsteps along a wooden floor. He'd only been there a few times but he could picture it quite clearly. The scrubbed pine floorboards of the Islington house that Annabelle had bought with his money. The three floors into which their furniture had been jammed; furniture which Annabelle had successfully argued she was entitled to. The children's bedrooms with posters of their music idols but no photographs of him, their father, who would have done anything in the world for them.

'Roderick?'

The sound of his ex-wife's stringent tones jolted him. One minute.

'I was waiting for Helena,' he said coolly. 'I haven't got long.'

'She's doing her homework.'

'Bollocks. She's watching television, isn't she?'

'I'm sorry, Roderick, but I don't want you to talk to her. It always upsets her.'

He could feel his body begin to shake. 'That's bloody rubbish and you know it. You just don't want me to have any contact.'

'It's not what I want. It's what the court said.'

'But I'm allowed to ring, dammit. You know I am. And if you hadn't told all those lies, I'd be allowed to see them as well. You wait, Annabelle. And what's this about Bridgewater House . . .'

'Time, Roddy, time.' Genevieve tapped him on the shoulder from behind.

'You'd better go, Roderick.' Annabelle's voice was dangerously sweet. 'I can hear you're being called by your girlfriend.'

'It's the Telephone Monitor, for Christ's sake. Not some fucking girlfriend.'

Out of the corner of his eye, he could see Genevieve wince. Too bad. This was more important.

'How long have you known about this bloody development?'

'Roddy, it's *time*.' Genevieve's voice was angry and final.

'I'll ring again tomorrow,' said Roddy hastily. 'And this time, you'd better let me talk to the kids or you'll be getting another solicitor's letter.'

Click. She'd slammed the phone down.

Roddy rubbed his eyes. 'I didn't mean what I said, Genevieve. It's just that she always does this to me.'

To his horror, his eyes began to prick with tears. Genevieve's face crumpled with sympathy. 'You poor man,' she murmured. For a minute, he considered putting his head on her shoulder. It would be so comforting and he might, with any luck, feel the soft, warm shape of her breasts.

'I don't suppose,' he whispered, drawing nearer, 'I don't suppose you know where I can get a drink? Just a little one. Just something to help me through this.'

Genevieve stepped back as though he had scalded her. 'Are you mad, Roddy? You'll get us both thrown out of here. And believe me, if you've been to some of the places I have, you'd know that this isn't as bad as the rest of them.' She shook her head at him. 'You've got to be strong, Roddy. And then maybe one day you'll get your kids back.'

Miserably, he walked slowly along the corridor towards the lounge. No one was there; it was a relief in one way and depressing in another. Slowly, he sank down on the vinyl armchair – he hadn't realised they made such dreadful things until he'd got here – and picked up the paper.

As he did so, the *Country Life* magazine fell to the floor. Only then did he notice the date. June – the month they were in now – but the year was wrong. The magazine was a whole year old. Why hadn't Annabelle's note pointed that out? A whole year old? That meant Bridgewater House had been carved into flats in the same month that he'd been incarcerated in this place. His home, his beautiful home, had been picked over like a chicken's carcass. How tragic. How utterly utterly tragic.

'All right, mate?'

Kevin sat down next to him, extracting something from his teeth with his forefinger. Roddy edged away, picking up the *Telegraph* from the table before him, and pretended to study intently the news on the front page. 'Kids Need Dads'. That looked interesting. Swiftly, he tore out the article and tucked it in his pocket.

Maybe, he thought, walking back to his room, maybe there was a way out of this after all.

Five

CAR OWNERS!

Please park with consideration on the drive. Recently, we have
had two incidents in which residents or their guests have
blocked someone else in. Thank you for your co-operation.

Bridgewater Residents' Association

'Shall we start unpacking?'

Nick's voice echoed round the drawing room, sending a
shiver down her spine at the strangeness and unfamiliarity of
it all. It only echoed, she knew, because the curtains weren't
up yet and because of the high ceilings.

It was one of the reasons she had bought an apartment here
instead of a three-bedroom modern box which would have been
in the same price range. Number 4, Bridgewater House might
be a glorified flat but at least it had character, like their old
home. It would, she had felt, be easier to make the transition
from a house that had been worth a generous six-figure sum.

She could, if she'd followed the solicitor's advice, have fought
to stay. The courts apparently looked favourably on women
with children still at home. But she hadn't wanted to; not with
the memories. Every time she looked at the phone by the bed,
it reminded her of that night when her world had been blown
apart. The night when Jonathan had phoned her from the office
and said he wasn't coming home again. The night he had told
her about Gemma.

Perhaps, because the shock was still sinking in, she hadn't wanted to be one of those women who fought tooth and nail for the family assets in revenge for what their husband had done. Besides, she could still remember all too clearly the bitter financial arguments between her own parents when they'd divorced during her teenage years, and she didn't want the children upset any more.

'We'll split it down the middle,' she had told the solicitor firmly. 'I don't want him throwing accusations at me about getting his money.'

The solicitor had pointed out that it wasn't 'his' money; that Louise had earned her share by giving up her job years ago and bringing up the children. But she had been adamant. And now here she was.

'I could start unpacking the stuff in my room – I mean ours,' said Nick. He was trying hard, her wonderful eldest boy. She owed it to him to do the same.

Forcing herself, she made her voice sound light. 'That would be great. The men have almost finished bringing everything in now. And after that, we could go out for fish and chips if you like.'

'Naked!' said Tim. 'I'd forgotten it was Wednesday.'

It had been a tradition that on Wednesday evenings, they would go down to the rather nice upmarket fish takeaway and bring it back to munch in front of the television in the kitchen. In the early years, Jonathan had been home early enough to join them but recently he had been later and later. At the time, she had believed him about working into the night. What a fool she'd been . . .

'Where do you want this, love?'

Two rather portly removal men stood sweating in the doorway with her grandmother's sofa. Their presence was reassuring, made her feel she wasn't the only adult in charge.

'In here, please.'

She watched them squeeze it through the doorway, easing one set of legs through first and then the other. It was such an art, moving furniture. Like a dance with the leader knowing exactly which steps to take. Once upon a time she'd thought her marriage had been like that.

'Blimey, it's big, isn't it? Going to take up a heck of a lot of room.'

Louise ran her hand over the fabric. She wanted to smell it; breathe in its comforting fragrance that reminded her of her childhood and the years when everything had seemed so innocent. 'Can you help me put it here?' she said. 'In front of the fireplace.'

That was better. She sank into it, testing its position. Yes, it felt good and it looked in keeping with the room, too.

'What about your other stuff, love?'

She looked at the Victorian oak side-table that she had bought at an auction when Nick had been a baby. That could go by the sofa but there might not be room for the pair of Georgian chairs that had come from her mother. She'd have to think of that one later.

'Right, love. That's it then. We'll drop that trampoline over a bit later, if that's ok? And we'll be off now.' The portlier of the two men – why was it that removal men were often so bulky when they had so much exercise? – was hovering. Of course! He was expecting a tip. She rifled through her purse, feeling awkward. She didn't have much cash, if they were going to have fish and chips. Correction. She didn't have much money, full stop. She'd have to start adding things up as she had done in the early stage of their marriage before Jonathan had earned what he did now.

Her heart sinking, she fished out a £5 note, leaving only ten next to it. 'Sorry it's not more.'

The man slipped it into his pocket with a look that signified he felt the same way. 'Ta, love. Shall I shut the front door behind me?'

'Thank you.'

Louise walked across to the two large bay windows. They really were beautiful. And the window seats were perfect for curling up on and reading a book – if she ever got to that relaxed stage. She watched the removal truck wend its way down the wide drive; as it disappeared out of sight, she felt ridiculously bereft and alone. Too late, she thought of all the things she could have asked them to do, like moving one of the beds to the other side of the boys' room. Or helping her to find the fuse box which the agent had told her was in the kitchen but which she couldn't find.

'You've got to sort that kind of thing out now,' she told herself firmly. 'And you will. You can.'

If only her best friend Amanda hadn't moved last year. If she was still here, she'd be helping. There were a couple of other friends – not nearly as close as Amanda – who had vaguely offered to help out but, in the event, were now away on holiday and another who worked full-time whom she didn't like to bother. It was strange how a marriage break-up affected your circle. Another friend had distinctly avoided Louise since the news broke, as though it might be catching.

'Mum, are we going to get Hector now?'

Heavens, she'd almost forgotten! She'd put the dog into kennels for the day, feeling, quite rightly as it turned out, that she couldn't possibly manage to keep an eye on him *and* move house. But if she didn't get a move on, the kennels would be closed. 'Coming with me?' she asked, grabbing her bag.

'Course,' said Tim, pulling on his beanie.

'I'll stay,' offered Nick. 'Someone needs to be at home for Justine. She's just texted me to say she'll be here soon.'

'Right.' Louise tried to sound perfectly normal but inside her heart was churning. If Justine was on her way here, would Jonathan come in too?

'Won't be long then. Bother, that's my phone. Can you see it?'

'There. In your bag.' Tim reached into it for her. What was wrong with her? Why was she incapable of the simplest things like finding her mobile? And, talking of finding things, where had she put the torch? Since Jonathan had left, she had taken to sleeping with one in her hand for reassurance.

'Hello?'

'Hi. It's me. How are you doing?'

The sound of Guy's calm deep voice made her feel instantly better. 'Well, we've moved in. In a manner of speaking. But it's a terrible mess. I'm just off to the kennels to get Hector.'

'The children will feel more settled when he's there.'

She nodded. It was true. Even though he didn't have children – or a wife – Guy had this instinctive way of understanding them and of saying things that many men, at least in her experience, didn't think of. It was one reason why he'd remained such a good friend. Louise couldn't remember a time when Guy hadn't been around. They had virtually grown up together, each being an only child who happened to live next door to each other. Their mothers had been friends and, as children, the fact that they were of different sexes hadn't mattered. They had climbed trees, played tennis in the park, dug for Australia in the garden and, later, gone to teenage parties together. He'd also been a rock when her parents had divorced. But never once had there been anything romantic about their relationship. At different times during their adolescence, Louise had sometimes wondered if Guy had feelings for her; certainly she occasionally had feelings for him. But each time, she was reluctant to do something about it in case it spoilt their special friendship.

She and Guy had had an agreement that when they met someone special, they would 'run' him or her past the other. So she'd been extremely relieved when, after meeting Jonathan at university and bringing him home for her parents' and, subconsciously, Guy's approval, the two men seemed to get on well.

Initially, it was true, Jonathan had expressed worries that her 'best friend' was a man but he soon realised that there was no more to it than that. Over the years, Guy had become Jonathan's friend as much as hers. Sometimes she'd wondered if he had done this intentionally, as though to prove he wasn't a threat. Either way, it went without saying that he adored the children. Guy lived in London which was only an hour's drive away so he, and whichever girl he was escorting at the time, was a frequent visitor, much to the children's delight.

'Thought I'd pop over later this week, if that's all right.'

'That would be great.' She turned slightly away from the children, cupping her hand over the receiver. 'Have you seen Jonathan?' she asked softly.

'Yes. We had supper together the other night.'

Supper?

'And no, Gemma wasn't there. Are you all right, Lou?'

'Sort of.' Why did her voice come out so small and pathetic?

'Can I have a word with the children?'

'I'll hand you to Nick. Tim and I have to dash for Hector now. Bye. And thanks for calling.'

'It will be all right, you know.' His voice was deep and reassuring. Almost enough for her to believe him.

'I hope so. See you maybe later in the week, then.'

Guy was right. Getting the dog instantly brought smiles to the boys' faces, took away that strained pinched look.

'Get off, you daft dog,' yelled Nick in delight as Hector hurled himself towards him, having been released from the car. 'Get *off*!'

Someone appeared at an upstairs window as the two boys rolled around on the ground in hysterical laughter with the dog on top.

'Shussh,' said Louise, alarmed. 'You're making too much noise. I told you, we've got neighbours all around us now. We have to be quieter. I'm sorry. I know it's difficult.'

Nick, who was wearing a t-shirt with 'Socially Dysfunctional' on it, wrapped an arm round her. She still found it amazing that at eighteen, he towered over her. 'It's not your fault, Mum,' he said, patting her back. 'Come on, Hector. This way, boy. Come and see your new home!'

That was another reason why she'd bought this place: the rooms were a good size for the dog. But even now, as she watched Hector leaping on to the sofa, panting with exhaustion after what Justine called 'pawplay', she wondered exactly how four of them and an overweight chocolate brown Labrador were going to fit in.

'Don't excite him,' she pleaded. 'Or he'll start barking and the neighbours won't like it.'

'Stuff the neighbours,' said Nick dismissively. 'Bet they've got habits we'll have to put up with, too.'

'Look,' said Tim. 'Justine's here! And Dad!'

Oh God, now she couldn't breathe again and her chest was tight. Too late, she wished she had taken those tranquillisers the doctor had given her. Quick! She had to make the place look nice. Show him she could manage. Frantically, Louise began to tip open the boxes, ripping open the sticky brown tape and delving inside. She was sure the cushions were here somewhere; and that throw which would look rather good on the carpet in front of the fire.

'What a mess!'

Justine stood behind her, surveying the room disdainfully. 'I thought it would be sorted by now.'

Louise ran her hands through her hair, reminding herself that it was difficult for her daughter. 'Yes, well, it takes time. Where's Dad?'

'He had to get going.'

'Oh.' Louise felt half-disappointed, half-relieved. 'Well I'll try and get your room sorted out after supper. But I thought we'd go out for fish and chips as a treat.'

'Treat?' Justine's eyebrows arched in amusement. 'Dad and I went to Pizza Express on the way. I'm not hungry.' She glanced at the packing cases still in the hall. 'Which ones are my clothes in?'

Louise felt another wave of panic. She had no idea. Just like she had no idea which box contained the tea bags or the boys' washing kit or even the dog food. So far the scribbled names on the boxes like 'Kitchen' or 'First Bedroom' had provided few clues to the things she really needed. 'I'm not sure. You'll have to open some and see.'

'Great. Thanks.'

'Mum, I'm starving!' Tim burst in, ignoring his sister. 'Are we going to get supper now?'

'Yes. Hang on a tick. I just want to finish this box and then we'll go.'

Justine sniffed. 'Aren't you going to get Hector from the kennels?'

'Got him, stupid. Mum and I went when you were out with Dad.'

'Then where is he?'

Louise's throat tightened. 'He's in the house, isn't he?'

'Don't you mean flat? I'd have seen him if he was.' She looked around her disparagingly. 'It's small enough, isn't it?'

Louise's heart began to race. 'Did you leave the front door open?'

'Yes. There are still boxes outside, so I thought you were bringing them in.'

'Hector!' wailed Tim. 'He could have run down the drive and on to the road.'

'Wait there.' Louise grabbed her coat.

'I'm coming with you, Mum.'

'No.' The last thing she needed was the children finding Hector slumped in the road. She began to shake. The kids adored the dog; and during the past weeks, he had been their – and her – one constant. They would sit by the Aga, talking to him; whispering things into his ears; taking him for walks which was, said the doctor, a wonderful way of letting it all out. How would they cope if something had happened?

'Look!' Tim pointed out of the window. Right at the bottom of the drive, heading straight for the main road, was a large brown bundle of fur.

'Quick,' yelled Justine, running outside. *'Catch him or he'll get run over!'*

Six

PRIVATE PROPERTY!

Access only to residents and guests.

At first, Mollie thought the dog was the effect of the three double gin and tonics she'd managed to get hold of during the funeral reception. Two for her and one for Gideon. But as her husband had disappeared by the time she'd procured the last glass (something he had also done occasionally when he'd been alive), Mollie had had to drink it for him. The result was that she felt pleasantly distant; enough to be able to ignore her son and his ghastly wife who kept reminding her, as if she was likely to forget, about the will reading at the solicitor's office the following day.

Thanks to the gin, she had retorted by firmly declining Nigel's invitation to drive her back home after the reception (Julia and Flora had returned with other relatives), insisting that one of the many young actresses and actors who had attended Gideon's send-off could do so instead. But Nigel had overridden her and now there they were, halfway up the drive to Bridgewater House in her son's new leather-seated Jaguar, when suddenly a large brown dog ran out in front of them, narrowly missing the tyres.

'Bloody hell,' said her son. 'Mother, don't get out! That thing looks vicious.'

Mollie sank to her knees, fully aware she was casting an elegant figure in her high heels and black sheer tights which showed off her legs to their best advantage. 'Nonsense. Come here, darling. What's your name?' She fiddled with her bent fingers until she located the large silver tag on the chain round his neck. 'Hector. Good strong name. Gideon played a Hector once. In Witherham-on-Sea, I seem to recall. Nice stage but terrible acoustics.'

'Mother, for God's sake. He might bite us.'

'Don't be so pathetic, Nigel. He's gorgeous. Look how he's slobbering over me. Thirsty are you, darling?'

'What the hell are you doing?'

'Putting him into the car, of course. You don't want him to run into the road, do you? He clearly belongs to someone in the house. We'll have to take him back.'

Nigel's face began to turn a mottled purple. 'You are not putting that great big muddy dog into the back of my car. Even if he doesn't turn on us, he'll scratch the leather.'

'Nigel.' Mollie took a deep breath and looked her son straight in the eye. How had she ever managed to produce such a wimp of a son? 'I do understand that you're scared of dogs after your experience as a child. But it was a long time ago and you weren't actually bitten, were you? Just frightened. Now this dog is not going to hurt us. Trust me. I have an instinct for this kind of thing. If you honestly think that I am going to leave this dog to roam the countryside and end up a bloody mess on the verge along with my tattered conscience, you are very much mistaken. And before you accuse me of being histrionic, please remember that I have just been to your father's funeral and that it is your duty to pander to me.'

Reluctantly, Nigel started the engine. 'Well, all right. But I'm only taking this thing to the house. And if we don't find its owner, we're calling the police.'

Mollie began to stroke Hector's fur. It felt soothing, rhythmic. She and Gideon had always wanted a dog but it would have been impossible with their jobs. No matter that his paw had ripped her 10-denier tights. He was a real beauty and he had a surprisingly calming effect on her. 'There you are, see. Good as gold. Clearly used to cars.'

Nigel glanced petulantly at her from his rear mirror. 'I thought there was something in your lease about not having pets. I'll have to look into that if it does belong to someone at Bridgewater House. The last thing we want is dog mess all over the place.'

'For God's sake, Nigel, will you stop being such an old woman. Can't you talk about something else? Like your father?' Mollie's eyes began to water. Hector looked up at her with deep brown eyes and she fingered his fur. 'You understand, poppet, don't you? And we've only just met.'

God, she missed Gideon! It was all very well him turning up every now and then. When he'd first died, she'd thought that was it and it was such a relief when he made an appearance, as he had always promised he would. But these appearances were unexpected and unpredictable, rather like performing ad hoc on the stage without a script.

She blew her nose just as Nigel crunched to a halt on the gravel by the front door. They all had their own front doors here, thank heavens. None of these shared entrances that led off corridors to flats. She'd been to set-ups like that belonging to less able friends; former acting friends who could no longer manage to walk properly and who now lived in warden-controlled establishments. She'd rather die than go somewhere like that, despite Nigel's clumsy hints.

'What the hell is that dog doing?'

'Careful, boy, careful,' she crooned. Too late, she tried to put her hands under his paws to save the seat. Oh dear. Already, there was a criss-cross of lines in the leather where he was furiously standing on his back legs, nose pressed against the window, barking.

'Is that your owner, poppet?'

Nigel was already out of the car and opening the rear door. Mollie stifled a giggle as the dog leaped forward, almost knocking her son over.

'Watch out.' Nigel was brushing down his Gieves and Hawkes suit. 'Is this animal yours?'

A pretty blonde woman – not young but not old either – was kneeling on the gravel, her arms around the dog. Three children – biggish children – came running up, yelling and screaming. 'Hector, you're safe.'

'Thank you so much.' The blonde woman stood up, holding out her hand to Nigel. 'We literally spotted him seconds ago, racing towards the road, and we were so scared. The children had already started running.'

They were breathless, Mollie noticed. The older boy was leaning over, hands on his knees, gulping in the air. Had they passed them on the drive? If so, she hadn't noticed. When she was young, she had noticed everything.

'Don't thank my son,' said Mollie smoothly. 'He would have abandoned your Hector to the juggernauts. I insisted we brought him back.'

Nigel had the grace to look ashamed.

'How did you know his name was Hector?' demanded the younger one who had a wonderful smattering of brown freckles. Very Just William-y. Nigel had been born with a pale skin that had done him few favours.

'It says so, darling, on his nametag.' Mollie beamed at him. 'Have you just moved in? I heard that the house next to mine had been sold.'

The girl – who sported a crop of angry spots on her forehead – scowled. 'It's not a house. It's a flat. We used to live in a house but now we've got to live in this snothole.'

Mollie drew herself up to her full five foot three and a half inches. 'I'm sorry that's how you see it, dear. Once you get to know our beautiful Bridgewater House, you will realise it's not a snothole at all, as you so graphically put it. And in fact, most of the residents do refer to their homes as houses because they're not typical apartments.'

The blonde woman was nodding. The skin below her eyes was slightly dark, suggesting lack of sleep. 'Exactly.' She held out her hand to Mollie. 'I'm Louise. Louise Howard.'

'Mollie de May. I'm very pleased to meet you, dear. Something tells me we shall be excellent friends.'

Nigel sighed audibly and Mollie shot him a look of pure irritation. He hated it when she acted impulsively, but that was her; and she was proud of it. Her gut instinct was infallible. And she knew that this pretty woman with sad eyes was someone she could understand. So they were downsizing, from what the girl had said. One more widow perhaps? Or yet another marriage casualty? Life was so full of them; she simply couldn't understand why it hadn't happened to Nigel and his wife. They were certainly thoughtless and self-centred enough.

The woman – what was her name again? – was looking at her in a way Mollie had grown over the years to enjoy. It was a look of recognition. A look that said . . .

'I'm so sorry to ask, but aren't you the actress, Mollie de May?'

She did a little bob. 'One and the same.'

Nigel coughed. 'Please excuse us. My mother is very tired. We have just returned from my father's funeral.'

The woman gave a little gasp, putting her hand over her mouth. 'Of course. I'm so sorry. I read about his death in the paper.' She blushed. 'He was wonderful. My mother used to talk endlessly about his films.' Her eyes became milky with compassion. 'It must be very difficult for you. Please tell me if I can do anything to help.'

'Thank you, dear. That's very kind of you.'

'We are managing perfectly well,' said Nigel stiffly. 'As I said, we really have to go, Mrs er . . .'

'Louise,' she prompted.

Ah, yes. Of course. Mollie felt like stamping. Only a few years ago, she used to boast she never forgot a name or a word, like so many of her contemporaries. What was happening to her?

'Louise,' said Mollie graciously. 'Would you like to come for coffee tomorrow morning? Around eleven?'

'I would love to.'

'Mother – we've got the appointment tomorrow.'

'What appointment?'

'The solicitor's appointment.'

Nigel's irritated voice sounded like crunched gravel.

'I know that, dear.'

How could she have forgotten?

'I was thinking afterwards. Maybe the afternoon would be best? About four?'

Louise was looking at Nigel questioningly. 'If you're sure it wouldn't be too much.'

'Quite sure, dear. I can tell you all about this place and who to avoid.' She looked at Nigel. 'As well as who is a good sort. We will see you then, including the children. And please bring Hector.'

Nigel made a spluttering noise which he followed by a great show of producing a white handkerchief and blowing his nose.

'Goodbye, dear. See you tomorrow.'

Later, when Nigel had finally gone, taking with him one of his father's bottles of 1907 claret as a 'gift' for the solicitor tomorrow, Mollie sank back on to the chaise-longue which she and Gideon had found in an enchanting antique shop in Guildford some years ago. If she closed her eyes, he might come.

'Gideon,' she whispered softly. 'Gideon, are you there?'

There was a soft russle of breeze through the open window and she could smell the tobacco plants outside. The curtains were still open but outside it was getting dusky. Almost 9 o'clock now. Not nearly time for bed and yet she was tired. So very tired.

Through the wall she could hear Hector whining. Not a loud whine; not enough to be irritating, even if she was the kind to let a dog do that to her. But a sad, plaintive whine. Maybe he was used to more space. No wonder he had tried to run free. If she could do that, she would run as well. Down to the road, past the gate, into the road and into Gideon's waiting arms.

'Shut up, Mum. *Shut up!*'

A girl's voice – shrill and angry – rose above the dog's whining. It was coming from the same direction. Mollie took a slug of gin. That woman – Louise, wasn't it? – had seemed rather sweet and almost ethereal in a Dante-like way. She could take to her. But she did hope the whole family wouldn't prove to be too noisy for their own sake. There were one or two people in Bridgewater House who would soon step down on them if they did.

One more sip. Long and deep. Slowly, Mollie swung her legs on to the floor and walked, slightly unevenly, over to the gramophone player that she and Gideon insisted on retaining, despite the bright modern CD system Nigel had bought them one Christmas. Topping herself up on the way back – nothing like Bombay Sapphire! – she leaned back on the chaise, closing her eyes. Ah, that was better. Strains of Chopin filled the air, taking her back to their first date where there had been a piano player at the Savoy. Lunch, Gideon had suggested. They had ordered salmon and new potatoes but had decided, before it had even arrived, to leave early. He had booked the room before lunch, without her knowledge. His confidence slightly unnerved her but her body by then had become melted butter, dissolving any misgivings.

So many years ago! If Gideon had managed just four more months, they would be celebrating their Golden Wedding. Her eyes began to prick.

'Now, now. None of that, old girl.'

'Gideon?' she called out.

The curtains rustled again. She stood up, wavered slightly and then steadied herself as she walked with her heart beating towards the window.

'Gideon?'

It was a whisper now. She could feel a pulse of anticipation as she put out a hand and felt through the material to the wall. Then, dramatically, she pulled them wide open. Nothing. Disappointment washed through her like a power-shower of pain. Outside, it was dark. So dark that maybe he was looking in; able to see her without her seeing him. She'd leave the curtains open and turn on the lamps in the drawing room. It might encourage him.

Whoops. Now she'd slopped gin on the carpet. Better get a cloth to mop it up or Nigel would accuse her of not being able to cope again. Not, she thought, as she went into the kitchen, that he could criticise the state of the rooms right now. Sally had been in as usual, bless her, and there was a fresh pine fragrance emanating from the worktops. She had left a note, too. How very, very kind.

Mollie sat down at her square, warm, honey-pine farmhouse kitchen table which had come from the props of a Pinter play many years ago, to read it.

> *Hope it all went all right. You're probably feeling like shit now so I've left you this. It's a homeopathic rescue remedy – quite safe. Love S.'*
>
> *PS. Someone called Poppy rang. Said she was sorry she couldn't make the service but will write. PSS. We need more lavender polish so I'll bring it next time to save you the trouble.*

Gideon loved lavender. It reminded him, he said, of that first summer they spent in Norfolk where the lavender fields cut swathes of purple and the heady scent made them sneeze as they lay on the ground. Since then, she had always sprayed the sheets with lavender scent, right up to the end when his senses began to go. Now, as she slid between the sheets, she could smell it still.

'Gideon!'

Shocked but elated, she stared down at him at the foot of the bed where he was lying on his front.

'I said I'd be back.'

'I know but . . . oh, Gideon! *Gideon!*'

She screamed slightly as he began to kiss her with his tongue; circle her with long slow licks up and inside. '*Oh.*' He was biting her now; sharp nips at her clitoris, making her gasp with pleasure. She gripped his head tighter, feeling her nails dig into his scalp.

'Now. *Now*,' she demanded. '*Please!*'

He was smiling at her as he eased himself on top. Gratefully, she felt his weight; weight which had dropped so sharply at the end but which was now the way it always used to be. She closed her eyes as he thrust himself in, pumping and kissing her neck at the same time. She never had to pretend with him; it had been a rule. No white lies. No fantasies. Straight talking. Pure fucking. Her chest tightened and she was breathing in her throat the way she always did when about to come. His breath was sharper and more rapid too and his mouth was twisted slightly; the sign that he was about to do the same. Now. Now. *Now.*

Gratefully, she sank back on to the sheets. 'Thank you,' she whispered. 'Thank you for coming back.'

Then she opened her eyes.

He had gone.

Mollie was fully dressed and waiting by the time Nigel arrived the following morning to pick her up. Surprisingly, she had slept deeply without her usual dreams. Nor had there been any noise from the new people next door, although she had seen one of the children – the smaller boy – walking the dog on a lead down to the lake.

'You're ready,' he said, taking in her appearance. She'd purposefully dressed carefully; pale green Jaeger linen suit and elegant wide-brimmed hat to match. Her usual string of pearls. Glossy 15-denier tights that showed off the shape of her legs and crocodile high heels that were taller than her usual kitten heels but which looked better with the suit as long as she didn't have more than one gin.

'You said you'd be here at 9.30 a.m., so here I am. Ready and waiting.' She brushed his cheek coolly but the contact made her cringe guiltily. As they walked to the car, she could see the boy coming back across the gardens with the dog and she waved at him. He waved back.

'We don't want to be late,' said Nigel, looking at his watch.

'Nigel,' she said sadly. 'People like you are never late. Please stop fretting.'

The drive into London took longer than expected. The solicitor was one they had used for years, when Gideon had started to get well-known; shortly before her fame had followed suit. The firm was just off Holborn but had its own private parking space. Something that no doubt was covered by the exorbitant fees. She had often suggested to Gideon that they switch to a smaller and less expensive firm but he had enjoyed the cachet. Besides, it had a good libel department and on the few occasions when they had needed to employ it – when something scurrilous had been printed, as happened in their profession – it made him feel secure and not a trifle smug to know their interests were fully protected.

Mollie allowed herself to be ushered into a waiting area with a large circular mahogany table covered in glossy magazines and broadsheets. On the walls were dark, stuffy portraits of legal-looking men; no women.

'Miss de May?'

Mollie uncrossed her legs slowly and rose, straight-backed. 'How do you do? I'm Amelia Rosani.'

She looked in confusion at Nigel. 'We usually deal with a Mr Griffiths.'

'He retired, Mother. Remember I told you?'

Had he?

'Please don't worry, Miss de May. Mr Griffiths left copious records and I can assure you that I have had several years' experience in this field.'

Mollie appraised the woman. Short. Black suit. Thick, hourglass pins. 'I'm sure you do.' She smiled. 'Besides, a will is a will. Gideon and I made them at the same time, together. So I know exactly what is in it.'

'Would you like to come this way?'

They sat at a table with a silver tray of coffee. Proper sugar lumps. Good.

Mollie stirred her cup as the woman started to speak. Words

began to drift in and out of her head. Annuity. No pension. Uncertain profession. It sounded important but she felt so sleepy.

'Wake up,' whispered Gideon urgently. 'Listen.'

'I don't understand.' Nigel's voice jolted her awake. 'Are you saying that my father has divided his estate four ways?

The woman with the bad legs was nodding. 'Precisely. Although he has left the apartment to Miss de May, his liquid assets in the form of building society accounts and shares are to be divided equally between yourself, your mother and two further beneficiaries.'

'Who are they, darling?'

Mollie's voice came out clearly as though she was projecting it to the back row.

'Poppy Marlowe and Rupert Bright.'

'What?' roared Nigel. 'What right do they have to our money?'

Mollie heard her voice reply, 'Because they're our friends, as you know. Part of the young crowd that come and see us every now and then.'

'I understand that you and your husband were very kind to younger actors and actresses you worked with.'

'Well, yes. We tried.' Mollie frowned, worriedly trying to make sense of what she'd just heard. 'We always keep up with the ones we got on with particularly well. We enjoy their company – they keep us young – and many would come to us for advice. Not just on their career but for other things too.'

'Great,' muttered Nigel. 'So now they're going to do us both out of what is rightfully ours.'

Mollie could feel her temples beginning to throb. 'I don't understand. Gideon and I made our wills at the same time. My share was to go to him and then our son. His to go to me and then Nigel. I can see that he might want to help others but surely not at my expense?'

'He didn't tell you that he made a new will?' said the woman lawyer softly.

'No.'

'When did my father do this?' demanded Nigel. Little red veins stood out at the side of his neck, Mollie noted, the way they had done when he'd been an angry young man.

'Earlier this year. April the eighth.'

'Can we challenge it? Was he in his right mind?'

Mollie frowned. 'Of course he was. He was in his right mind almost up to the end. You know that perfectly well. April. That was just before that diagnosis.'

'Do Poppy and Rupert know about the will?' Nigel sat forward urgently, making his ridiculous potbelly protrude even more clearly through his smart striped shirt.

The solicitor picked up her pen. 'We will be writing to them.'

Mollie began to stir her almost empty coffee cup. The froth was sticking to the underside of the teaspoon. She would like to have licked it off. She'd have liked to have been sitting back in her kitchen with Gideon who could, she was sure, explain all this quite simply.

'Poppy rang last night,' she said quietly. 'To apologise for not being at the service. She's a nice girl.'

Nigel scowled. 'May I ask how old she is?' enquired the solicitor.

Mollie smiled sadly. 'Early twenties, I think. So difficult to tell nowadays. She was in that television comedy that was on the other month. Tall, pretty dark-haired girl with Helena Bonham-Carter eyes. Now what was it called?'

Nigel waved his hand impatiently.

'Of course,' she continued, 'we haven't seen Rupert for a while now although I do remember he used to spend a lot of time with Gideon, talking about his marriage. Poor man. His wife left him, you know, because he was gay. So sad when that happens. In our day . . .'

'Mother, I don't think you realise how serious this is.' Nigel reached out across the table and took her hand. His own felt hot and clammy. 'I'm not just upset for myself, you know. It's you too. Your share of the money will only just cover the maintenance charge on the house and your daily expenses. I shall, of course, make over my share of the money to you . . .'

'Nonsense, darling,' said Mollie faintly.

'I insist, Mother.'

The solicitor tapped her pen lightly on the pad of paper in front of her. 'Perhaps Miss de May has private means of her own?'

'No.' Mollie shook her head ruefully. 'We used to pay my earnings into Gideon's account. He said it was simpler that way and it's what we did in those days . . .'

'Bloody marvellous,' muttered Nigel, sinking his head into his hands. 'It's worse than I thought.'

Mollie felt a shiver of fear pass through her. 'I'm not moving, you know. Gideon and I adore Bridgewater House and we've only been there for a year. I have no intention of going.'

'Mother.' Nigel lifted his head and he looked so red-eyed and weary that she almost felt sorry for him. 'If you can't afford to live there, you have no choice.'

'No choice? What do you mean?'

He rubbed his eyes. 'No choice but to come and live with us. That's what I mean.'

Seven

**BRIDGEWATER RESIDENTS' ASSOCIATION
MEETING REMINDER**

You are all cordially invited to our monthly residents'
meeting on Friday 27 June at 7.30 pm at number 6.
Items on the agenda include the following:

Maintenance charges
Preparation of the summer barbecue
Any other issues

This is an excellent chance for newcomers to meet the neighbours!

Cool, thought Marcie, picking up the bright red piece of paper
which had fluttered on to the ground. *Excellent chance for
newcomers to meet the neighbours*. So far, the only person she
had spoken to had been the dull flat woman from number 6
whose name she remembered Sally telling her was Lydia
Parsons. It was strange, really. She'd had visions, when David
and she had first moved in, of everyone meeting up for cookies
and chat. But it wasn't like that at all. The individual occu-
pants (heavens, she'd nearly said inmates there for a second)
seemed to live very separate lives.

Any other issues . . . Marcie sucked in her breath. What she'd
really like to do is talk about that dog. She was glad now she
hadn't had time to go round with cookies. Only yesterday she
had almost walked in dog mess on the drive that had made her
stomach turn. If she had been pregnant and had come into

close contact with it, it could have given her toxoplasmosis! David had been livid but when he'd gone out to investigate, it had gone.

Presumably, the woman must have got rid of it with her poop-a-scoop but it wasn't, as David said, what they'd expected in an exclusive development like this. As for the noise – that electric guitar in particular – well, maybe someone else would say something at the meeting and then she needn't stick her neck out.

Summer barbecue . . . That sounded nice. Really neighbourly. When were they planning to have it? She hoped it wouldn't be during the last two weeks of July. She and David had just booked up for Italy; one week in Florence and another in Rome. She'd always wanted to go to Italy, had hankered after it, especially after reading *A Room with a View*. Even better, Virginia was joining them in Rome and then coming back here for two more weeks. Marcie felt sick with excitement. Maybe by then; just maybe, she'd be pregnant!

Friday 27 June at 7.30 pm. There was no way David would be back at that time. She'd have to go alone. And Robert and Katy were arriving after school on Friday so she'd have to take them. The last time she'd left them alone in the apartment, they'd nosed around and told their mother about the new Hockney painting which, she was sure, had led to those demands for increased maintenance. David had agreed – they had the money after all – but it didn't strike her as being fair, especially now Diana had a new boyfriend who was clearly well off.

Was there an RSVP? Marcie examined the invitation one more time. The English could be so formal about these things, although the red paper was a nice touch. Kind of cute. Carefully, she pinned it on the kitchen noticeboard along with reminders about garbage collections and emergency electricity numbers.

'Hiya, Marcie!' The knock at the kitchen window made her almost leap out of her skin.

On the other side stood Sally. But she looked different from last time. In fact, she had pink streaks in her fringe! 'Be round in a minute. Just got to pop into Mollie's first. Won't be a sec!'

It took Marcie a couple of seconds to register. Tuesday. Ten. Even though it was actually nearer 10.30. Sally. Cleaning woman. Or cleaning lady as the English called it. Marcie frowned; Sally had been wearing that rather scruffy fleece again. If those were the kinds of standards she kept, she would have to be very firm.

She didn't want to be known by her first name, either. In fact, how dare Sally address her as Marcie? This Mollie woman might not mind, but in Marcie's view, it was very important to keep the distinctions separate. If she got too chummy, how could she tell her if the floor wasn't up to scratch? That was the weird thing about the English. Sometimes they could get so worked up about class distinctions – like David's mother – in a way that it was virtually Dickensian. And at other times they pretended they had known you for years after a few seconds, like that man from the wardrobe-measuring service who had come round to give a quote the other day.

Knock, knock. Marcie straightened her back – Virginia always said it made you feel stronger inside – and went to open the door. Sally was holding out a bunch of dahlias. 'Really sorry about being late but I had to check up on Mollie, poor thing. Thought you'd like these – from my garden. Got masses of them. Call it a sort of moving-in present, although I know you've been here a bit, haven't you?'

'A month,' said Marcie stiffly.

Sally flung her fleece on the back of a chair and adjusted one of her silver hoop earrings. She had a small silver chain round her ankle too, noticed Marcie.

'Bet it's a bit different from America, isn't it? Where do you come from? New York?'

Why did everyone presume that Americans came from New York?

'San Francisco, actually.'

'Wow!' Sally's face lit up. 'How *amazing*! Have you seen the Golden Gate Bridge? And does it really look as though it's made of gold?'

Marcie's face began to smile without the rest of her body's permission. 'No, it doesn't. It's kind of brown. But yes, I have seen it. In fact, I've often walked over it. It's really windy.'

'I've always dreamed of going to America.' Sally looked wistful. 'I think I'd like to start in New York, though. Ever been to France? I went to Lille on a day trip last year. For my fortieth, it was. The kids treated me.'

'Is that so?'

Marcie was beginning to feel panicky. If she wasn't careful, she'd be asking this woman if she'd like a coffee before she'd even started to do any work. Besides, she needed to get on. There were all those notes to transcribe from her recent trip to the British Library and she needed to email her tutor.

'Right, well, can't stand here all day.' Sally rubbed her hands as though the delay was Marcie's fault. 'Why don't you tell me where you keep all your stuff?'

Relieved, Marcie showed her the neat plastic basket of dusters and polishes and disinfectant she had stocked up on.

'It will take me a bit longer than usual to get some decent results at first,' said Sally, shaking out the duster as though it had been used when, in fact, it was brand new. 'It's always like that when there's a fair amount to do.'

Marcie's eyes narrowed. 'I'm not sure I'd say there was that much.'

Sally sucked in her breath. 'Well, those windows could do with a good going over for a start. Pity you're so near the front of the house. You get all the dirt from the cars pulling up. Still, we'll sort it out.'

Marcie began to wish she'd taken the reference offer up after all. 'Who else do you clean for, apart from the girl you mentioned?'

'Girl?' Sally tilted her face questioningly.

'Mollie.'

'Mollie's not a girl!' Sally roared with laughter. 'I'll tell her that. She'll be well chuffed. Mollie's an old lady. Well, she's in her seventies. Used to be a famous actress. You probably heard of her. Mollie de May. She was married to Gideon Winter. Died a couple of weeks ago, poor sod. Mollie's bereft without him but then you would be, wouldn't you, if you'd been married that long?'

Mollie de May? 'I saw her once on Broadway in *Lady Windermere's Fan*,' she said breathlessly. 'I was a teenager and it was the first play I'd ever gone to. She was amazing.'

'Yeah.' Sally nodded, her eyes sparkling. 'She is. So was he. I take it you haven't met her yet, then?'

'No. But we've got a residents' association meeting coming up. Maybe she'll be there.'

Sally shook her head. 'Not in the state she's in. Keeps talking to her old man and thinking he's talking back to her.'

Marcie frowned. 'But he's dead.'

'Exactly.' Sally's mouth tightened. 'It's the shock, I suppose. Quite sudden it was, at the end. I mean he'd had the cancer for a while but they thought they'd got it. Then it went to his brain and it was all over in weeks.'

Marcie felt goosebumps prickling her arm. Instinctively, she felt the urge to change the topic of conversation. 'Who else do you work for here?'

Sally waved her hand airily; her nails were short, Marcie noted, and her hands worn. 'Most of them. I was going to call on the new lot who've moved in, after you, to see if they want someone.'

'So you're short of work?'

Sally shrugged. 'I lost a couple of people, not here but in town, at the beginning of the year. One went to Saudi and the other got divorced.' She looked at Marcie sharply; when she didn't smile, she seemed almost threatening. 'Don't worry. I wasn't sacked. And when I'm late, I make up the time. Ask the others at your residents' association thing.'

Marcie coloured. 'I don't need to.'

'Right.' Sally was nodding as though she'd said the right thing. 'I'll start with the windows then, shall I? And by the way, when you get round to coffee, mine's two sugars. Second thoughts, let's lay off the coffee.'

Marcie was beginning to feel increasingly confused. 'Why?'

Sally patted her on the shoulder. 'Not good if you're trying to get up the spout. In fact, I brought some green tea with me, just in case you didn't have some. Get the pulsatilla, did you?'

Marcie felt unable to do more than shake her head.

'Thought not.' Sally patted her pocket. 'Brought some of that and all. You can pay me when you sort out my wages. Oh, and by the way, I did say I prefer cash, didn't I?'

The apartment was still gleaming by the time the children came over on Friday night. Sally might be a little weird but she did a good job. Katy's and Robert's rooms looked wonderful and Sally had even gotten rid of those cigarette marks that Robert, who shouldn't be smoking at his age anyway, had left on the dresser in her bedroom.

'Hi. How're you doing?' called out Marcie from the front doorstep as Diana's red Saab convertible pulled up, scattering gravel at her feet. She had always been determined, since meeting David, that she was not going to be one of those second wives who resented their husband's first family. It made it easier, of course, that David had been divorced for a couple of years before she'd met him, so no one could accuse her of being a marriage-breaker. Not that you would think so from Diana's frosty manner.

'Feel like a coffee?' she called out as the kids unloaded their gear from the trunk.

Diana stared stonily ahead, without putting down the window. She'd had her hair cut into a spiky style that made her look even harder. Sometimes Marcie would feel a frisson of panic at the fact that she was so different. How could David have ever fallen for someone like that? Had he chosen her because she was different? And if so, or even if not, what did it say about her?

'Ask your mom if she wants to come in, can you?' she said to Katy who was already walking past her without so much as a hello.

'Forget it,' said Robert, slamming the trunk. 'She can't stand you. Doesn't know what Dad sees in you. Says you're young enough to be his daughter.'

Marcie tightened her lips. The weekend always started like this when David wasn't around. As soon as he returned from work, the kids would stop being outright hostile and be cool but polite to her.

Well, as she'd told herself enough times already, if that's how they wanted to play it, she'd go along with their game. It was an awkward age, seventeen and thirteen. She could remember exactly how she'd felt then. On the other hand, like Virginia said, she couldn't let them go on being impossible for ever. If only they could be awful to her in front of David, then he would do something. But when she'd started to tell him about their nasty remarks, something strange flitted over his face and her gut instinct told her not to push it. He was their father, after all.

'I've made your favourite supper,' she said, standing at the doorway as they slung their bags on to Robert's bed. Already, there were scuff marks on the carpet – maybe cream hadn't been such a great idea after all – even though they knew they were meant to take their shoes off. 'Spaghetti bolognese with gluten-free pasta.'

'Ugh,' said Robert, making a face.

'Come again? Last week, you said it was your favourite.'

'Yeah, well I've gone off it now.' Brazenly, he opened a packet of crisps and proceeded to eat them, one by one, openly challenging her with his eyes to say something.

Katy threw herself on the bed, her shoes still on. 'Me, too. Can I have one of those, Robert?'

Don't let them get the better of you. Don't. She took a deep breath. 'Well, I could get a gluten-free pizza out of the freezer.'

Silence.

'Would one of you tell me if you'd like that?'

Katy made a great show of finishing her mouthful. 'We're waiting till our mouths are empty cos that's polite, in case you didn't know.'

Robert looked mildly interested. 'What kind of pizza?'

'Margherita,' she said hopefully.

He turned away. 'Don't eat tomatoes.'

'I've got pepperoni too.'

'No, thanks.'

'You had it last week.'

'We've gone off it now.'

'Fine. So what do you want?'

'Scampi.' Robert lay on his stomach on the bed and reached for the remote. 'I fancy scampi and chips.'

'You can't. They're not gluten-free.'

'Then we're not hungry, are we, Katy?'

'Nope.'

One, two, three. 'Give me those crisps now, please. You're not meant to have those either.'

Katy yawned. 'We would give them to you if we had any left.'

Robert pointed the control at the television, almost hitting Marcie's face. 'Can't you just go out and leave us alone?'

'No way!' hissed Marcie. 'The last time I left you two, you nosed around all my private bits and pieces, tried on my make-up, didn't put the top back on my foundation so it leaked, helped yourself to my scent, went through my underwear drawer and snagged a new pair of tights before putting them back in the packet and reported back to your mother about everything you'd found. And Robert burnt my dressing-table by stubbing out the cigarettes that he's not allowed to smoke. Satisfied?'

They both looked at her wordlessly although their eyes said it all. Open war. We hate you and now you've just told us how much you hate us. Now it would be so hard to make it right before David got back.

'Just get out, Marcie, can't you?' said Katy, sulkily. 'We're not hungry anyway. We ate at Mum's. Can't you see we're trying to watch telly?'

Eight

WINDOW CLEANER AVAILABLE!

Reliable and reasonable.
Specialists in sashes.

Contact Wunder Windows on 07999 5678.

'Visitor for you, Roddy.'

He flipped over quickly, fumbling with his jean flies in an attempt to do them up without being noticed. Christ, how embarrassing!

Kevin stood at his door, smiling. He must have seen him wanking over the magazine. Shit, shit, shit. Still, what the hell were you meant to do in a place like this?'

'Who?' he said huskily.

Kevin put his finger on his chin, pretending to think. 'Let's see. It could be your wife, Annabelle. Or it could be one of the many girls you fooled around with before she threw you out. Or one of your old Eton mates . . .

'Ok, ok,' said Roddy weakly. Not for the first time was he beginning to deeply regret having confided in Kevin during one of their Soul-Baring sessions. It had been part of the therapy and it was meant to be confidential. 'Just tell me who it is and then I can decide if I want to see her or not.' Automatically, he put a hand through his unfamiliar hair.

'Don't worry. You look stunning, as usual.' Kevin glanced down at the magazine on the bed. 'Mind you, I'd hide that if I were you.' Too late. Footsteps were already coming down the corridor.

'Roderick!'

'Peregrine?'

'No need to look so surprised.'

Behind him, Roddy could see Kevin smirking. He'd deliberately misled him into thinking his visitor was a woman. Meanwhile, his stepfather was looking round the bare room with distaste. The idiot was wearing a three-piece suit! Either he wanted to show him up or else he had no idea what this place was like.

'Is there somewhere we could sit? I have a rather important matter I need to discuss with you.'

A tremor of apprehension shot through Roddy. 'Mother isn't ill, is she?'

'No, although it's nice to see you care.'

Roddy grit his teeth. 'I have always cared, Peregrine. That's precisely why I was so concerned when she married you.'

His stepfather held up a warning finger and Roddy bristled. How dare he treat him like a child.

'If I were you, my boy, I'd listen to what I have to say before you start insulting me. You might just regret it.'

'Very well, then. Fire away.'

Roddy sat at the head end of his bed, watching Peregrine perched on the uncomfortable steel-tubed chair that he'd had brought in for his visitor.

'Let me get this straight,' he said, leaning his head back against the wall. 'You're offering me a deal. If I promise to give up drink properly, you'll let me live in your flat at Bridgewater House, rent-free, even though the house should be mine by rights.'

Peregrine stood up, adjusting his already tidy tie. 'If you're going to talk like that, there is no point in continuing this conversation.'

'OK.'

Roddy waited until his stepfather reached the door. 'C'mon. We both know I didn't mean that.'

Peregrine stopped, his hand on the door handle. 'I'm only

doing this for your mother. She's worried about you and I'm worried about her. No, she's not ill but neither of us are getting any younger and at our age, worry can bring on things.'

Roddy looked away. 'So can the pain of not being allowed to see your own kids.'

'If you hadn't become an alcoholic and behaved so badly, you'd be able to see them like any other divorced father. Now let me go over this proposal one more time. When your mother – I repeat, your mother and not me – sold Bridgewater House, she did so to pay back the debts that your late father left. No, don't look like that. You know it's the truth. However, one of the conditions of the sale was that we would be 'given' one of the apartments by the developer for our own private use. I am offering to let you live there on condition that you stop drinking. It's accessible to London and it's not that far from your children. It might not be Knightsbridge but if I was in your position, I'd see that as a plus. Daniel and Helena might enjoy being in the country if – or hopefully when – the visiting arrangements are altered. You remember the lake?'

'Of course I bloody remember the lake. I grew up there, didn't I?'

'All the residents have fishing rights. Just the thing to bring you and the children together.'

Roddy swallowed hard, remembering the long afternoons spent with a rod in his hand next to his own father.

'And how will you know – that I'm not drinking, I mean?'

Peregrine gave him a hard look. 'Because you're going to give me your word of honour.'

He almost laughed. 'Is that it? You're not going to put me under twenty-four-hour surveillance?'

'To be honest, I would prefer to. However, your mother seems to believe that you are totally trustworthy. I am hoping that your love for her will prove her unswerving maternal loyalty to be correct.'

Roddy swallowed again. 'It will.'

'So you're accepting my offer?'

'If it means I can get out of this place.'

Peregrine wiped his brow with a large blue and white spotted handkerchief. He'd put on weight, especially round his jowls, since Roddy had last seen him and it didn't suit him. 'It will certainly cost me a lot less. Although it's clear that they spend most of it on heating that you don't need.'

Roddy thought of the long cold winter nights he'd endured during the last year. 'It's bloody freezing sometimes.'

'Mixed company too,' continued Peregrine. 'I didn't think much of that chap who showed me in – Kevin, I believe his name was. There's just one more matter, Roderick.'

Peregrine gave him the kind of look that made him feel as though he was back in the headmaster's study. 'You can stay rent-free for the first month. After that, you will have to find a job and make some kind of contribution, depending on your wage. I don't care if it's fifty quid or five. The point is that you have to get back into gainful employment. Believe me, it's the only way to self-respect.'

'And what the fuck do you expect me to do? The bank's not going to take me back, not after what happened.'

'I agree. But you can do something else. Maybe something manual. I've seen the things you made for your mother. Not bad at woodwork, are you? And I gather you've been making some furniture here, too.'

'It's hardly going to make money.'

'Well, David Linley did it. And I've got some good connections I can pass your way. Just think about it. If not, there's always shelf-stacking at the supermarket. I gather they've opened a big one just down the road from Bridgewater House.'

'You *are* joking, aren't you? No, I take that back. You never joke. It's part of your problem.'

'Don't push me, Roderick. Or I might just retract my offer. Now, do you want to get out of here and move to Bridgewater House. Or not?'

'Scratch your hairy crutch.'

'I *beg* your pardon.'

'I said thanks very much.'

Peregrine stood up. 'Nice to see that you're grateful. Oh and just one more thing.'

Roddy braced himself. 'What now? I thought you'd finished.'

'If I were you, my boy, I'd stop subscribing to those kinds of magazines.' His eye travelled to a glossy tit that was peeping out from under the bed. 'They won't do you any good.' His eyes twinkled. 'Much better to have the real thing.'

A picture of the ghastly flabby Peregrine making love to his mother flashed through his head. Try as he did, he couldn't get rid of it. How could she have married such a toad? How could she?

'Bastard,' muttered Roddy as he watched his stepfather walking out the door. Bastard, bastard, bastard. Still, Bridgewater House . . . He was going home, at last. Home to the only place where he had ever really felt totally at home. But what would it be like after so long? And could he really cope with sharing his childhood home with a bunch of total strangers?

Nine

**BRIDGEWATER RESIDENTS' ASSOCIATION
MEETING REMINDER**

You are all cordially invited to our monthly residents'
meeting on Friday 27 June at 7.30 pm at number 6.

It was just over a week since she'd moved in. Sometimes it seemed
like a day and sometimes a month, thought Louise, as she clutched
the invitation in the palm of her hand, crushing it in her nerv-
ousness as she crunched her way across the gravel to number 6.

How ridiculous to be apprehensive! She'd been through so
much and yet the prospect of meeting new people could still
make her feel jittery. Not so long ago she had never been worried
about going to parties or walking into a crowded room. But
that was when she'd had Jonathan to hold on to . . .

Pathetically, she had even tried to persuade Justine to come
with her. 'Give me a break, Mum,' her daughter had said,
sprawled in front of the television. 'What do I want to go to
an old people's sherry party for?'

'It isn't a sherry party. It's a getting-to-know-you residents'
association thing.'

'Whatever. Forget it. I'm watching the finals of *Teen Idol*.'

It should be *Teen Idle*, thought Louise ruefully. Still, at least
Nick was working on his A-level Geography course work, promising at the same time to keep an eye on Tim. So here she was,
outside number 6, which had a rather nice dark mahogany front
door but a too shiny brass knocker. Almost as soon as she

touched it, she could hear footsteps as though someone had been hovering on the other side.

'Good evening!'

A well-made-up woman, possibly in her late fifties, beamed at her, reeking of a heavy, rather overpowering scent. Louise took in her blonde coiffeured hair, her kitten heels, black skirt just below the knee and pale sage green cardigan. It was similar to one she had fingered in Laura Ashley the other week but reluctantly relinquished because of the price – something she wouldn't have had to worry about this time last year.

'You must be from number 4. Louise Howard, isn't it? Do come in.'

How did she know her name? The only other person she had met was Mollie. Did that mean she'd moved into a place where everyone talked about everyone else?

Her heart sinking, Louise stepped into the hall, breathing in the smell of beeswax, lilies and gleaming mahogany furniture. 'This way, dear. Most people are here already. No, don't worry, you're not late. Drink?'

Louise found a glass of something bubbly being pressed into her hand. Champagne seemed somewhat over the top for a residents' association meeting – even a well-heeled one – but it would seem rude to say that it always left her with a pulsating headache.

'Now, this is Suzette White from number 1. She's one of the old-timers. Bought the very first apartment, didn't you, dear?'

Suzette, who seemed the same sort of age as Lydia, beamed at her. She was wearing a stunning metal chain necklace and a plunging v-neck silk t-shirt that hinted at a well-endowed tanned chest beneath. Several rings on both hands, including her wedding finger, made it difficult to see if she was married or not. Presumably that was the aim. Ever since she had taken her own off, Louise couldn't help examining other women's hands. It was always comforting to see someone else's bare left hand; in a selfish way it was consoling to know she wasn't the only one.

'I did indeed buy the first flat. Not that I spend much time here.'

'Suzette often goes to France to see friends,' said Lydia. 'More drink anyone?'

'Yes, dear, I'll have another,' drawled Suzette in a rather gravely voice. 'Freedom, as I'm always saying, is one of the perks of being divorced. Are you married, Louise?'

She could feel the heat searing through her. 'Yes. Well, not exactly. My husband and I have separated. We're waiting for things to go through.'

Both women nodded. 'Difficult time,' said Lydia kindly. 'We understand, don't we, Suzette? But you'll get through it and now that you're one of us, we'll help you.'

'Certainly will.' Suzette narrowed her eyes, as though appraising her. 'You're still young; you will easily find someone else.'

Louise shook her head. 'To be honest, that's the last thing I'm thinking of. I was married – have been married – for nearly twenty years. I can't imagine being with anyone else. Besides, I've got the children to think of. I just want to focus on them.'

Lydia tutted. 'But they'll grow up and leave you. Two of them are teenagers, aren't they?'

Was there anything she didn't know?

'The years will shoot by before you know it and if you don't start building your own life now, you'll find it even more diffi-cult when they've gone.' She patted her hand reassuringly, start-ling Louise with such an intimate gesture on the strength of a mere few minutes' acquaintance.

'Lydia, darling, are you going to get the show on the road soon?' A very petite and extremely beautiful woman with the most exquisite porcelain complexion and startlingly blue eyes had glided up. She looked even more striking than when Louise had seen her before. She was just about to thank her again for her role in rescuing Hector when Mollie spoke.

'Darling, please start the proceedings.' Mollie patted Lydia's arm. 'We're already frightfully late and Gideon will wonder where I am.'

Louise was beginning to feel she had wandered into a madhouse. Wasn't Mollie's husband dead?

Lydia, however, seemed totally unfazed. 'Don't fret, dear. We're just about to start. Aren't we, Suzette? Now, Mollie, I believe you've already met Louise Howard, haven't you? She and her children have just moved in.'

Mollie held out her hand and gave Louise's a gentle squeeze. It felt incredibly soft and left her own with a slight rose fragrance. 'Absolutely. She's got the most *adorable* dog, haven't you, darling? Now don't forget tea, will you. We said next week, didn't we? Thursday, I believe. Now please excuse me. I really have to powder my nose before Lydia begins.'

'Barmy, poor dear. Absolutely barmy,' said Suzette, watching Mollie walk graciously across the room towards Lydia's cloak-room. 'She's convinced Gideon comes back to see her.'

'She asked me to tea the other day,' said Louise quietly. 'When I went round, there was no one there. I thought she'd forgotten. But obviously she thought she'd said next week.'

'Very sad.' Suzette shook her head slowly. 'Right, we'd better be quiet now. Lydia's about to begin. Pity there aren't more people. Oh good, here comes that American girl. Goodness me, she's brought those teenagers with her. I know they can't be hers. Sally tells me that . . .'

'Please come in.' Lydia projected her voice towards the door. Everyone looked and, not surprisingly, the American girl looked deeply embarrassed. Poor thing! The accompanying children stared moodily at the floor. She should have brought Justine to have joined them, thought Louise. They could have had a mass sulk-in.

Lydia beamed round the room. 'We're here tonight to discuss any issues that might be concerning us and also to meet some new faces. One or two of us have only just met so I think the best thing is for our new people to stand up and say who they are.'

This was worse than school.

'Louise, dear, would you like to go first?'

All eyes were on her. How awful! She could feel herself burning up in a pyre of sweaty shame.

'My name is Louise,' she stuttered.

'Speak up, dear,' commanded Lydia. 'Or they won't be able to hear at the back.'

'I'm Louise Howard,' she repeated. 'I've just moved in with my three children.'

It still felt strange, saying that. The absence of the word 'husband' immediately flagged up the fact she was on her own. Too late, she wished she'd just used the word 'we'.

'And do you have any issues you'd like to discuss?' persisted Lydia. No need to ask her to speak up.

'No. Not yet, thank you.' Louise felt her voice tailing off. 'It's early days.'

'Absolutely. Now who else would like to introduce themselves?' Lydia beamed. 'Maybe us oldies should carry on. I'm Lydia Parsons and this is Suzette White.'

'I am Mollie de May,' Mollie stood up very straight and made a little bow. 'My husband Gideon could, sadly, not be with us this evening.'

Someone whispered loudly and someone else said 'Shhh'. Clearly, thought Louise, they were humouring the poor woman. Rather sweet actually, as though they'd formed a protective rank around her.

'I'm Marcie Gilmore-Smith.' The soft American twang seemed to make itself felt more strongly in the room than Louise's own voice. Here was someone who obviously didn't mind public speaking. She wasn't even standing up but spoke from where she was sitting on the floor, her back against the wall. She was wearing cowboy boots, cut-off jeans and tinted sunglasses poised on the top of head. Gosh, she looked young.

'We moved in about a month ago. And actually I do have a couple of issues I'd like to raise.'

'Good.' Lydia beamed. 'Please go ahead.'

Heavens, the American was staring right at her in a hostile fashion. 'Louise. I'd like to discuss your dog. It *is* your dog, isn't it?'

She nodded silently.

The American's glossy lips tightened. 'I nearly trod in dog muck the other day. There was a horrible pile of . . . well, mess, on the drive.'

The young girl next to her tittered.

Louise went extremely red. 'I'm very sorry. I did actually clear it up afterwards and I can assure you, it doesn't normally happen. It's just that Hector is used to having . . . we used to have a big garden where he . . . what I'm trying to say is that he's getting accustomed to a new environment.'

'I'm afraid that's not good enough.' The American was standing up now, her hands in her jeans pocket aggressively. 'My husband has checked the lease and it says very clearly that dogs aren't allowed in Bridgewater House without permission of the residents. Is that right, Lydia?'

Lydia looked awkward. 'I'm afraid it is. Actually, Louise, I was going to bring this point up myself. Didn't your solicitor point this out to you before you moved in?'

'No, he didn't.' Louise began to sweat. She couldn't possibly stay here without Hector; it would kill the children. They'd have to move; they'd have to . . .

'Why don't we have a show of hands?' suggested Mollie brightly. 'All those against Hector staying, raise your right hand.'

There was a tense silence. Marcie's hand shot up in the air and so, waveringly, did Suzette's. 'I'm sorry, dear, but I don't like the idea of mess myself. And dogs can be very noisy.'

Lydia's hand remained firmly down, as, of course, did Louise's.

'That's it then,' said Marcie triumphantly.

'I think you'll find it's a draw, dear,' said Lydia challengingly.

'Is she allowed to vote?' demanded Marcie, nodding in Louise's direction. 'Even though it involves her?'

'She is, under the rules,' said Lydia firmly.

'I *like* dogs,' said one of the children next to the American. 'Stop being so boring, Marcie.'

Suzette looked worriedly at Lydia. 'I'm really not sure what we can do to . . . Hello? Can I help you?'

A very tall, slimmish man, about her age, with a mop of dark brown hair flopping over one eye, Bryan Ferry-style, opened the door. 'Sorry to bother you but the front door was open and I'm looking for someone who can tell me where the fuck I can find my fuse box. My lights have blown. The name's Roddy Pearmain, by the way.'

'Number 3!' said Lydia triumphantly, as though she was playing Bingo. 'I'd hoped you might show up. You're in Peregrine's flat, aren't you?'

The stranger snorted, tossing his hair out of his eyes. 'Actually, this whole bloody house used to be mine.'

He'd been drinking, realised Louise with a start. After Jonathan, she could tell the signs. It wasn't just the slur in the voice, it was the challenging look in the eye and the slightly wobbly stance.

'Really?' asked Lydia curiously.

'Really.' He said it mockingly, as though taking off her home counties accent. 'I'll tell you all about it sometime. In the meantime, can you tell me where the fucking developer put the fuse box. I can't even see where to pee.'

The girl next to Marcie began to giggle.

'Absolutely,' said Suzette stiffly. 'It's by the front door, on the right. But since you are here, I wonder if you'd like to join our residents' association meeting.'

'Residents' association?' he grinned. 'I don't believe it. Do those kind of things still exist?'

'Very much so, darling.' Mollie beamed at him. 'And in fact, you have made your entrance with impeccable timing. We were just voting on whether Louise here should be allowed to keep her wonderful dog.'

For the first time since appearing, he looked interested in something. 'What kind of dog?'

He looked at Louise hard and she felt herself tremble involuntarily.

'A Labrador. A chocolate Labrador.'

'Labrador! Fantastic animals. Of course she should. Great deterrent against burglars, too. I went on a fantastic walking holiday with one once.' He grinned rather disarmingly. 'With a dog, that is, not a burglar. So count me in for the 'Fors' as it were. Now if you'll excuse me I'll leave you residents to it while I cast some light on my whathaveyou. Good evening, Ladies.'

'I don't believe it!'

Guy slapped his thighs, laughing. She was laughing too, realised Louise, for the first time in goodness knows how long.

'And then what happened?'

'Well,' began Louise, as she allowed Guy to pour her another glass of Chardonnay that he'd brought round to celebrate moving in, 'then he went and everyone was quiet for a few seconds, although I was so embarrassed that it felt like ages! Marcie made her excuses and left – with the boy and that girl who could have given Justine a run for her money in terms of sullenness – and I haven't seen her since. I'm dreading bumping into her. After that, Lydia topped us all up with more champagne by which time my head was throbbing – you know I can't take that much drink – and somehow I found myself agreeing to join the yoga classes which they're going to hold in the pavilion.'

Guy's eyes danced with enthusiasm. He'd cut his hair, Louise noticed. It suited him. 'You mean there's a pavilion in this place?'

Louise nodded. 'It's Victorian. Rather beautiful, down by the lake. It might be a bit cold when winter comes but it's perfect for the summer. Lydia's found us an instructor and we start next weekend. It's Astanga yoga apparently and if there's enough interest, we might have a tai chi class too.'

He studied her carefully. 'It sounds as though you're falling into a pattern.'

She traced an imaginary circle on the table with her index

finger. 'In a way. In a way, not. It's really weird being somewhere different. It's not just the space – or rather lack of it. It's just odd not having Jonathan at home in the evening, even though I wouldn't want him here, if you see what I mean. And when there's just one of you, there's so much to do! The children don't help as much as they should, even though I nag.'

'It must be difficult.' Guy squeezed her hand sympathetically but briefly. 'Listen, Lou, I know what you really want to ask me. So I'll tell you. Yes, I have seen him. They came to dinner last week.'

'They?' asked Louise weakly.

Guy fiddled with his cuffs before looking up. 'He asked if he could bring her and I didn't like to say no. I hope you don't think it's disloyal.'

'Not really. Did they seem happy?'

He looked her straight in the eyes as though it was an effort. 'Yes. I'm sorry, Lou. I really am.'

She shivered. 'He's coming over tomorrow to take the children out. I can't get used to it. I really can't. It's so weird. How can a father take his children out when he's meant to live with them?'

'It happens to lots of families nowadays, Lou,' said Guy softly.

'I know.'

She couldn't stop the tears now. 'But it wasn't meant to happen to us.'

'Mum, Mum.' Justine arrived breathless in the doorway of the kitchen, her spots standing to attention on her forehead. 'Tim's taken the batteries out of the remote control again and I can't work the telly.'

'Ok, I'll sort it.'

'You'd better. Hi, Guy.'

'Hi, you.' Guy rumpled her hair affectionately. 'Giving your mum a hard time, are you?'

'Yeah, well, it's what teenagers do.' She glowered at Louise. 'Have you told him about Tim?'

'I will.'

'Tell me what?'

Louise waited until Justine had gone into the sitting room and turned on the television. 'Tim's started to be really difficult. He should be doing his homework now and you can hear him, playing his drums. I've already had a note from school; his year tutor wants me to go in and see him. Oh God, do you think this is because of what's happened?'

'Do you want me to talk to him in his room?' he said, ignoring the question.

She smiled sadly. 'As long as Nick isn't there. They have to share now, you now.'

'Good for them,' said Guy briskly. 'It means they can help each other.'

She hadn't thought of it like that.

Together they walked to the boys' room with the Keep Out notice that Tim had put up. 'Can we come in?' asked Guy.

'If you want,' said Tim sullenly. He was lying back on the bed, strumming his guitar.

Guy pulled up a bean bag and perched on it. It made him look slightly ridiculous with his long legs but he didn't seem to mind. 'Your mum says you're meant to be doing your homework.'

Tim glowered at Louise. 'Telling tales again, are you, Mum? Can't you give me ten minutes to relax? Do you know how hard it is, being a kid?'

Guy put a hand on Louise's shoulder. 'Why don't you go and sit down for a bit, Lou. I need to talk man-stuff here.'

Louise looked at her youngest who had turned over so his back was facing them. Guy might just get through where she couldn't. 'Ok. But don't be too long. I've actually made an apple pie in your honour.'

'Apple pie? Every bachelor's favourite. We don't want to miss that, do we, Tim?'

Later, when by some miracle the kids had joined them for pudding and then gone off to watch television, Guy said he had to go.

'I suppose you've got some girl waiting for you?' she said lightly.

'Well, not tonight but I've got an early start. I promised to take Karen punting in Cambridge.'

'So you're still seeing her?'

He shrugged. 'She's a nice girl. You must meet her sometime.'

Guy looked at her worriedly. 'Sure you'll be ok?'

She nodded.

He seemed reluctant to go. 'I hope my talk with Tim will help things a bit. What have you got lined up for the week?'

'More unpacking. And then I'm going to have to start thinking seriously about getting a job.'

'Run the options past me again.'

'Well, I've been out of journalism so long that I don't know how easy it will be to get in. I thought I'd make a few phone calls to people I used to know and take it from there. If necessary, I'll have to look for something locally. Anything. Even stacking shelves if necessary.'

He looked shocked. 'Surely it won't come to that?'

'There isn't much money, you know. With three kids, the outgoings are incredible and even though the mortgage isn't huge, it's enough.'

He frowned with concern. 'Do you want me to help out?'

'Of course not.'

She felt hideously awkward, hoping he hadn't thought she'd said that to get some assistance.

'Well, let me know how it goes, won't you?' He stood up and, not for the first time, Louise was struck by his height as he leant down to hug her goodbye. His cheek felt slightly rough against hers. 'It will be all right, Lou, you know.'

She swallowed. 'I hope so.'

While standing at the door to wave him goodbye, a car drove past. It was the American girl at the wheel. She shot Louise a nasty look and Louise felt a wave of unease. All she needed now was an enemy on her doorstep.

Hector growled as the car shot off, close behind the American's. Louise lent down to kiss him on the nose. 'It's ok, Hector. It's ok.'

As she spoke, the sound of Tim's guitar pierced the ear. Someone banged a window from Suzette's direction and Louise groaned as she went inside to tell him to turn it down. As she passed the phone in the hall, she noticed there were two messages winking at her. She'd heard it ringing once during dinner but had ignored it.

'Hello. Mrs Howard. It's Steven from Steven Stevens Removal speaking. We've discovered a couple of small items in the truck that seem to have been left behind from your move. I can drop them off next week if you like. Please call.'

Delete.

Play.

'It's me. I just wondered how you were doing. Look, I know I'm picking up the kids tomorrow but I need to talk to you urgently.'

Urgently? Why? Getting out her address book to find his new number (how ironic that she had to do the same with her husband as she did for the removal man), she rang immediately.

'Hi!' said a woman's voice brightly.

Gemma? Louise's chest quickened as she dropped the phone. How could he? Had Jonathan intended this to happen? Or – as was more likely – was he just bloody thoughtless? If only she could cry; if only she could let the anger out. Why, instead, did she just feel this paralysing sadness?

Ring. Ring.

Louise listened to it ringing. If it wasn't Jonathan, she didn't want to talk. And if it was, let him think she was out.

A woman had to have some pride, after all.

Ten

RUBBISH ALERT!

Unfortunately, we appear to have a litter problem.
Recently, certain items such as crisp packets and
cigarette butts have been found by the lake. Please help us
to keep the grounds tidy by taking home your rubbish.

Bridgewater Residents' Association

'So we're going to have a barbecue next month. Sounds fun, although it won't be the same, darling, not if you won't be there. So do try to make it.'

Gideon made a non-committal noise as he leaned back in his chair with *The Times*, blew his nose on a blue spotted silk handkerchief and lit up a cigar. 'Did you read what this new reviewer chap said about Vanessa? Absolutely disgraceful. She'll be terribly hurt. You'll have to ring her and tell her to ignore that man.'

Mollie took a mouthful of gin, ran it round the inside of her cheeks to get the maximum flavour and felt it slide down her throat. 'I will. But more importantly, darling, what on earth were you thinking of when you changed your will?'

'Ah, that.' Gideon emitted a puff of cigar smoke and she breathed it in. Loved the smell. Always had done. It was so him. 'I meant to mention that but then everything started to give up so bloody fast.'

Mollie shivered, remembering the speed with which the cancer had spread during the last weeks. 'Don't.'

'I just felt I wanted to do something for those kids. They're a talented bunch and it's so difficult nowadays to make it; even harder than in our day.'

Mollie sat forward, running her fingers up Gideon's thighs. 'But darling, we don't have that much money. Nigel's ranting and raving and saying I'm going to have to live with him.'

'Nonsense.' Gideon blew out another cloud of smoke and drained his whisky glass. 'There should be enough if you live reasonably carefully. Come on, Mollie. It's not like you to be selfish.'

'But I'm not. It's just that . . . Gideon? Gideon?'

She stared in disbelief at the empty chair, still with the indentation of his body in the seat. He knew she still needed to talk to him. How could he do that? He'd already said he had no control over his entrances or exits but surely one could try something? She'd have to tackle him on that one next time but in the meantime – damn – the door-knocker was going. Of course! She slapped her hand to her forehead. That's why he'd gone so fast. He'd known someone had turned up unexpectedly.

'Clever you,' she said to the chair. 'I should have realised.'

The door-knocker went again. Goodness, some people could be so impatient!

'I'm just coming,' she called out, making her way carefully across the hall. Sally had polished the wood last week and it was still a little slippery.

'Mollie, I'm *so* sorry!' The beautiful tall girl on the other side of the door flung her arms around Mollie, kissing her warmly on both cheeks. 'We both are. We'd have done anything, anything in the world, to have been at the funeral but filming didn't finish until last night and we got here as fast as we could. Didn't we, Rupert?'

The young man with such gaunt features that he almost looked rat-like, wearing ripped jeans and a too small black leather jacket, nodded. Somehow Mollie had never warmed to Rupert. It was Poppy whom she'd always had a soft spot for.

Poppy with the flawless skin and bubbly voice; her dark brown hair, shot through with natural red highlights, worn scooped up under a cap which showed off her long turquoise earrings. She too had ripped jeans and a denim jacket with fur at the collar and neck. Below was a skimpy apricot t-shirt and a flat bare stomach with a navel ring.

'Poppy, darling! How lovely to see you. Please come in.'

She led the way to the drawing room. 'Now make yourselves comfortable. Would you like a drink?'

'No, thank you.' Poppy draped herself at Mollie's feet, looking up at her adoringly like a puppy. 'We want to know how *you* are. It must be so difficult without him.'

'Well, yes. Although he's still with me, you know.'

Rupert nodded. 'My mum says that about my dad. She can feel him all the time.'

'Exactly.' Mollie glanced at Gideon's empty chair which Rupert was now making his way towards. 'Although there are a few complications.'

'What kind of complications?' frowned Poppy.

Her concern indicated she knew nothing about the will. 'Oh, nothing I can't handle,' she said airily. 'Now tell me about this filming. It sounds awfully exciting.'

'It is!' Poppy's eyes shone. 'Mine was only a small part – Rupert's was a bit bigger – but it could lead to something else. The director said he'd try me out for a script next month so I'm hoping he won't forget.'

Mollie glanced at her young friend's navel. 'I'm sure he won't.'

Poppy looked pensive for a moment. 'In this business, people make promises and then they forget they ever made them.'

Mollie sighed, remembering her own earlier struggles. 'Well, things are about to look up for you both as I'm sure you've discovered from the solicitor handling Gideon's affairs.'

'What?' Both young people looked at her, confused. So they didn't know.

'You haven't got the letter?'

'We've only just got back. Rupert stayed the night at my

place – I've got a mound of post but haven't had time to go through it yet. We both wanted to come straight round here.'

'Gideon has left you a legacy each. It was his intention that you should use it to live on until you both make it. It was his – our – way of saying that we know you will get there one day.'

'My goodness!' Rupert gasped. 'How very decent of him. And you.'

'Are you sure?' said Poppy quietly. 'I mean, I don't want to be rude. But can you afford it?'

Such a *sweet* girl!

'Absolutely,' said Mollie brightly. 'There's plenty left to go round.'

Poppy's face relaxed. 'That's wonderful! I mean, it's terrible about Gideon – oh, how insensitive of me – but it was so kind of him, and you. Gosh, I don't know what to say.'

She flung her arms round Mollie's neck. 'There's no need to say anything, dear,' said Mollie graciously. 'Now, you will stay to lunch, won't you? I've got some poached salmon in the fridge and some perfect new potatoes that Sally – she helps me with the cleaning – grew in her garden.'

'That would be lovely.' Poppy sprang to her feet. 'Let me help you. I can take out your glass and this ash tray, for a start.'

They both looked down at it. Gideon's cigar still lay in it, smoking quietly. 'Silly, isn't it,' said Mollie, quickly. 'But I find it rather comforting to have a puff every now and then.'

'The smell makes me feel as though he's sitting right here,' said Rupert wonderingly.

Mollie smiled. 'I know exactly what you mean.'

They'd almost finished lunch when there was a knock on the door. 'I'll get it,' said Poppy jumping up. 'No, honestly, Mollie, I insist.'

She could hear a man's voice in the hall and, for a second, she thought it might be Gideon. Silly man, that really would really put a cat amongst the pigeons.

'Miss de May.' The same tall young man who had come late to the residents' association meeting last week strode into her drawing room with an assurance usually possessed by the acting profession or aristocrats. 'Roddy Pearmain.' He shook her hand firmly. 'We met last week. I'm *so* sorry to disturb you but I wondered if I could possibly trouble you for a tea bag. I know it's very disorganised of me but I can't find mine anywhere – still unpacking you know – and no one else seems to be in.'

'Of course I don't mind, darling. Would you like Earl Grey, Darjeeling or builder's?'

'Gosh, that's wonderful.' The man was looking at Poppy as though transfixed. 'Earl Grey would be perfect.'

'Have you just moved in?' asked Poppy lightly.

'Yes. A few days ago. Although actually, my family used to own this place.'

'They *did*?'

Rupert's eyes widened almost as much as Poppy's.

'Owned it for several generations, actually. I grew up here with my sister. It was an amazing place to spend your childhood in, as you can imagine. In fact, it's built on the site of an even older house which burned down in the eighteenth century.'

He paused. 'But then my father died and the death duties were staggering. My mother married again but my stepfather saw fit to sell Bridgewater House to a developer. Peregrine – my stepfather – got an apartment as part of the deal and that's where I'm living now.'

'Do you have a family of your own?' asked Mollie, returning from the kitchen with the tea bags.

'Two children.' He smiled tightly. 'They live with my ex-wife.'

'Poor you,' said Poppy. 'That can't be easy.'

'It's not.' He looked out of the window as though searching for something. A good stage trick, thought Mollie. Gave one time to collect oneself. Not surprisingly, he was studying Poppy again.

'Don't I recognise you from somewhere?'

Poppy tilted her head to one side. 'Perhaps.'

'She's an actress,' said Mollie proudly.

'We both are,' said Rupert. 'I mean, I'm an actor.'

'Please excuse my ignorance, but what would I have seen you – both – in?'

'My recent one was *Summer Love* with Brad Pitt but you probably wouldn't have noticed me. Not really. I was only on for a few minutes. One of his former girlfriends, you know. Film girlfriend, of course.'

Rupert coughed. 'And I was in the new play at the Shaftesbury. Quite a sizeable part actually, although I do top myself at the end.'

'How amazing.' Roddy raised his eyebrows. They met in the middle, Mollie noticed, as Gideon's did. 'Well, it's nice to have some interesting neighbours.'

'Oh, we don't live here,' Poppy assured him. 'I wish we did. It's beautiful, isn't it? No, we're just visiting Mollie. She and Gideon were – are – like surrogate godparents. They're wonderful to lots of us; we come and tell them all our troubles.'

Both Rupert and Poppy looked sad; poor children, thought Mollie. They were missing Gideon too.

'Well, I mustn't keep you.' Roddy rose to his feet. 'Thanks for these. I'll try and replace them this side of Christmas. And it was great to meet you both.' His eyes held those of Poppy. 'Hope to see you again soon. In the meantime, I'll look out for you on screen or on stage or whatever.'

'I'll see you out,' said Rupert.

'Nice man,' he said, coming back.

'Not your sort, darling.' Poppy smiled lovingly at him.

'I know. Still, one can only dream.'

Mollie looked at Gideon's chair. 'Very true.'

'We must be going too,' said Poppy. 'Now are you sure there's nothing you need?'

'Nothing at all,' said Mollie firmly.

'I'll ring you next week.' Each planted a kiss on one side of her face, like twins.

'No, don't get up to see us out. We'll be fine.'

She watched them through the window, their heads bent towards each other, deep in conversation. Dear children. They were probably worrying about her.

Botheration! Nigel's car was snaking its way up the drive. *And* he was getting out. What was he telling them? She would kill him if he told them that the will had left her with precious little money.

They were saying goodbye now. Rupert's little car was making its way down towards the main road and her son was striding towards her front door.

'Don't answer it,' commanded Gideon from his armchair. 'He'll think you're asleep. Here, come and sit next to me. He'll look through the windows and think you're resting.'

'Good idea.' She nestled next to him, resting her head on his shoulder. 'Actually, darling, I'm feeling really sleepy anyway . . .'

Goodness knows how long she'd been asleep for when the phone rang. The first thing she realised was that there was an empty cold space next to her. The second was that the phone was next to her when she could have sworn she had left it on its hook in the hall.

'Hello?'

'Mollie, it's me. Poppy.'

'Darling.' Mollie tried to gather her thoughts. 'It was so lovely to see you today.'

'You too. Listen, we bumped into Nigel on the way out and he told me.'

'Told you what, darling?'

'Told me how the will makes it difficult for you. I can't take the money. I really can't. Especially as Nigel has given you his share.'

She was sitting up now, awake. Trust Nigel to smugly flaunt his own good deed. 'But you must. Gideon wanted you to and it would be extremely bad luck – not to mention bad manners – to refuse it.'

'But it means you will hardly have enough to live on.'

'I'll get by.'

'Actually, I had an idea. Well, it was Rupert's actually. You might not like it but, please, give it some thought. The lease on my little flat is running out and my landlord won't renew it. I was going to move in with Rupert but I have to confess that it didn't really appeal. We have such different lifestyles.'

'I can imagine,' murmured Mollie.

'Rupert would give his share to you as well but between you and me, he's seriously in debt. Gideon's gift was a godsend.'

'I wouldn't hear of it anyway,' cut in Mollie.

'But supposing I paid you rent and moved in with you? I won't be there all the time. Especially not if I get this new role. And I promise not to get in your way.'

'I'm not sure . . .'

'Brilliant idea,' growled Gideon gently behind her.

Mollie hesitated. 'But why would you want to come and live with an old woman?'

'Mollie, you're not old. You're young. In spirit anyway.'

Gideon guffawed. 'Just like me.'

'Rupert's going to find out how much a competitive rent payment would be.'

'I'm not sure, dear. You know it's very quiet here.'

'Your dashing neighbour didn't look the quiet type to me,' twinkled Poppy's voice down the phone. 'Did you know that he's actually a lord? Rupert looked him up.'

'I didn't know. Well, dear, if you're sure about coming here . . .'

'She is,' said Gideon quietly. 'And it would make me feel easier if there was someone to look after you.'

'I don't need looking after.'

'I know you don't,' pleaded Poppy. 'But we can be company for each other, can't we? Please say yes. *Please.*'

Eleven

**HELP NEEDED PLEASE,
FOR THE FORTHCOMING BARBECUE!**

Contact Suzette White at Number 1

'Meanwhile, Mrs Gilmore-Smith, I suggest you do something to help take your mind off the situation.'

Marcie glared at him. 'Take my mind off the situation, Dr Wolfe? Have you any idea what it's like to want to be pregnant? To think about it every waking moment? To feel as jealous as hell when you see a kid walking down the street, her hand in her mom's? What exactly do you suggest? Bridge? Running the local fete or barbecue? That's what you English do, isn't it?'

Dr Wolfe doodled on his notepad. 'Some of my patients find yoga helpful. Another has been doing autogenic therapy which is a type of meditation programme.'

David coughed. 'It might be worth considering, Marcie. Do you have any leaflets on the autogenic idea?'

'I'm afraid not but no doubt you could find it on the net.'

Marcie leaned back in her chair, grateful that she had worn her shades so the doctor couldn't see her angry tears. Through the consulting rooms window, she could see a park. Swings. Children. A red pushchair. 'Let's get this straight,' she repeated. 'According to your tests, there is nothing that suggests there's anything wrong with me.'

Dr Wolfe shook his head. 'As I've pointed out before,

Mrs Gilmore-Smith, we prefer not to use the adjective "wrong" because it suggests blame in one direction or the other. What I can say is that there is nothing that suggests why you have, so far, been unable to conceive a child.'

'And you are suggesting,' cut in Marcie, tapping her immaculate nails on his desk, 'that we carry on making love at "the optimum time" of my cycle in the hope that something will, one day, happen.'

Dr Wolfe nodded tautly.

Leaning forward across the desk, she had this crazy urge to yank this man's ghastly spotted tie. 'In addition, I am to keep taking my vitamin pills, forget we're trying to have a baby and take up yoga.'

David put a hand on her arm. 'Marcie, darling, I know it's frustrating but what else can we do?'

Marcie's eyes flashed. 'We could start on some kind of a programme, surely? We don't have to keep IVF for when we're old and desperate. Just because I'm young, doesn't mean we can afford to sit around and wait for a miracle to happen. And what about pulsatilla?'

Dr Wolfe rocked back on his seat, the tips of his fingers together as though in prayer. 'Ah, yes, the homeopathic route. Some of my patients do dabble in alternative remedies but in my opinion this isn't wise if you are taking conventional medicine. We don't have enough evidence to show whether they conflict or not.'

'Hang on.' David was sitting forward now, alert, his handsome face questioning the doctor. 'But we aren't taking any conventional medicine yet. You've told us to keep trying. So why can't we try herbs or whatever?'

Thank you, said Marcie silently to herself.

'Personally, I wouldn't recommend it but, of course, it's up to you.' Dr Wolfe picked up his pen again. 'Supposing I see you in two months' time? Then, if there aren't any developments, we will consider our options.'

'Consider our options,' muttered Marcie as they pushed open

the heavy black door and walked out into New Cavendish Street. 'He doesn't know how I feel.'

'How *we* feel, Marcie,' corrected David quietly, reaching out for her hand. 'And I'm sure he does. You're just upset and understandably so.'

They both fell silent as they walked along. He was right, thought Marcie ruefully. But why couldn't she do something which David and his first wife Diana had achieved so effortlessly; so very effortlessly in fact that they had *had* to get married – something which, as David had often said, his eldest must never know about.

'I'm sorry,' she said, as they approached David's office near Wigmore Street.

'Don't be.' David hugged her briefly. 'It's not your fault.'

Overcome with emotion, she leaned her head on his shoulder hoping for more than a cuddle (just a kiss would help) but David was already hailing a taxi for her, to take her back to Marylebone. As luck would have it, a taxi was passing and Marcie wiped her tears away quickly.

'All right now?' he said tenderly, opening the door for her, as though her outburst could make everything good again.

She nodded, not trusting herself to speak. He stood outside his office, waving as she left. She turned round to catch the last glimpse of him. A tall, oh-so-English gentleman in his pin-striped suit and crisp blue and white striped shirt. Then, as soon as he was out of sight, she sank back into the seat miserably.

'It's not your fault,' he had said.

But the terrible thing was that it was.

Her train was up on the indicator at Marylebone but without a platform number. There was a large crowd of early evening communters milling around in front of the board, waiting. What was it with the British, that they couldn't run trains on time? Irritated, Marcie headed for the Italian tea and coffee stand by the ticket office before altering her course towards the new Souper Douper stall.

'Avoid tea – unless it's green – and coffee,' Sally had urged. 'Plenty of fresh fruit and vegetables. And take these folic acid tablets too.'

Maybe, as David said, it was all in the mind. Perhaps she should have told Dr Wolfe the truth. But how could she, with David there? Virginia had told her to hang on in there but . . .

'I'm so *dreadfully* sorry!'

An extremely tall slim man with a floppy fringe, carrying some kind of a long musical instrument shrouded in a black case, stepped back after knocking into her.

'How awful! I've spilt your drink down you. Please, let me get you another.'

Marcie dabbed at the orange stain on her black t-shirt. 'No, it's ok. It had gone cold anyway.'

'Really?' The man's eyes were dancing at her beneath a rather unkempt fringe. 'Almost as irritating as British trains, you mean?'

'Precisely.' She glanced at the indicator. Still no platform number.

'And British dogs that leave unmentionable piles on the drive.'

She looked at him sharply and he took a mock bow. 'That's right. Roderick Pearmain. One of your neighbours. I saw you briefly at the residents' association farce the other night. Getting the train home, are you? Look, the platform number's up at last. Do you mind if I sit with you? I can fill you in on British eccentricities like cold carrot soup.'

By the time they had reached Chalfont & Latimer, Marcie was well acquainted not just with the history of Bridgewater House – which was truly riveting – but also with Roderick's colourful past. Her gut instinct warned her that the latter had been strongly edited but, in a way, that made it even more exciting. It was all she could do not to get out her notepad and write it down so she would remember every little detail for her next letter to Virginia.

'So your children live with your ex-wife because you didn't want to disrupt their lives?' she repeated disbelievingly.

Roderick ran his hand through his hair – he seemed to do that an awful lot – and nodded, his eyes fixed on hers. 'There's nothing worse for a child than to feel torn in two. Do you have kids?'

Marcie looked away. 'Not yet. David has two from a previous marriage and they stay with us every other weekend.'

'Is that difficult for you?'

'Not at all.' She rustled in her bag for her ticket. 'I love having them over. Wow, we're here already.'

'Yes, and we're only ten minutes late.' Roddy shook his head in mock amazement. 'Not bad at all. I don't suppose you need a lift?'

'No, thanks. I left my car in the car park.'

'Me too. Well, Marcie, it was very nice to see you.'

He shook her hand firmly. 'Sorry about your stained top.'

'It will wash. And if it doesn't, well, there are worse things.'

'You're more understanding than I thought.'

'What do you mean?'

'Well, that fuss about the dog.' He looked sideways at her as they got off the train. 'It doesn't do to fall out with new neighbours, you know.'

'I didn't want to fall out with them.' Marcie felt the anger in her chest rising. 'But when there's a group of people living close to each other, they have to have some respect.'

'I agree.' He patted the case. 'So just let me know if my guitar music gets too loud.'

Him too? The family with the dog already had a kid who played those wretched drums *and* the guitar. She needed her peace to write. It was one reason why they'd moved into the country.

'Don't worry,' she said, zapping her car door open. 'I will.'

'So you see,' she wrote, the following day, 'I've already managed to argue with two of my neighbours. Well, one and a half. I haven't exactly fallen out with the aristocrat whose family owned this place; just rubbed him up the wrong way, as David says. Still, he told me some amazing stuff about Bridgewater House. Apparently . . .'

'Cooee, only me!'

Marcie put down her pen and waved half-heartedly through the open window as Sally went past. She'd have to go out now. Two weeks' worth of Sally had taught her that writing was impossible when she was around. She'd pretend to tiptoe round as though she had some respect for what Marcie was doing but would then say, 'Sorry to interrupt, Marcie, but do you prefer lavender polish to beeswax? I've got both.'

As if she cared!

Still, she had a good excuse this morning. The yoga class was starting in the pavilion; it had been decided at the residents' association to hold it on Tuesday mornings as well as Saturdays. She was already dressed in a pale blue tracksuit and trainers to match.

'Going to yoga, are you?' Sally nodded approvingly as Marcie let her in. 'Good. Anything like that helps.'

Marcie shuddered with distaste at the uninvited familiarity.

'Taking the pulsatilla, are you?'

'Yes.' Marcie gritted her teeth. 'Look, Sally, I know you're trying to be helpful and I appreciate it. But I find it difficult discussing my gynaecological problems with someone I don't really know.'

The girl was regarding her coolly with an amused look in her eyes. 'That's fine with me, Marcie. Only trying to help. See you later. Enjoy the yoga.'

Well done, Marcie told herself as she headed over the lawn towards the pavilion. That was the third person she'd managed to frost off that week. Now Sally would probably steal the silver or help herself to her Chanel body lotion. David's mother had warned her about that. If she did, she'd have to go. In fact, maybe she'd have to go anyway. Not immediately – that would look too spiteful – but soon. It would be too difficult to have her long term after the conversation they'd just had.

Voices were already coming from the pavilion. Sounded as though quite a few people had turned up. Marcie hoped the yoga wouldn't be too basic; she'd done a few courses back home and it would be boring if it was just for beginners.

'Shut up, Mum. I told you. It was only an 18. Stop fussing. Do you know how many porn movies Nick's watched?'

Porn movies? Marcie turned round sharply as a boy sprinted past her, barefoot, from the direction of the lake, closely followed by the woman with the dog. She winced as the dog sniffed at her ankles before running on.

'Sorry.' The woman was panting. 'Hector, come *here*. Tim, come back.' She glanced at Marcie. 'Are you going to the yoga class? Can you tell them I'm coming but I might be a few minutes late. Thanks. Hector, come *back*.'

Marcie watched her run towards the house. Porn movies? That kid didn't even look old enough to be a teenager. When she and David had kids, they would never let them behave like that.

Twelve

IF ANYONE IS INTERESTED IN RESEARCHING THE HISTORY OF BRIDGEWATER HOUSE,

please contact Lydia Parsons at number 6.

'For Chrissake, Annabelle, I've told you. I'm clean. And I haven't had a drink for a nearly a year. Or a fuck, come to that, but I don't suppose you're interested.'

Her voice showed not one hint of amusement. What had happened to the woman's sense of humour? 'No, Roddy, I'm not interested. And I'm still not giving in. In fact, I could tell my solicitor that you're harassing me.'

Roddy lay back on the sofa which was too short for his long legs, eyes closed, mobile pressed to his ear. 'Come on, Annie B. Be reasonable.' He kicked his shoes off with frustration, watching them hit the floor. 'I just want to see my kids. They'd love it here. It's part of their history. It's where I grew up. It's where you and I first . . .'

'I don't even want to think about that.'

Years ago, he could remember a completely different Annabelle. An Annabelle straight out of St Mary's who had fallen in love not just with him but with Bridgewater House itself. He could see it in her eyes, picturing life in this fantastic house where they could bring up loads of children. And then his mother had married bloody Peregrine and everything had started to go wrong.

'I can understand that, Annie B.' He dropped his voice, speaking slowly and soporifically, the way he used to talk to her in bed. 'But I want to take Daniel fishing in the lake, like my father took me. And I want to throw Helena a fantastic party in the summer . . .'

'What? In your tiny apartment?'

He winced. That bloody notice from Lydia Parsons had already put his back up when it had come fluttering through his letter-box this morning. How dare someone else dig into his own house's history. It made his ex-wife's comment about his reduced circumstances even more galling. 'We could put up a marquee in the grounds,' he said defensively.

'Sorry, Roddy. It isn't working. You've lost your charm along the way and, quite frankly, I don't think you're responsible enough to have the children for an hour, let alone a weekend.'

'Really.' His voice cut down the phone. 'Well my solicitor thinks differently. He's lodging an appeal – based on a recommendation by the clinic – so I can see the children every other weekend.'

'Over my dead body.'

'It may well come to that.'

The words were out of his mouth before he could stop them.

'I knew you hadn't changed.' Annabelle's voice was triumphant. 'I'm recording this conversation, by the way.'

Shit, shit, *shit*.

'I may not have any physical bruises any more, Roddy. But the mental ones will be there for ever.' She was hissing now. 'And I will never ever forgive you for that.'

'I'm sorry.' His voice came out cracked. 'It was only the once. And I wasn't responsible for my actions. You know that.'

'You never were, Roddy.' She sounded sad now. He preferred it when she was angry. It made him feel less of a heel. 'You're not going to have the kids. You know that, don't you?'

'Just one weekend, Annie B. *Please.*'

Was that a slight hesitation?

'Fuck off, Roddy.'

Maybe not.

Click. She'd put the phone down. Roddy closed his eyes. Did anyone understand that terrible emptiness; that grief of not being near your children at a time in their lives when they needed a father?

'Helena,' he murmured. 'Daniel.'

His eyes travelled towards the Queen Anne corner cupboard where Peregrine had left a bottle of Johnnie Walker. He knew why, the bastard. It was a test. Well, he was going to show them all. Walking across to the cupboard, Roddy opened the door. There it was. Red Label. Full. Absolutely full with a whisky glass next to it. Slowly and deliberately, Roddy took the bottle out, holding it up to the light. The morning sunshine danced through it so it shone like amber. A couple of swigs – maybe three – and it wouldn't seem so bad. A few more and he might, for a bit, be able to forget all this.

Swiftly, he put the bottle back and turned the key.

Out. Go out. Get away from the cupboard and Peregrine's little tricks. Walk away from the phone and Annabelle and the children she wouldn't let him see. Down to the lake. That's where he'd go. The lake where not so many years ago life had seemed simple.

What the hell was happening? Roddy picked his way over a dog turd and glanced through the doors of the pavilion which his great-great-grandfather had commissioned. An array of coloured leotards were seated, lotus-style, in front of what he could only describe as an extremely fit, nubile young lady with well-good tits, as Kevin from the clinic would have said.

'Bit of a milf, isn't she?'

He turned to find himself face to face with a tall, freckled boy in ripped jeans and a t-shirt with the group slogan 'The Wattevers' written on the front.

'What exactly is a milf?'

'Don't you know?' The boy was staring at him condescendingly. 'It stands for "Mother, I'd like to have your kids". Well, actually, it's "Mother, I'd like to f—"'

'Ok. I get it.'

Roddy studied the boy. Somehow, he reminded him of himself at that age. That devil-may-care attitude. The total lack of respect for adults.

'I'm Roddy Pearmain. I've just moved in.'

The boy held out his hand. 'Tim. We've moved in too. Mum says you saved our dog.'

'I did?'

'Yeah. You voted for him at the residents' meeting the other week. Thanks.'

'Not at all. I like dogs.'

'Gum?'

'Thanks.' He took a piece from the packet which the boy was offering.

'Do you like it here?'

The boy looked away. 'Sokay. We used to live in a proper house. With a big garden. And my dad.'

Roddy's chest lurched. 'I see.'

They began to walk, as though in mutual agreement, towards the lake, the dog running ahead. 'Do you see your father still?'

'Yeah. Every Saturday.'

'That's good.'

'Is it?'

'Why isn't it, then?'

The boy's eyes narrowed. 'Because his girlfriend is with him. That's why he left Mum.'

Roddy's skin began to prickle. 'I'm sorry.'

'Why? It's not your fault.'

'No, I know. But it's the kind of thing you feel you should say.'

'Why?'

Roddy grinned. 'I used to argue like that, at your age.'

'Did you get told off?'

'All the time. Still do.'

The boy's mouth twitched. They were at the lake now. Together, they stood by the side of the water, looking at it.

'Hector, come back.' The boy tugged at his sleeve. 'I don't know if he can swim.'

'He'll be all right. Dogs are natural. See, he's loving it. Shit, he's coming out now. Watch out – he'll be soaking!'

'Hector! Don't!'

They both fell about laughing as the dog bounded up to them, shaking himself so close that the water sprayed up at them.

'Sorry about that,' said the boy.

'I don't mind in the slightest. My dog used to do the same. Say, have you ever been fishing?'

'No.' The boy looked wistful. 'My dad was going to take me but he never did.'

'Why don't you go with friends?'

The kid's face darkened. 'I started a new school last year and I don't like it. I did have a best friend – his mum was Mum's friend too – but they got moved to Florida.'

Roddy remembered what that was like all right. He'd hated his senior school for the first two years. His only real friend had left at fifteen to go and live with his father in Yorkshire. 'Well, I've got a spare rod or two,' he said casually. 'Ask your mum if it's ok and we could come down here, if you like.'

'Ok.'

Was that a pleased ok or an I've-got-to-be-polite-to-an-adult ok?

Roddy glanced at his watch. Bloody hell. He'd be late for his solicitor's meeting. 'Look, I've got to go now. But I'll call in on your mother later on to sort out the fishing if you like.'

The boy nodded. 'Cool.'

'See you later, then.'

It was only when he got back to the house that the doubts began to creep in. What was he trying to do? Find a substitute for his own son? That kid was nothing like Daniel. Besides, the boy may not have a full-time father but at least he had one that was allowed access. Or was he trying to go back to his own youth? The words of the clinic psychologist came back to him. 'Forget the past because you aren't going back there.'

Maybe the fishing trip wasn't such a good idea after all. Perhaps he should quietly forget about the whole thing.

'So you see, Lord Pearmain, I'm afraid you haven't made life very easy for yourself.'

The woman solicitor – standing in for his usual one who was on paternity leave, for heaven's sake – eyed him narrowly across the table. This firm had acted for his father and his father's father and his father's father's father. He'd never be able to afford them were it not for Peregrine, who had offered to foot the bill. Much as he hated to take hand-outs from the man, he had no choice.

'Threatening your wife on the phone isn't going to do you any favours,' she added.

It was hard to take women like this seriously. How old was she? Thirty? Thirty-five at the most. Sparkling diamond on her left hand. Seriously big. Awful hourglass legs. A chin that was on its way to becoming two of a kind.

Clothed, as Daniel would say.

'I beg your pardon, Lord Pearmain?'

'Nothing.' He drained his coffee. 'Just thinking of something my son said on the phone. You see, that's the whole trouble.'

He leaned across the table, resting his elbows on the shiny mahogany surface. 'That's all I can do. Talk to my children on the phone. How can they have a meaningful relationship with a father that way?'

'You're allowed to email.'

He groaned. 'That's not what I'm trying to say. Isn't there anything you can do? All I want is the right to see my children once or twice a month. Ideally, I'd like to see them every weekend but I'm prepared to compromise.'

The woman was looking through her papers. 'Well, the report from the clinic is very encouraging. I was going to suggest we launched an appeal on the basis of that but, unfortunately, your wife taped your recent telephone conversation. It really isn't wise, Lord Pearmain, to use phrases like "Over your dead body".'

He looked sulkily out of the window. 'It's just a phrase. You said so yourself.'

'But not particularly apt in the circumstances, wouldn't you agree?'

'I suppose not.'

'And in view of the fact that your ex-wife is remarrying . . .'

'What?'

He stood up, knocking over the coffee as he did so. A cup went flying over the table, spilling its contents over the carpet and her black skirt.

'She's getting married again?'

'I gather you didn't know.' The bloody woman was looking at him as though it was his fault. 'Would you mind passing me that napkin? Thank you.'

She began dabbing furiously at her skirt.

'Who is he?'

'The letter doesn't say. However, a new union has obvious implications for your relationship with your children.'

'It bloody well does.' Roddy was already fumbling for his mobile in his jacket pocket to call Annabelle. 'It means another man is going to be bringing up my kids. The children that I'm not even allowed to see . . .'

'For reasons which the courts felt were perfectly valid.'

'Whose side are you on, for Chrissake?'

She'd finished sponging her bloody skirt now. 'Your side, Lord Pearmain. I will do my best but I cannot make any promises.'

Annabelle was on the phone, dammit. Probably to her new fiancé. Well, he'd go round right now!

'And please don't consider going round to your wife's home or doing anything stupid like that. That would render an appeal impossible.'

If he wasn't a man, he'd be crying. He focused hard on the Monet print on the wall. 'Then what am I meant to do?'

She was looking sorry for him now. That was even worse.

'Try and concentrate on something else, Lord Pearmain. Your work, perhaps . . . your stepfather tells me you're starting a furniture line.'

He snorted.

'I will start an appeal process and will be in touch as soon as I have any news.'

'But it won't work.' He glared at her. 'You said so yourself.'

'It's worth trying. As you said.'

He walked out without his customary smile at the pretty receptionist. Lawyers! Damn the lot of them. Well, there was something he could do. He hadn't been sure at first – they seemed a weird lot – but now Annabelle and the solicitor had given him no choice.

Punching in the number (he'd taken the precaution of adding it to his mobile phone address book), he continued walking along the street towards the tube. 'Hello? Is that Kids Need Dads? Good morning. I spoke to you the other day. The name's Roddy Pearmain. Listen, about that meeting. I'd very much like to come after all.'

Thirteen

DON'T FORGET!

As already notified by the electricity board, our main supply
will be turned off between midday and 3 pm on Wednesday
so urgent works can be carried out.

Friendly reminder from the Bridgewater Residents' Association

Traditionally, they always had fried eggs for breakfast on
Saturdays. Nick was in charge of the toast and Justine was meant
to be doing the eggs. In the old days, it had been Jonathan's job.

'Crap. I've dropped shell in it and I can't work this stupid
cooker.'

'Justine!' Louise felt her voice rise to a crescendo as she
helped her daughter scoop the shell out of the pan and turn
the front ring down. 'No wonder Tim's picked up that horrible
word. Can't you think of something else to say?'

Justine scowled at her. 'Like what?'

'Well, like Andrex or something.'

'You're sad, Mum. Really sad.'

'How about Shandrex?' suggested Nick, fishing a piece of
burnt toast out from the toaster. 'The "sh" bit makes you feel
you're going to say . . .'

'Ok, we get it,' said Justine tiredly. 'This toaster's crap, Mum.
Why can't we have Aga toast?'

'Because we don't have an Aga,' said Louise tightly.

'Why can't we get one, then?'

Don't lose it. Don't lose it. 'Because there isn't room in the kitchen and because we have an electric cooker instead.'

Grumpily, Justine pulled up a chair and began eating. 'But it's not the same. And it won't keep us warm in the winter.'

Nick dug her in the ribs. 'Quit moaning, Jus. Can't you see it's difficult for Mum? Now hurry up or we won't be ready for Dad.'

'What time's he coming?' asked Louise, trying to sound as though she wasn't bothered.

Nick glanced at his watch, the watch they had given him for his sixteenth birthday when she had been blissfully unaware of Gemma's existence.

'Any minute now. Where's Tim? Shaking hands with the unemployed again?'

'What?' asked Louise.

'It's their disgusting way of saying he's having a pee,' said Justine, making a face.

What would they come up with next? Louise was still grappling with the toaster which appeared to be overheating, even though it was on the lowest setting. She had to get it to work; she couldn't afford another. 'Actually,' she said, 'Tim's still doing his homework. I said he had to do his French before he went out with Dad. I'd better go and hurry him up.' She glanced at her daughter's pushed-away plate. 'Are your knife and fork having an argument?'

'What?'

She was trying to make a joke, to lighten the atmosphere. 'Then put them together nicely, please.'

'You're mad, Mum, really mad.'

Ignore it. 'More toast?' asked Louise lightly.

'No thanks,' sniffed Justine. 'I'm good.'

Why did kids say they were good when they didn't want something? It was particularly ironic bearing in mind that 'good' was probably the last adjective she'd apply to her daughter, thought Louise, going out into the hall. She glanced at herself in the mirror; the beautiful gilt one that had hung before in the sitting room of the old house and which now looked too grand for the apartment.

Her mascara was already smudged under her eyes from where she'd rubbed them (something that seemed automatic nowadays) and her hair needed touching up at the roots. She used to go to the wonderful Michaeljohn up in town; now she'd have to investigate a local cheaper hairdresser instead.

'Tim?'

The room he shared with Nick was dark, curtains still closed.

'Tim? I thought you were doing your homework.'

She drew back the curtains and opened the windows to get rid of that stuffy, stale, cheesy smell so indigenous to teenagers. The gardener was mowing the communal lawn and a lovely fragrance of freshly cut grass pervaded the room.

'Tim?' she repeated, drawing back the covers. Her son was lying face-up to the ceiling and fully clothed. She'd given him breakfast an hour ago before sending him off to do his French. What was happening?

She sat down on the edge of the bed next to him. 'Do you feel ill?'

'No.' He turned over, away from her. What was happening to him? How could a child change so fast? What had she and Jonathan done to him?

'Are you all right?'

'No.'

'Why not?'

'Because I can't be arsed.'

She bit back the Don't-use-words-like-that phrase that was coming to her lips.

'Can't be bothered to do what?'

'Write out the school rules. I got a detention yesterday.'

'I see.'

Writing out the school rules was one of the punishments dished out by school. It was a long, arduous process that made the children's wrists ache and which was meant to deter them from repeating the same misdemeanour.

'What did you do this time?'

'Threw something.'

'A ball?'

'No.'

'What then?'

'Glue.'

'Glue?'

Tim rolled over to face her. 'It was a game. And it was only a supply teacher anyway. It doesn't matter.'

'Tell me exactly what happened.'

Tim groaned. 'I threw a bottle of glue at Birkin and he threw it back. The top was on but then it came off and some of it went on his jacket and some on mine . . .'

'Glue? On your blazer? Where?'

She stood up to find it. There it was, on the ground with the rest of his school uniform that she'd been meaning to pick up last night to wash but had forgotten about, so it was now on the ground like a worm cast. 'Tim, this is awful. I'll never get it off. That means buying another and they're so expensive.'

'Sorry.'

'You don't sound it.'

'I got a detention too. Next Friday after school.'

'But that's your confirmation class. You'll have to miss it again.'

For some ridiculous reason, the detention slot – a standard one for all pupils – was after school on Friday at exactly the same time as confirmation class. Tim seemed to be the only pupil affected by this clash; clearly the other confirmation candidates were not the detention type.

'You know you're meant to be confirmed at Christmas. At this rate, you'll have missed so many classes that the rev probably won't let you.' She sighed heavily. 'I'll have to talk to him again.'

Tim rolled over away from her once more. 'Have you told him about Dad?'

'Yes.'

'I asked you not to.'

'I had to, Tim. They needed to know.'

'Then they've got to make excuses for my behaviour, haven't they?'

'No, Tim, they haven't. It doesn't mean you can do what you want. It just means they know what's going on. It's not easy for teachers, you know, when kids play up.'

'If I was a teacher teaching me, I'd quit.'

She almost laughed. 'Me too. Now come on. Why don't you get up? You'll have to do your French later or you'll be late for Dad.'

'I don't want to see him.'

Part of her was pleased. No, that wouldn't do. It wouldn't do at all.

'Don't be silly. Of course you do.'

'I don't.' Tim sat up. 'Anyway, I said I'd go fishing with that bloke that's moved in.'

'Which bloke?'

'The one that you told me about; the one that voted for Hector.'

'Fishing? He hasn't asked me. Anyway, you can't. Dad will be really upset.'

'I don't care.'

There was the sound of a hoot outside. Louise looked out of the window. Jonathan was standing by the car – a new one. A make she didn't even recognise. Justine and Nick were already there, talking to him. The beep was clearly for Tim; he couldn't even be bothered to come in.

'Are you sure you don't want to see Dad?'

'Certain.'

'What shall I tell him?'

'I don't give a monkey's . . .'

'Ok.'

Smoothing her hair back, she walked through the apartment towards the front door. Jonathan was coming through at the same time and they almost collided.

'Sorry.'

It gave her a shock to stand so close to him. How can you live with someone for so long and then forget the exact shape of his eyebrows, the way his nose bent very slightly at the top; the broadness of his shoulders . . .

'Where's Tim?'

'He doesn't want to come.'

'Why not?'

'He won't say. He's being really weird at the moment. Swearing and being rude.'

'That's not like him.'

'I know.'

For a moment, she could almost pretend things were normal; a husband and wife discussing a child who was fast becoming a teenager.

'Are you blaming me?'

She shrugged. 'Not necessarily. Could be his hormones. It's not a great hormone combination in this house. I'm probably premenopausal; he's teenage hormonal; and Justine's hormones are flying all over the place.'

'And I suppose you think I'm male menopausal.'

'You said it.'

Wrong thing to say, Louise. Wrong thing.

'Listen, I tried to get hold of you last night. I left you a message.'

'I know. I thought I'd see you today so I didn't call back.'

'There's something I need to talk to you about.'

He put a hand on her arm and her heart leaped. 'What?' Her mouth was dry. 'Do you want a coffee?'

'No.' He looked around. 'The kids are waiting outside and I wanted to tell you first.'

She could feel her chest beating in her throat. 'Tell me what?'

'It's Gemma.' He looked her straight in the eyes, the way he hadn't done before when telling all those lies. 'She's pregnant.'

'Pregnant?' she whispered.

'Yes. I'm sorry.'

'Are you?'

'What?'

'Sorry?'

He shifted from one foot to the other. 'Well, put it this way. It wasn't planned but neither was . . .'

'Stop. Right there. You always did blame me and I've told you. It takes two for that sort of thing just like it takes two right now. Well, I hope you'll be very happy. The three of you.'

'Please, Louise, don't be like that.'

'Don't be like what?'

She could feel the anger coming now; it hurt but at the same time it felt good, like pus finally oozing out of a wound. 'You lie and cheat to me for over a year, maybe longer if I knew the full truth. Then you leave me with your three children and, hey presto, you have another. What will you do when you get bored with Gemma? Leave her too with the kids you have with her? Or is she the One? The One I wasn't?'

He was trying to hold her now but she shook him off. 'Get out, Jonathan. Get out. I don't want to see you again. Next time you pick up the kids, carry on hooting outside. Do you hear me? Now go. Please. Just go.'

She watched him turn and stride towards the front door, his shoulders back and straight. Numbly, she made her way to the kitchen and sank her head on to her arms.

'Mum?'

She turned round. Tim was standing pale-faced at the door. 'I heard you talking. Is Gemma really pregnant?'

She nodded.

Wordlessly, he padded barefoot across the lino towards her. Wrapping him in her arms, she breathed him in. Her youngest. Her baby. The child that had shown the cracks in a marriage that, until then, she had thought impermeable.

He drew away from her, too soon, his face hard and hurt.

'Why didn't you go with Dad?'

'I didn't want to.' His face was stony hurt. 'Can I go fishing instead?'

'What?'

'You know, fishing. I told you. Roddy's waiting outside for me now.'

It was all too much to deal with. 'I want to see him first.'

He considered her face. 'You're red.'

She splashed herself with tap water and dried her cheeks and forehead on a tea-towel. 'Better?'

He nodded. 'Sort of. Come on. He's waiting outside.'

How much had he heard? Putting on her sunglasses as camouflage, she went to the window.

'Hello.'

Her voice came out shakily. Pregnant. Gemma was pregnant.

'Tim says you've kindly offered to take him fishing.'

He was leaning against the wall but stood straight when he heard her voice. 'Is that all right? Just down by the lake. We'll be back by lunchtime.'

'That's very kind of you. Thank you.'

He was looking at her strangely. He must be able to see she was upset.

'It's a pleasure. See you later.'

She watched Tim walk over the lawn with the neighbour before sitting down again at the kitchen table. It dwarfed their new kitchen but the familiarity of the pitch pine and the grooves made by the children over the years comforted her. That was better. The tears were coming now. Fast and furious. Hot and gushing.

'Louise?'

For a moment, she thought she was imagining it. A pair of arms around her, from behind. Holding her, giving her strength. A male angel who would lift her up from all this and set her down, gently, in the past so she and Jonathan could begin all over again.

'Guy?'

'The door was open. Are you all right?'

'No.' She buried her head in his jumper; it smelt woolly and safe.

'Jonathan rang me from the car. He said he'd told you. I was nearby so I came straight round.'

She lifted her face to his.

'You knew before?'

His eyes were apologetic. 'I couldn't tell you. It wouldn't have been right. Not from me.'

But he had been her friend first, she wanted to say. Before Jonathan's.

'I'm so sorry.' His arms tightened around her. 'It will be all right, you know. You might not think so at the time, but one day . . .'

'Hello? I'm sorry. The door was open and this was so heavy, I just came in.'

They both stepped apart. Louise fumbled for a piece of loo paper up her sleeve to blow her nose. It took her a few minutes to recognise his face. Of course, the removal man. He'd left a message. Along with Jonathan's.

'These are the boxes that were left behind in the truck by mistake. Shall I put them here?'

'Thanks.'

He glanced at Guy. 'Settling in all right then, are you?'

'I'm not living here,' he said quickly.

'We're fine, thanks.' Louise bent down, pretending to examine the box in order to shield her tear-stained face.

'Good. Well, I'll be off then.'

'Thanks.'

'Are you all right?'

Guy stood over her as she undid the box.

'Yes. No. I don't know. It's such a shock. How pregnant is she?'

'Not very. I didn't ask but she's not really showing.'

Louise winced.

'Want a hand with that?'

'It's all right, thanks. They must have wrapped this up well.' She yanked the last bit of tape off. 'Oh God.'

'What?'

He squatted down beside her.

Louise pushed the box away. 'It's the photograph albums. All of them. Look!'

She laughed hoarsely, picking one up. 'Our wedding album. Can you believe it? Remember?' He nodded. Guy had been one of their ushers. 'The beginning of it all.' She pointed to her writing at the bottom of the wedding picture. 'If only I had known.'

'Lou, don't torment yourself.' He gathered her to him again. 'Please. Don't.'

His lips were brushing her cheeks now; his forehead on hers; his arms wrapped comfortingly around her. 'It's all right. It's all right.'

'No, it's not. It's all wrong . . .'

'Shhhh.'

He made a movement towards her. He's going to kiss me, she thought. The realisation shot through her like an electric current.

'Mum!'

The kitchen door opened. Instantly they jumped apart.

Tim stood there, in his wellington boots, rod in hand. 'Guy?' His young voice came out strangely. 'I need a drink. Roddy forgot to bring some.'

'Here.' Louise went to the fridge, her hand shaking. How much had he seen?

'I must go.' Guy was putting on his jacket. 'Actually, I was wondering if you wanted to go to the cinema next weekend, Tim?'

'Maybe.' He turned to her. 'When's Dad coming back with Justine and Nick?'

'I don't know.'

This wasn't right. This wasn't right at all.

'I'll ring.' Guy brushed her cheek coolly and ruffled Tim's hair. 'See you, mate.'

'Mum?' Tim stared at her, barely waiting for Guy to leave. 'Were you just kissing him?'

'No.' Her hand shook violently as she poured the juice into a plastic flask. 'Of course not. He was just giving me a comfort hug, like I do to you when you're upset.'

Tim was still staring at her with an expression that she hadn't seen before. A hard expression. One far beyond his years.

'Because if you were – kissing him, I mean – I would never forgive you. Never.'

But why, she wanted to ask. Your father and I have separated. He's got someone else. Why can't I?

Yet she couldn't. It was too soon after Jonathan. She wasn't ready. Besides, the kids had been through so much. They'd already had to cope with their father going off with Gemma and now they would have a half-brother or -sister to contend with. How could she make their lives more complicated?

As she watched her son walk back over the lawn towards the lake, she felt more confused than ever. Guy had – she was sure – been about to kiss her. She had been scared but, at the same time, she'd wanted him to. Or was it just that she'd been starved of love for so long that she was confusing desire with simple comfort from her oldest friend?

Fourteen

AT HOME

MOLLIE DE MAY

**WEDNESDAY, 30 JUNE FROM 10.30
ONWARDS. COFFEE AND SPIRITS FOR THOSE
WHO'D LIKE THEM.**

RSVP

'It's a ridiculous idea!'

Nigel was wonderfully unaware that he had a piece of spinach in between his front teeth. Mollie watched in fascination as he barely swallowed his next mouthful before carrying on with his tirade. People at the next table were beginning to look. At the noise, that was – not the spinach. How utterly delicious!

'You can't possibly invite some floozy of an actress to move in with you,' said Nigel, helping himself to more new potatoes, despite the fact that his stomach was bulging over the top of his brown corduroy trousers. 'She'll hold wild parties and leave ring stains on the furniture. She might even help herself to the silver.'

'How dare you!'

Mollie drew herself up to her full height and gave her son a well-practised Lady Bracknell-handbag-look. 'Poppy isn't like that.'

'How do you know what she's really like? How well do you know her?'

'Your father and I met Poppy when she was still at RADA. We were invited to a production and instantly spotted her talent; something we're rather good at, actually. Just look at Hugh.'

Hugh had been one of her success stories – more so than Gideon's. It had been she who had spotted his star quality and had persuaded an old director friend to give him the first leg up the ladder. And now look at him! He hadn't been the first either. She and Gideon got a tremendous thrill from helping younger actors to get their first break. A psychologist would, no doubt, have put it down to the fact that they only had one child – and a child who had never been interested in the theatre. But it was more than that. It was part of the creative drive inside her, a drive that made her want to mould others and help them maximise their potential. The way she'd had to learn herself, the hard way. Gideon had been the same. That's why they had been so good together. They knew what it was like to struggle.

'Humph!' said Nigel, tucking into his rare steak. A waiter worried behind him. Nigel had a reputation for making complaints. This restaurant, a short drive from Bridgewater House, had heard them all before but still Nigel came back, mainly because it had a reputation for celebrity guests who lived in nearby Henley.

She touched his arm. 'Poppy won't be any trouble. She's testing for an amazing part later this week. If she gets it, she'll be filming in Canada most of next month.'

'And if she doesn't get it?'

Mollie smiled. 'She will. I've spoken to the director and he's already smitten.'

'Don't you think that's interfering, Mother?'

She regarded the piece of spinach between his teeth, which had grown bigger after the last mouthful. Couldn't he feel it?

'Nigel,' she said, putting her knife and fork together on the plate, 'you know me. I'm not the interfering type.'

'I beg your pardon?' asked Gideon at her side.

She ignored him. This was not the time and he knew it.

'So you see, Nigel, I won't need to move in with your after all. However, I am, of course, grateful for the offer.'

'Very grateful,' added Gideon in a teasing tone.

Nigel pushed the fat from his steak to one side. 'I'll agree on one condition. That you let my lawyer draw up a lease so that if you want to get rid of this Poppy girl, you can without any hassle.'

'Agree?' said Gideon astounded. 'What gives him the right to agree?'

'Absolutely,' said Mollie. 'It's not up to you to agree, Nigel. This is my decision.'

'But as the executor of Father's will, it's my obligation to look after you.'

'Well done,' hissed Mollie to her left. 'I told you not to make Nigel an executor.'

Gideon shrugged. 'I thought he'd be all right. He's always been very business-minded.'

'Very well, Nigel.' She leaned back in her chair and mopped her mouth elegantly, making sure she didn't leave a lipstick stain. 'Get your man to draw up a lease, but don't make it all mumbly jumbly.'

Nigel looked offended. 'It has to be done properly, you know.' He looked across the room, caught the eye of the maître d'hotel and clicked his fingers. The man instantly came scurrying over. 'This meat.' Nigel jabbed a thick index finger at it. 'It's virtually raw. I asked for medium rare.'

'I beg your pardon, sir. I will order another immediately.'

'No.' Nigel pushed the plate away. 'I'm not hungry now. You can waive the bill instead.'

'Of course, sir. Of course.'

'Nonsense.' Mollie opened her purse. 'I won't allow that. Mine was extremely nice; you must allow us to pay.'

She shot a fierce look at her son. 'I insist. Absolutely insist. And by the way, Nigel. Did you know that you have a large piece of spinach between your teeth. Doesn't he?'

The waiter shifted uncomfortably and Mollie looked up at Gideon for approval. But he had gone.

'Damn his stage exits,' she muttered.

'What, Mother?' Nigel said irritably, getting his credit card out.

'Nothing.' She smiled brightly at him. 'Trust me. You wouldn't understand.'

The following day, she was feeling a bit stiff. Probably the yoga. Well, she'd need to loosen up before her coffee morning. The latter had been Gideon's idea.

'You could invite those new people, the woman with the children and that rather dashing lord. Give them a chance to get to know each other. And it will be company for you too.'

'You're just saying that because you think I'm lonely,' she'd said. 'I'm all right, really. I still have you to talk to, even though it's not the same. And there's Sally. Besides, Poppy will be here later in the week. Friday, I think she said.'

But she'd thought about it and decided that maybe Gideon had a point. It might be nice for that mother – Louise, wasn't it? – to meet the neighbours properly. She looked so sad whenever she saw her; life wasn't going to be easy for her. Mollie's matchmaking instincts, which had been so helpful where dear Jude had been concerned, told her that, sadly, the mother and Lord Pearmain weren't right for each other but that didn't mean they couldn't enjoy each other's company. And they might even help to unwind that rather stiff American girl who was trying – according to Sally – to get pregnant, poor thing. Goodness, she knew what that was like.

She re-read her invitation. Coffee and spirits for those who'd like them. The last bit had been a rather clever touch, she thought. Especially as she had no idea if Gideon would turn up or not.

'Cooee, only me!'

Sally let herself in, using the key Mollie had given her months ago. It had seemed a good idea, especially towards the end, when she didn't want to leave Gideon's bed to answer the door.

Sally cast a quick look around. She was wearing, unusually

for her, a slim-fitting turquoise skirt which finished neatly just below the knee, showing off a rather nice pair of legs.

'You look brown,' observed Mollie, 'or are you wearing tights with a very fine sheen?'

Sally did a twirl, Angela-Rippon style. 'Nope, they're all me. Well, it's nice to go bare-legged in the summer and I found this great self-tan stuff from the department store. Got them to give me one of their free samples, I did, and another for my sister.'

'I didn't know you had one,' remarked Mollie.

'I don't.' Sally grinned. 'But I knew one sample wouldn't get me far. When I run out, I'll go somewhere else. Now let's get on with this, shall we?'

The apartment did, Mollie had to admit, need tidying up. A pile of *Stage* magazines sat on the low Indian cane table which she and Gideon had brought back from Delhi when he was doing a Merchant Ivory film. The hand-woven maroon and green rug, purchased at the same time (Gideon adored haggling), had biscuit crumbs on it. And Mollie's own heavy glass whisky tumbler sat on the occasional table by the chaise from last night.

'Everything ready for your coffee do?'

'Not exactly,' said Mollie. 'Sometimes, I don't know where the time goes. I probably should be getting ready now.'

Sally was already getting the Dyson out of the cupboard. Mollie admired her figure. She had the kind of breasts – even after three children – that one took for granted at that age.

'You go and change,' said Sally kindly, 'while I sort this lot out and find some cups. I brought some coffee just in case you're out. I presumed you'd be well stocked on the spirits front?'

Mollie smiled quietly. 'Very well stocked.'

'Great. Heck, I can hear someone at the door already. Don't worry. I'll see to it. Oh, and Mollie?'

'Yes, dear?'

'I hope you don't mind me saying, but you've still got face cream on your cheeks. You might want to rub it in.'

Through the bedroom wall, which had to be a stud wall

since the noise was quite clear, she could hear voices. The American, who was early – such bad manners! – and the dashing duo, Suzette and Lydia. Gideon had had rather a soft spot for Suzette. Or rather for Suzette's ample chest. It had been one of their little jokes between them. Mollie had never been the jealous type. In fact, she'd believed in pointing out pretty women to her husband, knowing that by doing so, he would compare his own wife favourably.

As though on cue, she felt his arms cradle her from behind. Weak with pleasure, she leant her head back into his shoulders.

'I didn't really fancy Suzette,' he whispered into her ear.

'Yes, you did, you naughty boy. Admit it.'

'Well, just a bit then.'

He held her to him; his chest was naked too. Skin on skin. His left hand sidled down towards her crutch; his right gripped her buttocks.

She moaned softly.

'Not now, Mollie. Not now. You've got guests. Later.'

'Please, Gideon, please!'

Too late. The room was empty with just a hint of a breeze through the window, even though she could have sworn she had closed it that morning.

'Everything all right in there?'

Sally was knocking at her door.

'Fine.' Mollie's voice came out cracked. Her body felt hollow and unfulfilled, crying out to be loved. 'Just coming.'

'So you see,' the pretty but earnest young American woman was saying, 'Victorian novelists were really ahead of their game. By the way, are those really Oscars on the mantelpiece?'

'I believe so.' Lord Pearmain's eyes weren't looking at the intent young woman addressing him. They were focused on the girl who was standing in the doorway, suitcase in hand, looking slightly paler than usual, Mollie thought, but still just as gorgeous with her red-brown hair tumbling down to her shoulders.

'Poppy, darling! What a lovely surprise.'

Mollie drew her in, kissing her warmly on both cheeks.

'You were expecting me, weren't you, Mollie?'

'Of course, dear.'

Had she got it wrong again? Maybe it was Wednesday and not Friday.

'I'm having a small coffee morning to welcome our new neighbours. It's a wonderful time for you to arrive because you can meet them all. Louise, this is Poppy. She's an actress and she's coming to stay with me for a while.'

Dear Louise – or was it Laura? – looked stage-struck with admiration. 'An actress? Gosh, how wonderful! You'll have to excuse me – I haven't been to the cinema or theatre for a while – what have you been in recently?'

Mollie left them to it, moving on to Roddy who clearly needed rescuing from the American.

'If you ask me, Mrs Gaskell was no better than . . .'

'Lord Pearmain! How nice to see you.'

The American – heavens, what was her name? – frowned at the unwelcome interruption.

'Please, call me Roddy.'

'Then you must call me Mollie. Now, have you both got a drink? I believe Sally is just coming in with coffee. Alternatively, would you prefer something harder? Gideon has a very good whisky here.'

Something flickered in his eyes as he looked away from the bottle. 'Coffee is fine, thank you very much.'

'Me too,' said the American quickly.

Mollie wracked her brains for her name but it wouldn't come. She'd have to blunder on without it. 'Did you know that Lord Pearmain used to live in this house as a child. It's been in his family for centuries.'

The American was transfixed. 'That's just incredible! Does it have a ghost?'

What was it with Americans and ghosts?

'It does, actually. Thank you.' Roddy took a mug of coffee

from the tray that Sally was holding out. 'He's called Henry. I used to talk to him when I was younger, but after I got sent away to school, he didn't appear again.'

The American was grinning now. She had perfect, even white teeth. 'You're teasing me, Lord Pearmain.'

'Not at all.' He was stirring his coffee. Somehow Mollie hadn't put him down as a two-sugar type.

'He was a Roundhead, judging from his clothes. And that makes sense. Oliver Cromwell stayed here, you know, and apparently planned one of his strategic battles in the grounds.'

'And how do you know he was called Henry?' asked Mollie.

'He told me. He was my imaginary friend or real friend, whichever way you look at it. He'd come and go and no one else could see him. My family used to think I was making him up.'

'And have you seen him since you moved in?' asked Mollie quietly.

'Sadly not. But I'm keeping my eyes open.'

That pretty woman, Louise or Laura, was coming up to them. Good. She wanted to know more about her; find out how she was getting on.

'Lord Pearmain . . .'

Roddy waved a gracious hand. 'Please. Just call me Roddy.'

Louise coloured slightly in what Mollie thought was a rather attractive way. 'I just wanted to thank you for taking my son fishing. He had a wonderful time.'

'Not at all. I've said we'll do it again if you're happy about it.'

'That would be very kind.' She seemed to be worried about something. 'The only thing that worries me is the lake. It's quite deep, isn't it and I wondered if . . .'

'Excuse me,' said Mollie quickly. 'I think that's my phone.'

She went towards the kitchen to take the call away from the noise.

'Mollie?' said a rich deep voice. For a moment it sounded like Gideon. 'Yes?' she said, her breath catching in her throat.

'Mollie, darling. It's Alan. Look, I know this probably isn't a great time for you, but something has come up. A fantastic opportunity. And before you say no, I want you to give it some serious thought.'

'I agree,' said Gideon in her ear.

Mollie felt her pulse quickening, the way it did before she was about to go on stage.

'Do tell me more,' she said, sitting down.

When she finally put down the receiver, she sat for a moment at the kitchen table, reflecting.

'Are you all right?' asked Gideon, his hand softly on her shoulder.

'Fine.'

'Are you sure?'

She looked up and it was Roddy, not Gideon at all.

'I think so.'

She took a deep breath. 'That was a director I used to work with, years ago. He wants me to do a voiceover. For a face cream advertisement, can you believe?'

'A voiceover? That's wonderful.'

'I've never done one before. To be honest, Gideon and I used to think it was like selling yourself. But yes, you're right. At my age – and given that I'm too old to tread the boards again – it *will* be wonderful.'

She could feel the excitement bubbling up inside her. 'In fact, I can't wait to go back to work again! It could be just what we – I mean I – need!'

Fifteen

DO YOU HAVE ANY CLOTHES YOU NO LONGER NEED?

If so, please leave them outside your front door next Tuesday
and they will be collected by a local charity.

'This doesn't look like a doctor's waiting room,' said Katy,
picking up a round rubber ball and examining it. She was
wearing, noted Marcie distastefully, such a short skirt that it
might as well be a scarf round her middle.

'What's this meant to do, anyway? It's got funny little spikes
in it.'

'It's a stress ball, stupid,' said Robert, throwing it up and
down in the air, nearly hitting the ceiling. 'They have them in
that inventions shop in Oxford Street. Mum says they're for
saddos.'

Marcie gritted her teeth. 'You're meant to squeeze it to get
rid of your stress.'

Robert tossed her the ball and she only just ducked in time.
'Well get squeezing then, Marcie. Mum says you're the most
uptight person she's ever met, although actually she doesn't
reckon you're a person at all. She says you're uptight and made
of plastic – American Express, she calls you – and she can't
think what Dad sees in you.'

'You could have hurt me, throwing the ball like that,' said
Marcie, shaking with anger. Picking up the ball from the floor,
she automatically squeezed it hard to stop herself punching the

boy. Honestly, what had got into her? She had never ever been a violent person yet these kids made her feel like doing things she had never thought of.

David, unfortunately, simply didn't see that side of them. When their mother had rung to ask if they could have them over an exeat – some weird British term for a day off school – he had immediately agreed, even though he wasn't the one who'd be looking after them. In vain did she tell him she had a doctor's appointment without, of course, going into too many details because her gut instinct warned her he would disapprove. He merely told her to take the children along with her and promised that he would be home early from work so they could 'do something fun' for the evening.

Fun! Marcie squeezed the ball harder so the veins stood out on her wrists. There was never any fun when these kids were around. And she could swear she smelt something alcoholic on Robert's breath.

'Have you been drinking?' she demanded sharply.

He gave her a scornful look. 'Course not. I just had one of Katy's sweets.' He handed her the packet. 'Want one? They're Jelly Willies.' He rolled one round on the tip of his tongue and closed his eyes in mock delight. 'Mmmm . . . delicious!'

Marcie turned away amidst their peals of laughter. 'That's disgusting.'

'It's not as bad as some things, Marcie,' said Katie naughtily. 'Do you know what masticate means?'

Was this another of their trick questions?

'Of course I do,' she said firmly.

'Are you sure?' Katy smirked. 'You're not muddling it up with masturb—'

'Be quiet,' hissed Marcie. 'Someone might hear you.'

'I doubt it.' Robert waved a leaflet at her. 'And if they do, it must be because they've had this hopi candle treatment. This piece of propaganda says they clear your ears. It's a really weird place, isn't it? All these notices about clearing your past channels and tuning in to your own wavelength.

You're not going mad, are you, Marcie? This isn't some kind of a loony bin?'

'No, It's not. It's an alternative health centre where they treat you as a whole and not just the symptoms.'

'What are you on, Marcie?'

'I'm not even going to dignify that with an answer.'

'Shit, Marcie. You really need help, don't you? You've squeezed that ball so hard there's a hole in it. Look.'

It was true. The ball was deflating now, in the palm of her hand. Marcie could feel the tears pricking her eyes. When Sally had suggested coming to the Crystal Alternative Health Centre, she had felt a ridiculous glimmer of hope. But now these horrible children had made her feel even worse than ever. How could she ever hope to get pregnant if her mind was in such a mess?

'Marcie Gilmore-Smith?'

A very thin, angular woman in a white coat put her head round the door. 'I'm sorry to have kept you. Would you like to come this way?'

'Can we go too?' asked Katy.

'No,' snapped Marcie. 'You can't. Read your magazines instead.'

'But I've finished my *Heat*.'

'Yeah, and we haven't got anything else to do.'

'Then find something.'

'I'm sure our receptionist can find them some more magazines,' said the woman in the white coat smoothly. 'Why don't you go through there, both of you, and ask her. We'll be back as soon as we can.'

Marcie sat on the chair, watching the woman fill in the form. It was taking such a long time. All she wanted was to get on with whatever treatment might help.

'May I ask how you heard about me, Mrs Gilmore-Smith?'

'Through my cleaning lady. She's into this sort of thing.'

'And can you tell me why you are here, specifically?'

Marcie felt the familiar lump rising into her throat, the same lump that came up every time a stranger asked if she had children. 'I've been trying to get pregnant for over a year. My husband and I have been seen by a private consultant and had various tests. Apparently, there's no reason why we can't conceive but it just isn't happening.'

The woman put down her pen. 'Then the teenagers in the waiting room aren't yours?'

'My husband's. From his first marriage.' Marcie laughed drily. 'No problems there, as you can see. Which means it must be my fault.'

'We prefer not to use words like "fault".' She spoke softly, almost hypnotically. 'Now, I don't know if your friend told you anything about the work we do here but there are indeed some treatments that might be able to help. You tell me you've already been taking pulsatilla that you purchased over the counter?'

Marcie nodded.

'As a homeopath, I'd like to ask you some more questions and do a skin test to make sure you're taking the right treatment. I am also a cranial osteopath and I would suggest an approach which might just help the natural energies flow better within your body. I'm not promising this will resolve the problem but it might well help.'

Marcie nodded again. For the first time since she'd come into this place, she was beginning to feel there might be an answer after all.

'I'd like to start with the osteopathy. Can you slip off your jeans and lie on the couch for me?'

Jeans? She'd thought cranial was to do with the head. And, without wanting to sound politically incorrect, this woman did look a bit manly.

'I need to be able to manipulate your pelvis,' said the woman, as though sensing her apprehension. 'After that, I'll go on to other areas of your body.'

'Right.' Awkwardly, Marcie slid out of her new Calvin Kleins.

'You're very thin,' remarked the osteopath disapprovingly.

In the States, this would have been seen as a compliment. 'I can't help it. We've just moved house and it's been a bit stressful.'

The woman's hands were moving very gently over her pelvic bones; so gently that she could hardly feel it. 'Well, that's what we're here for. To reduce the stress. I know it feels a bit strange at first but we advise new clients to close their eyes and imagine themselves in a place that means something to them.'

Marcie's eyes were already drooping. She was sitting on her father's verandah, wearing beige shorts and a red skinny t-shirt, leaning back on the railings with a glass of lemonade in her hand. It was hot. Very hot. And then, in the distance, she could see the battered red Ford truck coming up the dusty drive . . .

'Are you all right?'

She had jolted awake.

Marcie began to shake. 'I'm not sure. I've just remembered something and I feel a bit spooked.'

'Lie back down again.' The woman's hands were working her skull now. That was better. The truck faded into nothing. She was almost asleep.

'Are you cured now, Marcie?'

Katy sniggered from the back of the car. 'Yeah. Are you sane now? Did that woman in the white coat make you better?'

She wasn't going to let them spoil this wonderful sense of well-being. 'What would you like for supper, you lot?'

'Whatever you haven't got.'

Marcie closed her eyes briefly and thought of the homeopathic tablets in her handbag which the therapist had given her. She was to take them along with the pulsatilla. Straight on to her tongue from the plastic bottle; no touching of hands in between. So barmy that it might just work.

'Actually, your father has suggested we go out for a Chinese.'

'Mum's new boyfriend's Chinese.'

'No he's not, stupid. He's from Kuala Lumpur.'

'Well, Mum says he's rich enough to own China. Say, Marcie, we got you another leaflet when we were waiting in that weird place. I'll read it out for you, shall I? It says, "Regress back into your past lives. Help clear the channels so you can deal better with the present." How weird is that?'

'Don't tell me,' said Robert in a voice which sounded deeper than last weekend, unless he was just putting it on, 'that you really believe these saddos at your centre can take people back into former lives?'

'And why not?' Marcie's hands tightened on the steering wheel. 'The chap who's just moved in – whose family used to own the house – said there's a ghost in the west wing. It's perfectly possible.'

'A ghost?' Robert snorted. 'That's *so* American, to believe in ghosts.'

'Fine. Have it your way.' Marcie swung off the main road, through the gates and up the drive. Every time she did that, it still gave her a thrill. 'Good. Your father's home early.'

For once, she added to herself. Why was it that David was late, night after night, when it was just her at home. But when the kids were here, he always managed to get the early train.

The Chinese was a good idea. For the three of them, that was. Marcie spent the evening trying to choose something that wasn't heavily coated in gluto-whatever. The therapist had advised her to stick to non-additives and had given her a list of diet do's and don'ts. The Chinese wasn't actually suitable for Katy, who was still on her no-wheat and no-dairy diet, but David appeared to have forgotten that and she felt it would make her even more unpopular to mention it.

'Yummy,' said Katy, licking her lips. 'Ooops, sorry, Marcie. I seem to have spilt some soy sauce on your lap.'

'No problem,' said Marcie tightly.

'Everyone had enough?' David paid the bill. 'Right. Time to go home, I think.' He yawned. 'I'm exhausted. But you two can watch a video if you like.' He patted his pocket. 'I got you the new Jennifer Aniston DVD.'

Katy sidled up to him, snuggling up against his shoulder in a way that instantly made Marcie feel out of it. 'But it hasn't been released yet, Dad.'

David touched the side of his nose. 'One of my clients works for Universal. He thought you might enjoy it.'

'Wicked.'

It made for a reasonable journey home, without the usual snide remarks about Marcie's driving. Thank goodness neither of them had mentioned the visit to the Crystal Alternative Health Centre, although Marcie had already figured out an explanation. She would just say that she was investigating it on behalf of Virginia, who was interested in that kind of thing.

'At last,' murmured David as they slid into bed together. On the other side of the wall, they could hear the DVD. Not too noisy but loud enough to block out any sounds at their end.

'Mmmmm.' Marcie slid into her husband's arms. It wasn't the right time of the month but what the hell? Sometimes it was nice to run the race without trying to win it.

'What is it? asked Marcie sleepily, turning over. It felt late, although she was too tired to focus on the clock. Moonlight was pouring in through the curtains and she shielded her eyes. David was climbing back into bed.

'Where've you been?'

'Katy was having a nightmare. About a ghost.'

His voice sounded cold and wide awake. 'She says you told them the house was haunted?'

'Not exactly. I just said that Lord Pearmain told me there was meant to be a ghost.'

She sensed him frowning in the darkness. 'That wasn't very sensible, was it? It's really freaked them out.'

'They didn't seem freaked out when I told them. In fact, they started the conversation about people having lived before.'

'They told me.' David sounded even grimmer. 'Where exactly did you take them today?'

Marcie groaned into the pillow. 'To an alternative health centre, if you really must know. I got some osteopathy and some homeopathic tablets to try and make me more fertile. I didn't tell you because I knew you and that stuffy consultant would disapprove. There. Satisfied?'

'Well what's all this about going back into previous lives?'

'I didn't do that.' Marcie beat her fist on the pillow. 'Katy picked up some leaflet about a woman at the centre who specialises in that, but I didn't see her. Why would I? All I want to do is have a baby.'

Hot, heavy tears slid down her cheeks.

David patted her arm. Angrily, she moved away.

'I didn't mean to get cross but Katy is really upset. I've had to let her sleep with the light on. And it's bound to get back to Diana.'

'Go on. Say it.' Marcie sat up, feeling nauseous. 'If I was a proper mother like your ex, I wouldn't have mentioned ghosts. I would have known it might have scared them.'

'Well . . .' David hesitated.

Marcie swung her legs out of bed. He put out his hand and touched her thigh. 'Where are you going?'

She shrugged it off. 'To the kitchen to make myself a drink.'

'Don't be mad.'

Her head began to pound the way it always did during confrontations. 'I'm not. Just crazy, according to your bloody kids.'

She sat at the breakfast bar for a while, nursing a glass of cranberry juice. Sometimes, just sometimes, she wondered if she'd done the right thing. Moving to England and falling in love with a true British gentleman had seemed so romantic; Virginia had been really bowled over and so had her friends. It was what they had all dreamed of when studying Jane Austen and the Brontës. But now the harsh realities might be better suited to a Gothic novel. She'd never get the better of those children; and what's more she couldn't be bothered. All she wanted was a baby of her own.

Getting up, she walked towards the window. The moonlight had bathed the grounds in a white pool. Towards the bottom, she could see the lake glimmering. It was all so beautiful. So very, very heartbreakingly beautiful.

Impulsively opening the window, she leant outside. The stocks, which the gardener had planted in the tubs outside in the drive, were heavenly.

'Gosh, sorry.'

She withdrew her head. The man walking by had almost bumped into her face but he hadn't seemed to notice. He was tall, very tall, although he had a slight stoop, indicating an elderly person from the back, and he was wearing a velvet smoking jacket.

He looked familiar somehow; Marcie wracked her brains to think where she had seen him before. Maybe he was one of Suzette's many gentleman friends. Still, it was no business of hers if someone chose to take a midnight walk. She wouldn't mind taking one herself.

Why not? It would do David good to worry about her.

Pulling her dressing-gown closer around her, she slipped into a pair of sneakers by the front door and put it on the latch behind her. The air was already beginning to calm her throbbing temples. The man was some distance ahead. She didn't want to catch up or he might think she was following him. Somehow she didn't feel scared; with so many people living here, this place seemed so safe. It was one of the things she liked about it.

She rounded the east wing. The man in front had disappeared. Just as she'd thought. He'd gone into Suzette's door. Marcie's lips twitched despite the traumas of the evening. Good on Suzette! Whoever said sex was just for the young – or for making babies?

Sixteen

**THIS IS A NEIGHBOURHOOD
WATCH AREA!**

If you see anything suspicious, please contact Lydia Parsons at
number 6, Bridgewater House.

Roddy woke up from an amazing dream in which he managed
to drink an entire bottle of whisky without feeling in the slightest
bit tipsy.

He stretched out, feeling cheated by the dream and at the
same time wonderfully relaxed. It really was fucking amazing
to be in a proper bed without a cellmate next to him. He'd
thought that every day since leaving the clinic, although occasionally, to his consternation, he missed one or two other
inmates. Not Kevin. Christ, that man had been irritating. But
every now and then Genevieve's green eyes and lithe brown
body swam into his mind.

No. He wouldn't torment himself any more, Roddy told
himself, swinging his legs over the side of the bed. Besides,
he had other things to think about now. Such as his meeting
this afternoon with Kids Need Dads. When he'd first made
the appointment, he'd felt hopeful for the first time in months
about sorting out this whole bloody mess about Daniel and
Helena and Annabelle getting married again. But now he was
beginning to feel less certain somehow. What could they do
to help him? The law was hardly going to be changed
overnight.

His third thought was that someone was banging on the door. And at this time of the morning! Either that or the headache – which had started sometime in the middle of the night and couldn't even be blamed on alcohol – was getting worse.

'Coming, coming,' he called out irritably, pulling on a pair of boxers. Only wimps like Kevin, in Roddy's opinion, wore anything in bed.

'Hi there.' A pert youngish woman, her hair in a pony-tail with a pink fringe, stood facing him. Her eyes travelled slowly down to his boxers and back up again with a bemused smile. 'It was meant to be nine o'clock, wasn't it?' she asked questioningly.

If this was a dream, it was one he could do with more often. 'I beg your pardon?'

'Sally.' She tossed back the pink fringe carelessly. 'I'm the cleaner. I usually do this place at this time for your stepfather. He said to carry on, even though you're here now.'

'He did?' Roddy ran his hands through his hair. 'That's fine. Come on in.'

'Tell you what.' Her pony-tail was bobbing. 'I'll do next door first and come back later. You can leave a key if you like, in the usual place, if you're out.'

'And where might that be?'

'Under the stone slab by the front door. That's where Peregrine normally leaves it. Oh, and by the way, I do mending too. If you're interested.'

It wasn't until he'd closed the front door behind her that he realised what she'd meant. Oh, shit. Oh, shit. There was a big hole in his boxers at the back. And to his horror, the front seemed a bit fuller than it normally was. Had she noticed? Well she couldn't have failed to.

Knock. Knock.

Now what did she want? He pulled on some jeans quickly. 'Yes?'

'Tim!' What was this? Piccadilly Bloody Circus? 'What can I do for you?'

The kid was standing there expectantly, rod in hand. Even as Roddy spoke, he had a sinking feeling. Surely he hadn't promised another fishing trip, had he?

'You forgot.'

The kid spoke flatly; it wasn't a question. He turned. 'It's ok. I can do something else.'

'No, wait.' A vision of Daniel shot through Roddy's head. Daniel with that look on his face when he'd come downstairs one night to find his father with a whisky bottle in one hand and his mother, slumped on a chair, weeping. So many disappointed kids in the world. So many disappointed fathers. 'I was just getting up.'

'Honest?'

The kid's face lit up.

'Honest.' Give me five, Roddy would have liked to have said. That's what he'd used to do with the kids on the good days. They'd raise their hands and slap their palms together playfully. But he and this boy didn't know each other well enough for that. Come to think of it, he'd better be careful. 'Does your mother know we're going down to the lake?'

'Yeah. I told her. She's gone for a job interview anyway.'

Roddy felt a flicker of interest. Pretty woman, Tim's mother. But too sad-looking for his taste.

'What about your dad? Is he coming over today?'

Tim shuffled his feet, looking down at them. 'Don't think so.'

Shit, life stank. 'Just wait there. I won't be a sec.'

Leaving him in the hall, Roddy threw on a t-shirt and put on the kettle. He had to have a cup of coffee first or he wouldn't get through the morning. Funny. He used to think that about whisky. Well, that bottle was still in the cupboard. He'd been amused to discover Peregrine had put a very discreet cross on the label so he could tell if he drank it and then replaced it. No need for that. He was going to prove the bastard wrong.

'Right. I'm ready now.'

Tim was looking at the paintings on the wall. 'These are

weird, aren't they? Sorry, I didn't mean to be rude. But they don't mean anything. They're just circles in bright colours.'

Roddy cast them a disparaging look. 'They're not mine, believe me. My stepfather collects that sort of stuff.'

'Bet they're worth a bit, though.' Tim was still looking. 'My parents took us to the Picasso museum in Paris before they split up. These paintings look a bit like those.'

Roddy's eyes narrowed. 'They do a bit, don't they? But sadly they're not. Ok then, off we go. Thought we could head past the temple on the way. There's something I thought you might like to see.'

'The temple?'

'Haven't you found it yet? I'd have thought you kids would have explored every inch of this place by now. It's a sort of Gothic extravaganza that my great-great-grandfather built at around the same time as the pavilion. Come on. I'll show you.'

The temple wasn't in as great shape as he'd remembered. In one way, he was relieved that the developers clearly hadn't done anything with it. In another, he was cross that such a piece of history had been left in this state. The stones around the outside were badly broken in places and the roof – still its original slate blue – had holes in it. But the wisteria and winter jasmine were still entwined around the cast-iron pillars.

'Cool,' said Tim, kneeling down and examining the pictures on the stone slabs. 'What are these?'

The excited look on the boy's face gripped him. He should be doing this with his own son, not a stranger's. The pain was almost too great to bear. And now Annabelle was getting married again, another man would be sharing these moments. Just as he was, with this kid, whose father had left him.

Roddy knelt down beside him. 'That's Mars, God of War. And that babe next to him is Venus. When I was your age, my sister and I used to make up stories about them and pretend they lived here.'

'Like Henry?'

'Who?'

'The ghost. Mum said you knew a ghost here, called Henry. She overheard you telling that American woman he was a childhood friend.'

Roddy looked away, embarrassed. 'Yeah. I had an overactive imagination at that age. It was just a pretend friend really but you know what these Americans are like. They love a ghost story and everyone seemed so bloody – I mean so very – excited that I'd lived here before that they wanted to know about the history. It seemed a shame to disappoint them.'

'That's telling fibs.'

'I know. I shouldn't do it.'

'I do sometimes.' Tim leant back against the wall. 'Not big ones. But little ones. To stop Mum getting mad at me.'

Roddy thought of the pale blonde woman he'd seen, flitting between the car and the house. 'She doesn't seem like the kind of person to get mad.'

'Well she does. She's got really different since Dad left. You never know what she's going to be like.' Tim was pulling grass out of the wall and tossing it angrily on the stone slabs. 'Sometimes she cries and then I feel sorry for her but I don't know what to do. It's, like, difficult. And sometimes she yells at us for no reason.'

Roddy began to pull out the grass vehemently. 'Don't be too hard on her. It's not easy when you're left.'

Tim looked at him. 'Is that what happened to you?'

'Sort of. Except it was my fault.' He looked away. 'I drank too much. It made me say and do things I shouldn't have.'

'Did you do drugs too?'

'Of course not.' God this was getting difficult. The boy was only a kid. And not his own, either. They shouldn't be talking about this kind of stuff.

'Say,' he said, changing the subject, 'did you know that your part of the house was the old dairy? And the American woman's bit was the cook's quarters.' His mouth twitched. 'She won't like that very much.'

Tim grinned. 'No, she wouldn't. I feel like telling her. She's always going on at Mum about the dog. The other day, she said our rubbish bin smelt.'

Roddy suddenly felt bored with all this small talk. That's what happened when people lived too close together. In fact, it made him want to have a drink.

He jumped to his feet. 'Come on. Or we won't get any fishing done at all. And I've only got a couple of hours because I've got to be somewhere.'

'You don't have to take me fishing.' Tim's eyes narrowed again.

'Actually,' said Roddy, picking up his own rod. 'I want to. And you're doing me a favour by coming along.'

'Really.'

Roddy grinned. 'Really. I could use some company before I hit town this afternoon.'

It had been ages since he'd last been in this part of London. Clapham wasn't an area he knew well, thank God. And it had taken him ages to get through the traffic. It might have been all right if he'd left earlier, but how could he have disappointed that kid? They'd only caught a couple of pike – and thrown them back – but the boy had been as happy as he had been at that age.

Now it was time to face reality.

Roddy walked past a parade of shoddy shops. One, with the sign 'Past It' on the façade, had a brass chandelier hanging in the window and some dusty pine furniture – Victorian, surprisingly – on the pavement outside. He ran his hand over the edge of a bevelled dressing-table mirror. Almost immediately, a man came out of the door.

'Nice bit of work,' he commented.

The man nodded curtly. He was wearing the kind of navy blue fleece that Kevin used to favour in the clinic. 'Actually,' said Roddy, 'I was looking for Bevan Road. You don't happen to know where it is, do you?'

'Second on the left.'

'Thanks.' Roddy's fingers were now working their way over a mahogany chest of drawers. He couldn't help it. Wood always did that to him.

'Make things, do you?'

'Used to. I've had a bit of a break but I'm thinking of getting back into it.'

'What kind of things?'

Roddy shrugged. 'Tables. The odd chair. Boxes. I restore things too.'

'Got any pictures?'

'I have, actually.' Roddy fished in his pocket for the Polaroid he always carried, along with the pictures of the kids. It was a large box he'd made for his mother years ago for her to store documents in, and had been so successful that her friends had all placed orders too. It had made him feel good which was why he had it in his wallet. That had been one of the more useful suggestions that the clinic therapist had made.

'Not bad.'

The man handed it back. 'If you want to bring some stuff down here, we can sell it for you. Fifty-fifty.'

'Thirty-seventy.' Rod slipped the photograph back in his wallet.

'Forty-sixty.'

'Ok.'

The man handed him a card. 'Here's my email. Get in touch and we can talk more.'

Roddy continued down the road, feeling jauntier than he had done before. He knew damn well that the owner of Past It would pass his work off as original but so what? It wouldn't be the first time.

Second left. Right. He was here. The house was a run-of-the-mill Victorian terrace with an untidy front garden and weeds growing through the slabs. The door needed a wipe too, and so did the wide windowsills. He raised the knocker. Perhaps this was a mistake.

'Come on in.'

A very tall, broad-shouldered man had opened the door almost immediately. He was wearing brown cord trousers and a crisp checked shirt. Roddy began to feel slightly better. 'I'm Peter Sussex, chairman of Kids Need Dads. Nice to have you on board.'

Roddy wanted to say that he wasn't on board yet and wasn't sure that he was keen to be. But he was already being led through the long narrow hall and into a square room with a tiled fireplace and several chairs grouped round the outside. There were at least twelve men there – rather like a jury – and for one of the few occasions in his life, Roddy felt somewhat intimidated.

'Hi, I'm Roger.' Someone got up and shook his hand.

'I'm Will.'

They all introduced themselves in turn. Politely. It wasn't what he'd expected.

'Take a seat, Roddy. I can call you that, can't I?' Peter took out a notepad. 'Now, I know you'll probably have read up on us but I'd like to spend a bit of time telling you what our aims are. For a start, we're not the aggressive organisation that the papers like to portray us as. We're simply a group of fathers who, through various reasons and often no fault of our own, have been denied contact with our kids or who don't have as much contact as we'd like. Roger here has kids who live in Cornwall. Their mother took them there after the divorce and because Roger's job is demanding and he doesn't earn much, he can only afford to see them once a month.'

'And even then it's at McDonalds or whatever bed and break-fast I find to stay in,' added Roger. 'The courts decreed that they should come to me for two weeks every school holiday but their mother says it isn't practical. My solicitor is meant to be on the case but it's taking months and costing me an arm and a leg.'

Each man, it seemed, had a different grievance. Kids moving away seemed to be a common one. One man was even fighting his wife's decision to emigrate to Australia.

'Do you want to tell us about your situation,' said Peter gently.
The room went quiet. Roddy cleared his throat. 'It's tricky.'
Everyone nodded understandingly.

'Actually, I've probably got myself to blame, although I've
changed. I really have.'

No one spoke.

'I used to drink. Quite a lot. It made me do things I shouldn't
have. I didn't hurt the kids. But I did scare my wife a bit.'

'You hit her?' asked Peter.

Roddy looked away. 'I don't really remember much about
it. But yes, that's what she says. After that, she got an order
against me. I wasn't allowed to see the children. My stepfather
paid for me to go to a clinic and I'm ok now. But she still won't
let me see them. My solicitor is doing what she can – at least
I think she is – but now Annabelle, my ex, is getting married
again and I'm scared, so bloody scared, that I've lost my kids.'

Oh, shit. He was crying. He was actually crying. Roddy sat
down, his head in his hands.

'It's ok.' Peter was standing over him, his hands on his shoulders. 'We've all been there in different ways, haven't we, boys?'

There was a chorus of assent.

Roddy lifted his tear-stained face.

'We can help you, Roddy,' Peter was saying. 'We can really
help you.' He crouched down in front of him, his face on the
same level. 'And I think you might be able to help us too.'

Seventeen

CURRICULUM VITAE

Louise Howard
Age: 45
Qualifications: English degree 2:1 from Sussex University.
Previous experience: magazine journalist.
Currently having a career break to bring up children.

Louise shifted uncomfortably in her chair as the employment agency woman read her CV. She'd spent ages getting it right and Nick had sweetly suggested different fonts to make certain bits stand out. Not that they were worth highlighting. She hadn't worked for so long that she was surely unemployable. Which was precisely why she had left out any dates.

'So you read English at university and trained as a journalist.' The woman sounded surprised.

Louise nodded.

'But you gave up to have a career break after your second child was born?'

She nodded again.

'So when exactly was that?'

Louise reddened. 'About sixteen years ago. It was difficult with three children. And when I was married, I didn't really need to . . . But I have done the odd bit of freelance work for the magazine I used to be on. Just a few articles, over the years.'

'And have you tried finding work as a journalist?'

Louise smiled ruefully. 'It's not the kind of career that lends itself to taking breaks. Once you're out, it's hard to get back. Most of my contacts have moved on and either become free-lance like me or become editors. I did email someone I knew who is now editing a big glossy monthly but she hasn't even bothered to come back to me.'

'Are you qualified for anything else?'

'Not really. But a lot of journalists go into public relations so I wondered about that.'

The woman shook her head. 'We don't have anything like that on our books. What about computer skills?'

'Well, I can type, of course, and I'm familiar with Word.'

'Spreadsheets? PowerPoint?'

Louise shook her head. 'Sorry.'

'Are you willing to go on a refresher course?'

'Provided it doesn't take too long. As I explained, I'm a single mother now. I need to earn money.'

'But you also need more qualifications.' The woman was flicking through a thin pile of papers on her desk. 'Would you say you were good with people?'

Louise thought of the blazing row she'd just had with Justine over her DT coursework that morning. She was meant to have handed it in by last week and it still wasn't finished. 'Yes. You have to be, as a journalist. And I don't think you lose that skill unless, of course, you're related to people. I certainly seem to manage to rub my own children up the wrong way.'

The woman's lips moved slightly into something that might or might not resemble a smile.

'I think we all feel like that.' She picked out a sheet of paper and handed it over.

'This might suit you. The Crystal Alternative Health Centre needs a receptionist. Unlike most of the PA jobs we handle, it doesn't actually need a wide knowledge of computer skills. It's mainly dealing with clients and making appointments. Doesn't start until next month but they're interviewing now.'

Louise felt a weight in the pit of her stomach. If someone had told her, in the heady days of *Charisma* magazine, that in twenty-odd years time she'd be doing the kind of job that was more menial than that of her own secretary, she would have been appalled.

'How much does it pay?'

The woman named a rate that would scarcely have paid her weekly supermarket bill in the days when she had considered herself happily married.

'I'm not sure.'

The woman's eyes narrowed. 'Don't dismiss it. I don't have anything else that you're qualified for, but you'll be lucky to get this, if I'm honest. I've already sent five applicants down and none of them were thought suitable.'

Louise swallowed. 'All right. I'll apply.'

The woman picked up the phone. 'Good. I'll see if I can arrange an interview.'

At least, Louise thought as she came out of the agency, her preliminary interview with the agency woman had stopped her thinking about everything else for half an hour. But now, as she made her way to the car park, it was crowding her head again. Gemma was pregnant. Guy might or might not have been about to kiss her. Nothing seemed real any more.

No one was home when she got in. Home? Louise mentally ran her tongue round the word. She'd considered their previous house to be home for so long that it seemed almost unfaithful to call Bridgewater House the same. Yet it did feel homely, mainly because of her neighbours, like Mollie.

Roddy was friendly too. It was nice of him to take Tim fishing again; he'd rung to ask her permission, explaining he'd had to cut short their fishing trip yesterday because he'd had to go to London, and asking if they could go for longer today. Part of her felt slightly uneasy about Tim going off with a stranger, but the other part felt bad at even thinking such a thing. He was a father himself, wasn't he?

The only real problem was the American woman. Louise felt uneasy at having upset her but, then again, you couldn't please everyone.

'Hello, you,' she said, kneeling down and ruffling Hector's fur. He lay on his back, willing her to tickle him more. 'Want a walk?' Putting Hector on the lead, she made her way across the drive. As she did so, she saw Jonathan's car coming up. But he wasn't driving. He wasn't even in it.

'Hello, Louise.' A slim woman with a creamy complexion and kohl-rimmed eyes slid out of the car and eyed her coolly. 'Jonathan couldn't pick up the kids so he asked me to come.'

Louise felt sick. How had this woman known who she was? Had she seen a picture? 'I presume you are Gemma?'

She was so pretty. So unbelievably pretty, with sleek hair that fell in soft curls to her shoulders. Small too. The kind that would head for the Petite range.

'You presume right. I guessed it was you because of the dog.' Gemma almost seemed to be laughing at her. Why was her heart beating so fast? Why was she scared of this woman when she was perfectly in her rights to yell – lash out even?

'Are they ready? Only we're going out and we don't want to be late.'

Louise struggled to sound normal. 'I'm afraid I don't know where they are. Were they expecting you?'

'Of course they were. Jonathan arranged it last time. We've got tickets for a play in the West End.' She looked around angrily. 'They must be somewhere. Isn't that Timothy walking up?'

'Tim,' said Louise. 'He's known as Tim.'

'Whatever.'

'Mum.' He began running towards her. 'We've had a great time and . . . oh. Hi, Gemma.'

'I didn't know you were going out with Dad tonight,' said Louise. 'I've got supper organised.'

It wasn't true but she might have done.

'Sorry.'

'Where's Nick and Justine?'

'They said they'd make their own way to Dad's.'

'Nice of them to tell me.'

Gemma smirked.

'Everything all right?' asked Roddy, striding up, fishing rod in hand. Gemma's eyes swivelled towards him. He did indeed make a dashing sight, Louise thought. Hair tousled, Marco Pierre White-style, large green wellies, damp baggy cords.

'I just hadn't realised the children were going to Jonathan's,' said Louise. She could tell from Gemma's face that she had put two and two together and made five. But so what? It might just give Jonathan something to think about.

'Want me to run Tim over for you?'

His eyes twinkled. He had had the same thought, she could tell. Part of her was embarrassed and part amused.

'There's no need,' said Gemma, her eyes still fixed on Roddy. 'That's why I'm here. But you're not coming like that, surely, Tim?'

'Don't worry.' Louise put a hand on her son's shoulder. 'I'm quite capable of cleaning him up first. Why don't you wait in the car?'

'Oh. All right. But don't be long. This isn't lastminute.com, you know.'

Louise turned to Roddy. 'Thanks for taking him fishing.'

She nudged Tim to remind him of his manners. 'Yeah, thanks, Roddy.'

'My pleasure. We had fun, didn't we? We'll do it again, soon. Oh, and by the way, you had a delivery when you were out. We took it in for you.'

'Flowers,' said Tim, his eyes narrowing. 'Who are they from?'

'I've no idea.' Louise felt herself reddening. 'Not until I see the card.'

'There wasn't one. We looked, didn't we, Roddy?'

Why was everyone looking at her like that? 'Well it must have fallen off then. Probably a moving-in present.'

Gemma was looking at her watch again. 'You know, we're really going to be late.'

Louise was damned if she was being bossed around by that woman. 'We won't be long. Come on, Tim.'

Later, when they'd gone and the house was empty, apart from Hector who was dreaming noisily in his basket, Louise unwrapped the roses from their expensive plastic wrapping. Twelve of them. Tall-stemmed. Deep red. And Tim had been wrong. There was a note but thankfully it was right at the bottom, in the wrapping where no one else could see it. Had he requested that?

She studied the card carefully, half smiling, half scared. For a message, it was brief. But clear. Slowly, with her right index finger, she traced the outline of the writing. One x. One kiss. And the initial G after it.

Her heart quickened. But at the same time, she felt a terrible weight. It was no good. She really wasn't ready to think about anyone else so soon. Surely Guy must see that?

Deliberately, but almost regretfully, Louise tore up the card into tiny little pieces, watching them flutter into the bin. Then, just to be sure no one found them, she tied the bin liner at the top and took it out to the dustbin outside.

Eighteen

I'M TOO KOOL FOR SKOOL!

'So you see, my dear, I am going back to my work. And at my age!' Mollie inhaled triumphantly on her Marlboro in the slim black ebony holder that Gideon had given her years ago after her lead role in the unforgettable *When We Are Married*.

Poppy leaned back against the chair in what Mollie had come to recognise as her usual position, legs crossed over rather like one of her yoga positions, her ethnic blue and pink patterned dress revealing bright fuchsia leggings underneath. Poppy always dressed to reflect her name; it had been one of the traits which had made her stand out when Gideon and Mollie had first met her.

'That's fantastic. Just run the details past me again. A face cream company, you say? Which one?'

Mollie stubbed out her cigarette with more force than usual. 'I can't quite remember. Silly, I know, but I have found – since Gideon, you know – that I can't quite find the words to match the names. I'm sure it will pass. It wasn't Elizabeth Arden. At least I don't think it was. And it certainly wasn't that one which dropped that model (what was she called, now?) when she got to forty. Anyway, it's a big name. And they're paying a rather decent sum of money, which will help.'

Poppy squirmed. 'I feel so awful about Gideon's will. At times, I feel like turning it down and giving you the money instead.'

'Nonsense.' Mollie lit another cigarette. 'I wouldn't take it.

This is a much more civilised arrangement. You needed somewhere to live and I need a little cash.'

'When does the job start?'

'Next week. Monday, I think they said. Or was it Tuesday? I've written it down somewhere. I've got my script. There really isn't very much to say but I think I can stamp it with a mark of my own. Rather like Louise's children. At least I presume it was one of them. Have you seen the graffiti on the wall by the old vegetable garden.' She chuckled. 'I'm too cool for school. At least I think that's what it meant. Wonderful spelling, although I'm rather afraid that they'll get into trouble over that one from Lydia and her cronies.'

Poppy grinned. She had a lovely girl-next-door grin thought Mollie fondly. Rather like that pretty young American actress Cameron whatever her name was. 'I have seen it. But getting back to you, Mollie, I always thought it was a shame you retired at all. I mean, this voiceover is great but I hope it's the beginning to you going back on stage.'

Mollie giggled, almost girlishly. 'That's very sweet of you, dear. But I'm an old woman. I can't move the way I used to.'

'Want to bet?' growled Gideon.

She dug him playfully in the ribs before glancing at Poppy to see if she'd noticed. That was one problem with having a tenant. She and Gideon could only really be open with each other in the bedroom or when Poppy wasn't in.

'More coffee, dear?'

'No thanks. I've given it up actually. I'm into green tea.' Poppy stood up. 'Like some of mine?'

'I wouldn't mind trying some.' Mollie stood up. 'Shall we go into the garden? It's such a beautiful morning.'

'Good idea. Actually, I've been dying to open the French windows for some fresh air.' Poppy coughed, a pretty little cough with the back of her hand to her mouth.

Mollie's mouth tightened slightly. 'I hope my cigarettes don't bother you.'

'Well, since you've mentioned it, I'm not keen on smoking.

It really gets to my chest and sometimes, if someone smokes a lot, it affects my voice. But I don't want to intrude. It's your home, after all.'

'Yes, it is.' Something inside Mollie made her stomach flutter. 'But Gideon was always telling me to give up. So maybe I should.'

They'd been sitting in the garden a while (heaven knew where Gideon had gone), basking in the late June sunlight, when they saw the car coming up the drive. Poppy shaded her eyes with her hand, squinting into the light. 'Goodness, doesn't that look like Max Walker?'

Mollie felt her body jolt. 'Max? Where?' She stood up so fast that she almost fell against the chair. 'Just tell him I'm not in, will you.'

'I can't. He's seen us. Look.' She waved. 'Hi, Max!'

A bulky man with a short beard that belied his bodily mass puffed towards them. 'Mollie, darling. And Poppy! What an unexpected pleasure. Are you staying for lunch too?'

'I don't recall inviting you to lunch, Max.'

Poppy was looking at her, surprised at her uncustomary rudeness.

'You didn't, darling. But I thought that if you didn't invite me, I would ask you out to lunch instead.'

Mollie looked at her watch pointedly. 'We're about to go out ourselves, aren't we, Poppy?'

'What a shame. I was merely passing and wanted to make sure you were all right. We didn't have much of a chance to talk at the funeral.'

'Perhaps,' said Mollie coldly, 'I didn't want to. Excuse me, I believe that's my phone.'

It wasn't, but she needed to give herself space, time to breathe. That awful man could still make her feel so jittery. Right, she'd better go back now and get rid of him.

'. . . and Cannes would be a wonderful chance to make some contacts.'

'That would be amazing, Max. Thank you so much.'

'No,' said Mollie interrupting the conversation. 'No.'

They both turned to her. 'What do you mean?' asked Max, frowning.

She ignored him, addressing Poppy directly. 'Don't fall for it. He's only asked you so he can take advantage of you.'

Max rose unsteadily, grasping the back of the chair as if for support. 'Mollie, I know you've been through a difficult time but I have to say that I take extreme umbrage at your implied suggestion.'

Mollie's eyes flashed. 'Do you? Then how do you explain the fact that you have taken several young girls to Cannes and other places over the years – and that not one of them has made the kind of "contact" they'd expected?'

'I think you're still upset after Gideon, dear. So it's totally understandable if you're not quite yourself. I'll be in touch when you feel a little better. It must be very difficult for you. So nice to know you have a young friend to help you. Poppy tells me she is staying with you.'

Mollie picked up her Oscar from the mantelpiece as though she was going to throw it at him. 'Get out, Max. Get out now. And if you go anywhere near her, so help me, I'll kill you.'

'Mollie!' Poppy's eyes were wide.

'I'm going, I'm going.' Max waddled through the gate leading to the drive. 'Goodbye.' He lifted his hat, half-mockingly. 'Thank you so much for having me.'

Poppy waited until he was in the car and halfway down the drive before she spoke.

'Do you want to tell me what that was all about?'

Mollie was still shaking. Somehow she managed to stand up and walk into the drawing room. She returned, bearing a photograph.

'Who does this remind you of?'

Poppy examined it carefully. 'Max, as a young man?'

Mollie shook her head. 'It's our son, Nigel.'

Poppy frowned. 'I don't understand.'

Mollie sat back on the garden chair, her spine very straight, looking out towards the lake. She spoke slowly as though Poppy wasn't there. She'd never told anyone about this before, ever. But somehow the words were just coming out of her mouth as though they belonged to someone else.

'Shortly after Gideon and I were married, Max made me a similar proposition to the one he has just made you. He was an up-and-coming director then – not as famous as he is now but quite famous nevertheless – and I was flattered. I thought he might be able to help me. There was never any question of intentional impropriety. Gideon indeed encouraged me to go with him to a film festival at Monaco where, he said, he could help me make the right contacts.'

She fell silent.

'He took advantage of you,' said Poppy softly. 'And you got pregnant.'

'I didn't dare tell Gideon at first. I was too ashamed. I thought it might have been my fault. I kept wondering if I had led Max on. I tried to resist but he was too strong for me. I couldn't possibly have cried rape. In those days it wasn't so acceptable for a girl to make a fuss – especially over an important man like Max – and I was scared too that Gideon would see me as tarnished and possibly leave me. We'd always had a torrid relationship; he was a very volatile man, you know.'

Poppy nodded. 'But couldn't you have had an abortion?'

'In those days it was much harder. Very risky. Besides, Gideon was desperate for a baby and there was a chance it might have been his. I didn't know until Nigel was born.'

'But didn't Gideon see the resemblance?'

'I often wondered but he never said anything although I think he got suspicious when Nigel began to look more like his real father at the age of nine or ten. By then, thank God, Max was working in the States so we didn't see him for years. If he'd seen more of him, Gideon might have put two and two together. By then, we'd been trying for years to have another baby but it was clear, at least to me, that since I'd already had a baby, it was Gideon who was unable to father a child.'

'Did you ever tell him the truth?'

Mollie lit another cigarette. 'A year ago. Just after Gideon was diagnosed with that awful cancer. I felt I had to confess or I would never be at peace with myself after he'd gone.'

'And how did he take it?'

'Philosophically. Better than I'd thought. Even said that he'd had his suspicions over the years because Nigel wasn't anything like him.'

'And is that why you don't like your son?' Poppy leant forwards. 'Forgive me, but I've seen how you are with him. Cool and distant. Not really motherly.'

'I can't help it.' Mollie tried to light the cigarette but the lighter kept going out in the breeze. 'Every time I look at him, I remember how that man dared to . . . I can't even say the word.'

'Wow!' Poppy rocked back and forth on her chair. 'It's quite a story, isn't it?'

'Yes, my dear, it is.' Mollie looked firmly at her. 'Now do you want to tell me *your* story?'

'What do you mean?' Poppy's voice wobbled.

'Well it's quite clear to me.'

'What is?'

'That you're pregnant yourself, my dear. I've heard you, retching in the morning. And you've taken to wearing loose dresses. You've given up coffee. And you turned down that film part in six months' time, even though I told you it would be good for your career. Do you want to tell me about it?'

Poppy took the old woman's hands and squeezed them gently. 'I can't. I promised him.'

'He's married?'

Poppy nodded. 'Very much so. With two young children.' She laughed hoarsely. 'I fell for the oldest trick in the book. He said he'd leave his wife but when it came to it, he couldn't. So here I am.' She spread her hands out. 'If it wasn't for you, I don't know what I'd do. I knew I was pregnant when I moved in but I didn't dare say.'

Mollie took her into her arms, patting her gently on her back. 'Well I'm glad you are here. I can look after you. And maybe when the baby is born, I can look after it – I'm sure Sally will help – while you work.'

'Goodness, I wouldn't impose on you like that.'

Mollie beamed. 'It's no imposition, my dear. It would be wonderful, absolutely wonderful, to have a baby in my life. And this time, a baby that I really want.' Her eyes sparkled. 'In fact, it's the best news I've had for a long time!'

Nineteen

THE BRIDGEWATER RESIDENTS' ASSOCIATION

would like to express its disappointment and disgust at the
recent graffiti on the garden wall. We would appreciate it
if the culprit would clean it off immediately.

*'So you see, Virginia, by the time you get this letter I'll know for
sure. In fact, I'll have probably phoned you! I know I shouldn't get
too excited but it's amazing the way a few little pills helped. Unless,
of course, it's coincidence. But I'm sixteen days late and my breasts
feel tender. I can't stand the taste of coffee any more and I'm quite
sure my waist is thickening.'*

Marcie put down her pen. If she pretended hard enough, she
could make out that the pavilion and the fantastic grounds around
it were all hers, instead of one-seventh. David would love to have
a place like this, although it would be an awful lot of upkeep, as
his mother put it. And 'help' was so intrusive! Marcie had only
come out into the grounds to escape Sally who kept talking when
she should have been dusting and kept asking about how she was
getting on at the Crystal Alternative Health Centre. She 'tidied
up' things, too, when Marcie didn't want her to. She still couldn't
find her new Calvin Kleins, even though she could have sworn
she'd hung them in the wardrobe. If Sally wasn't at least two sizes
bigger than her, she might have suspected her of taking them.

'Hi. How are you doing?'

She smiled briefly at her neighbour as he strode past. Now

that was a man who looked as though he still owned the place. It must be really galling at times.

'Great thanks. And you?'

Roddy waved a large piece of wood in reply. 'Better now I've found this.'

She ran her finger over the rough texture. Oak maybe. Or elm. She was never great at that kind of thing.

'Oak,' he said, as though reading her mind. 'I make things. Furniture, mainly. And I restore things too.'

'Really?' She was interested now. 'I must tell my husband. His mother gave him some kind of chest which has been in the family for ages. The hinge is broken at the back. Maybe you could have a look at it.'

He gave a mock bow. 'It would be my pleasure. Would you like to show me now or later?'

'Now would be fine but you'll have to excuse my cleaning lady. She tends to go on a lot but the trick is to ignore her.'

'Will do.' Roddy grinned. He had very good teeth, Marcie couldn't help noticing. And, she noted to her consternation as he strode, rather ungallantly ahead of her, a really cute Darcy-like rear to boot. 'By the way, it wasn't one of your stepchildren who defaced the garden wall, was it?'

She was shocked. 'Certainly not.'

He looked thoughtful. 'Pity. I thought as much.'

What, pondered Marcie, did he mean by that? Honestly, the English were so weird!

'Hi, Sally.' Roddy greeted her cleaning lady with such familiarity that Marcie realised she'd made an awful mistake with her earlier comment about the woman.

'Nice to see you've got your pants on today,' said Sally, looking him up and down.

'Especially for you. And they don't even need darning.' He glanced at Marcie. 'It's a sort of an in-joke. Don't mind us.'

'The chest is through here,' she said meaningfully.

'See you later then, Sal. And don't forget to dust under my bed.'

She raised her eyebrows. 'Depends what you've got there.'

Marcie let out a small sigh of exasperation and looked purposefully at her watch.

'Sorry, am I keeping you?'

'It's just that my mother-in-law is coming to lunch.'

'Right. Let's take a look then, shall we? At your chest, that is, not the mother-in-law, unless her chest is worth examining too.'

Sally giggled.

'Goodness. Is that it?' Roddy crouched down beside the chest which stood in the drawing room in front of the chaise-longue. 'Rather nice, isn't it? Georgian, I'd say at a guess. Ah, yes, I see what you mean about the hinge. Should be able to sort that out all right. You don't want to replace it, of course. Would ruin the value. But I think I can do something.'

'Any idea how much it would cost?'

'Not really. But don't worry. I won't fleece you. I'll take it now, shall I? So happens I've got a bit of time at the moment.'

'Ok.' Marcie began to feel slightly uneasy. It had seemed like a good idea at the time but now – partly because of that over-friendly banter between Roddy and the cleaning woman – she wondered if she'd done the wrong thing.

'Sally will give me a hand to carry it,' continued Roddy. As if on cue, Sally appeared almost instantly from the bedroom where she'd been cleaning, as though she'd been listening. 'Want to shift it now?'

'As long as it doesn't take too long.' Marcie forced herself to sound firm. 'I have a guest for lunch, Sally.'

'Don't worry. I'll only be two ticks.'

David's mother was ten minutes early and Sally was still vacu-uming when she arrived. Fortunately, the table was already laid and the salmon soufflé in the oven.

'Marcella, how lovely to see you.'

Ruth, who was wearing a very formal black and white checked suit, bent her cheek coolly against hers. Marcie resisted the temptation to remind her mother-in-law for the umpteenth time that everyone called her Marcie, and took her jacket instead.

They were having pre-lunch drinks outside on the patio when Sally interrupted them. 'I'll be off then, Marcie.' She waved the cheque Marcie had left on the kitchen table. 'Say, do you have any cash instead? I'm a bit short.'

'Sure.' Marcie jumped up. 'Sorry, Ruth, back in two shakes.'

Her mother-in-law eyed her steelily when she returned. 'Marcella, dear, it doesn't do to be too friendly with the help. Your girl really shouldn't have interrupted us like that.'

'I know. But I don't want to get on the wrong side of her.'

'In my opinion, people worry far too much about upsetting staff. It's the staff who should be worried about getting on the wrong side of their employers.'

She was probably right but Marcie wasn't going to give her that satisfaction. 'Actually, Ruth, lunch is ready. I'll just bring it out.'

'Let me help you, dear.'

That, Marcie knew, was code for 'let me take a good look at what you've done to the place'.

'Where have you put the chest, dear?'

Marcie's own chest tightened. 'It's in one of the bedrooms. Goodness, this soufflé is more than ready. Would you mind taking the salad outside for me?'

Two glasses of Chablis later and Ruth was becoming slightly more mellow. Marcie made the coffee – Ruth was clearly so used to help that she didn't offer it herself – and excused herself. Phew. It was a relief to lock the bathroom door behind her and have a few minutes to herself.

No. Oh, no. No!

And she'd run out of loo paper. Could she move? No. Impossible. Slumping back on to the seat, Marcie reached into her jeans pocket and reluctantly called Ruth's mobile number.

'I'm sorry,' she said, shakily. 'Yes, I am still in the house but I've got a problem. Er, Sally doesn't seem to have replaced the paper. Yes, that's right, the loo paper. There's some more in the kitchen cupboard. Would you mind putting a roll outside the door?'

'Goodness gracious me! I've never heard anything like it!'

The disapproving surprise in her mother-in-law's voice said it all. Marcie sat there miserably waiting. After what seemed like an age, there was a sound on the other side of the door.

'There you are,' trilled Ruth sharply. Marcie waited for the sound of footsteps to disappear before opening the door and grabbing the roll. How terrible!

Ruth, who was clearly as embarrassed as she was, had her nose in a magazine when she finally came back to the sitting room. She looked up tautly. 'You really should have a word with that cleaner of yours. Replacing that sort of item is a very basic task.'

Marcie nodded.

Ruth looked at her sharply again. 'Are you all right? You look a little pale.'

'It's just my time of the month,' said Marcie flatly.

Ruth winced at the expression.

'What a shame. I was hoping your colour might indicate a different kind of state altogether. I would so love another grandchild. I know you are very involved in your dissertation, dear. But don't leave it too late to have a baby, will you?'

Amazingly, the Crystal Alternative Health Centre had an appointment early that evening. A cancellation, the girl at the other end of the phone said, as though she was doing Marcie a favour. Ruth had gone, thank God, and David was going to be late home again tonight. Plenty of time for her to get there and be back in time to cook his supper. Plenty of time to sit and cry over what might have been.

Angrily, Marcie screwed up the letter to Virginia, tearing it into tiny pieces before dropping it into the bin. As she did so, she could make out the words 'late' and 'sore'.

It wasn't fair. It really wasn't fair.

'There must be some mistake,' she said angrily to the girl on the desk when she arrived. 'I clearly booked an appointment for the homeopathic consultant.'

'I'm sorry but I've got you down for Caterina.'

'And what does Caterina do exactly?'

'Let's see.' The girl studied the list in front of her. 'Sorry, I'm a temp. You'll have to give me a second. Ah, yes. Caterina specialises in past lives.'

'Past lives! I'm not interested in past lives. I'm interested in the present. And the future.' Her fingers gripped her bag so tightly that her nails left a mark in the plastic handle. 'Don't you understand? I'm trying to have a baby. That's why I'm here. And your treatment isn't working.'

She could feel her body shaking with sobs. Then suddenly, she was aware of a cool pair of hands on her shoulders from behind. The coolness seemed to seep through her body; slowly, her sobs grew quieter, although the horrified expression on the receptionist's face was enough to show her she'd already made a complete fool of herself.

She turned round. A small, slightly plump woman with dark skin was regarding her with concern. 'I'm Caterina.' She had a low, almost manly voice. 'I'm sorry there has been some confusion. You are clearly upset. It might help to see me now, even though I am not the person you booked.'

Something in her voice – almost hypnotic but definitely soothing – connected. Marcie's gut instinct made her follow her into a room just off the reception. Quiet music was playing and there was the sound of water. She looked around. A small fountain contraption tinkled in a pewter bowl on a low bamboo table.

She sat where Caterina indicated, a chair opposite hers. The woman reached out for her hand. It seemed natural, not overfamiliar. 'Sometimes, Marcie, we need to know what happened in our past lives in order to make sense of the present. We call it clearing. We ask spirit to clear whatever confusion may have happened in the past and that helps us to go forward. Would you like me to do that?'

'I don't know.' She was feeling so tired; the crying had taken it out of her. 'It sounds a bit spooky.'

Caterina shook her head. 'That's a common misconception. But there is nothing to fear, I promise you. Will you trust me?'

David would be horrified. So, too, would Virginia. But for some crazy reason, she *did* trust this woman whom she had barely met. She nodded.

'Good.' Caterina clicked on the tape machine. 'Some of my clients find it helps to re-play the session. Now I want you to empty your mind of external noise and feel waves of peace and calm flood through you.'

It was amazing. It sounded like mumbo-jumbo but she really was beginning to feel calmer now.

The woman was swinging a crystal, suspended on a thread, over a chart in front of her. 'You were hurt as a child. Abused.'

Marcie gasped. 'How did you know?'

Caterina was speaking as though in a trance. 'I can see a red truck. Someone you trusted let you down, badly.'

She almost fell off the chair with shock.

'And now you are trying to have a baby but it may not happen with the man you are with. It could go either way.'

Marcie felt a wave of panic.

'But David can have children. He's already got two.'

Caterina was closing her eyes. 'You've been through this before.'

She could hardly get the words out. 'When?'

'1817.'

This was unbelievable.

'How can you be so certain?'

'Spirit is telling me.' The crystal was swinging faster. 'You could not have your husband's child so you took a risk.'

Marcie gasped. 'What kind of risk?'

'You slept with his brother. Just once. He had always been attracted to you but you had turned him down to marry your husband. Then when you found you couldn't get pregnant, you slept with him in order to conceive.'

But she wouldn't do anything like that.

The crystal was slowing down. Something was wrong. She could tell.

'What else?'

'You got found out.'

This was awful!

'By my husband?'

Caterina nodded.

This was rubbish. It had to be.

'What was my husband's name?'

'David.'

Marcie froze. There was no way she could know that. She hadn't given David's name when registering at the centre.

'But he doesn't have a brother.'

'He might not now. But he did then.' Caterina was looking at her, eyeball to eyeball.

'Do you know what happens to us when we die? Our spirit leaves our body and has a time of reflection – maybe eighty, ninety years – before coming back to this world. Often, we are with people we were with before. Your husband's brother might be a friend or colleague or even a casual acquaintance.'

Marcie tried to think of any possible candidates. David had several friends but not one whom he was particularly close to.

'Spirit is telling me something else too.' Caterina's eyes were squeezed shut with concentration. 'What is this big house? A bit like a stately home. With a pavilion and a lake.'

Marcie gasped. 'That's our home. Well, not all of it. Just an apartment.'

'All right, all right.' Caterina spoke as though she was soothing a child. 'I'll tell her.'

She opened her eyes once more. 'You've lived there before. It's where you got pregnant. And it's where you'll get pregnant again.'

'With my husband?'

Caterina looked slightly sad. 'Maybe. Maybe not.'

'But he'll find out again?'

'Spirit, I command you to clear all past channels of confusion and misunderstanding and deceit.'

The crystal spun faster. Was she making it do that or was it doing it itself?

'There. I've done what I can.'

'But will it be all right?'

'That depends,' said Caterina, 'on how you define all right. But I can tell you one thing. You will have your baby eventually. But not in the way you expect.'

Twenty

Dear Mrs Parsons and the rest of Bridgewater
        Rezidents Association,

        I am verry sorry I wrote on the wall. It
was becos I was board. I will not do it again.

        Tim Howard

He'd forgotten how soothing it was. You needed to be gentle but
demanding at the same time. Just like sex. Lovingly, he ran his
hand over the wood which he'd smoothed with the plane. It
would make a nice box. Boxes had been one of his popular lines
before the clinic. People used them for all sorts of things. To
store precious things, keep documents safe. Legal documents.
Divorce papers. Custody papers.

Bugger. Roddy cursed as his hand slipped. Sucking the
blood which was seeping from his finger, he went into the
kitchen to find a plaster. The thought of legal documents had
made him lose his concentration. He hardly ever hurt himself;
a careful craftsman didn't. A careful father didn't lose his
children.

The men at the meeting had helped. But only a bit. Their
pain was as raw as his, even though some had lost their kids
years ago. It was grossly unfair. How could so many men be
denied access to their children?

But they'd given him the name of another solicitor. A male
solicitor (he was fed up with women) who had a reputation for
dealing with custody cases. Roddy had already rung him and

they were meeting next week. He didn't hold out huge hopes but it was something.

Or was it? Roddy put the plaster on his finger and found himself walking towards the drinks cupboard. There it was. A wonderful large full bottle of Johnnie Walker. His favourite.

Slowly he lifted it down. The glass was cool. The liquid inside slopped slightly. He could taste it; feel it soothing his throat. He held the top between his thumb and index finger. One twist and it would be his. One twist and Peregrine would know he had opened it. Except that he wouldn't, because he could go and buy another, marking it with the same childish cross that his stepfather had left.

No one would know.

Only him.

Roddy slammed the bottle back inside the drinks cupboard. A promise was a promise. Not to bloody Peregrine, but to himself. If he wanted his children back, he had to do the right thing. And if going teetotal was part of the deal, so be it.

'You daft twit, you've left a ring mark.'

Sally began rubbing at it with a cloth, while Roddy leant back against the wall, admiring her legs and wondering whether to be amused or affronted. Sally said what she thought about him and everyone else, as far as he could make out. But she didn't do so with malice. It was all done in such a matter-of-fact way, often with a dollop of common sense and some fascinating tip that he'd never heard of. It had been Sally who'd suggested milk thistle tablets for his queasy stomach the other day. And they'd worked.

'What's it from?' She was still rubbing. 'Wine? Whisky?'

'Water actually.' Roddy was annoyed with himself. He'd drunk several glasses of the tap stuff after locking the drinks cupboard. He was normally so careful about using coasters; as a craftsman, he knew better than most not to stain wood. But he'd been in such a state after not having the whisky that he could have done anything without remembering.

'Is it coming off?'

'Not very well. Bit better though than the stain on the chest.'

He felt himself go cold. 'What stain?'

'That old chest in your workroom. You must have put a glass on that as well.'

Shit. Oh, shit. He tore into the second bedroom which he was using now as his workroom. There it was, bang in the middle of the lid. A round water mark on that American woman's heirloom. How could he have? How? A dim memory of stomping around the flat, a tumbler of water in his hand, after putting the whisky back, flashed into his head.

'Actually,' said Sally, beside him, 'I've just had a thought. It's still damp, isn't it? I'll blot it with kitchen roll and you go and get a hair-drier.'

'A hair-drier? But I don't have one!'

'Then borrow one. Fast.'

'Why?'

Sally gave him a scathing look. 'Because, if we're quick enough, we can hold the heat against the ring and it might just dry out and save your bacon. Isn't this the chest you're doing up for Marcie?'

'Yes but . . .'

'Then for pity's sake, move it. Because otherwise, I can tell you, she'll soon move you and not in the way you're used to.'

Who could he borrow a hair-drier from?

Clearly not the American. Mollie was still asleep – Sally had already told him so – and he didn't want to disturb her. Lydia and Suzette were in Spain. Louise maybe?

She took a while to open the door and when she did, her eyes were red. To his embarrassment, he could see she'd been crying. He didn't know whether to ignore it or say something.

'I'm really sorry to bother you but I wondered if I could borrow a hair-drier?'

'A hair-drier?'

'Yeah.' He shifted uncomfortably from one leg to the other. 'I know it sounds daft, especially with the way mine's thinning at the moment, but I need to dry something out.'

She smiled palely at the thinning bit which, for some reason, pleased him, made him feel better about himself. 'Right. I see. Hang on a minute.'

She came back almost immediately and thrust the drier into his hand, half-closing the door at the same time.

'Thanks. Er, are you all right?'

'Fine.'

Her voice was tight; she wasn't fine at all. But what could he do? He didn't know her well enough to push it.

'I'll bring it back in a few minutes.'

'No. Please. Just leave it for a while.'

Chastened, he went back to his flat.

'Buck up.' Sally was still kneeling over the chest. 'Quick. Plug it in.'

He watched as she held the nozzle over the water mark. 'Make sure it doesn't burn the wood.'

'That's why I'm moving it round in a circle.'

Spellbound, he watched the mark fade.

'Give it a good wax and you might just be all right.'

He crouched down beside her to take another look. There was a faint smell of perfume. Nice. Fragrant and soft. As for the ring . . . she was right. It might just be ok.

He stood up. 'How do you know about this kind of thing?'

Sally sniffed. 'My husband was a bit of a handyman. Too much so, as it turned out.'

He'd noticed she wasn't wearing a wedding ring.

'Still, it's all helped me to become independent.'

He was already opening the tin of Jacobean-coloured beeswax. 'I'm really grateful. Can't think how it happened. By the way, I borrowed the drier from Louise. She seemed a bit tearful. I didn't say anything because I didn't want to impose. I heard on the grapevine that it was her son who wrote that stuff on the wall.'

'Really?' Sally frowned. 'I'll go round when I've finished here.'

'Is she having a bad time?'

Sally gave him an are-you-completely-daft? look. 'Any woman who had to move from a six-bedroom house to a three-bedroom apartment because her husband ran off with the office floozie might be said to be having a bad time. Especially if your kids are a bit of a handful.'

'I'm sorry.'

'Don't be.' Sally flicked her pony-tail. 'We get used to it in the end.'

We? He looked at her.

'Yeah, that's right. Happened to me too. Except that my house didn't have six bedrooms.'

Somehow he hadn't thought so.

She grinned at him with a smile that made him feel better already about that bloody water mark. 'It had seven.'

Roddy parked outside the school gates, turned off the engine and waited, trying to forget the new solicitor's advice.

'Whatever you do, don't try and have contact with the children without their mother's permission,' he had said on the phone yesterday. 'I know you're desperate to see them but we've got to do this the right way.'

Sally had unwittingly given him the idea. 'These yours?' she'd asked when taking down the framed photographs to dust a younger version of Daniel and Helena. He'd nodded.

'Hope you see them more than my ex sees his. Only time he ever bothers is when it suits him. Can't even pick up the kids from school when I need him to.'

What would he give to pick up his own children? Talk to them properly instead of those artificial conversations on the phone. It was impossible, of course. But no one had said he couldn't park outside the school gates and watch them come out. Just as long as he didn't try to make contact.

He stiffened. Here they came now. He watched hungrily as a stream of children poured through the gates in their expensive maroon and gold uniform. There was only eighteen months between them so they usually came out at the same time.

Roddy held his breath as a tall girl with long blonde hair and very straight posture came out, walking closely next to a slightly taller boy. Helena's hair had grown. It seemed blonder too. Had she had it coloured at her age? And Daniel, his features had filled out. He was still a boy but he could see glimpses of the man he would soon become. And even from this distance, he could see the similarities between his son and his long-dead father.

'Dad!'

They'd seen him. Quickly, he leapt out of the car.

'Dad!'

Helena was burying her head in his neck. Daniel was holding his arm awkwardly.

'What are you doing here? Mum said you weren't allowed to see us.'

So Annabelle hadn't stuck to their agreement to pretend he was working away!

'What exactly did Mum say?' he asked carefully.

'That you were in some clinic because you drank too much and that the judge said you couldn't go near us in case you hurt Mum.'

Roddy felt sick. 'It's not exactly like that but it's hard to explain. What I do know is that I miss you.'

'We miss you too, Dad. Can't you come back with us?'

His hand tightened round the back of her head, running his fingers through her silken hair. 'I can't, princess.'

'No, he can't. He might hurt Mum again.'

'Please, Daniel, don't. That was an accident. A stupid accident. I'm not like that now. You've got to believe me.'

Daniel hesitated and he could see the doubt in his serious young eyes. 'Mum says you're an alcoholic. That drink makes you do things you shouldn't.'

God this was hard.

'There was a time when that was true. But I don't drink now. And I'm living at Bridgewater House where I grew up as a boy. I really want to show you children what it's like. Your grandfather lived there. And your grandfather's grandfather and . . .'

'Roddy, what the hell do you think you're doing?'

He swivelled round as a tall, slim, smartly-dressed woman with sunglasses and a pink bouclé suit swung her legs out of the Aston Martin that had parked behind him.

'I'm not doing anything, Annie. I just wanted to see the kids. I wasn't going to talk to them but then they came up and . . .'

She'd already whipped out her mobile.

'What are you doing, Mum?'

'Ringing my solicitor.'

'No, don't.' Daniel knocked the mobile out of her hand and it fell on to the pavement. 'Why can't we see Dad? We've missed him. It's not fair. You told us he was a drunkard but he seems perfectly normal to me.'

Annabelle put her arm around her son. 'Have you forgotten, darling, what he did?' Her voice was rising and more than one passing mother threw curious looks at them. 'He pushed me down . . .'

'For Crissake, Annie, I didn't mean to. I'd had a drink and I don't drink any more. Will you just give me one more chance?' He bent down to pick up the mobile and handed it to her. 'I heard about you getting married. I'm happy for you – yes, I mean it – but I don't want my kids to forget about me because they've got a stepfather.'

'We'll never do that, Dad,' said Helena firmly.

'I can see you've brainwashed them already.' Annabelle put her other arm around their daughter. 'You were always good at making other people do what you want.'

'That's not fair, Mum.'

'No, it's not.'

'Annie . . .'

'Don't you Annie me.'

'Annabelle, please hear me out. All I want is to see the children regularly. I'll come to you, if you'll let me, and you can sit in the same room if you don't trust me.'

'Can't we go to you, Dad? I haven't seen Bridgewater House for ages.'

'Yeah, it would be cool.'

He looked at Annabelle. For a minute, he thought he could see the woman he had once loved so very much.

Then she frowned and took off her sunglasses. Without the protection of the dark shades, he could see her forehead creased with anger lines. 'Do you really want them to go to you, Roddy?'

'I'll look after them. I promise.'

'The way you looked after me?'

He sighed. 'No, not the way I looked after you.'

'Sorry Roddy. No, Helena, don't look like that. You're too young to understand. The answer's no. Very definitely, unequivocally no. And if you ever try to see them again, you'll be back in court faster than you can lie. And believe me, that's no mean feat.'

'But, Mum . . .'

'Stop it, Helena. When you're older, you'll understand.'

Numbly, he watched her march the children away from him. As they got in the car, Helena looked back. Her face was crumpled. What had her mother told her in those few brief seconds?

He waited until they had driven off, Daniel's face pressed to the glass. Then he got out his phone. 'Peter. It's Roderick Pearmain. Listen, about your idea. I'd like to say yes after all.'

Twenty-one

BIN REMINDER!

Don't forget, everyone, that refuse collection dates have been changed. From now on, it will take place on Wednesdays instead of Tuesdays.

Louise slid into the designer jeans she'd found at the local charity shop (such a bargain!), hoping they were the right thing to wear for her interview together with a crisp white blouse. Smart casual, the agency had advised her. She glanced at herself in the mirror. Losing weight after Jonathan had been one of the few pluses. Heavens, was that the time?

She ran into the kitchen, trying to put on her pearl stud earrings at the same time. 'Tim! You haven't eaten your cereal! If you don't hurry up, I'm going to be really late.'

Her youngest son pushed away the bowl. 'I'm not hungry. It's too early. Anyway, late for what?'

'My job interview, Tim. And you must have breakfast. It's the most important meal of the day. Damn! Now I've dropped my earring. I told you all last night that the agency had got me one. Don't you ever listen?'

He grinned. 'Sometimes. When I want to.'

There it was! Under the kitchen table along with a ball of dog hairs. Gratefully, she put it on. This place needed a good clean but she'd been too tired to do anything about it. The roses had helped for a time but now they seemed absurd. She and Guy were friends and it would be crazy to ruin that relationship. Secondly, he'd had too many girlfriends with whom he'd failed to commit. She wasn't going to end up as one of his broken-hearted floozies. Nor was she going to upset the children. It was difficult enough for them as it was. That's why, she knew, Tim wrote on the garden wall. She'd told him off and he'd promised he wouldn't do it again but deep down she knew it was her own fault – hers and Jonathan's – for breaking up the family.

'You're so rude to Mum,' snapped Justine, coming in, fully dressed, thank heavens.

'So are you!' Tim glowered at his sister. 'At least she's not a sad Goth.'

Louise groaned. Justine had taken to wearing black and lining her eyes heavily with the same colour. She was naturally pale anyway and the overall effect was anaemia crossed with eggshell white.

'Choad!' Justine hissed back at her younger brother.

'What,' asked Louise, searching for the car keys, 'is a choad?'

Tim sniggered. 'It's shaped like a cylinder. And it's really big.'

'In your dreams,' sniffed Justine. 'It's a penis, actually, Mum. The kind Tim hasn't got. Ouch!'

'I have got one. And I can do a pearl necklace.'

'A what?'

'It's when the bloke drips you know what round a girl's neck and . . .'

'Ignore them, Mum,' said Nick firmly, coming into the room to catch the conversation.

How could she?

'Tim, that's disgusting. You're not getting your pocket money this week now. And you did do those corrections for your French homework, didn't you?'

'Nope! If I don't get it wrong, I won't learn, will I?'

Louise groaned. Tim simply wasn't interested in his school work and his spelling seemed to be getting worse rather than better. She'd have to go and talk to his form teacher.

'Nick, have you got your UCAS form?'

He looked awkward. 'Stop fussing, Mum. It's only a rough draft. It doesn't need to be in until next term.'

There was so much to remember when there was only one of you running the house. And now there was precisely twenty minutes to drop them off at school before she could get to the Crystal Alternative Health Centre. She was going to be late.

She could work here, thought Louise, looking around. It was actually very pleasant. Pale beech desk, comfortable chair, low coffee tables with magazines, quiet background music which was so different from the racket at home and clients who were polite and needed reassuring.

She used to be good at that; she'd had a reputation on the magazine for dealing sympathetically with interviewees who had a tragedy to tell. It was her own family she wasn't good at dealing with. Why was it so much easier to be nicer to strangers than your own 'loved ones'?

'Excuse me, can you tell me more about acupuncture? Does it hurt?'

Louise, who'd been sitting by the front desk waiting to be called in for interview, smiled reassuringly at the older woman who'd been sitting nervously chewing her fingers. Instinctively she had a feeling the woman was here to quit smoking.

'I'm afraid I don't work here but I've had it myself. For hayfever, actually. And no, it didn't hurt.'

'Did it work?'

'It did. And I hardly felt the needles going in.'

The older woman looked reassured. 'Thank you.'

'Mrs Howard? Please come in.'

Louise followed a small, trim woman, who'd introduced herself as Mary, into a side room. She glanced at her watch. 'You arrived late. Why was that?

Louise flushed. 'The children . . . I mean, the traffic was worse than I'd thought.'

Mary regarded her coolly. 'We expect our staff to be on time here. Still, I was impressed with how you reassured the client in reception. We need someone to sit at the front desk. Nothing taxing. Just a matter of taking down clients' names and answering the kind of question you did out there. The hours are 9 to 5, although two nights a week you'll have to work to 7 p.m. There's half an hour for lunch. I believe the agency told you how much we paid.'

She nodded.

Mary looked down at the form in front of her. 'You haven't had much experience, have you?'

Louise shifted awkwardly in her seat. 'No. I was a journalist but I gave up when my children were born. Now I need to get a job.'

The woman automatically glanced at her left hand. That's right, thought Louise. No ring. Desperate single mother in search of a job.

'I was looking for someone with reception experience, but I also want someone who's mature. We'll give you a month's trial. How does that sound?'

The woman got up, signifying that the short interview was already at an end. 'Just one more thing. I see you have three children. You do realise that you'll be expected to work through the summer holidays.'

'Of course. Actually, my eldest is eighteen, so he's more than capable of looking after the others.'

'Good. We run a tight ship here and everyone's expected to pull their weight.'

Louise shivered as she walked out into the car park. She hadn't warmed to Mary but the money was the important thing. As for working when the kids were on holiday . . . well, that's what all single mothers had to cope with. And she would cope. She *would*.

A smallish truck with Steven Stevens Removal on it was waiting outside when she got back. Her first reaction was irritation as he got out of the front seat but the man's friendly face made it seem churlish to show her annoyance.

'I'm sorry to turn up like this but I'm desperate for those empty storage boxes.'

They walked together to her front door, past the overflowing rubbish bin which she'd put out, forgetting the change of date. Embarrassed by the smell of rotting cabbage, Louise hoped the man wouldn't notice. The storage boxes were already in a pile in the hall. Nick, bless him, had got them ready.

'Kids not back yet?' he asked.

Louise felt slightly uncomfortable about being alone in the house, although the man seemed nice enough. 'It's the last day of term.'

'They'll be celebrating like mine, then,' he said equably. 'Goodness knows how I'm going to keep them busy in the holidays while I'm working. They're teenagers like yours. Not quite old enough for a holiday job, although they'll help a bit in the office so I know where they are.'

She must have looked curious because he added. 'I'm like you. A single dad.'

Unable to stop herself, she glanced at his wedding ring. 'My wife died last year,' he said quietly. 'Multiple sclerosis.'

'I'm so sorry,' she said.

He nodded in acknowledgment. 'Actually, I wanted to say something last time but it didn't seem the right moment. There's a group of us who meet up in town once a month. Not a dating group or anything like that. Just a group of single mums and dads who want some adult company. We call ourselves Starting Again. Look, here's one of our notices. If you feel like joining, just come along.'

She nodded. 'Thanks.'

He looked around at the hall. 'You've made it look nice.'

'Well, it's not the same,' she began.

'But you wouldn't want it to be, would you?' He looked at her kindly. 'Life has to start again in a different way. That's what I've found, anyway.'

He was right, she thought after he left. Life did have to start again in a different way. And if other people could do it, like the removal man, so could she.

'I don't know what to put on my UCAS form,' groaned Nick that night before supper.

'Let's see.' Louise wished Jonathan was here. He was good at this sort of thing. 'Why don't we ring Dad?'

'No.' His face glowered. 'We can do this without him.'

'Why don't you say something like "I've always wanted to read geography because I . . ."'

She floundered.

'See? It's shit, isn't it?'

'What's shit?'

'Guy!'

She looked up at the tall man grinning slightly sheepishly as he came into the room.

'Sorry. The door was open so I just came in. Hector's in the drive outside. Did you know?'

Nick leapt up. 'Not again! I'll get him.'

Guy waited until he'd gone. 'Did you get the flowers?' he asked quietly.

She nodded. 'Thank you. They were lovely.'

He moved nearer. His body was big, broad under his suit.

'The children . . .' she started to say.

He reached out for her hand. 'Louise, I need to know if you feel the same way.'

She began to shake. 'I don't know. It's so soon after Jonathan. And it's sort of weird, isn't it? I mean, you and me.' His hand fell away and she wanted to take it back. 'But I've always loved being with you. We all do.'

'I see.'

His face was crestfallen. She had this sudden urge to fling her arms around him but it was too late. Here was Nick.

'Tim's got to stop leaving the door open or Hector will escape.

Guy, you haven't got any good ideas for my personal statement for the UCAS form, have you?'

'The what?'

'In our day, it was UCCA,' said Louise quickly, grateful for a neutral subject. 'Nick's finally decided on Manchester with Southampton as his insurance. But he's got to fill in the form by next term and it's a nightmare.'

'Let's have a look.' Guy pulled up a chair. He was careful, she noticed, to studiously avoid the odd look she couldn't help shooting at him.

She wanted to make amends. 'Would you like to stay for supper?'

'If you're sure there's enough.'

'There is.'

He looked up and her heart lurched. 'That would be very nice, Louise,' he said formally. 'Thank you.'

After they'd finished supper and the children miraculously, because of Guy's presence, had helped clear away, the kids had gone off to walk the dog in a rare moment of sibling friendliness, leaving them alone in the kitchen over coffee.

'What would you put on your personal statement if you had to do one?' asked Guy, leaning back in his chair. He seemed more relaxed now.

She smiled. 'Well, I'd say that bringing up three children has taught me enough diplomacy to qualify me for the UN. Except that in the heat of the moment, I forget the diplomacy stuff and start yelling instead. What would you say?'

He helped himself to milk. 'I'd say that I hadn't reached my full potential yet.'

'That's very honest but it wouldn't earn you a university place.'

'I wouldn't want it to.' He looked at her. 'There's only one thing I want it to earn.'

'What's that?' Her voice came out as a whisper.

'You.'

He said it so quietly she could hardly hear him.

'It's always been you, Louise. But there never seemed to be the right time to tell you. Either you were with someone or I was. And then, when you fell in love with Jonathan, I finally realised I should have said something. But it was too late.'

'But all those girls . . . all those girls you've seen over the years . . .'

'None of them matched up to you. And I couldn't take second-best even though you were no longer available. Oh God, Louise, I love you. I really do. I always have done. I just didn't realise until it was too late.'

Somehow he was there, in front of her. Cupping her face in his hands. Brushing her lips with his mouth. Softly at first and then hard. He tasted as though they'd been kissing for ever. Natural and yet exhilaratingly new at the same time. Sweet. And yet serious. Deadly serious. Electric. She wanted it to go on for ever. Then a vision of Tim's little face swam into her head and she broke away.

'Guy, I can't.'

He frowned, confused; hurt in his eyes. 'Why not? Don't you feel the same?'

'Yes. No. I don't know. It's too soon.' She stared at him pleadingly. 'You must see that. I can't just go from one relationship to another. Besides, the children . . .'

'They'd understand. After all, they know me.'

She took a deep breath. 'Tim saw you cuddling me last time. He said that if we had a relationship, he'd never forgive me.'

Guy took her hand. 'But that's not fair on you; or me. We didn't do anything wrong first. And besides, friendship is surely a fantastic basis for love because we know each other so well.'

It was true. 'But this has been a huge thing for the kids to get used to and I can't allow it to be more complicated. You do understand, don't you?'

He nodded silently and then got up. 'I do. And I think you're a brilliant mother as well as the most gorgeous woman I've ever met. But I also think we're going to regret this, Lou. Sometimes, we have to put ourselves first. Look, I'll give you a ring sometime. Don't worry, I'll see myself out.'

Twenty-two

THINKING OF SELLING?

Why not discuss it with Desirable Homes Estate Agents first? Due to
a number of disappointed would-be buyers, we are actively seeking
properties for sale in your area!

It had started off well. They sent a car for her – very thoughtful,
commented Gideon who sat in the back to run over the script
with her. As Gideon pointed out, she hardly had anything to
say. And there was a limit to how much emotion you could fit
into 'Silk Face Cream smooths away the years'.

Personally, she made her own face cream out of yoghurt.
Had done for years, although her agent had said it was best
not to mention that during interviews. And there were bound
to be some interviews, apparently. Mollie had caused a lot of
disappointment amongst her fans when she'd retired. This could
be the start of something new.

'Miss de May!' The advertising agency girl was in the foyer
to greet her. It was a very modern building with blue-tinted
glass and an outline which seemed to sway when she looked
up at it from outside. She turned round to say as much to
Gideon but he had gone. So disconcerting.

'It's so wonderful to meet you,' gushed the girl as she
bounced ahead in what looked to Mollie like tennis shoes. They
certainly seemed at odds with the short flared skirt, bare legs
and purple vest thing on top. She had green hair too – Mollie
still wasn't sure about Sally's pink fringe but at least it wasn't

all-invasive. 'My mother is a huge fan of yours and so was my grandmother.'

Mollie winced. This girl could almost be her granddaughter. But why not? Crazy to think that time stopped still just because you got older. There were so many young people now, all with the same driving ambition that she and Gideon had had; all waiting to take their place. And now, here she was, hoping to make a comeback. For a brief second, she wished she was at home with Sally's comforting background chatter and that wonderful view down to the lake.

'This way, please, Miss de May.'

The studio was small, without windows. A tubular chair stood behind a desk on which was a microphone and a jug of water.

Mollie placed her script neatly on the surface, smoothed back her hair, rearranged her terracotta silk scarf round her neck, cleared her throat and sat down.

A schoolboy gave her the thumbs-up, behind a glass panel in the wall.

'We're ready,' said the girl excitedly.

Mollie tilted her head in agreement and the familiar wave of excitement mixed with fear washed through her. She looked around for Gideon. Still not there.

And then she started.

'I'm afraid we're going to have to do it one more time.'

The advertising girl was looking – and sounding – less patient. Mollie didn't blame her.

'They're not easy words to say,' she protested. 'The "s" in the "silk" and then the "s" in the smooth makes the tongue trip up.'

'But that's why it works, Mollie.' The girl had long ago dropped the Miss de May bit. 'Perhaps you need a rest. There's a couch next door, if you want.'

'I'm not that old,' she snapped.

'Mollie, I didn't mean you were. Lots of people need a rest when they're recording, especially for the first time.'

What a cheek! 'It's *not* the first time. I've been an actress for longer than your mother can remember.'

'Easy,' said a deep voice.

She jumped as Gideon touched her arm.

'There you are.' She glared at him accusingly. 'Where have you been?'

'Sorry?' The advertising girl was looking at her worriedly. Mentally Mollie cursed herself. She kept forgetting other people couldn't see her husband in the same way as she could.

'Just take it slowly.' Gideon began stroking her arm. 'And project your voice more, as though you're talking to the back row of the stalls.'

She nodded, listening carefully. She and Gideon had always coached each other like this. 'And don't fight the words. They might sound daft but they're actually very sensuous. Silk and Smooth. Run them round your tongue as though you had me in your mouth.'

She smiled. The advertising girl's face relaxed.

'Feeling like trying again, Mollie? Good.'

She signalled to the boy on the other side of the glass wall. He'd stopped doing the thumbs-up a while back.

Mollie sat forward in her chair. Gideon's arm was still round her shoulders. She could do anything providing she could feel him.

'Silk face cream smooths away the years. Trust me. I should know.'

The girl's face lit up. 'Fantastic. Much better. I love the way you said Silk and Smooth. But can we try it just once more?'

'Silk Face Cream Smooths Away the Years. Trust me. I should know.'

Not one slip-up. The words were gliding out of her mouth. Just like Gideon was beginning to glide away now. She was learning to recognise the signs.

'Don't go. Not yet.'

The girl glanced at the boy behind the screen. She knew what she was thinking. Crazy. Batty.

'If we're going to make this work, you've got to stop talking to me out loud,' said Gideon in her head.

She nodded. But she'd have to be a really good actress.

'Sounds fantastic,' said Poppy, raising her glass of water flavoured with lemon in celebration. 'Almost makes me want to rush out and buy some of that stuff. What was it called again? Silk?'

'It can't be very effective if you can't remember the name,' said Nigel sulkily. 'Either that or you weren't listening.'

'Nigel, that's very rude.' Mollie turned off the tape the girl had given her (it was going to be aired surprisingly soon) and shot him a warning look over the silver teapot. Nigel was always dropping in, unannounced. She'd been able to cope with it before but now Poppy was here, it was more awkward, especially as Nigel seemed incapable of hiding his dislike for her new tenant.

Poppy stood up. 'I think I'll leave you two to it. Besides, I feel absolutely shattered.'

'I should think you do, dear. How did your antenatal go?'

'Very well, thanks. But I seem to be what they call rather big for my dates. I thought I was fifteen weeks but it looks as though I might be nearer twenty.'

Nigel's face turned red as he stared unashamedly at Poppy's stomach. 'You're pregnant?' he spluttered.

'Yes. Didn't you know?'

'Sorry, Nigel, I meant to mention it. Although I rather thought you'd have guessed. Poppy's beginning to show quite a lot now, aren't you, dear?'

'But that's ridiculous. I mean, you can't possibly have a baby here? It would scream and yell and do all the things that babies do. My mother is far too old for that at her time of life.'

'I think, Nigel, I'm quite capable of knowing what I can and can't do at my time of life, as you so sweetly put it.'

She looked around for Gideon for reassurance. Typical. He was always good at keeping out of trouble when Nigel was around.

Poppy's sweet face was puckered with concern. 'I really don't want to cause problems.'

'I think you've done that already.' Nigel got to his feet. 'Max warned me the other day to keep more of an eye on you.'

'Max?' Mollie could feel her breath catch. 'What business is it of his?'

'He rang me the other day. Rings me quite a lot, as a matter of fact. He's worried about you, Mother. We all are.' He threw Poppy a filthy look. 'I'll be back tomorrow to collect you for lunch. You haven't forgotten, have you?'

'No,' lied Mollie. 'I hadn't.'

They both waited until they could see him getting into the car.

'Are you sure he doesn't know about Max?' said Poppy, standing next to Mollie at the open window.

'Quite sure. He'd have said something.'

'And does Max know? That Nigel is his son, I mean?'

'I'm sure he doesn't. He's not the kind to keep quiet about that kind of thing. He'd have accused me long ago, if he had suspected. Now, why don't you go and have that lie down.'

'I think I might. I really do feel awfully tired.'

'Pregnancy does that to you.' Mollie patted her arm kindly.

She continued sitting by the window, watching Nigel's car snake its way down to the road. The view rested her; made her feel calmer. It was so lovely and the lake at the bottom was glistening in the late afternoon sunlight. She could hear children too; of course, the summer holidays had begun. It would be nice to have some life around the place.

There was a rustle in the border outside the window.

'Gideon?'

Silence.

Funny. She could swear she had seen something. A shape. A shadow. It had gone now but a sense of unease filtered through her. Could someone have been in the border below when she and Poppy had been talking? And if so, was it possible they had heard what Poppy had said about Nigel and Max?

Twenty-three

TO ALL RESIDENTS WITH CHILDREN

Now it's the summer holidays, we understand that children
will want to play in the grounds. But please make sure they
do not disturb the other residents. We would be particularly
grateful if parents could ensure that music levels are
kept to a minimum.

It wasn't fair. Why couldn't David understand?

'It's because it's the summer holidays, darling.' David leant
towards her in a conciliatory manner. 'They've broken up now
and Diana needs to drop them off early because she's been
called to Nice for a meeting.'

Marcie flopped her head back on the pillow in frustration.
'But I've got my appointment at the centre. I may not be here
when they arrive unless they're early. And they'd better not play
their music as loudly as they did last time. Have you seen that
notice that was dropped through the door by the residents'
association?'

'I have and frankly I think it's a damn cheek. These grounds
belong to everyone and if people don't like the noise, they
shouldn't have moved to a development like this in the first
place.'

David pulled on his suit trousers. He had put on weight, she
observed. Weird. Ever since that Caterina woman had told her
that stuff about her past life, she'd begun to feel critical about
her husband. Of course, it might not be true, even though it

had been really scary when she'd mentioned the truck. On the other hand, she'd read how people like that could 'read' your inner fears and then present them as predictions for the future.

'Anyway,' he added, fastening his cufflinks. 'If you do have to go before the children arrive, we can leave a key.'

She sniffed. 'The last time I left them alone, they went through my stuff.'

'Marcie, please. Are you going to bring that up every time? Just give them a chance.'

He dropped a kiss on her forehead. Not her mouth, Marcie noticed.

'Ok. Have it your way.'

'It's not my way.'

'Isn't it?'

David straightened his tie. 'I'm not getting into this kind of argument. Besides, it's the last time we can see them before Rome.'

'We're only going for two weeks.'

His eyes flickered with hurt. 'When we have a baby, Marcie, you might realise how painful it is not to see your children regularly.'

She pummelled the pillow with her fists. 'That's not my fault. Your marriage was over long before us.'

'I know.' He sat at the edge of the bed, taking her hand in his. 'Look, I know this is difficult and I'm sorry. Who are you seeing at the clinic?'

'The homeopath again. She's trying to get my periods sorted out. Then I might stand some kind of chance of conceiving.'

'Well I just hope it doesn't interfere with any treatment that the hospital decides to give you.'

She ignored him. 'You'll be home early then, if the children are here? Not like last night or the night before that.'

He shook his head. 'I always try to get back as soon as I can, Marcie. But I don't have a nine-to-five job. You know that.'

She waited until the door had shut (David never slammed doors, even after an argument) before throwing the pillow across the room. It landed on top of the dresser, knocking over a picture of the children. Marcie felt a juvenile sense of pleasure. She'd read about other couples having trouble with stepkids. And she'd read about couples falling out because they couldn't have a baby. But coping with both was something else. A scary thought flitted through her. Were they up to this?

Sally had come in – late – so Marcie had been able to leave the children with her which made her feel better. At least it did until she got to reception.

Surely that wasn't that Louise woman with the dog?

'Hello.'

Don't say the woman *worked* here?

'Can I help you?'

'I've got an appointment. At 5.30.'

'It's Marcie Gilmore-Smith, isn't it?'

'Correct.'

'Please take a seat.'

She did so but all the excitement she had felt about coming had evaporated at the sight of that woman who had spoken in such a clipped polite way. She made Marcie feel mean because she'd complained about the dog – which wasn't fair. Still, maybe she should try and mend bridges. David was right. It didn't do to fall out with the neighbours.

'I didn't know you worked here,' she ventured.

Louise's head jerked up from the notes in front of her. She looked tired, Marcie noted. Her eyes had black shadows underneath. For a second, she almost felt sorry for her. 'I've started this week.'

'Do you like it?'

'So far, although the hours aren't ideal. I have to work late two days a week which means leaving my eldest one in charge of the others.'

'Including the dog.'

Marcie hadn't been able to resist that one.

'Including the dog,' repeated Louise. Her previous tone – which had been verging on warm – cooled.

Marcie watched Louise lean over for some papers on the other side of the desk. Hang on. She was wearing a pair of Calvin Klein jeans that were exactly like the ones she couldn't find in her wardrobe.

'I like your jeans,' she began cautiously.

Louise looked as though she wasn't sure how to take the compliment. 'Thanks.'

Marcie couldn't stop herself. 'I've got a pair just like them. I bought them in the States.'

Louise self-consciously fiddled with her waist. 'I got these at a charity shop down the road.'

'A charity shop?' repeated Marcie.

A buzzer sounded somewhere.

'Would you like to go in?' said Louise smoothly. 'It's the third door on the left.'

Marcie's head was reeling. Katy had picked up that notice from the charity people and asked if she had anything to give away. Marcie had said no. She clearly remembered it. Surely not even Katy could have given away her new Calvin Kleins? And, even worse, what a horrible coincidence if that Louise woman had bought them.

In some ways it had hardly been worth going, thought Marcie irritably. The homeopath had simply asked her about her periods – erratic still – and told her to continue with the tablets.

Louise looked up from the reception desk as she passed. 'Would you like to settle now?'

'Just send me the bill, can you?'

'I'm afraid it's our policy to ask clients to pay their bills before leaving.'

Sighing audibly, Marcie pulled out her card. She hated Louise for that bloody dog and she hated her for taking her jeans.

'I'm afraid we don't take credit cards. It's cheques or cash.'

'Well I don't have either. And I don't like your attitude either.'

'I'm only explaining the clinic rules.'

'How much did you say?'

'I didn't. But it's £60.'

'That's £10 more than last time. Are you sure you've got it right?'

'I'm afraid our charges have gone up. There's a notice up there about it.'

Furiously, Marcia opened her Gucci wallet and pulled out six crisp notes. She flung them on the table. Louise's smug expression made her seethe. It was all right for her. She had three kids. She knew what it was like to be pregnant.

'Thank you very much. Have a nice evening.'

'There's no need to be sarcastic,' snapped Marcie.

Louise didn't bat an eyelid. 'I'm sorry if you see it that way.'

'Well I do.'

Marcie flung open the doors and marched towards the car. What was getting into her? She always seemed to be losing her temper nowadays and usually on occasions when it wasn't her fault. It was the disappointment, that was all. But then, what had she expected? For the homeopath to wave a magic wand and make her conceive overnight? Resting her head on the steering wheel, she burst into tears. All she wanted was a baby. Was that too much to ask after everything that had gone wrong in her life?

The flat was suspiciously quiet when she let herself in. Sally, of course, had gone but she'd left a note.

I introduced Robert and Katy to Louise's kids because they all seemed at a loose end. They're round there. Sorry about the bathroom but ran out of cleaner. Will do it next week. Hope the appointment went well. Love S.

Marcie crunched the note into a ball of paper. What did Sally think she was doing? She was here to clean, not to organise the children's social lives. At a loose end, indeed! They had the television, didn't they? And all those grounds to walk about in. At their age, she'd have been happy curled up with a book. But now she had to go to that woman's house and find David's kids.

Slightly to her relief, there was no reply when she knocked on Louise's door. She couldn't even hear that bloody dog. Maybe they were outside. Honestly, this really wasn't on. The lamb chops which she'd left in the oven would be over-done if they didn't turn up soon.

She strode across the lawn, towards the pavilion. 'Robert? Katy?'

Heavens, now she was sounding like that awful Louise who always seemed to be yelling for her kids in the evening and whose garbage bin was always overflowing with unhealthy stuff like pizza packets.

The pavilion was empty. Then she heard something. A giggle. Someone going hush. There it was again. Coming from the boathouse. She flung open the door.

'Marcie!'

Two horrified faces stared up at her.

'What on earth do you think you're doing, Katy?'

Too late, the girl was trying to stump out her cigarette next to that kid who had apparently scrawled graffiti on the wall.

'Katy. You know you're not allowed to smoke. And you, Tim, isn't it? Does your mother know you're doing this?'

He shook his head.

'Actually, Katy, I want a word with you. Did you put out my new jeans for that charity collection the other week?'

The guilty look on the girl's face said it all. Marcie's lips tightened. 'Well, we'll see what your father has to say about that. Where's Robert?'

'How am I meant to know?'

There it was. That giggle again. Outside. Behind the boathouse.

Marcie stomped round. And stopped. Robert was lying on his back, his shirt off next to a half empty bottle of wine. And lying next to him was Justine.

With her top off.

Twenty-four

Dear Louise,

I thought you should know that I have just discovered your daughter and my stepson near the boathouse. Your daughter was not fully clothed. They had also been drinking.

Yours sincerely,
Marcie.

The plan was simple. In theory, at any rate. Roddy had rung an old friend of his father's who was in the House of Lords, asking if it was possible to have some guest passes. He'd felt a bit guilty about it; the old boy, who had known him since he was a baby, had immediately agreed after Roddy had given him all that flannel about wanting to see where his father had spent so much time. If he knew the real reason, thought Roddy, he would be horrified. No, he wouldn't think about that now. He was doing it for a good reason and his father would, he was sure, understand.

'I'll do it on one condition,' Roddy warned them at the meeting the following week in Peter's London house. 'When you're caught – because they will get you now security is so tight – you're to say that I didn't know you were going to do anything. They might not believe you but on paper it's got to look as though I'm not involved. I don't want any more trouble.'

'Point taken, Roddy,' said Neil, leaning back with his pad of notes. He was a taxi driver and meticulous with his note-keeping, not to mention the organisation's accounts. 'But to be honest, you haven't got much to lose, have you? Your wife won't let you see the kids anyway – which in our view is bloody unfair. So if your name *did* get into the papers, it would highlight your predicament.'

Roddy shuffled awkwardly in his chair. 'I doubt if the solicitor would agree. He's told me to keep my nose clean.'

'So are you changing your mind again?' asked Adam with a slight sneer. Adam was a former banker who had given up work when his wife had left him and taken the children to New Zealand.

'No, I'm not doing that. I'm just saying I want to minimise the damage.'

'We're not going to hurt anyone, Roddy,' said Peter clearly. 'You know that's not our style.'

Roddy did or he wouldn't have agreed to help in the first place. Even so, things could so easily go wrong.

'Well just make sure you don't.' He flipped open his diary. 'The best time is the week after next. Normally it would be the recess but they're all going to be in then, to discuss the health service emergency.'

'Well now they'll have something else to think about,' said Robin.

Roddy felt a shiver of apprehension passing through him. 'As I said, I'm only going to help out if there's no trouble.'

'Don't worry,' said Peter, clapping him on the shoulder. 'There won't be.'

There was a wonderful smell of pine as he opened the front door. Roddy breathed it in. Sally must be here. In the few weeks since he'd been here, he'd grown to look forward to her weekly visits. It wasn't just that she had this knack of transferring the flat from a bit of a shambles to something that resembled home as he had once known it. It was also the way her cheery smile put a completely different complexion on life.

Besides, not many women could make jokes about seeing a half-dressed client.

'Hiya!' She looked up from the bath where she was scrubbing a thick white cream into the enamel. 'Got your smart togs on today, then. Slightly more presentable than your birthday suit!'

'Ok, ok.' Roddy grinned ruefully. It had become a ritual that she usually opened the conversation with a remark like this. He would usually parry it and then suggest coffee which she always turned down.

'Coffee?'

'Not for me, thanks. Had my green tea earlier on. That reminds me. Did you know you're nearly out of coffee and tea? You could do with some loo paper too. Oh, and the American has been over twice. Wants to know if her chest is ready. Felt like telling her there was a bit of a boob there – all puns intended – but I don't think she'd have relished the joke.'

'Nor me.'

Roddy felt slightly sick. He'd convinced himself that the mark had almost gone but in a certain light you could just about see it.

'You know,' said Sally, bending down with a bath scourer. 'I tell my kids that when they've got to do something they don't really want to do, they're better off getting on and doing it.'

'You're right.' He took a deep breath and tried not to look at her rather neat rear. 'You can hardly see the mark anyway. Can you?'

Sally looked up at him. 'Why is it that men can lie so well, even to themselves?'

'Don't say that.'

'Say, want a laugh? What's the difference between an elephant's bottom and a post box.'

'They're both red?'

'Just say you don't know.'

'I don't know.'

Sally grinned. 'Then remind me not to give you a letter to post!'

She jumped up, raising her hand for a high five. It seemed natural – the kind of thing he'd do with a kid sister. 'Very good,' he said as his hand met hers.

For a second he held it. Was that his imagination or was she holding his, too. Then she dropped it.

'Go on then,' she commanded, kneeling down on the ground again, back to him as she continued with the bath. 'Get it over with.'

He'd hoped Marcie would be out. Then he could put a note through the door and tell her it was ready for collection. Procrastinating it might be, but what the hell?

But no. Here she was, opening the door in what looked like some kind of yoga stuff (he'd seen them practising earlier in the pavilion), her hair tied up and no make-up on her face. Funny, thought Roddy, how some women – like Sally – could get away with that but not others. Without the help of mascara or that black stuff they put on the inner lid, Marcie's eyes sort of faded into the rest of her face.

'Ah good, it's ready then.'

An older woman came up behind her. A rather well-bred woman. Roddy had grown up with the type. Salmon-pink trouser suit, bouffant hair, heavy gold earrings, over-pronounced English accent. 'I'm glad to see we've got it back safely.'

She had beady eyes that bore into him. 'My daughter-in-law tells me you are a furniture restorer. I am Ruth Gilmore-Smith.'

He held his hand out to her. 'I am indeed. Roddy Pearmain. Pleased to meet you.'

She was reassured by his accent, he could tell. 'I used to know a Pearmain when I was younger. The Hon. Henry. Do you know of him?'

'One of my uncles, actually.'

'Really?'

He could see her doing genealogical maps in her head.

'Then you must be . . .'

'Lord Pearmain,' he said helpfully. Her admiring expression showed that he definitely had the old girl on his side now. At times, his background was a badge, a sign that he was in the right camp. It didn't always work – definitely didn't help in the clinic – but hopefully it would get him out of this particular hole.

'I believe I once heard your father speak in the House of Lords,' she gushed.

'Ah, yes. He rather enjoyed that. Not sure what he'd have made about all the changes though.'

Ruth tutted sympathetically. 'I quite agree. Presumably you don't have a seat yourself?'

'Not any more, I'm afraid.'

'Say, this chest looks great,' said Marcie, bending down to look at it. 'Thanks, Lord, . . . Roddy, you've done a great job.'

'Good heavens! What's that terrible mark there?' interrupted the old girl sharply.

'What?' asked Roddy and Marcie together.

'That mark. It looks like a ring, as though someone has put a glass on it.'

Roddy examined it carefully on his knees. 'I hadn't noticed that. Must have been there before.'

'Marcie,' said the woman sharply. 'That chest was perfect when I gave it to David. It's virtually priceless – I'm sure Lord Pearmain knows that, given his experience. In fact, without being rude, I'm surprised you didn't take it to someone in London, Marcie, to have it restored.'

He took a deep breath. 'It is indeed a very fine example.'

'So how could you have let it get spoilt in this way, Marcie?'

Oh, God. The poor girl's neck was going blotchy. 'I don't know. I didn't notice it, like I said. I just knew the hinge needed fixing.'

Roddy leapt up to his feet. 'I'm afraid I have to go now. So sorry, but I have another client waiting.'

The old bat suddenly remembered her manners. 'Of course, Lord Pearmain. How nice to meet you.'

Marcie was opening her purse and handed over a wadge of crisp £20 notes. 'I believe this is what we agreed.'

Feeling like a complete heel, he took them. 'Thanks.'

'Would you be able to restore the ring mark? asked the older woman.

He hesitated. 'I could try. But to be honest, I think I would rather you took it to one of your own contacts. I would feel very embarrassed if anything went wrong.'

'Of course.' She shot Marcie a very unkind look. 'Well, as I say, nice to meet you. I'm sorry it wasn't under more pleasant circumstances. By the way, how is your uncle Henry? It's been years since we met.'

'Dead, I'm afraid. Cirrhosis of the liver. Drink caught up with him. Runs in the family, unfortunately. Bye, Marcie. See you at the barbecue on Friday?'

She was understandably flustered. 'Maybe. It depends if my husband is home on time.'

'By the way,' added Marcie's mother-in-law, pursing her lips together as though she had just remembered something. 'Didn't I hear somewhere that you haven't been . . .' she coughed delicately . . . 'very well? That you'd been in some kind of clinic?'

Roddy put his head on one side quizzically. 'Me? Definitely not. That would be one of my cousins.' He shook his head soulfully. 'A bit of a lost cause, that one.'

For the rest of the evening, Roddy tried to put the whole horrible episode out of his mind. Of course he felt awful about it. But what else could he have done? Confessed that it was he who made that stain? Then they'd have made him pay for the whole bloody thing and he didn't have that kind of money. He was glad Sally had gone by the time he got back. Somehow he knew that he couldn't have lied to her about what had happened.

Damn. The phone.

'Darling, I thought I'd ring to see how it's going,' trilled a familiar voice down the line.

He'd wondered how long it would be before Peregrine would check up on him. Although it was his mother at the other end, he bet his stepfather was listening on the extension.

'Fine, thank you very much. I'm doing a bit of woodwork, your flat is still intact and so, by the way, is the whisky bottle with the little cross on the label that Peregrine left so thoughtfully. So do tell him, won't you?'

His mother laughed awkwardly.

'Have you met Mollie de May yet? Wonderful character. Peregrine and I got on very well with her and her poor husband before he died. We used to play bridge together.' She laughed throatily. 'He was a very attractive man. Peregrine used to get quite jealous at times.'

He hated it when his mother got all girlish like this. She was in her seventies, for goodness sake. 'I have indeed met Mollie.'

'It must be difficult for you, dear, not being able to see the children. But Annabelle told me what you did the other day. That was very silly, if you don't mind me saying. However, I'm ringing with a little bit of good news. I've managed to persuade Annabelle that you only acted as you did because you were desperate – understandably – to see Daniel and Helena. So she's agreed they can come over to visit you on Friday.'

'Mother, that would be amazing. Really amazing. Actually, we've got a barbecue then. In the grounds.'

After they'd finished their conversation Roddy put down the phone uneasily. If Annabelle was going to be more sympathetic, he could always tell his father's friend that he didn't need the House of Lords guest passes after all. On the other hand, what he really wanted was to see his kids regularly and she hadn't agreed to that.

The phone again. Bet it was Annabelle, changing her mind. 'Yes, this is Roddy Pearmain speaking? Really? That's great. Thanks very much.'

The shop in London had sold his boxes! And they wanted

more! Maybe, he thought, as he sat back on the sofa, life was beginning to look up after all. It had been a good idea to come back home. And he couldn't wait for the children to be here too.

Twenty-five

HELP STILL NEEDED FOR THE BARBECUE!

In order to arrange events like this, we need as many
volunteers as possible! Please see Lydia Parsons at number 6.

'But I made the appointment for 2.30. I'm quite certain of that.'

Louise checked the clinic diary once more. 'I'm sorry but I
have 2 o'clock here.'

The client – a well-dressed woman in her forties – clucked
impatiently. 'Then you must have written it down incorrectly.'

The older woman who'd accompanied her nodded firmly. 'I
was with her when she made the phone call and I heard 2.30
as well.'

Had she got it wrong? Since hearing about Justine with that
boy and the wine – which had led in turn to a furious argument with her daughter – Louise had been unable to think
straight. She was also paranoid about the children making too
much noise – that notice had really hurt her feelings. Mollie
had let slip it had come from Lydia and Suzette. She hadn't
thought they were like that.

The worry was affecting her work. She had already charged
one person too much this morning (she'd misread the price
list) and had forgotten to write down an appointment yesterday.
Luckily, the homeopath had been able to slot the client in but
it was unlikely she'd be able to do the same with this woman.
The 2.30 appointment was due in any minute.

'I apologise for any misunderstanding but I'm afraid there

aren't any other appointments. Can I offer you one later in the week?'

'Is there a problem?'

Blast. Mary, the office manager, was coming through the doors. Briefly, Louise outlined the situation.

Mary, tightlipped, was going through the diary. 'We can fit you in at 3 o'clock tomorrow afternoon and there will, of course, be no charge.'

The woman sniffed. 'That's not a very convenient time but I suppose it will do.' She shot an angry look at Louise. 'Your receptionist here made me feel as though it was my mistake, not hers.'

'I really didn't mean . . .' began Louise but Mary interrupted.

'We will look into it, I assure you. In the meantime, we look forward to seeing you tomorrow.'

Mary waited until the pair had left, before speaking. 'Louise, this isn't the first mistake you've made and, as you're aware, this first month is a trial period only. I'm afraid that unless you can prove you are more efficient, I won't be able to offer you full-time employment.'

Louise had never felt so humiliated. Was it really only twenty years ago that she'd been a confident magazine journalist? And now, here she was, unable to hold down a menial office job.

'I'm sorry. I've had a lot on my plate at home.'

Mary's eyes grew even colder. 'We cannot allow ourselves to bring our home problems into the work environment.'

Oh, no. Her mobile was bleeping now, indicating she was receiving a text message. She waited until Mary left until furtively scrabbling in her bag for the phone.

'*Dinner tmrrow nt? Pls be free. Will rng to confirm. Lts of lv, Guy xx*'

She could just pretend she hadn't received it. No, that was cowardly.

'*Sorry. Can't make it. L.*'

She sent it quickly, scared she would change her mind if she didn't. And then she dived into the Ladies, locked the door of the cubicle and wept.

After drying her eyes and reapplying her mascara, she rang home to tell the children she had to work late that night. Justine – whom she'd reprimanded severely after the lake incident – was distinctly offhand but Louise needed the extra time to go through her paperwork and check she hadn't made any more mistakes.

'Not gone home yet?' asked Susan, one of the homeopaths, coming out of her room.

Louise smiled wanly. 'In a few minutes. You're late too.'

'That's because a journalist rang to interview me. You know the recent fuss about Prince Charles's comments on homeopathy? Well she was trying to get a different angle.'

Susan had published several books on the subject and was making quite a name for herself in the field.

'Which magazine does she write for?'

'Charisma.'

'Really!' Louise felt a pang. 'How funny. I used to write for that myself.'

Susan perched on the edge of her desk. 'You did?'

So Louise found herself telling her about her short but successful career as a journalist and how she'd given it up after Nick was born because childcare wasn't as easily available then.

'The journalist who called me was a Mandy McCourt. In fact, she was the editor. Do you know her?'

Louise leaned forward excitedly. 'We trained together. And we started on *Charisma* at the same time. She left after me to go on to another magazine. She must have gone back. Gosh, the editor. That's incredible.'

'Yes and no.' Susan was considering her carefully. 'You can do all kinds of things if you put your mind to it.'

'Faith moving mountains?'

'That's one way of putting it. You ought to talk to Caterina about that.'

Louise had read about Caterina's work with spiritual guidance and so-called past lives from her leaflets and been surprised when more than one seemingly sensible matron went in for an appointment.

'I don't think so,' she said quickly. 'To be honest, Susan, that kind of thing makes me feel really uncomfortable.'

Susan smiled sadly. 'It's not scary. Still, if you feel like a bit of a boost, maybe you should come to me for some treatment. We have a good staff discount.'

She flushed. 'I really can't afford it at the moment, thanks. Besides, I'm only on probation here and I've made a few mistakes already.' Her eyes became misty. 'Mary's already given me a warning.'

'I'm sorry. I didn't know. Well, I hope it works out. You've got a good manner with the patients, I've seen you.'

Louise felt a flush of pride. 'Thank you.'

There was the sound of the Highland Fling from Susan's right top pocket in her white coat. 'My five-year-old son's just downloaded a new tune – corny, isn't it? Excuse me.' She turned to go back into her room but Louise could hear her talking.

'No, of course I don't mind some more questions, Mandy. Fire away.'

And Louise, listening to Susan talking to a girl whom she had once worked with in another life, felt even more like a failure than she had a few minutes earlier.

Getting into the car to go home an hour later, she saw she had a voice message on her mobile.

'Hi, it's Steven from Steven Stevens Removals. In case you're interested, our group is having a meeting next week. Wednesday about 9 at Jolie's wine bar in town. Don't bother ringing back. Just turn up if you can make it.'

The sound of his voice was surprisingly reassuring. Even though it would be a bit scary meeting new people, she also wanted to. It meant she wasn't the only one in this position. And it would be good to know how others coped too.

Partly because of the message, Louise felt more uplifted as

she opened the door. Gosh, that smelt good! Something garlicky that tingled her taste buds.

'Justine, that smells divine . . .' she began. And then she stopped.

The children were all sitting at the table and, at the cooker, wearing her blue and white striped apron, was her husband.

'Hi.' Jonathan smiled hesitantly. 'Hope you don't mind. But I came round to see the kids and they hadn't eaten, so I thought I'd whip something up.'

'I had to work late.'

'I know. They said. But to be honest, I was starving too and I thought it might help if I made a start.'

When had Jonathan ever made a start on dinner? He had barely known how to work the microwave when he left.

'Where's Gemma?'

'At the gym. Want a cup of tea? You look all in.'

'That's because she *is* exhausted, Dad. She's been working full-time since you left.'

Louise threw Nick a grateful look.

'I know. Look, have a glass of wine. I brought a bottle. I think this is ready now. Shall I serve?'

She'd thought it would be awkward and it was, but only for the first ten minutes or so. Jonathan made a huge effort, she had to admit, and was asking the children about their end-of-term exams and what they had planned for the holidays. In fact, he was showing them far more attention than when he'd been at home. And when the children had slipped down from the table to watch *Pop Idol* in the next room, he started asking her about her new job.

'I've made a few mistakes already,' she confessed. 'But my mind hasn't really been on it.'

A wave of guilt flitted across his face. 'I'm sorry.'

'It's not just that – well, it is – but it's also Justine.'

He frowned. 'What's happened?'

She filled him in on the lake episode.

'They weren't having sex then?'

'Well, no. I don't think so. But they'd drunk over half a bottle of wine! I read her the riot act and told her about the damage she could be doing to her kidneys. She said she wouldn't do it again so I'll just have to keep an eye on her – and Tim too. Justine said he was smoking and I could smell it on his clothes. But he said it was Katy, one of the American woman's stepchildren.'

He reached out and touched her arm lightly. His kindness was almost unbearable; he was being so much nicer than before. 'Louise, Justine's sixteen. Nearly seventeen. You were only a bit older than that when we met. And I definitely remember . . . well, doing things that we probably wouldn't want our daughter doing now.'

She smiled wanly. 'Maybe. But it's difficult to know what is acceptable when you have to bear responsibility for everything.'

'You could have rung me.'

'I didn't want to get Gemma.' Her eyes misted. 'I don't know how you could fall for someone like that, Jonathan. She was a real bitch to me when we met the other day.'

Jonathan pushed his plate away.

'Look, Louise, I know it's difficult but Gemma wasn't the reason for this. We'd had problems for a long time.'

She was stung. 'Well, I wasn't aware of these problems. And it would have been far more mature if you had discussed them with me before launching into an affair.'

'You're going to keep on throwing that at me, aren't you?' He stood up. 'I'm off now.'

Her chest was pounding. In one way, she wanted him to go but in another, she wanted him to stay; to go back to where they'd been just a few minutes ago when they'd actually managed to talk about Justine like an ordinary married couple.

'Jonathan, there's something else.' She hated asking but she had no choice.

'What?'

'You haven't given me this month's cheque.'

'Don't worry. You'll get it. I've set up a direct debit to make it easier.'

She felt a wave of panic. 'So when will the money go in?'
'Next week.'

Next week? 'But I haven't got enough until then. I don't get paid at the centre until the end of the month.'

Sighing, Jonathan got out his wallet and peeled off £50 in notes. 'It's all I've got, I'm afraid.'

Silently, she took them, feeling horribly humiliated. Not so long ago, she would have spent this amount of money at the supermarket without even thinking about it. Now she would have to stretch it out to feed them all until the monthly cheque came in.

Jonathan picked up his jacket. 'I must go now. That bitch, as you called her, will be waiting for me.'

And as she watched him leave through the window, Louise wondered if she had ever really known her husband at all.

Twenty-six

Thank you for the wonderful response to our plea for barbecue volunteers. We also need help in clearing up after the barbecue. Please see Lydia Parsons at number 6.

'Darling, Mollie,' said Lydia, lightly kissing her on both cheeks. 'Goodness, that barbecue's smoky, although the steak smells really good. Now what's this I hear about you being on television? I only have to go to Spain for a week and you're up to something already! Gideon would be so proud of you!'

Mollie hated it when Lydia assumed a proprietorial relationship with Gideon, as though she could possibly know what Gideon would and wouldn't have been proud of. She'd only known him through their bridge foursome for heaven's sake and besides, Gideon couldn't stand the woman.

'It's only a voiceover,' said Mollie grandly. 'Although my agent seems to think it might lead to other things.'

'How exciting!'

Mollie bent her head graciously in acknowledgement. Lydia was wearing a bold red checked pair of trousers – was that her idea of a barbecue outfit? – together with jangling gold bracelets that accentuated her tanned skin. Mollie had always considered gold bracelets to be very nouveau. Tonight, she herself was wearing a beautiful jade bracelet which Gideon had bought her some years ago when he had been filming in Malaysia. It looked very striking against her terracotta shift dress, even though it was a little on the cold side. That was the trouble with barbecues in England. They always seemed like a good idea but when you were shivering in temperatures of well under 15 degrees, despite these patio heaters that someone had brought out, they weren't really much fun.

Especially since Gideon had failed to turn up.

The barbecue might have been more amusing if Poppy had come with her but the dear girl had been invited to a party. Mollie had gently suggested that it might all be too much, given her condition but Poppy could be surprisingly firm. 'Rupert is coming to get me,' she had said. 'Please don't fuss.'

Mollie had been horribly hurt, although she forgave her when Poppy came to say goodbye. She had looked beautiful in a violet, velvet ethnic-looking dress that merely hinted at her bump.

Mollie looked around at the other guests shivering under the patio heaters. Oh good, here was that nice woman with the dog and children.

'Laura darling, how are you doing?'

'Actually, Mollie, it's Louise.'

Of course it was. How stupid of her. She should take some more of those ginseng tablets that Sally had left her.

Mollie prattled on to cover her own confusion. 'Now is there anyone here whom you don't know? You must tell me and I can introduce you. Is this your eldest?'

A rather haughty young girl – who somehow reminded her of Nigel at that age, although he would never have had the gumption to insert a ring in his stomach like this young thing – scowled. 'No, that's Nick. He's coming later with my younger brother, Tim.'

'Tell me,' asked Mollie, still riveted by the sparkly belly ring. 'Did it hurt to have one of those put in?'

Louise groaned. 'Don't. Justine had it done on the last day of term and I'm still furious about it.'

'I actually think the ring is rather interesting,' said Mollie quickly. 'My husband tells me it's quite the fashion nowadays for young men to have one inserted down below. Apparently, it gives them more pleasure when they have intimate relations.'

Well she'd obviously said the right thing there to break the ice! The child – what was her name again? – was grinning from ear to ear although she seemed to have embarrassed her dear mother.

'You must forgive me, darling,' she said, touching the younger woman lightly on the arm. 'I tend to say what I think and sometimes it isn't always appropriate.'

'I think it's great,' said the girl. 'I wish Mum would think like you. She's so boring.'

'Thank you,' said Louise tersely.

'Don't worry too much about her,' commented Mollie as they watched Justine swan off into the crowd by the barbecue. 'It's a difficult age. My son was absolutely appalling.'

Louise looked slightly reassured. 'When did he start to get better?'

'He hasn't,' said Mollie shortly. 'Now tell me, how are you managing on your own?'

Louise sighed. 'It's difficult.' She lowered her voice. 'It doesn't help when Lydia and Suzette complain about the noise my boys make. Now it's the school holidays and I'm working, I have to leave them alone during the day. Nick's old enough to be in charge but Tim and Justine can be quite a handful.'

'They can always come to me if they have a problem,' suggested Mollie. 'Did you know I'd started work again?'

Heavens, it was good to say that! And the impressed look on Louise's face brought back some of the old feeling when someone recognised her.

'I'd heard! It's a voiceover, isn't it, for Silk? I used to buy it myself although now I'm on a budget . . .'

Her voice tailed away. Mollie's heart went out to her. 'My dear girl, you will let me know if there's anything I can do, won't you? Do you have any parents or family to help?'

Louise shook her head. 'My mother died young and my father lives abroad. My closest friend moved away a year ago . . . before it all happened.'

'So there's no one?'

'Well, there is a family friend but he's also a friend of my husband which makes it a little awkward.'

'You need to get out.' Mollie tapped her hand firmly. 'Join some groups. Take up a class. The yoga group is fun, isn't it, especially when I noticed Suzette's toe polish was gloriously chipped. Take a good look next time. Exercise is wonderful because it takes your mind off things. Of course, it's slightly different for me because I still have someone.'

'Careful,' hissed Gideon in her ear, suddenly appearing.

'You do?' asked Louise, her eyes widening.

'Yes,' said Mollie quickly. 'My new lodger. Poppy. You must come round and meet her sometime. She's having a . . .'

'Shut up,' implored Gideon.

'She's having a little break from acting at the moment,' continued Mollie smoothly. 'Now, why don't we grab a glass of that bubbly stuff that's being passed off as the real thing and mingle, shall we?'

Goodness, she really couldn't take much more of this. Lydia had been monopolising one of the few interesting people here – Roddy – although she wouldn't mind talking to his children before she left. She also wondered whether she ought to mention to Louise that her daughter was in the boathouse with the American woman's tall spotty stepson.

'Nonsense,' said Gideon interrupting. 'Let them have some fun.'

He was right, even though he was still nowhere to be seen. Recently, rogue thoughts had been creeping into her head, thoughts that suggested that the voice wasn't actually Gideon's but her imagination. No, that was too uncomfortable to consider.

'Hi,' said Mollie, approaching a lanky boy who was swigging back a glass of bubbly. 'You must be Roddy's son.'

The boy shook her hand nicely. 'Pleasure to meet you. My name is Daniel and this is my sister Helena.'

Mollie was enchanted. 'Of course, you must know this

wonderful place very well. Your father tells me he spent his childhood here.'

'Yes, but we haven't been here very often,' said the girl clearly. 'Daddy's usually in some clinic and we're not allowed to see him.'

'Shut up, Helena,' said the boy. He glanced at Mollie. 'Sorry.'

She wanted to hug them both. 'Not at all. It can't be easy for you. But if it helps, we all have our little problems. See that American woman over there? She's got two stepchildren that she can't stand *and* she's trying to get pregnant which is why she's so ratty all the time. She's also fallen out with Louise over there who's just split up from her husband, because she doesn't like Louise's dog.'

'Is that the dog down by the lake?' pointed out Helena.

Mollie shaded her eyes against the evening sun. 'I believe it is.'

'I've always wanted a dog but Mum says it's not practical in town.'

Mollie nodded. 'She's right. But it would be wonderful here. Perhaps you should ask your father if you could have one. Then you could see it at weekends.'

'Cool,' said Helena, her face lighting up.

Mollie felt justifiably pleased with herself. She'd always been good at sorting out younger people's problems.

'Do you mind if we do go down to the lake?' asked Daniel.

'Of course not, dear. I've got plenty of people to talk to. Off you go now and have fun. See you later!'

Twenty-seven

VEGETARIAN OPTION AVAILABLE ON THE OTHER TABLE!

If he shut all these people out of his head, he could imagine he was here alone in the home that should rightly be his. There, across what used to be the croquet lawn, were his two children striding purposefully down to the lake and in his hand was a second glass of bubbly.

It was only cheap stuff. It couldn't count. And besides, he had to have something to cope with the situation.

God knows how his mother had persuaded Annabelle to agree to let him have the kids. Roddy felt as though he could burst with happiness. His children were here with him at Bridgewater House! They were actually talking to him as though they were almost a proper family again. Yes, there were some awkward bits in the conversation, especially when it got round to their mother's forthcoming wedding. But it had been a start.

And tomorrow he was going to take them fishing. Part of him wondered if he ought to ask Tim too but, sod it, he had his own kids down for the weekend. He needed time with them.

'Another drink, sir?' asked Sally mockingly.

He put his hand out and then changed his mind. 'No, thanks. Hey, I thought you were meant to be a guest here; not a skivvy.'

'I am – a guest, that is. But we all have to do our bit, don't we?'

She gave him a searching look and he tried not to return his gaze to her chest, which swelled in a rather nice way under her slightly tight white t-shirt. God, if women knew what an erotic combination tight t-shirts and jeans were, they wouldn't bother spending their money on anything else.

'We do indeed,' he said, floundering for something interesting to say. Funny, he didn't normally have this problem with women but somehow Sally always made him feel slightly unsure of himself.

'I see that Marcie's husband has graced us with his presence,' said Sally, glancing to the side.

Roddy followed her gaze to a tall, pin-striped man (why hadn't he changed into something more casual?) who was talking earnestly to Suzanne.

'What's he like?'

'Stuffy. And extremely pernickety.'

Just what he didn't need, thought Roddy, in view of the mess he'd made of the chest.

'Where's your son?' he asked, changing the subject.

'With my mum.'

'You should have brought him.'

'He's younger than your lot. 'Sides, there's too much space for him here; he'd get lost.'

He laughed. 'That's the whole point. I was always getting lost.'

She looked at him slightly sadly. 'And you still are, aren't you, Roddy?'

'Excuse me,' he said abruptly. 'There's someone I need to talk to.'

Bloody cheek, he thought, as he strode off towards the American woman. How dare Sally assume such familiarity just because she'd seen him in his Calvins and cleaned for him?

'Marcie,' he said, beaming. 'How are you?'

Her face tightened as she turned towards him and his heart sank. His father's words came back to him. Face your enemies. Never run.

'Enjoying yourself?' he asked.

'It's all right.' Marcie looked away as though searching for her husband. To his relief, he could see him some distance away talking to someone he didn't recognise.

'Only all right? That must mean you need another glass of bubbly.'

Marcie covered her glass with her hand as though scared he was going to forcefully top her up. 'No thanks. I'm on orange juice.'

'Me too.'

If only. Funny how even two glasses of that cheap stuff had made him feel slightly unsteady. Still, at least it wasn't whisky. That was one promise he'd made to himself that he would definitely keep.

'Are you pleased with your chest?'

It was a dangerous gambit but it had to be brought out into the open.

She looked steadily at him. 'It would be very nice if it weren't for the ring mark.'

He sighed. 'You know, sometimes, restoration can bring out marks that have been camouflaged by dirt and age.'

Her face cleared. 'I see.'

He was almost there; he could feel it. 'Actually, you were lucky to get me when you did. I've just received a rather nice commission from a certain lord.'

Her eyes widened. 'Really? Who?'

He laughed, lightly brushing her arm. 'I couldn't possibly say who. But when I've finished, you'll be reading about it in one of the glossies.'

'Gosh.' The American looked really impressed now.

'By the way,' added Roddy. 'Nice to see that your stepkids were able to join us tonight.'

She groaned. 'Don't.'

'Did you know that your stepson is rather friendly with Louise's daughter? Well, I'm not sure if I should tell you this but I did happen to spot your stepson going into the boathouse with the belly-ring daughter a few minutes ago.'

'You did?' gasped Marcie.

'Afraid so.'

This was such fun that he was almost tempted to take another drink from the tray that was going around.

'Then I must find them. Or at least find David.' Marcie looked around anxiously. 'Goodness, what's going on down by the lake?'

'Someone's shouting.'

'What's going on?' asked Lydia.

And then they heard it.

'Help,' yelled a woman. *'Help!'*

Roddy couldn't even remember running. Nor could he recall precisely when he first knew, with that terrible parental instinct, that it was one of his children in trouble. All he did know was that when he arrived at the edge of the lake, his legs were shaking like jelly and he could feel that awful bubbly stuff rising up his throat.

That bloke in the pin-stripe suit was floundering around in the water and for a minute he thought it was him who was drowning.

'He's looking for a kid,' said someone and cold fear grabbed his chest.

'Daniel! Helena!' he yelled out.

Oh my God, where were they?

It was then that he saw him. Marcie's husband, rising to his feet, carrying something across his shoulder. A wet rag. A limp rag. And another child clutching his legs, yelling.

Roddy was in the water before he knew it. 'Helena,' he screamed, pummelling Marcie's husband's chest to put her down. 'Is she alive? Oh my God, Helena!'

David laid her gently on the sand. 'Put her in the recovery position,' someone said. Roddy knelt down beside his daughter. Her eyes were open. 'Dad, Dad!' she spluttered.

Roddy looked around wildly. 'Call an ambulance, someone.'

'Let me through, please,' said Suzette firmly. Roddy dimly remembered being told Suzette was a retired doctor. 'Helena, can you hear me? Good girl. That's right. You be sick. Bring up all the gunk. Now I'm going to take your pulse.' She looked up at Roddy. 'Go and get a blanket, can you? And hurry.'

'Dad,' asked Helena later, after he'd got her checked out at casualty (she was fine) and finally brought her back. 'What would you have done if I had drowned?'

He shuddered, holding on to her hand. 'Don't.'

'Would you have cared?' Her grey eyes, so like Annabelle's, focused steadily on him.

What kind of question was that? 'Of course I would have done. How can you even ask?'

Helena turned away. 'Because Mum says that if you cared about us, you wouldn't have done what you did.'

He stroked her shoulder, biting back the emotions that were tightening his throat. 'Helena, I adore you. And Daniel. But sometimes adults do daft things, like children. The difference is that people don't always give them a second chance.'

She turned back to face him. 'That's not fair.'

He held her to him. 'No, it's not.'

'I love you, Dad,' she said, her voice muffled against his shoulder. 'And I've missed you.'

He could hardly get the words out. 'I've missed you too, darling. But we're going to see more of each other now. I promise.'

'So you won't drink any more?'

She looked at him searchingly.

'I won't drink any more,' he repeated steadily.

What he really needed, he reflected ruefully after Helena and Daniel had fallen asleep, was a decent shot or two. But he couldn't. Not after that conversation with his daughter. Even so, he could bloody do with one. It had been one of the scariest moments of his life. He couldn't even go down the 'what ifs'. If he hadn't had two glasses of that awful bubbly stuff, he might have been more alert. If he hadn't been worried about that bloody ring on the chest, he might have been with his kids. If they hadn't been playing games with that dog in the lake, they wouldn't have gone in after him.

But now the kids were safely tucked up in bed and he'd impressed upon them the urgency of not telling their mother what had happened or they'd never be allowed down here again, another implication struck him.

He owed the life of his kids to the American woman's husband.

The same man to whom he had lied about the bloody chest. And try as he did, Roddy couldn't get that out of his head. It was a debt of honour. A gentleman had to have principles.

It was too late to be knocking on someone's door, especially after an evening like this. But he had no choice.

Luckily, it opened before he got to the third knock.

'Look, I'm sorry,' Roddy began as a tousled-haired David finally appeared in maroon striped pyjamas. 'I just wanted to say thank you again.'

David rubbed his eyes. 'You thanked me enough at the time.'

'Actually, there's something else. It's about the chest.'

David's eyebrows rose. 'The chest?'

'Yes.' Roddy felt terribly sick. 'I told your wife the ring mark had been there before.'

'Yes?' David was looking at him now in a way that made Roddy feel highly uncomfortable.

'But it was my fault. I stood a glass on it by mistake.'

'I see.'

'I'm sorry.' Shit, he felt as though he was back at prep school.

'And what do you hope to achieve by telling me this now?'

Roddy felt even worse. 'Well, I wanted to come clean.'

'And you think I'm going to say it's all right?'

He felt even more stupid now. 'I know it's not but . . .'

'That chest was an heirloom. It has been in my family for years. My wife had no right to give it to you to "restore".'

'I'm sorry.'

'Don't be. It was her fault in the first place, although you should have been honest earlier. Still, these things are done. And compared with a life, it's not important, is it?'

Roddy felt an unexpected surge of relief. 'So it's all right?'

'Well, I'm not very pleased. But let's just say that we'll let it go, shall we?'

'Thank you.' Roddy wanted to hug him. 'And more importantly, thank you again and again for saving Helena.'

'I only got her out. She would probably have done it on her own anyway.' The man was looking even more austere now. 'Look. Want my advice? It's bloody hard work looking after teenagers. I know that from my two. But I couldn't do it if I messed around with a bottle or anything else. So just keep clean, will you?'

Did everyone know, wondered Roddy as he made his way back to bed, that he'd been in a clinic and was now occasionally allowed to see his kids? If so, who had told them? Sally probably. Or maybe that bitch of a gossip, Lydia. Still, he was clean now. And for the sake of the kids, he would try, he really would. He'd do anything to make sure he could keep seeing them.

Even if it meant breaking the law.

Twenty-eight

DOG OWNERS. BE RESPONSIBLE!

The local authority can impose a £100 fine for not cleaning
up after your dog.

'I'm so proud of you, darling.'

Marcie ran her hands down the fine line of dark hairs on her
husband's chest. Unfortunately, she wasn't anywhere near her
ovulation period but what the hell? There were times when she
almost forgot what fun it could be to have sex for the sake of it.

'Nonsense. I only did what anyone else would have done.'
David stretched out languorously with a self-satisfied smile on
the bed as the morning sunlight flooded in. She loved it when
it was like this. Quiet. Peaceful. Just the two of them. No Robert
or Katy. Such a shame it was a work day.

Very gently, she bent down and licked the hair beneath with
the very tip of her tongue in the same way that usually drove
him wild; well, as wild as David ever got. 'I thought you were
incredible. You saved a child's life. That drunken lord should
be permanently grateful.'

'He was. Besides, he isn't a lord and he wasn't really drunk,
just a little tipsy, which wasn't surprising given the quality of
the drink.'

Why wasn't David more aroused? She bent down again.

'In fact, that lord of yours was so grateful,' he continued
calmly, as though she wasn't doing what she was doing, 'that
he confessed he'd made the ring mark on my mother's chest.'

'No!' She was stunned. 'So he lied to me.'

'Of course he did.'

'You think I was wrong to let him have it in the first place, don't you?'

'Well, it wasn't one of your most brilliant ideas.'

She moved away. 'I was only trying.'

David raised himself up on one shoulder. 'Sometimes, Marcie, you need to think a little first.'

A little chill passed through her. That was the kind of thing her father used to say. 'I did,' she said in a small voice.

'It's like the clinic business,' added David. 'Diana says Katy is still having nightmares about ghosts.'

Nightmares? Rubbish. She was making it up just to get back at her. Marcie pushed back the duvet. 'Perhaps she should have nightmares about giving other people's clothes away without asking for their permission.'

David sighed. 'I know that was wrong of her. But we've been through this so many times. I've spoken to her and she's sorry. You got another pair of jeans, didn't you?'

'That's not the point.' Marcie got out of bed, glancing back at her husband to see if her naked form might be able to achieve some kind of reconciliation but David had already turned over.

Something had got into him recently. Maybe it was work or the strain of commuting but whatever it was, she didn't like it.

Hopefully going away would help. Meanwhile, she couldn't wait to see Virginia in Rome. There was so much to tell her; so much that only her sister would understand. Suddenly a vast wave of homesickness overpowered her. Bridgewater House now seemed horribly oppressive after the chest business and her stepkids. Still, thought Marcie, putting on the kettle and knocking back a couple of herbal calming tablets, it wasn't long before she could get her husband away from here and his bloody kids.

Then it would be all right.

Marcie glanced at her watch impatiently. Her suitcase and David's were waiting in the hall and the taxi would be here in the next half-hour. Where was David? He had promised, absolutely promised, to get back by now. She'd known it was a mistake for him to go into the office this morning but he'd insisted. She was just about to check she'd put her homeopathic tablets in her bag when the phone rang.

'Marcie?'

Whatever happened to 'darling'?

'Look, Marcie, I'm sorry but I'm going to be late. I'm going to have to see you at the airport.'

She knew it.

'We'll miss the plane.'

'No, we won't.' He spoke smoothly in his glib office tone as though she was a child. 'I'll see you at the check-out desk. Must go.'

She replaced the receiver, shaking. It wasn't fair. And where was the taxi? It should be here by now.

Marcie opened the front door and went out into the quad, picking her way through the gravel and keeping her eye out for dog mess. Oh no! The wind had blown the door shut and now she was locked out. Marcie felt her chest tighten with panic. What was she going to do? David would accuse her of not thinking again and then . . .

'Are you all right?'

She spun round. A tall lanky man with jeans slung low down on his hips was looking at her. So tall in fact that she had to stare upwards in a way that made her feel even more at a disadvantage.

'I've locked myself out.'

His eyes sparkled as though this was highly amusing. 'Does anyone have a spare key?'

She tried to think. 'The cleaning lady. But I don't know if she's in. What am I going to do? I'm meant to be meeting my husband at the airport and the taxi is coming any minute.'

Was it her imagination or did his face change slightly when she mentioned the word 'husband'. And why did she feel so strange; so uncomfortable in the presence of this stranger as though she was doing something she shouldn't?

'Tell you what, I'm about to visit a friend of mine who lives here. Roddy Pearmain. Would he have a spare key?'

'You've got to be kidding.'

The stranger regarded her with amusement. 'No, I'm not sure I'd trust him either.'

It was hard to tell from those dancing eyes if he was joking.

'Well, we could break into your apartment, or condo as you Americans call it. Such a strange word, condo, isn't it? It almost sounds rude.'

'Break in?' she repeated, horrified. 'You can't do that. David would go crazy.'

'If I did it carefully, it wouldn't even break the lock.'

'But how . . . I mean when . . . have you done this sort of thing before?'

'I'm not a professional burglar, if that's what you're thinking. But I have managed to help a few people out now and again. Oh dear, is that your taxi coming up now?'

So it was. If they didn't get into the apartment now, she'd have to turn up at the airport without the cases. David would blame her and it would get the whole holiday off to a wrong start.

'How much would you charge?' she heard herself say.

'Please.' The stranger put his head on one side. 'I don't want paying for helping out a beautiful woman.'

She flushed. 'Ok. Do you, er, need tools?'

He took out a bulky wallet from an inside pocket of his jacket. 'I've got everything I need in here. Persuade the taxi driver to wait a few minutes. By the time you come back, it will be sorted.'

Part of her was horrified. But another part – which she hadn't even known she'd possessed – felt thrilled and excited. This stranger knew what he was doing. David wouldn't have a clue how to break in to someone else's house!

The taxi driver hooted impatiently.

'Hurry up.' He grinned again. 'These cabbies don't like to be kept waiting.' He held out his hand. 'By the way, I'm Kevin.'

She smiled nervously. 'And I'm Marcie.'

He was right. The driver was extremely bad-tempered, even when she explained her predicament. 'I'll give you five minutes, lady, and if you're not ready, I'm on me way.'

Marcie raced back round the corner, terrified about what she might find. Her front door was wide open! Shaking, she went in. Kevin was sitting down on the sofa, reading a magazine, as though he lived there.

'All done,' he said. 'And as you can see, no mess. The lock's still in good working order, so you don't have to worry about someone else breaking in when you're away.'

'But the burglar alarm?'

In the panic, she had forgotten to warn him about that.

The stranger smiled ruefully. 'Ah yes, that took me by surprise. But luckily I know how to sort those out too. Well, most of them.'

She looked up at him, conscious that she was beginning to sweat in a most unbecoming way. 'What are you? What do you do?'

'All kinds of things.' Those eyes sparkled again. 'But I used to work in a rather special kind of force, if you take my meaning.'

'You're not a spy?'

'Not exactly. Look, shouldn't you be going?'

Of course she should. She grabbed the cases.

'I'll take those.'

His hand touched hers as he took them from her and an electric shock went through her.

'Make sure you put the alarm on and lock the door,' he warned, half-mockingly. 'You can't be too careful. And don't worry. I haven't any plans to break in myself.'

She couldn't deny, as he walked with her to the taxi, that she hadn't been worried about that.

'How can I thank you?' she said quietly.

'Well, next time I'm around, I'll pop over and you can buy me a drink.'

David would be horrified! Yet she found herself nodding.

'Goodbye then,' she said, leaning out of the taxi window. 'And thank you.'

David was waiting at the airport, elegantly attired as usual in his pin-stripe and a beige summer cashmere coat.

He frowned before brushing his smooth cheek against hers. 'You're late.'

'The taxi driver got lost.'

It was frighteningly easy to lie.

'You've got your passport?'

She nodded curtly, cross that he always thought she was going to mess up. What would he have said about the suitcases if she had had to come without them?

'Good.' His face relaxed and he kissed her lightly on the cheek. As he did so, a vision of the handsome stranger swam into her head. His cheek, she instinctively knew, wouldn't be smooth like David's. It would be rugged and fierce and . . . oh God, what on earth was she thinking?

'Right then. Better check in. Are you excited about seeing your sister?'

For the past hour, she hadn't even thought of it. 'Sure.'

She did feel excited too. She felt a tiny frisson of electricity pulsing through her veins in a way that she hadn't felt since she was about sixteen. But it wasn't the thought of seeing Virginia that was doing it.

It was that man.

Kevin.

Twenty-nine

GOING ON HOLIDAY?

Tell your local Neighbourhood Watch representative.
Lydia Parsons, number 6.

If Louise had thought it was hard getting to work on time during the school term, it was worse during the holidays.

'Please get up soon,' she said, after having brought Justine a cup of tea in bed while the boys were still fast asleep. 'I can't just leave you lot in bed while I go to work.'

'Why not?' asked Justine blearily, still wearing yesterday's panda eye make-up. 'We'll be fine.'

But there were so many things that could go wrong. They could set the place on fire (after the Aga, they weren't used to the cooker). There was the lake which now, after Roddy's daughter's accident, seemed sinister rather than beautiful. And there was Justine and that boy. According to Lydia, the American woman had gone away for a fortnight but how did she know that Marcie's stepson wouldn't turn up, looking for her daughter?

If only she had someone to talk to, but Guy had taken her at her word; he hadn't phoned and, after what had passed, she couldn't bring herself to ring him.

'I'm off now,' she said again to Justine's back. 'Lunch is in the fridge. I'll ring during my coffee break. Remember to walk the dog. And get the boys to turn down their music or we'll get another note.'

Justine covered her head with the duvet. 'Shut up, Mum; I'm trying to sleep.'

Heavens, was that the time? She half ran towards the car, fumbling in her bag for the keys.

'Off to work, darling?'

Mollie was walking up from the lake, dressed in a pale blue tracksuit.

'I'm afraid so.'

Mollie patted her hand. 'Be positive, dear. Work is vital for the mind; I should know. You should try power walking too, like me. Every morning I walk once round the lake to get my grey cells working.'

Louise smiled weakly. 'I don't have time. In fact, I don't mean to be rude but I must dash or I'll be late.'

Mollie glanced towards the drawn curtains of Louise's apartment. 'Children not up?'

Louise shook her head.

'Nigel was a lazy little bugger too,' said Mollie equably. 'Don't worry. I'll pop in during the day to check they're all right. Give me your mobile number, dear, and I'll call if there are any problems.'

Gratefully, Louise scribbled it down.

'Off you go then, darling, and remember, chin up, as my husband says.'

Miraculously, work seemed to go all right that day, although she had to work through her lunch break to catch up on yesterday's paperwork. She just managed to snatch five minutes outside to check her phone messages.

Darling, it's me. The children are fine and got up at lunchtime. Your lovely dog did seem a little over-excited but your youngest son said he was about to take him out for a walk. I'll pop in again after my afternoon power nap. Byeeee.'

Louise pressed the Reply button and left a message for Mollie, expressing her thanks. None of the children were picking up their phones so she could only hope they were all right. She was a born worrier; something that had annoyed Jonathan but which Guy had understood. How she missed talking to him! Unable to stop herself, she scrolled down to his number. Her finger hovered over the green button. No. How could she give him false hopes when it made life too complicated?

'You'll feel better soon.'

Louise sipped her glass of wine. 'How do you know?'

The woman – who'd introduced herself as Sheila – smiled ruefully. 'Because we all do, eventually.'

She was very pretty with shoulder-length auburn hair cut in an expensive-looking bob. Her t-shirt looked like silk and her jeans were beautifully cut. In comparison, Louise felt dowdy in her work clothes which she hadn't had time to change out of. In fact, she hadn't intended to come along to Starting Again at all and it was only a phone call from the children to say that Jonathan had picked them up early to take them out to supper that had persuaded her. The prospect of coming back to an empty house was not appealing. It was then that she'd remembered. Jolie's wine bar. Nine o'clock. Wednesday. Why not?

Luckily Steven and his group were sitting near the entrance so she didn't have to wander through like a lemon, looking for him. He'd introduced her to Sheila who had immediately started chatting.

'Just take each day at a time,' continued Sheila. She looked up. 'Hi, Derek.'

An older man with thinning grey hair sat down at their table. 'Louise, Derek. Derek, Louise. Derek's a vet so keep in with him and you might get some advice for your dog.'

Derek laughed deeply. 'It's my only chat-up line at the moment. Don't get me wrong. Steven's probably explained we're not a dating group. We just meet up and share our thoughts.'

'It's therapeutic,' said Steven, looking around. 'Kim hasn't arrived. That's unlike her.'

'She's got a date,' said Sheila promptly.

Derek looked a bit disappointed. 'Good for her.'

'You see,' said Steven kindly to Louise. 'Life does go on. Kim's been on her own for a few years now and swore she'd never find anyone else.'

'I'm not looking,' said Louise firmly. 'I just find it difficult being on my own, that's all. And besides, I don't think I can ever trust anyone else again.'

'You will,' said Sheila, sliding into the empty seat next to her. 'But right now, you're in the wilderness and it's daunting, isn't it?'

Louise nodded. 'How long have you been divorced?'

'I'm not yet. Another six months for the paperwork to come through. I won't pretend it's been easy.'

'Do you have children?' asked Louise.

There was a pause. 'Yes, but they're not with me.'

Sheila fumbled in her bag for a cigarette and Steven brought out a lighter with an easy familiarity. Inhaling deeply, she said quietly, 'My husband has got them. When I first left, I took the kids but they missed their friends. So my husband suggested they went back for a bit and now his solicitor is claiming they should stay with him because now they're used to it.'

'That's terrible,' said Louise, appalled.

Sheila nodded. 'You're not as badly off as you thought, are you?'

'I think we all need another round of drinks,' said Steven, standing up. 'Glass of wine, Louise?'

She looked doubtfully down at her sparkling water. 'No thanks. I'm driving.'

'Come on,' said Sheila. 'You can have one glass. You know what?'

'What?' asked Louise nervously.

'I've got the distinct feeling that you need to start living. Your kids sound hard work. Maybe it's time you started doing a few things for yourself.'

Steven raised his glass. 'Here's to that! Cheers, Louise. And welcome to our little group.'

* * *

The following day she caught herself humming during a brief respite from the phone.

'Someone seems happy,' said Susan going past.

Happy? She'd almost forgotten what that was.

'I went out last night,' she said almost apologetically.

Susan raised her eyebrows. 'Anyone nice?'

'Not like that. It was with a group of people.'

'Best way at first. I did the same.'

She was surprised. 'You've been on your own too?'

Susan perched on the edge of her desk. 'My husband left me when my daughter was little. I couldn't work; in those days, there weren't the nurseries that there are now. Besides, Tabitha has special needs. But when she was older, I trained as a homeopath. So you see? Life has this weird way of working out. And keep smiling. It suits you. Oh, and I've been meaning to say to you. Watch out for Mary. She's quite sharp. In fact, she upset our last receptionist so much that she left. There goes your phone again!'

'Crystal Alternative Health Centre. How can I help you?'

'Hi. This is Mandy McCourt. Can I speak to Mary, please?'

Louise did a double-take. 'Mandy? You're not going to believe this. But it's Louise. Louise Howard, although I used to be Louise Thomas when you knew me. You probably don't remember . . .'

'Louise!' Mandy's voice rang down the phone with delight. 'Of course I remember! How are you? The last time I heard about you through the grapevine, you'd just had a second baby.'

'Well, now I've got three. And they're not babies. They're stroppy teenagers.'

'And you're still living the life of married bliss?'

Louise's hand tightened on the phone. 'Not exactly. Actually, Jonathan and I have just split up.'

'No! Shit, Louise, I'm so sorry. I'll never forget your wedding. You seemed so right for each other.'

Louise winced. 'Yes, well, it turned out that we weren't.'

'Are you still writing?'

'No. I freelanced for a bit but stopped when Tim – he's our youngest – was born. I'm working as a receptionist here at the centre.'

'I see.' The sympathy in Mandy's voice made her cringe. 'Look, we must get together sometime.'

'That would be great. Shall I put you through to Mary now?'

'Thanks. And I'll email. Promise.'

What was the point, thought Louise? What would they have in common now she was just a receptionist and Mandy was a high-flying editor? She said she'd email but she hadn't even given her the address. No. Not the phone again.

'Louise?'

Mollie?

'Darling, I'm so sorry to bother you at work. I don't want to worry you but I think you'd better come back. As soon as you can.'

Thirty

LOST!

A small gold watch of great sentimental value. If anyone finds
it, could they please contact Suzette White at number 1.
Possibly mislaid near the lake.

Of course she shouldn't be here, Mollie told herself as she
examined a silver-framed photograph on Marcie's hall table.
But Sally hadn't been able to open the window lock in the guest
bedroom to clean the frames properly while the Gilmore-Smiths
were away, and somehow Mollie had found herself offering to
show her how the locks worked.

It was the day after she'd helped Louise out with her little
emergency.

In fact, by the time Louise had got back, Hector was shaking
violently under the table. Immediately, she realised he was
having a fit.

'Has he done it before?' Mollie had asked, alarmed.

'A couple of times. But Jonathan was there when it happened.'
Louise knelt down to stroke him. 'Hector, are you all right?'

'Calm down, dear. You won't do him any good if you sound
so panicky. What did Jonathan do?'

'He rang the vet who gave us tablets. But I don't know where
I put them after the move.'

'Then we'll ring him. What's his name?'

The vet had come out within the hour, by which time
Hector had actually finished fitting. But he'd given him a

tablet to calm the dog down and left some more in case it happened again.

The experience had rather excited Mollie, made her feel extra-neighbourly. It was so nice to be appreciated. Towards the end, Gideon had stopped being appreciative and had become decidedly bolshy instead. It had been very hard.

'The window lock is just like mine. See?' She turned the key to the right once and then to the left. 'It's a bit fiddly if you don't know how.'

'Thanks, Mollie.' Sally's pinny was stained with pink window cleaner. 'I'm usually good at that kind of thing but that really foxed me. Nice place, isn't it?'

Mollie looked around disapprovingly at the polished floor-boards without rugs and Shaker furniture. 'Rather minimalist for me, dear. I prefer more warmth; chintz roses and rugs.'

Sally shrugged. 'Maybe. Fancy a cup of coffee?' She nodded towards a cupboard. 'There's some great stuff in here.'

'Absolutely not,' said Gideon firmly. 'It's very rude to intrude in someone's home when they're away, let alone drink their coffee.'

'Coffee would be lovely,' said Mollie, appalled at herself. 'Goodness! She could open a shop with this lot.'

Sally tutted. 'I told her not to drink coffee if she was trying to be pregnant but she won't listen to me. Mind you, didn't stop her going down to the clinic at my suggestion, did it?'

'That nice woman Louise works there, you know. As a receptionist.'

Sally spluttered. 'She does? That won't go down very well with Marcie. She loathes her. Always going on about that dog.'

Mollie leaned back in one of Marcie's ergonomically designed chairs. She felt ridiculously sleepy for this time of the morning. 'We'll have to do something about that. People must get on with each other if they're going to live in a place like this.'

'Well there's not much you can do if they don't,' pointed out Sally. 'Bloody hell. What's that funny noise?'

'I can't hear anything.'

'It's from Roddy's flat.' Sally picked up a large wooden figure. 'No, Mollie. You stay put.'

Nonsense. Mollie waited until Sally flew out of the door and then, picking up the other wooden figure as a weapon if necessary, she followed her cleaning lady outside.

'What are you doing here?' demanded Sally.

A tall lanky man with bad teeth, whom Mollie vaguely recognised from hanging around the grounds last week, stubbed out a cigarette, leaning languorously on the wooden draining board.

'I could ask you the same question,' he said, leaning against the sink.

'I'm Lord Pearmain's daily.'

The man gave her chest an appreciative look. Mollie half expected him to whistle. 'Who's a lucky boy then?'

Sally's lips tightened. 'And you are?'

'Kevin.' He held out his hand. 'Pleased to meet you. I'm waiting for my mate,' he said. 'Lord Pearmain.'

'And has he given you permission to break in?' demanded Mollie imperiously.

'I didn't break in, love.' He was grinning with amusement.

'I heard you. Doing that thing with your credit card.' Sally held out her hand. 'If you didn't break in, give me the key.'

The man held up his hands mockingly, as though giving himself up. 'All right, you win. But Roddy won't mind. Here he is now.'

Roddy clearly looked astounded at the gathering in his kitchen. 'What's going on?'

'Hi, Rods, mate. This lady thinks I've broken in.'

'Well you must have done.' Roddy was livid; Mollie could almost feel the heat. 'I certainly didn't give you permission to come in.'

Sally sniffed. 'I thought as much.'

'Rodders.' Kevin's face had suddenly turned very serious. 'I came to see you because I've got a message. From that fathers' group you belong to.'

Roddy turned to Sally and Mollie. 'Look, thanks for your

help. I really appreciate it. But it's ok, it really is. Kevin and I have some things to discuss.'

After so much excitement, thought Mollie, she'd be glad of a lie-down. But who was this, waiting by the door? A uniformed chauffeur? Mollie wondered if she'd wandered into one of her dreams again, the kind where she and Gideon were touring and everyone was clapping.

'Are you ready, ma'am?'

Mollie drew herself up to her full height. When in doubt, look tall. 'Ready for what, my man?'

He looked at the pad of paper in his hand. 'I have got the right place, haven't I? Miss Mollie de May for the Elstree studios?'

'You forgot, didn't you,' said Gideon accusingly. 'You've got another voiceover. It's in the diary; I tried to tell you but you were too busy snooping round that American woman's place.'

Mollie flashed one of her most charming smiles at the driver. 'Can you give me a couple of secs? Do come in and wait.' She pulled a large bag of Marcie's coffee out of her bag. 'I can make you a drink.'

'I'll wait out here, thanks. But we'd better be sharpish; the traffic's terrible.'

Mollie raced around her room, applying her make-up and changing out of her tracksuit into a more suitable skirt and twin set.

'A professional never forgets a date,' muttered Gideon in her ear.

'Do shut up, Gideon,' she hissed back as she rushed back out to the car. 'Everyone can make mistakes. You almost sound jealous, as though you want to be doing this.'

'Well I should,' he retorted, getting in after her. 'I wasn't that old. And I've still got so much to do.'

Mollie's eyes swam with tears. 'I know, darling, I know. But I'm going to do this for both of us. Together, we can carry anything off.'

'Even murder?' asked Gideon nastily.

A horrible prickle ran down her spine as she settled into the back of the car.

'Don't use that word,' she said testily. 'You know it wasn't like that.'

'But a jury might not believe you.'

'Gideon, will you stop it!'

Heavens, she must have said that bit out loud; the chauffeur was looking at her in the mirror.

'As you wish,' said Gideon sulkily.

He said nothing for the rest of the journey to Mollie's relief although it didn't stop her head from spinning. Since he'd passed on, Gideon had really changed. And she wasn't at all sure that she liked it.

Thirty-one

Certain residents have expressed concern about security issues
at Bridgewater House. We are discussing the possibility of
installing electric gates. Could you please send your
views in writing to Lydia Parsons, number 6.

'What the hell do you think you were doing?'

Roddy's eyes were blazing and he had to clench his fists to
stop himself lashing out at Kevin.

'You can't just break into someone's house like that. You do
realise I could get you back in jail simply by ringing the police,
don't you?'

Kevin was leaning against a kitchen cupboard, smiling amusedly. 'But you won't, will you, Rodders? Because if you do, I'll
tell the boys in blue that you're planning something with that
loony fathers' group.'

Roddy felt a cold sweat pass through him. 'What do you
mean?'

'When I let myself in – purely because I was tired of waiting
outside, you understand – your phone went. Don't worry. I
didn't pick it up.' Kevin grinned. His teeth seemed even worse
than Roddy had remembered. 'Anyway, I didn't need to. It was
someone called Peter from your fathers' action group and he
was indiscreet enough to leave a rather full message.'

Roddy felt a wave of apprehension hit his stomach.

'He wants you to ring back with details of your proposed
little trip to the House of Lords. I do hope you're not planning something silly, Rodders.' Kevin looked around the designer

kitchen with unmasked admiration. 'It would be a shame if you had to leave this place. I wouldn't mind living here myself.'

Roddy spluttered. 'In your dreams, mate.'

Kevin shook his head. 'I don't think so. In fact, I think I've found rather a satisfactory answer to our problems. You wouldn't want me telling anyone of your rather foolhardy plans to get the PM to listen to your mad dads' group, would you?'

'They're – we – aren't mad. We just want rights; to see more of our kids.'

'Whatever.' Kevin grinned again. 'Frankly, I'm not interested. But I am interested in this place. My rented London flat is pretty basic. And damp. I'd like to stay here for a bit. Not all the time because my business takes me around the country. But I'd like to be able to pop in here when I like. With a key, that is, and not a credit card.'

Roddy spluttered. 'You've got to be joking.'

Kevin took out a piece of filter paper from his inside pocket and proceeded to fill it with something from a tin. 'Oh, but Rodders, I'm deadly serious. If you don't accept me as an occasional houseguest, I'll tell the police that you're planning to storm the House of Commons with your dads' brigade.'

'I don't even know if we're going to do this thing,' said Roddy desperately. 'I haven't made up my mind yet.'

'Ah,' said Kevin, lighting up. 'That reminds me. There was another message on your answerphone. From your lovely wife, or should I say ex-wife. Perhaps you'd better listen to her, although I'd advise turning down the volume. She seems a little upset.'

His throat tight with anticipation, Roddy pressed the Play button.

'Roddy? I know you're there. Pick up! Helena and Daniel have told me what happened at the barbecue. They didn't want to but I could see they were upset when they got back. Do you realise Helena could have drowned? I let you have them, against my better judgment, because I felt sorry for you – yes, sorry – and you can't even keep an eye on them for one evening. I gave you a second chance

but now my solicitor says that no court in the land will allow you to have them after this.'

'Wow,' said Kevin, exhaling a cloud of smoke. 'That was even louder than I remembered the first time round.'

Roddy sank on to a chair, head in his hands.

Kevin patted him on the shoulder. 'Know what I'd do in your position?'

Roddy lifted his head wearily. 'What?'

'I'd go ahead with this little party of yours to the Houses of Parliament. After all, what have you got to lose? If the wife won't let you see the kids, maybe you're right to tell the prime minister and his crowd how unfair it all is. But do it properly, will you?'

'What do you mean?'

'Well,' said Kevin, flicking some ash off his sleeve and on to the carpet carelessly. 'You might need someone with you. Someone with my door and window-opening qualifications.'

'No thanks,' said Roddy firmly. 'This is meant to be a peaceful protest.'

Kevin shrugged. 'As you will. Still, I'm afraid my original proposal still stands.'

Roddy snorted. 'Threat, you mean.'

'It's up to you how you see it but I think it would be nicer all round if we saw it as an open invitation so I can stay when I like. Otherwise, I spill the beans.'

Roddy held up his hands in defeat. 'I haven't got much choice. But you'd better behave yourself. I don't want to fall out with the neighbours.' He glared at Kevin. 'You can't smoke that stuff near them. Or have any of your jailbird friends round. If you're going to be my houseguest, you behave like one. Talking of which, here's an ashtray.'

Kevin's eyes glinted. 'That's more like it, Rodders. Getting back to your old self now.' He opened a kitchen cupboard. 'Now, where do you keep your whisky?'

'I don't drink any more,' said Roddy tersely.

'Don't drink?' Kevin looked truly appalled. 'Well, I do. And

I know you always have the best stuff. Here it is.' He lifted down the bottle that Peregrine had left.

'Don't touch that,' roared Roddy.

'There's no need to get that upset.'

Roddy began to shake. 'Go and buy your own drink if you want some. But leave that bottle alone.'

'All right, all right. Keep your hair on. Know what you need, Rodders? A nice fat joint to keep yourself calm. I could do you one if you want.'

'No thanks.' Roddy glared at him. 'I'm going to use the bathroom. I would show you where it is but you've probably found out already. And when you do use it, clean up after you. Got it?'

Kevin nodded. 'In one. You know, Roddy, I think we're going to get on like a house on fire.'

Thirty-two

GOING-AWAY REMINDER!

Despite our earlier notice, certain residents have gone on
holiday without telling their neighbours, which has caused
some concern. In view of the spate of burglaries in the area, as
highlighted in the local paper last week, may we suggest that
you alert your neighbours and give them your holiday dates.

Bridgewater Residents' Association

Unusually for her, Marcie dozed off on the plane. She rarely
slept on short flights but the trauma of having to break into
the flat and then that weird stuff with Kevin – what was it
about him that made her feel so uneasy and yet at the same
time so alive? – had exhausted her.

Besides, dozing off meant she didn't have to talk to David.

She was still cross with him over Katy pretending to have
nightmares about the clinic. She tried so hard with his children yet he was always on their side. Well, now they were
going to see *her* family, or rather, the only person left in her
family.

Marcie wriggled uneasily in her semi-sleep, thinking about
Virginia. When she had first met David and they'd gone through
all that family stuff, he'd asked her to describe her sister.

But what could she say? Their relationship confused her, let
alone an outsider. Virginia was her older sister; she was always
there with advice but, at the same time, she had got her into a

fair amount of trouble with her mother. If Marcie had stepped out of line, such as when she'd skipped a school trip, Virginia would let her mother know 'for her own good'. But she'd also been her alibi; the only other child in a household where sadness swam like an undercurrent. Their parents had not been happily married, but carried on miserably. No one rowed; but no one laughed either.

As the eldest, Virginia had been able to escape before Marcie. She had gone to college on the west coast and that's when Marcie had really missed her, mentally blocking out the snide remarks her sister used to make and imagining her as a perfect friend. It was only when they saw each other for more than a few days that she remembered how difficult she could be.

Now she was going to see her after nearly a year. During that time, Marcie had forgotten her sister's traits, just as she'd forgotten them when she was away at college. But as the pilot's voice instructed them to fasten their seatbelts for landing, she felt a flutter of apprehension.

Supposing Virginia didn't get on with David? She hadn't ever met him before, not having been able to attend the wedding as she was at an advertising conference in Hong Kong. And suppose she told him about . . . No. Marcie shuddered. No. Even Virginia would never do that.

'There she is!'

Marcie flew ahead through the crowd, flinging her arms around a tall, beautifully groomed woman with a blonde chignon.

'Virginia, you look gorgeous. I love your hair!'

The woman gently eased her away, holding her at arms' length. 'I've been wearing it like that for ages,' said Virginia amusedly. 'Now let me look at you, little sis. Goodness, you look just the same but a bit paler. Must be the lack of sunshine, I suppose.'

She held out her hand graciously to David. 'Hi. You must be Marcie's husband.'

Marcie watched them both nervously as David shook her sister's hand. 'How do you do?'

Virginia laughed. Her laugh had changed, thought Marcie. It was lighter, more flirtatious. 'I love the English! So formal.' She turned to Marcie. 'A real English gentleman. No wonder you fell for him.'

Astoundingly, David seemed flattered.

'How very kind of you,' he said, bending his head as though in acknowledgment. 'Now, shall we find a taxi? I believe the hotel is quite close.'

'I've got one.' Virginia laid a hand on David's arm for a brief second. 'I've talked one into waiting for us outside.'

'How very clever of you,' said David. 'Let's go, shall we?'

She needn't have worried, thought Marcie, as she sat in the back of the cab with David and Virginia on either side. They were talking as though they had always known each other and Marcie, squashed up in the middle and sticky in the heat, almost felt in the way.

'Of course, when I came to Rome in the eighties, I was a backpacking student,' said David.

'No,' gasped Virginia. 'Me too. Which year were you here?'

'July 1980.'

'Incredible. Me too! Same month as well. Wow! Where did you stay?'

'At a rather basic youth hostel, not far from the Vatican museum. Now let me think . . . it will come to me in a minute.'

'Not the Casa de Roma?' asked Virginia.

David slapped his knee in a way Marcie had never seen before. 'I believe it was! Is that where you were?'

Virginia nodded excitedly. 'Imagine! We might have passed each other, even said hello!'

'Well it certainly is an amazing coincidence,' said David. 'Don't you think, Marcie?'

She nodded. Somehow, none of this surprised her. How could she have forgotten the way Virginia always managed to dominate the conversation; to make herself look so lovely in comparison with her. Ridiculously, she felt hurt. Somehow she'd imagined a cosy sisterly chat with the odd gesture to ensure David was included.

'Wow!' said Virginia excitedly, pointing out of the window. 'Look at that amphitheatre! Such amazing architecture, don't you think?'

David nodded. 'Did you know that it took nearly one hundred years to build that?' He tapped the guidebook in his knee. 'You must read this. It's pretty good.'

Virginia fished a book out of her bag. 'Got it. And guess what, it's exactly the same as yours!'

Fancy that, thought Marcie grimly as her phone began to bleep. Grateful for the intrusion, she opened her Inbox.

'Hope u got there ok. Nice to meet u. C u another time maybe? K.'

'Anything urgent?' asked David, as she hastily she pressed the Delete button.

How had he got her mobile number?

'Just something from my tutor.'

'How's your thesis going?' asked Virginia.

'Ok.'

'I guess you've got a lot of other stuff going on at the same time,' said Virginia coyly. 'Any luck with the baby department yet?'

'Not yet,' said David stiffly. 'Ah, this looks like the hotel.'

The taxi drew up outside a white stuccoed building. 'It's beautiful,' said Virginia, donning a cream straw hat. 'I'm so glad you chose somewhere old. I can't bear these new hotels. Wow, isn't this exciting!' She beamed. 'We're going to have a wonderful time!'

Why, wondered Marcie, did European hotels always have twin beds? Didn't they have sex out here? Or did people just choose to go their own separate ways at night when they'd finished the other stuff?

'Never mind,' said David, yawning. 'At least we'll get some sleep. We've had a busy day, haven't we? Your sister can walk, I'll say that for her.'

Marcie, slipping out of her nightie after her shower, thought of Virginia striding ahead in excitement as they had wandered round the Pantheon that afternoon and then spent hours in two huge, marble-filled museums, stuffed with so many treasures that for her, at any rate, they soon lost their 'wow' factor. Later, they'd had dinner, during which David and Virginia had talked non-stop about backpacking adventures.

'So you like her?' she asked, sliding into the bed next to his.

'I'm pleasantly surprised,' said David, leaning over to give her a goodnight kiss. 'One never knows about family, does one? And it's important that when you love someone you get on with their nearest and dearest.'

Marcie thought briefly of her mother-in-law and then of David's children. 'I suppose it does.'

'Mind you,' said David, turning over, 'you two girls probably need some time on your own to catch up. So I've suggested to Virginia that you both chill out in the hotel tomorrow morning. I've got a client to see anyway.'

'I didn't know that.'

'Didn't I mention it? It won't take long. I'll be back by lunchtime and then we can go to that restaurant Virginia pointed out this afternoon.'

Virginia had always been good at finding smart restaurants. 'Sure. Just going to the bathroom again for a bit.'

Locking the door behind her, she sat on the closed lavatory seat and turned on her phone.

'Nice 2 have met u 2. Rome very hot and sticky. Thanks 4 your help 2 day.'

The reply came back almost immediately.

'Hv fun.'

Marcie made her way back to bed, her feet cold against the marble floor. David was already gently snoring. She turned over, looking at the strange silhouettes of unfamiliar furniture in the semi-darkness. It was almost ovulation time according to the Boots device which Sally had got her to buy. They could have tried tonight if David hadn't fallen asleep.

Marcie sighed, wishing the air conditioner wasn't so noisy. It had been thoughtless of her sister to have mentioned that baby stuff in the taxi. But maybe David was right. What they needed was a proper sisterly chat.

Thirty-three

PLEASE DO NOT DISTURB!

'Your David is real cool,' said Virginia, sipping her cappuccino. She was wearing an elegant gauze lilac scarf wrapped around her head and shoulders as sun protection. Marcie suspected she was actually aiming for the Audrey Hepburn *Roman Holiday* look. Virginia had always been keen on old films.

'Glad you like him,' said Marcie, dunking her teaspoon in the froth of the cappuccino and sucking it.

Virginia frowned. 'Don't. It looks so touristy.'

Marcie only just prevented herself from apologising. 'How's work?' she asked quickly. Marcie never really understood Virginia's work, partly because her sister seemed almost purposefully vague about it. She knew she worked in the marketing department of a large advertising firm based in San Francisco, and she also knew this involved a lot of travelling, but that was as far as it went.

Virginia groaned. 'Don't. My boss has moved on and I can't stand the woman who's replaced him. She hates me.'

Marcie wasn't surprised. Virginia had always been the kind of woman who got on better with men at work.

'Will you find another job?'

'Maybe.' Virginia's eyes were fixed on a group of young Italian teenagers, giggling and laughing at a large table by the window.

'It doesn't seem that long ago since we were that age,' said Virginia quietly.

Marcie went cold. 'It does to me.'

Virgina looked at her with sympathy. 'Does it still hurt?' she asked soothingly.

Marcie nodded, not trusting herself to speak.

'Have you told him?'

Marcie felt a stab of panic slice through her.

'No,' she managed to whisper.

Virginia removed her sunglasses and looked severely at her. 'I think you ought to.'

Marcie stood up abruptly, holding the table to steady herself. 'I think it's up to me. I'm sorry, Virginia. I don't want to fall out but it's my business what I tell my husband and what I don't.'

Virginia shrugged. 'Up to you, honey. I might not be married myself but I've seen people who have hidden stuff and it never turns out right. Now, where do you want to go next?'

'To that church.' Marcie fumbled in her bag for her sunglasses to hide her tearful eyes. 'The one on the corner that we passed.'

'I didn't think you went to church any more.'

'I don't. But I feel like it right now.'

Virginia laid a hand on her arm. 'I understand, honey. I'll come too. Two lots of prayers have got to be better than one.'

The church echoed with silence. It was cold too and Marcie wrapped her shawl round her. For a small church, it was surprisingly full of people coming in and out, with little clusters of men and women in the enclaves at the side. Curiously, she watched other tourists lighting candles and suddenly she had an urge to do the same. But which altar should she go to?

'How about the Virgin Mary?' whispered Virginia loudly.

That was the thing about being sisters. However different you were, you often knew what the other was thinking. There had been no need to tell Virginia in words that she needed to light a candle to ask God to give her a baby. Virginia just knew.

Marcie dropped the euro into the candle box, hearing the

clang as it fell. Reaching out for a candle, she lit it from one of the others before standing it in the tray in front of the altar to the Blessed Virgin. There were several other candles already there, each asking for something different.

On her knees at the altar, she was conscious of Virginia kneeling next to her. Marcie closed her eyes and breathed in the incense. 'Give me a baby, please,' she said silently. 'I'll do anything. Anything.'

She glanced across at Virginia. Her sister's eyes were tightly shut and her mouth was moving silently. Eventually, she stood up and the two women made their way across the stone floor towards the door. Marcie was grateful to feel the sunlight.

'You're shivering,' said Virginia, putting an arm around her. 'Don't worry. I prayed for forgiveness.'

Marcie looked at her, startled. 'For what?'

'Forgiveness, on your part.' Virginia tucked her hand into Marcie's arm. 'Don't you see, sis? You'll only heal if you forgive that man. Maybe that's why you can't have a baby . . .'

'Stop.' Marcie pulled her arm away. 'I don't want to talk about it. I told you at the time.'

A man walking by looked at her. 'Shh,' said Virginia. 'I'm only trying to help.'

She knew that tone. The hurt tone her sister put on when she'd gone too far and was trying to regain the moral ground. Well this time, she wasn't going to appease her.

'I'm going back to the hotel,' she said. 'See you there.'

David wasn't in the room, so presumably was still at his meeting. Marcie closed the heavy wooden shutters and flung herself on the bed. There was something very calming about lying down in the middle of the day with dusky shadows glancing off the shutters while it was hot and bright outside. It reminded her of being ill as a child.

Marcie propped herself up in bed, with the large continental bolster behind her. Virginia had been right even though she hadn't liked her saying it. It was time to face the truth. Time to . . .

The phone's sharp tones startled her. Funny. One didn't expect the phone to ring in a hotel room unless there was a problem. Marcie's heart began to pound. 'Hello?'

'Is David there?'

A very well-spoken English woman's voice clipped down the line.

'No, he's not. Can I help you instead, Diana?'

'I presume that's Marcie speaking?'

'Sure.'

'Can you tell me when David is back? I need to speak to him urgently.'

Marcie forced herself to remain civil. 'He's at a meeting. Can I take a message?'

'Well, you can, provided you don't get it wrong. I've got to go to the States on business and there isn't anyone to look after the children. So I've booked them a flight to Rome for this evening.'

What? 'Can't David's mother have them?'

'She has a bridge party,' replied Diana crisply.

Only the English could put that first!

'And besides,' continued Diana, 'the children have never been to Rome. They'd like to come.'

'It is meant to be our holiday,' interrupted Marcie.

'Well the children would like one too. If you ever have children yourself one day, you'll understand that.'

Marcie winced. Had Diana picked up, through the children, that she was trying to have a baby?

'Give me the flight details,' she said flatly, 'and we'll be there to meet them.'

She was sitting on the balcony by the time David got back. It was after lunch but she hadn't felt like eating.

He glanced at the half empty bottle of wine on the table. 'You don't normally drink at lunchtime. In fact, I didn't think you were drinking at all at the moment.'

'Sit down.' She stared across the street. On the opposite side was another hotel with an almost identical wrought-iron balcony. It was strange how you noticed details at crunch times. It had been the same that afternoon when the red truck had rattled its way down the drive. 'I've got something to tell you.'

He pulled up a chair. 'If it's about the children, I'm sorry,' he began. 'Diana got me on the mobile after she spoke to you.'

'It's something else,' she interrupted. 'Something I should have told you when we first met. Virginia said I should come clean and I think she's right.' Marcie sighed. 'As always.'

'What?'

David sat forward like a worried small boy. Marcie closed her eyes. It was easier that way.

'When I was 15, Virginia and I used to hang out at a deserted house on the edge of town. Other kids did the same. We smoked and drank a bit. Nothing serious. But it was somewhere to escape.'

He nodded tersely. 'And?'

She closed her eyes tighter. 'One afternoon, I got there alone. Virginia was meant to be there after school but she wasn't. So I just sat there, waiting. Then I heard a truck coming up the lane. I thought it was one of the boys who used to take his dad's truck. Joel, he was called.'

She opened her eyes. David was watching her.

'It wasn't Joel. It was his older brother.'

Marcie felt the tears stream hotly down her cheeks. David reached for her hand but she pushed him away. Why hadn't she been able to push Joel's brother away like that?

'I couldn't stop him.' She was gulping now for air just as she had gulped for air then. 'He was too big for me and it was all over so fast. He drove away and then Virginia came.'

She was shuddering as David wrapped his arms around her. 'Shh, it's all right.'

'No.' Marcie pummelled her fists against her husband's shoulder. 'No, it wasn't all right. I got pregnant.'

He let go of her and as he did so, Marcie felt all the hope draining away. 'You got pregnant?' he repeated in an odd voice.

Marcie felt the bile rising into her throat. 'Virginia sorted it out. She knew this woman who did abortions but we had to keep it quiet. She said that if Mom knew, it would kill her.'

'But your parents could have taken charges out against the boy.'

Marcie was hysterical now. 'I didn't want anyone to know!'

There was a soft knock on the door.

'Leave it,' instructed David.

The knock came again. 'Marcie, are you ok?'

'Let her in,' sobbed Marcie.

She heard David walking across the marble floor, heard the whispers, felt Virginia's arms around her.

'It's all right, baby,' whispered her sister. 'You did the right thing in telling him.'

Marcie looked up through her tears. David was white; something had gone from his eyes. Something indefinable.

'Would you like me to go?' whispered Virginia.

'No,' said Marcie, hugging her. 'Please stay.'

Thirty-four

DOES YOUR CAR NEED CLEANING?

Responsible 13 year old avaylable for car washing.

Contact Tim Howard on 07930 9383.

Louise opened her latest bank statement, her heart sinking. How could she have got through so much money when she'd been so very careful? She ran over the payments, ticking them off against the credit card stubs. Justine had insisted she needed a new pair of jeans and Nick had definitely had to have another pair of shoes, although he would only consider designer brands. When she'd told him she couldn't afford it, he had looked at her in such a way that she'd felt terrible. So she'd paid the extra and now the consequences were in black and white before her eyes.

Then there were the bills and the recent vet fees.

The phone. Who could ring at this time of night?

'Hello?'

'It's me. How are you doing?'

Louise's heart rose and fell at the same time. For weeks now, she'd been half-hoping for and half-dreading this call.

'Ok-ish.'

'Tell me.'

It was so comforting hearing Guy's voice that she found herself telling him about Justine and the American woman's stepson, her work and how she had to do it even though she knew she could do something better. But she left out her worries about the bills because she didn't want him offering to help out again.

'Poor you. I would offer to come round and talk to Justine if it wasn't so late but I've only just got back. I've been in the States on business again.'

So that had been why he hadn't called! She felt ridiculously happy for a minute before yanking herself back to being practical. 'Did it go well?'

'It was good for work and I looked up a couple of old friends.'

Her heart lurched. What kind of old friends?

He sounded vague. 'A girl who used to work for me and someone else I was at Bristol with.'

'That's nice.'

'Look, Louise, there's something else.' He spoke quietly so she could barely hear him. 'I understand why you said what you did the other week. I've been giving it a lot of thought and I think you're probably right. I made things more complicated for you than they are already and I'm sorry.'

'Don't be,' she said quickly.

'Well, I am. But I want you to know that I'm always here for you as a friend.'

'Thank you.' Her voice sounded small and flat.

'I'll ring next week, then.'

'That would be nice. Sorry, Guy, I must go. One of the children is calling me. Bye.'

It wasn't true, she thought, putting down the phone. The children were all, miraculously, asleep in their own beds. But she couldn't cope with the conversation any more. A terrible sinking feeling inside her told her that she'd made an awful mistake. Guy, the kindest, nicest man she had ever met, had offered to help her make a new life. And, rightly or wrongly, she had turned him down.

The following morning, Louise was sorting out the washing in the kitchen. As she shook out a duvet cover, one of Justine's t-shirts that she'd been looking for everywhere fell out. It was, she thought sardonically, a bit like marriage. Everything seemed normal on the surface but the unexpected could fall out at any time.

'Morning, Mum,' mumbled a tired voice behind her. It was Tim. That was unusual for him to get up so early. He seemed to have woken the others too; she could hear them approaching and arguing at the same time. 'I'm going fishing with Roddy,' continued Tim. 'Have you got my jeans?'

Tim only had one pair of jeans that he would wear – he pretended the others were too small – and Louise always had to wash them overnight.

'Again?' Louise felt a stirring of unease, hating herself for doing so. Roddy Pearmain was a father, for goodness sake. So why shouldn't he take Tim fishing? All the same, one heard so much nowadays about child abuse.

'Does anyone else go with you?'

'No.' Tim was getting his stuff ready. 'Why?'

'It might be nice,' said Louise carefully, 'if you took some friends with you too.'

'They're all on holiday.'

'Yeah,' said Justine pointedly, pouring herself a glass of juice and slopping it over the side. 'Just like we would be if you and Dad hadn't split up. Where were we going to go again until you lot cancelled it? Cuba, wasn't it?'

'Justine, please mop up that mess,' said Louise tersely. 'And Tim, you've got to put on a jumper. You can't just go out wearing a t-shirt. You'll catch a cold.'

'Chill out, Mum.' Tim was pulling on his trainers. 'They've done some research proving you can't get a cold just because you feel cold.'

Sometimes she wondered if these survey people were out to make parents' lives a misery.

'Well take a hoodie anyway. And Justine, I want you to tidy your room today. It was a complete tip yesterday and so was the rest of the house. It's not fair when I'm at work all day.'

'I'll do it when I want.'

'Justine! Stop being so rude. When you're my age, you'll realise how hurtful it is.'

'When I'm your age, I'm going to live my life very differently,' said Justine coolly.

'Look, I'm older than you and I deserve some respect.'

Justine smirked. 'I know you're older. That's why you've got grey bits in your hair and your brain cells aren't as sharp as mine. Anyway, I can't tidy my room because I'm spending the day with Dad and Gemma.'

'You are?'

Louise felt a stab of hurt.

'Yes. They're taking me shopping, which is more than you ever do.'

Why hadn't Jonathan told her? They'd agreed to liaise on arrangements like this.

'And don't you try to tidy my room,' added Justine sharply. 'It's my territory, not yours.'

Count to ten, Louise told herself. 'What about you, Nick? Someone needs to be here for the dog. And haven't you got some work to do? It would be nice if you read a bit more.'

'I read loads on the net, Mum,' said Nick, putting a slice of bread into the toaster. 'It's no different from books. In fact, in a few years, there probably won't be any books cos everyone will be downloading them. Just go to work, can you? We'll be fine.'

Grey bits in her hair? Louise sat at her desk in reception, thinking. Was Justine being difficult just because she was Justine (she'd never been easy) or because of what had happened? Probably a mixture of both.

'You look pensive.'

Louise looked up as Susan came in. She smiled ruefully. 'I've just had a bit of an argument with my daughter.'

'Ah.' Susan smiled. 'Teenagers. I was a terrible one myself and now I've got all that to come. Still, you're at work now. You can get away from it for a few hours.'

It was true. It was a relief to be somewhere where someone

wasn't being rude or nasty to her or spilling juice without mopping it up.

Susan sat on the edge of the table. 'Someone told me, when my husband left, that one day you wake up and suddenly discover that life isn't as bad as you thought it was and that you actually rather like being on your own.'

'And is that what happened to you?'

Susan nodded. 'Then of course I met my husband, Jeff, but to be honest, I held out for quite a long time, especially as I then changed careers and trained as a homeopath. It gave me confidence, so I wasn't sure I wanted to commit to another man and risk everything all over again.'

Louise thought fleetingly of Guy. 'But you did?'

Susan smiled. 'And it was worth it. After that, we went on to have our son – I never thought I'd have another child – and we're still very happy. Be honest, Louise. Were you really happy with your husband? Before you found out what happened?'

'Not really. If I'm really frank, we don't have a lot in common apart from the children. But I just went on, like so many people, I suppose. Drifting apart didn't seem enough to end a marriage.'

'So now,' persisted Susan, 'you've got time to see what you do want and maybe find someone you do have more in common with.'

After that, she felt surprisingly calmer. Even so, there were still some difficult things she needed to do, like getting hold of Roddy on the mobile number her son had given her.

'Tim said you were taking him fishing and I just wanted to make sure that he wasn't in your way,' she said diplomatically.

'Not at all. It's nice to have the company. Hang on, Tim. You thread the bait this way.'

He sounded so nice that she felt awful about checking up. 'Thanks. It's very kind of you.'

'Not at all.'

'Er, he's not actually going into the water, is he?'

'No.' Roddy's voice cooled. 'Don't worry. I won't let him drown like I nearly let my daughter.'

'I didn't mean that,' she said hastily. 'It's just that he's not a strong swimmer.'

'Would you like me to take him home now?'

Now she'd offended him. 'No. Not unless he's in your way.'

'I told you. He's not.'

Louise looked up. Mary was heading this way, disapprovingly. 'Sorry, Roddy, I've got to go. Thanks anyway.'

Mary was coming up to her desk. 'Louise, I believe I've told you before that personal calls are not allowed at work except under extreme circumstances. I know you had a problem with your dog the other day and that's understandable. But it cannot become a habit.'

Louise flushed. 'I'm sorry.'

'Well don't let it happen again. Susan tells me you're very good with the clients. I wouldn't like to lose you.'

The threat was implicit. How would she manage to get by if she didn't work? Jonathan had already told her he'd had to take a drop in salary because he'd lost a client. So she couldn't ask him for more.

'Talking of personal calls,' continued Mary bossily, 'that journalist from *Charisma* rang last night after you'd left. She wants you to contact her. Urgently.'

'What do you think?' demanded Mandy.

Louise had had to wait until her tea break before being able to go outside and ring. And now she couldn't believe what Mandy had suggested.

'You want me to write a column, every month, describing what it's like to be suddenly single?'

'That's right.' Mandy sounded impatient. 'So many of our readers are in the same position; it would help them to know they're not alone.'

'Jonathan would kill me.'

'Do it anonymously. We could call it something like "Susie's Divorce Diary".'

'But I haven't written anything for years.'

'If you don't want to do it, Louise, tell me.'

'Yes, I do,' Louise heard herself saying. 'How many words do you want?'

'Eight hundred. By next Thursday. Start off with the break-up and that stuff you were telling me about your daughter. How she's making you feel bad even though it's not your fault.'

Louise felt a tremor of unease. On the other hand, it would be anonymous. And, even more important, she'd be doing something she had actually trained for. She could write in the evenings after work.

'There's one thing you haven't asked,' added Mandy. 'Don't you want to know how much we're paying?'

'Sorry,' said Louise.

'Don't apologise to me. God, that man's destroyed your confidence, hasn't he? We can give you £450 a column. It's not much, I'm afraid.'

Not much! Louise could hardly believe her luck!

'File straight to me,' continued Mandy. 'And don't overwrite. Email if you have any problems.'

Louise's head was still whirling when she got home that night. Was she up to writing a column after so many years of not doing anything? She'd always regretted giving up her free-lance work but, after Tim was born, there had been too much to do. Neither she nor Jonathan had liked the idea of anyone else bringing up the children. But now, too late, she could see how her decision had made her fall out of the job market. Well now was her chance to redeem herself.

As she let herself into the house, it seemed strangely silent. There was a note from Tim, saying he'd got back from fishing and had gone out with Nick to buy a pizza because some of Nick's friends were coming round. That was something. Over the last few weeks, he'd slowly invited some school friends over. And instead of looking down their noses at their new small house, they'd declared the lake to be cool.

Meanwhile, Justine was nowhere to be seen. Maybe that was

her now knocking at the door. She could hardly hear it over Hector's furious barking.

'Darling! Hi. Supper's almost ready.'

Her daughter pushed past her roughly. 'I'm going out with Dad. I've just come back to get some stuff.'

Jonathan was waiting in the car outside. A car she didn't recognise. 'Is this new?' she asked, walking up to it.

'It's Gemma's.' Jonathan was looking at her coldly as though she was the one who had caused all this mess.

'I'm ready, Dad.' Justine was flying back out of the house, suitcase in hand.

'I didn't know you were staying the night with Dad.'

'Hasn't he told you?' Justine was looking at her challengingly.

'Louise,' began Jonathan. 'Justine has been telling me about all the rows and how you're never there because of your job.'

'That's not fair!' began Louise.

'And that stupid residents' association won't let us play our music,' added Justine. 'So Dad said I could live with him for a bit.' She smirked. 'You don't mind, do you?'

Thirty-five

SPECIAL OFFER AT

* * WINO'S OFF-LICENCE! * *

Three bottles of French white wine for the price of two.
Free delivery, depending on size of order.

They were pleased with her voiceover. Her agent had rung to say so.

'In fact we've had an approach from another ad firm, wanting to know if you're available,' he'd told her.

Mollie leaned back in her chair, nursing her whisky glass. It had been half-full just now. Had Gideon been helping himself again?

'I would love to,' she'd said grandly.

'There's only one thing. They don't just want your voice, Mollie. They want you to appear on screen. It's for a vitamin company and they want someone of, let's say, a certain age who still looks good. What do you think, Mollie? Shall we go for it?'

Poppy was cocooned in Gideon's big armchair, her legs up on the little mahogany stool in front and a cushion supporting her back.

'It's a fantastic opportunity, Mollie,' she said. 'You can't possibly turn it down, especially with that kind of money.'

'I don't think Gideon would like it,' she said thoughtfully.

Poppy shifted her position. 'Bet he would. He was always one for taking gambles.'

Mollie frowned. She had never thought of Gideon like that. 'Oh, I don't know.'

Poppy smiled dreamily into the distance. 'I remember telling him about something that could potentially be amazing or terrible, depending on how it turned out. And he told me to go for it.'

Mollie put her glass down. 'Sometimes,' she said slowly, 'I think I can hear Gideon in my head.'

Poppy smiled sadly at her. 'That's very common when someone has died. My mother used to say she could hear her mother too.'

'No, but it's more than that.' Mollie stopped. How could she really tell the child that she actually *saw* Gideon every now and then when he chose to reveal himself? 'And I can definitely hear him warning me about this commercial. The public might just think I'm a sad old bag attempting to make a comeback.'

'Precisely, darling,' said Gideon.

'Go away,' she hissed. 'Can't you see we're talking?'

'What did you say?' asked Poppy, yawning. 'Sorry, Mollie, I'm so exhausted I keep dropping off.'

'Nothing, darling. I was just muttering to myself. Changing the subject, how did your antenatal go?'

Poppy yawned again. 'My blood pressure is fine and the baby is moving just as it should. It seems to be in the right position too.'

'And when exactly are you due?'

Poppy wriggled back in the chair. 'Ah, that's the only funny thing. You know I said I was further gone than I'd thought? Well apparently, I'm almost thirty weeks.'

Thirty weeks! 'But I was enormous at that stage,' cried Mollie. 'Surely you must have realised you were pregnant ages ago?'

'Well, no. As I said, I was irregular. I didn't get any sickness, thank God, and I only put on a few extra pounds. The doctor has given me a list of antenatal classes with other pregnant mums but they'll have partners and I don't really fancy going alone.'

'I'll come with you, darling.'

Poppy sat up straight. 'Really? You'd do that for me?'

Mollie felt a lovely warm feeling seeping through her. 'Of course I will. I'd enjoy it. We didn't have things like that in my day, you know.' She was silent for a bit, thinking how difficult Nigel's birth had been. Sometimes she wondered if that was another reason why she had failed to bond with him.

'There's just one more thing, actually,' added Poppy, smiling at her in that sweet way. 'You know my parents are still abroad?'

Mollie nodded. Poppy's father was in the Foreign Office.

'So I can't ask Mummy to be with me. And although Rupert has offered, I'm not sure he'd be very good at that sort of thing. So I wondered if you'd be my birthing partner. Would you mind?'

'Mind?' Mollie almost leapt off her chair in her eagerness to hold Poppy's slim, cool hand. 'My darling girl, I'd be deeply honoured!'

Later that week, after signing the contract, Mollie was putting the bins out when she saw Louise doing the same.

'Darling, you've been crying,' Mollie said. 'What's wrong?'

'My daughter has chosen to go and live with her father,' sniffed Louise.

'How awful for you.' Mollie put her arms around her. 'But why?'

'We haven't been getting on.' Louise moved away. Maybe she'd embarrassed her. 'We're always rowing about silly things. And I got upset when I caught her in a . . . in a compromising position with a boy. I probably overreacted.'

'No.' Mollie shuddered, thinking of her own experience with Max. 'No, you were right to be worried. Too many young girls get pregnant when it's not really the right time.'

Louise was crying openly now. 'I feel so rejected.'

'I can understand that.' Mollie drew her to one of the garden benches, patting the seat beside her. 'You know, sometimes we don't hit it off with our children even though they're our flesh

and blood. I've never really got on with my son. He's very difficult and, to be honest, I never bonded with him which probably made me difficult too.'

'Why didn't you bond?'

Mollie shifted uncomfortably on the wooden seat. 'It's a long
story. We rub along now all right, on the whole. Your daughter
will come back eventually. Trust me.'

Louise nodded doubtfully.

Mollie patted her arm. 'You're still young enough to find
someone else.'

Louise shook her head. 'It's far too soon. Besides, I don't
know if I could trust anyone again.'

Mollie nodded slowly. 'Sometimes, you have to take a gamble.'

Suddenly, she felt Gideon's arms around her. The relief was
immense and she sank into his warm embrace.

'When you find the right kind of love,' she said dreamily,
'there's nothing like it.'

Louise had stopped crying now. 'How do you know when
you've found it?'

'You just do. You can talk to that person for hours on end
about anything and everything.' Mollie leaned her head on
Gideon's shoulder, feeling his hand stroke her right shoulder,
rhythmically. 'When they touch you, it makes you melt.'

'But the children would be upset.'

'Sometimes,' said Mollie, 'you have to do what is right for
you. It's like me. I've been asked to do another ad, you know.
Not a voiceover.' She stood up straight. 'A proper one showing
me in all my frontal glory!'

She giggled.

'Steady on, old girl,' whispered Gideon.

'That's wonderful!' said Louise.

'Well it will be if people like it. It's a risk but it's one I have
to take.'

'All right then,' said Gideon quietly. 'Give it a go.'

'What do you think your husband would have said?' asked
Louise, gently.

'I think he might say I should give it a go. Just as you should give your own life a chance, my dear. Goodness, it's getting cold now, isn't it? Would you like to come back for a drink? I've bought a crate of some absolutely delicious French wine.' Mollie patted Louise's shoulder. 'I think it's what we both need, don't you, darling?'

Thirty-six

Would the person who scraped the side of my
BMW silver convertible please contact me immediately.

Suzette White, number 1

'Supposing they don't let us through?' asked Peter, sitting cross-legged on the floor of the house in south London. It was, thought Roddy, a horrible place with bare floorboards and the odd rug strewn around to hide the stains. Peter's house definitely lacked a woman's touch.

Their houses all probably did.

'I've told you,' repeated Roddy. 'I've got guest passes. You make your way to St Stephen's entrance . . .'

'Which one is that?' interrupted one of the other men. 'I went there last week to have a nose around and there are hundreds of bloody entrances, each with Christ knows how many policemen at the gate with guns the size of harpoons.'

Roddy reached inside his pocket for a pen and paper. 'You take this exit at Westminster tube and then you turn right.'

It was like explaining a school trip to a bunch of kids. Not for the first time, Roddy was having serious doubts. On the other hand, the situation for fathers without their children was intolerable. This way, the government might be forced into looking at the issue.

'Now when you go through the entrance at St Stephens, you show your guest pass. You'll then walk through the building towards the central lobby. Lots of stone steps and hangings on the wall. A bit like a museum really. When you get to the lobby, you turn right towards the Lords. Again, show your passes and ask for the Strangers' Gallery.'

'Then we play it by ear,' added Peter smoothly. 'Wait until I give you a signal and then I'll stand up and explain our cause. No silly games, mind you, like flour-bag throwing. We need to show them that we're responsible fathers.'

'We'll get arrested,' said a large man at the front.

'Quite possibly,' said Peter calmly. 'But if we do, we'll hit the headlines. And that's what we want, isn't it?'

'So when are you going on your little outing to the House of Lords?' asked Kevin nonchalantly. He was squeezing oranges on Roddy's juicer for breakfast.

'Shut up,' said Roddy irritably. 'By the way, it wasn't you who pranged that silver BMW outside, was it?'

'Not guilty this time, guv. Anyway, stop changing the subject. You'll have to make your trip fast. The PM and his cronies have only come back temporarily from their summer break to discuss this health service crisis. They'll be off again to their villas in Tuscany if you don't do it quickly.'

'I said shut up.'

Roddy was trying to repair the coffee machine.

'I'll do that. Look, you've put the screw in the wrong way.' Kevin grinned. 'If you can't sort this out, how are you going to break into one of the world's most venerable establishments?'

Roddy could swear Kevin read the dictionary at night to improve himself. 'We're not going to break in.'

Kevin's eyes lit up. 'Ah, you've got passes have you? Or are you going to pretend to be workmen? Trust me, you won't hack it with an accent like yours. You need someone like me with you.'

'No thanks,' said Roddy shortly.

'Spoilsport.' Kevin knocked back the glass of juice. 'I enjoy that kind of thing. And besides, I could be useful.'

'Fuck off.' Roddy sat down at the table with his mug of coffee. 'How long are you going to be here, anyway?'

'Let's see.' Kevin pretended to consider the question. 'I was offered a job in Croydon next week but, to be honest, I feel quite comfortable here at the moment. Besides, didn't you say that pretty little American neighbour of yours is coming back soon? There's something I need to say to her.'

'What?'

Kevin leaned back in his chair. 'I'm afraid that's private. Oh by the way, did I mention that the shop you've been doing some work for rang yesterday?'

'No, you didn't. What did they want?'

'Let's see.' Kevin walked languorously towards the phone base. 'I think I wrote it down somewhere. Maybe not. It was something to do with another commission. I think they want one of your boxes by tomorrow. That's right. A bit of a rushed job, I seem to recall.'

'Tomorrow? Bloody hell, you could have mentioned it earlier.'

'Sorry.' Kevin stretched. 'Think I'll go and have a shower now. Nice head you've got here, by the way. I do enjoy a bit of power with my water.'

Roddy rang the shop and found himself promising he could make the boxes by tomorrow. But he'd need some more wood first.

Memories of the wood store in the cellar when he'd been a boy came back to him. As a kid, Roddy had loved helping the gardeners chop the logs and stack them up against the stone walls. It was an outside chance but maybe, just maybe, there might still be some left.

As he went out of the front door, he almost collided with Tim carrying his fishing gear. 'Christ, I'd forgotten. Look, Tim, I'm sorry but something's come up. I can't go fishing today.'

Disappointment washed over the kid's face.

'I've got to look for something, in the cellar.' A sudden thought crossed his mind. 'Want to come with me?'

Tim's eyes lit up. 'Is it as good as the temple?'

Roddy laughed. 'See what you think.'

Amazingly, the cellar hadn't been blocked up. Roddy shone his flashlight round. 'Incredible. It's hardly been touched.'

The beam touched on a large pile of wood in the corner. 'Fantastic.' Roddy knelt down by it. 'Just what I was looking for.'

Tim was looking around. 'What's this?'

Roddy's heart fluttered. 'My trunk. I took it to boarding school. Afterwards, I used it to store stuff. I'd forgotten it was still here. Incredible that the builders didn't move it.'

'Can I open it?'

'Ok.'

The hinges were stiff and there was dirt and cobwebs all over it. But his name was clear. Roderick Pearmain. 121. His boot number. The number that Nanny had to sew or write on to everything to make sure it didn't get lost at school.

'Cor,' said Tim, peering inside. 'There's loads of stuff in here.'

'That's my coin collection.' Roddy lifted out a heavy book. 'Might be worth a bit now. And that's my stamp collection.'

'What are these?'

'Photographs.'

Roddy took the album from the boy and flicked carefully through.

'Who's that?' asked Tim, pointing to a beautiful young woman wearing an evening dress with a double row of pearls, clasping the arm of an extremely handsome man in uniform.

'My parents,' said Roddy shortly. 'Shortly before my father died.'

'Does it upset you to look at it?' asked Tim quietly.

Roddy nodded curtly.

'I know what you mean.' He spoke in a small voice. 'My mum took all the photographs of us. She said she'd get them duplicated for Dad but she hasn't got round to it yet and he keeps going on about it. But if he hadn't left us, he wouldn't have needed them, would he?'

It was one of the longest sentences the kid had ever come

up with and Roddy wasn't sure what to say that would help in return.

'Come on,' he slapped his shoulder. 'The trunk's too heavy to take now. We can come back for it. I really need the wood. Listen, I haven't time to take you fishing but if you want you can be my apprentice for the day. I've got to make a wooden box. Want to help?'

'Hiya, Rodders!' Kevin bounced in through the front door. 'Nice to see you're hard at work. Found your wood in the cellar, did you?'

Roddy glared at him. 'How do you know?'

'Keep your hair on. Saw you coming out when I was walking around, getting to know the place. And you've got a helper too. Tim, isn't it? I could do with some help when you've finished with Roddy here. I've got a couple of little jobs myself.'

'Bugger off,' growled Roddy.

'It's all right. They're quite legal. Actually, talking of legal, there's something I need to talk to you about, Rodders. In the kitchen, I think.'

Sullenly, Roddy followed him out.

Kevin leant back against the sink and, with a flourish, drew out a wadge of papers from his jeans pocket.

'I couldn't help finding these when you were out. Just a word of advice. If you want to hide something, next time put them in a less obvious place.'

'Give them to me.'

'I don't think so. Let's see. One, two, three, four passes for the House of Lords. Not long to go, have you, judging from the date? Want them back, do you?'

'You know I do.'

Kevin grinned. 'Only if you give me one too. I've always fancied going along to the House of Lords. Anyway, you never know, I might come in useful.'

'Over my dead body.'

'Don't say things like that or it might just come true.'

Kevin made to rip them up with his fingers.

'All right, you bastard. You win.' Roddy's eyes flashed. 'But I'm warning you. You do what you're told. Any false move and I'll tell the police, even if it means we all end up in jail.'

Thirty-seven

Furniture restorer available. All jobs considered. Will also
take private commissions for boxes and other objects.
Contact Roddy Pearmain at number 3.

Under the circumstances, thought Marcie wryly, it was just as
well that the children were coming out here. For the first time
since she'd met them, they'd be a welcome distraction.

After her confession to her husband, things simply hadn't
been the same between them.

'Of course I still love you,' David had said when they'd talked
about it later. 'I just need a bit of time to think about what you
told me.'

He stroked her arm but she still wasn't reassured.

'It must have been awful for you,' he continued.

She nodded. 'I had a bit of a breakdown,' she said quietly.
'I couldn't go out of the house for a long time. My mother
kept asking what was wrong but I couldn't tell her.'

'But why didn't you tell *me* before?'

'I couldn't.' Her voice came out all squeaky. 'There never
seemed to be a right time.'

'Not even when you saw the gynaecologist?'

He had moved slightly away from her now. The light from
the street outside shone through the shutters so she could see
his anxious face. 'You don't think that having an . . . an abortion,' his words faltered slightly, 'is why you haven't been able
to conceive?'

Suddenly she felt like snapping. 'Maybe. Lots of women have

abortions and go on to have babies. But perhaps I'm not going to be one of the lucky ones. Then you'll be able to divorce me and marry someone who can have kids.'

'Don't be silly.' He gathered her into his arms. 'I'm sure it will be all right.'

The following day, Robert and Katy arrived and they all – including Virginia – were there to meet them at the airport.

Katy, noticed Marcie disapprovingly, was wearing an extremely short denim skirt which left little to the imagination. Robert didn't even bother saying hello.

'This is my sister, Virginia,' said Marcie to the children.

Robert held out his hand and shook hers. 'Very nice to meet you.'

Marcie was aghast. He had never been that polite to her.

'Nice to meet you too,' said Virginia. 'I've heard so much about you kids, although I must say, Marcie, you didn't tell me how gorgeous Katy was. I just love that skirt!'

Katy flushed. 'Thanks. Mum got it for me for the trip.'

'Funny thing,' continued Virginia, 'that it goes with a pair of earrings I just happened to spot in town yesterday.'

Katy opened the small parcel. 'They're lovely. Gosh. Thanks, Virginia, that's really kind of you.'

They were round silver hoops, far too grown-up for the child in Marcie's eyes.

'I'll have to get my ears pierced now,' said Katy, squeezing David's hand. 'Won't I, Dad?'

'I ought to check with your mother first.'

'Oh, doesn't she have pierced ears?' cried Virginia. 'Well if your mother agrees – you could text her – I'd be delighted to take you to a jeweller's here to have them done. I've found the perfect place . . .'

The pair made their way towards the hired car, chattering as though they had always known each other. David was deep in conversation with Robert about his recent end-of-term exams and Marcie felt completely left out. She should have thought about getting Katy a present. It would also have been nice of Virginia to have mentioned it first so they could have shared it.

Memories of Virginia getting in first, being the daughter to give their father a birthday watch before she, Marcie, had finished saving up for one, came flooding back. She'd been away from Virginia for so long that she'd forgotten those little things that got on her nerves.

'All right?' asked David as he opened the passenger door for her.

'Fine.' Marcie forced herself to smile back. 'Just fine.'

They all went out to dinner that night. David had chosen the restaurant. It was, Marcie had to admit, a good choice, with tables outside in a pretty little square surrounded by potted green shrubs. There were Christmas lights everywhere, even though it was summer, and a man with a violin was going round from table to table, playing for families or couples.

'This is so lovely,' breathed Virginia, her eyes sparkling.

'It's pretty cool,' said Robert.

'What do you think, Katy?' asked Marcie, trying to get into the conversation.

'She's got her headphones on,' said Robert tersely. 'She's listening to her music.'

Marcie felt irritated. 'That's very rude.'

'She's all right.' David was considering the menu. 'She's on holiday. Let her relax.'

Marcie could hardly believe it. David was a stickler for table manners and at home the children were meant to sit up and behave.

'Katy.'

Marcie reached over to pull out the headphones. She knew she shouldn't but something inside her was making her act irrationally.

'Fuck off,' said Katy, pushing her away.

'David! Are you going to let her tell me off like that?'

David sighed. 'Now Katy, you know that's rude. Apologise.'

'No, I won't.' Katy's eyes were flashing. 'She was the one who was rude, trying to pull out my headphones.'

Virginia reached across the table and squeezed her hand. 'She doesn't mean it, sis. You remember what it was like at that age.'

'What was Marcie like as a teenager?' asked Robert suddenly.

Marcie felt a prickle of unease.

'Oh, just like any other kid,' said Virginia carefully. 'Curious, always wanting to know about things . . .'

'I think,' said David smoothly, 'that it's time to order. What would you like, Virginia?'

The following day wasn't much better. They spent the morning going round shops where Virginia insisted on buying Robert an expensive leather case for his phone. 'Just see it as a gift from your step-aunt,' she said. 'Please, I insist.'

Lunch was just like dinner the previous evening except that, instead of being plugged into her music, Katy was engrossed in her own phone which seemed to go off every few minutes. The tone was like an annoying musical waterfall.

'I can't help it if I'm so popular,' she said when her father gently suggested she turned it off for lunch.

'I hope they realise how much it costs to ring out here,' remarked Marcie.

'Their parents pay,' retorted Katy, slipping her hand into her father's challengingly. 'Just like Dad pays for mine. Anyway, Robert's the one who's always texting Justine, the girl he met at Bridgewater House. It's probably costing you loads.'

Marcie gave David a look which said, 'That's the girl he was caught in the pavilion with. Aren't you going to do anything?'

But David was leafing through his guidebook. Common sense told her he didn't want to tell them off during their precious time together. But that made her look like the bad guy.

'I thought we'd go to the Vatican museum, this afternoon,' he announced.

'Boring,' said Katy.

'I think you might find it quite interesting,' said Virginia quickly. 'I've been reading up about it. Apparently, there's one particular painting where the eyes follow you if you've been dishonest.'

'Is it done by computers?' asked Katy.

Virginia laughed. 'No, but maybe it should have been. You know, David, you've got a really clever daughter here.'

Katy glowed and David looked pleased. 'Thank you, Virginia.' He reached out for his daughter's hand. 'I'm really proud of my kids. They mean the world to me.'

Virginia always knew how to say the right thing, thought Marcie miserably as they queued up outside the Vatican. Since the kids had arrived, she had felt like an extra. And David had definitely been distant. She shouldn't have told him about what had happened; she really shouldn't.

'I'm just going to the restroom,' she announced when David returned with ice creams to occupy the kids while they were queuing.

'Want me to come with you?' asked Virginia.

'No thanks,' retorted Marcie coldly.

Inside the cubicle, Marcie turned her mobile on. Yes! There was a message waiting.

'How is it gng? Pretty dull here bt am planning trip to somewhere special. K.'

Something tingled through her body. K! It suggested a familiarity which somehow she didn't find unappealing. And it was nice to have someone who seemed to find her interesting for a change, someone who didn't treat her like a kid.

'Family complication,' she texted back. *'Not gt. Enjoy trip.'*

His return message came back within a few minutes.

'Family can b pain. C u wn u r bk.'

She felt better when she returned to the others, hugging her secret to her like a naughty child. It didn't mean anything. But it sure was good to know that there was someone out there rooting for her.

It took ages to get into the museum and by the time they did, they were all feeling hot and scratchy. After a few paintings, thought Marcie, you'd seen them all. But that didn't stop her trying to get Katy on her side.

'That's nice, don't you think?' she asked, pointing to a romantic picture of a dark count with his arm round a lady in green.

No response – and the child didn't even have her music plugged in.

Well, damn that. She made her way out of the room and wandered off down a long gallery of tapestries. How long it must have taken someone to have done that, she thought. Of course, more than one person would have worked on it but even so . . .

Further down was a group of people clustering around a guide. To her delight, they were Americans and she attached herself to the back. 'This,' the guide was saying, 'is the famous tapestry depicting Jesus. It is said that when you walk past, his eyes follow you if you have been deceitful in your life.'

There was an uneasy ripple of laughter from the group.

Marcie started walking. They had a whole week of this left. A week of Virginia currying favour with the kids and David pretending that nothing had changed between them. She wished now that they hadn't arranged for Virginia to come back to Bridgewater House for a month.

Marcie glanced up at the tapestry. The Lord's eyes were firmly on her. She walked past, steeling herself to look behind. What did the future hold now for her? Why was she pathetic enough to glean hope from some text messages from a man she didn't know? What kind of man would want to stay married to her, now he knew she had been violated as a teenager?

'Why didn't you struggle?' he had said.

She had tried to explain that she'd been frozen with fear; the shock had been so great she hadn't been able to think straight.

Marcie looked back. Jesus' eyes were still on her.

It was proof. Proof that she didn't even need.

She had been a bad girl and now she was doing it all over

again, with Kevin. All she wanted was David. But he didn't want her now. She had blown it; just like she had always blown the important things in life.

So what did she have to lose?

Thirty-eight

Due to the absence of so many residents during
the summer holidays, yoga lessons will be cancelled until
September. Can we also ask residents not to cut flowers from
the communal garden. They are there for everyone to enjoy.

It just wasn't the same with two children in the house instead
of three. When they'd all been small, it had been constant chaos
and non-stop demands. Often she had craved peace and quiet.
But now it seemed too quiet.

'I still can't believe my daughter chose not to live with me,' she
wrote, fingers flying across the keyboard. *'I've failed completely
as a mother.'*

The words came tumbling out just as they had when she
had done this as a real job.

*'It's Saturday and I'm exhausted after a week's work. But I've
joined a self-help group for single people and I've learned lots of
practical and emotional stuff. In fact, there's a meeting tonight and
I might just go along.'*

Funny. She hadn't really intended to until the words came
out. But seeing Sheila and the others suddenly seemed like a
good idea.

'I miss Justine so much,' said Louise mournfully into her second
glass of wine.

'When my kids went to their father, there didn't seem any point
any more,' said Sheila starkly. 'But you learn to adapt. Do you
talk to her?'

'We've talked briefly on the phone. Gemma took her shopping the other day and bought her a new pair of jeans. The same pair that I couldn't afford to get her.'

'Hey.' Derek patted her hand briefly. 'She'll come back eventually. It just takes time.'

Louise blew her nose. So embarrassing! She hadn't meant to get upset and, besides, they all had their own problems. Steve's wife had died. How bad was that?

'Did it take your children long to get over their mother?'

Steven gave her a half-smile. 'You never do.'

Of course you don't. How stupid of her.

'But you learn to live with it,' added Sheila quickly. 'You learn to live with everything eventually. Trust me. By the way, did you know you could get 25 per cent off your council tax if you're the only resident adult? You didn't? Well, ring them up for a form quickly!'

The house was lit up with a blaze of colour as she drove back and for one heart-stopping moment Louise thought it was on fire until realising it was the sunset reflecting in the windows.

Sheila was right. It was slowly getting better – and that practical stuff about the council tax was invaluable – although there were still some very dark moments. At least she didn't have to go home and face a distant husband; Jonathan had been so cold in the last few months before telling her what was really wrong.

'Hi!' Roddy strode up to her. To her surprise he greeted her with a light kiss on both cheeks. Louise was so taken aback, she could hardly think straight. She barely knew the man!

'How are you getting on?'

'Fine, thank you,' she managed to say.

He was looking at her carefully. 'I know what you're going through. You and I are in the same boat. But it will get better. I truly believe it will.'

Had he been drinking? She couldn't smell anything but there

had been persistent rumours, mainly from Lydia's direction, that Lord Pearmain had been in a clinic for alcoholics.

'Thank you,' she murmured. 'And thank you also for taking my son fishing.'

'Not at all. I enjoy the company. Well, must be off now.' He airbrushed her cheeks again. 'Looks as though you've got someone waiting for you.'

'What?'

Only then did she notice the smart silver and black sports car parked opposite. She ran across.

'Guy. I didn't know you were coming over!'

He looked at her coldly and her entire chest froze. 'And I didn't mean to interrupt your conversation.'

'You didn't. That was Roddy. Our resident aristocrat. You don't think . . .' She giggled. 'He wasn't really kissing me, you know. It's how people like him behave. And he's been very kind to Tim, taking him fishing and that kind of thing.'

'You don't need to explain.' He started the engine. 'I was passing so I called in to see if you're all right. The boys told me Justine had moved out.'

Tears pricked her eyes again. 'It's awful. I don't know how I'll manage.'

Something sad, regretful, flickered across his face. 'You seem to be doing all right.'

'No,' said Louise urgently. 'No. You've got the wrong idea about Roddy.'

He started the engine. 'See you sometime.'

Her heart sinking, she went into the house. All the lights were on but the boys were actually asleep, clothes strewn on the floor, dirty plates still on the side.

How ridiculous of Guy to get the wrong idea about Roddy! Still, maybe he'd tell Jonathan. It wouldn't do him any harm to realise that some people found her attractive.

The following day, the boys seemed intent on being as difficult as possible. Justine's departure had obviously affected them too.

'I want you to tidy your room. It's a real mess.'

'Chillax, Mum,' scowled Tim. 'You're always so uptight.'

'Guy came round last night,' said Nick, putting his plate in the dishwasher.

'I know. I saw him when he was leaving.'

'Why did he come?' asked Tim suspiciously.

'I don't know. To see if we're all right, I suppose.'

'Whatever.' Tim pushed his chair back, leaving his knife and fork haphazardly on his plate. 'I'm going out.'

'Where?'

'Just out. Stop nagging, Mum. You're always on my back.'

Why did they always get the better of her? 'You ought to give Dad a ring.'

Tim scowled. 'Why? I don't want to see him.'

'But you should do. He's your father.'

'Well he hasn't acted like one, has he? Shut up, Mum. You're really getting on my nerves.'

She'd forgotten how helpful it was to write it all down. *'The children are behaving really badly. In one way I'm glad Jonathan isn't here because he'd be cross with them. But in another, I feel like another single mother statistic, who can't cope with her kids.'*

She re-read her paragraph. It was far more open than she had meant it to be but it was anonymous. She'd finish it off in her lunch hour tomorrow.

It was almost – but not quite – enough to take her mind off Guy. And the funny thing was that for the first time in ages, the pain about Jonathan wasn't quite as raw as it had been, even though it still hurt. Did that mean she was finally coming to terms with it?

The text message came the next morning. Luckily Mary wasn't around to hear the tell-tale bleep.

'Sorry I overreacted on Saturday night. You're entitled to see who you want.'

She texted back immediately. '*I'm not seeing anyone. Roddy's just a neighbour. Need to talk.*'

His reply came within seconds. '*Have to go into meeting now but will ring.*'

It wasn't that satisfactory but it would do. Just what she would say to him when they did meet was a different matter. Meanwhile, she simply had to complete her column or she'd miss her deadline. Louise glanced at her watch. It was her lunchtime, or nearly. No one was around to notice if she finished it off on the office computer.

'May I ask what you are doing?'

Louise jumped as Mary spoke in clipped, polite tones behind her.

'I'm just finishing something off. It's a sort of letter, to a friend. It *is* my lunch hour.'

Mary looked at her watch. 'It's 2.30, Louise.'

She'd forgotten how fast time could go when you were writing.

'I'm sorry. But there haven't been any patients . . .'

'That's not the point.' Mary pursed her thin lips. 'You might have a way with the patients but we also need someone who can give her full attention to the job and not race home to look after sick dogs or write letters to friends on the office computer during work hours. You're sacked, Louise. And don't expect a reference.'

Thirty-nine

NEED HELP WITH YOUR IRONING?

Contact Sally on 07769 4444.

Mollie had forgotten how much she loved all this. Having her face and hair done, chatting to the stylist in the elegant little dressing-room they had given her and then, finally, sitting in the studio with the bright lights.

In one way, she wasn't surprised that Gideon hadn't shown up that day.

'Don't be jealous, silly,' she said quietly. 'I'm doing this for you as much as for me.'

'I didn't quite catch that, Mollie,' said the sound girl. 'Mind if I adjust your mike?'

She deftly moved the wires that ran up inside Mollie's elegant top from Frank Usher that wardrobe had found her. She was wearing a rather nice silk skirt of her own that Sally, bless her, had ironed before she'd left. 'Let's try that. Can you say something, Mollie?'

Of course she could. She could say, 'Come on out, Gideon, you silly old fool, from wherever you're hiding.' But that wouldn't go down very well. Now what were the words of the script again? She'd been practising them with Poppy. Ah, that's right. Mollie smiled serenely at the camera. 'Vital Vits will keep you young – whatever your age.'

'Lovely,' said the girl. 'Gosh, Mollie, you look fantastic. What's your secret?'

'Plenty of sex, darling.'

The girl laughed nervously.

'I mean it.' Mollie's mind flashed back to a couple of nights ago when Gideon had flipped her over in bed and taken her roughly from behind. Rather more roughly than usual, she recalled, as though he had been angry with her. 'It keeps you young. Now, am I sitting right?'

'You're absolutely perfect,' said the director, a youngish man with a wispy beard. 'Now straight into camera and speak.'

'Vital Tits . . .' said Mollie. 'Sorry, I'll do that again. Vital Vits will keep you young – whatever your age.'

'Darling, that's lovely. But can you say it with more caress? Seduce the words. Stroke them.'

Closing her eyes, Mollie recalled the wonderful way Gideon ran his tongue down her. 'Vital Tits . . . Vits will keep you young – whatever your age.'

The producer frowned. Gripping the side of her chair, Mollie repeated the phrase, getting it right this time.

'Fantastic. Nearly there. But just a tiny little more pause after the word "young".'

And so it went on. After nearly an hour, the director seemed satisfied but Mollie was exhausted.

'You did brilliantly,' said the sound girl, unhooking her afterwards.

'But it took nearly an hour,' said Mollie. 'They must have thought I was stupid not to have got it right the first time.'

'Nonsense. Lots of people take far longer.' She named a famous news reader who had apparently taken three hours.

Feeling slightly better, Mollie smiled graciously at the film crew as she made her way to the dressing-room.

'Not bad for an old lady, is she?' said one.

What a cheek, thought Mollie, tempted to turn round and give them a piece of her mind.

'No. Still, it didn't stop her old man from shagging every-thing in sight when he was alive, did it?'

Mollie went cold. 'What did you say?' she asked quietly, turning back.

The lads fell silent.

'Please explain what you meant,' she said again.

One of the boys, the shorter one, shifted his weight from one leg to another. 'Well, you must know,' he said at length. 'Your husband had a bit of a reputation, didn't he? As a ladies' man and all that.'

'All that?' repeated Mollie grandly, drawing herself up to her full height. 'And what precisely do you mean by "all that"?'

'Forget it,' said the boy. 'I shouldn't have said anything. Sorry.'

It haunted Mollie all the way home.

'What's wrong?' asked Poppy, who had been asleep on the chair, when she got in. 'Didn't it go well?'

'The shoot was all right,' said Mollie dully, rearranging the roses she had rather naughtily picked last week from the grounds because her own had proved exceedingly disappointing. 'It's something else.'

Briefly, she explained what had happened. 'I know Gideon loved to talk to women but he wasn't unfaithful.'

Poppy drew her knees up to her chest, covering herself with the throw she liked to cuddle up under.

'He loved you very much, Mollie. You know that.'

'Yes, but do you think he actually slept with other people?'

The girl stood up and held her in her arms. 'Look, Mollie, does it really matter? Lots of husbands and wives do things that their partners never know about. But I do know that Gideon was devoted to you. Now, are you too tired for my antenatal class tonight?'

Goodness, she'd almost forgotten.

'Of course I'm not. I can't wait!'

If only they had had this kind of thing in her day. Mollie marvelled at the way the girls talked to each other about personal things like how far you had to dilate before the baby could come out.

There were so many different options now, too, like water

births and home births and goodness knows what other kind of births.

It almost – but not quite – took her mind off what the boy had said about Gideon.

'Are you Poppy's mother?' asked one of the girls during the break in the class.

Mollie beamed at the compliment. 'I wish I was. No, I'm just a rather old friend.'

'A very dear friend,' said Poppy, squeezing her arm.

'My husband and I have known Poppy for years,' added Mollie. It gave her a warm feeling to be amongst these lovely girls, most of whom had brought their husbands. She felt so sorry for Poppy without a man. She wanted to make up for it.

'Don't I know your face from somewhere?' asked another girl.

'Mollie is an actress,' said Poppy proudly. 'She and her husband Gideon were really famous.'

'You're Mollie de May, aren't you?' gasped the first girl. 'Gosh, my mum idolised you.'

'Mine had the hots for your husband,' said another.

Mollie noticed Poppy giving her a worried look. 'Well, he was a very good-looking man. Lots of women admired him.'

She looked around. Still no sign of him. A slight feeling of unease spread through her. She hadn't seen him since the day before the filming. Odd.

'Isn't your partner here?' continued the first girl.

Poppy put on her it-doesn't-matter-to-me look. 'I'm not with him any more. No, it's fine. Honestly. I can manage on my own.'

'But you're not on your own, darling,' said Mollie insistently. 'You've got me.'

Poppy looked slightly sad for a minute. 'Yes, I know. Thank you.'

The following morning, Mollie slept in late. So much had happened the day before that she was exhausted. She was worried too that Gideon still hadn't shown up.

When Mollie had got out of her shower, she found that Poppy had gone out. The flat seemed strangely quiet. Outside, she could see a taxi unloading the American woman and her husband, plus the two teenagers she'd met before and another woman whom she didn't recognise.

Just after she'd got dressed, there was a knock on the door. For one wild, silly moment, she thought it might be Gideon. But it was Nigel. No doubt he'd come to tell her off about something again or tell her that she was too old to risk her reputation in front of the camera.

'Mother, I need a word.'

Not so much as a 'How are you', she thought wryly. 'Come and sit down, Nigel.'

'No thank you.' He glanced at the framed family photographs on the mantelpiece. 'I'd rather stand. There's something I need to tell you.'

She felt a prickle of alarm. 'What is it?'

He rubbed his eyes and instead of the small difficult boy she had always seemed to associate with her son, she saw a tired, anxious middle-aged man. An unexpected lurch of sympathy shot through her.

'The truth is that I'm not very well. Don't worry, it's not life-threatening. At least I hope not. But I've had to have a series of tests over the last few months.'

'What for?'

'They weren't sure at first but they think it might be diabetes. It can happen apparently in mid-life. Alternatively, it might be some kind of virus.' Nigel thrust his hands into his pockets nervously. 'The thing is, Mother, that they also need to take some blood from you. I'm sorry to ask you this but they want to confirm whether it might be genetic. It could affect Flora too, if it is.'

'Blood tests.' Mollie felt the words coming out like a squeak. 'From me? But is it really necessary?'

'It shouldn't be too much of an inconvenience. I'll take you to the appointment and all that. But I've been feeling bloody rotten, actually, and in one way I'm surprised you haven't noticed.'

'Noticed?' Mollie couldn't believe her ears. 'You haven't seemed any different to me.'

'Didn't you see how tetchy I've been?'

'You always are,' she said, unable to stop herself.

'That's typical.' Nigel's eyes blazed. 'You never understood, did you? Even when I was young, you never believed me when I was ill in the holidays. It would have interfered with whatever you and Dad were doing.'

Mollie lit a cigarette to give herself time to reply. 'I think you're a bit overwrought, Nigel, and it's not surprising if you're not well.'

'You're getting away from the point, Mother. I need you to have a blood test. Now will you have one for me, or not?'

Forty

Don't miss the next meeting of the Bridgewater House History Group. Lord Pearmain has kindly agreed to speak about his family memories. Details below.

Roddy couldn't think why they hadn't been stopped. For God's sake, what was wrong with security? The policeman had actually smiled at Kevin in that suspicious-looking shiny blue shell suit, before directing them through the entrance at St Stephens. They'd shown the passes again to another policeman ('Bloody pigs,' muttered Kevin under his breath) and then to another as they walked along the endless corridors and up the stone steps leading to the central lobby.

'Nice stuff,' murmured Kevin, admiring the tapestries on the wall.

'Keep your bloody hands off,' snapped Roddy. 'They're alarmed, anyway.'

He'd passed Kevin off as an assistant to the others. He'd also had some leaflets printed with an array of facts on the importance of fathers to families. All sane, level-headed stuff.

They'd got to the central lobby now. 'Bloody hell, isn't that Ian Paisley?' asked Kevin in a loud voice, nodding at a jowelled man leaning nonchalantly against a red seat, looking for all the world as though he was sitting on his own sofa at home.

'Quite possibly,' said Roddy. He was feeling sick now and his mouth was dry. Roddy had felt so upset about Annabelle's refusal to let him see the children that he didn't feel he could lose anything by being arrested. But now they were actually here, he was beginning to have doubts. Suppose Peregrine took the apartment away from him. Suppose . . .

'Can I see your passes, sir?'

He handed them over.

'Along there, sir. Straight on.'

They did as they were told although Roddy had to force his legs to work. Peter and the others looked similarly nervous; only Kevin seemed to be enjoying himself, looking around with a knowing smirk. Nearly there now. Apparently, the Lords were debating a bill on nurses' pay. Pity it wasn't more relevant to their cause, although Peter had some convincing statistics showing that troublesome teenagers often came from families where there was inadequate contact with fathers.

This was it. The entrance to the gallery. Roddy's mouth went even drier. He looked across at the others and then, suddenly, there was the most enormous bang from somewhere.

Bloody hell, what was that?

The whole building rocked and Roddy found himself being knocked sideways. For a few seconds, he could feel the floor shaking and, with a weird sense of distance, he waited for it to fall beneath his feet.

There was an eerie silence and the smell of smoke. Then the door to the gallery was flung open and a stream of people – mainly men, it seemed – streamed out, handkerchiefs clutched to their faces. Somewhere an alarm bell went.

'Is this something to do with you?' demanded Roddy, turning to Kevin.

'Don't be fucking stupid. It's a bomb. Didn't you hear it? We need to get out of here.'

Peter was white-faced. 'We can't just go without getting our message across.'

'Well we can't go in there now,' snapped Roddy. Fear always made him tetchy.

He grabbed Peter's notices and flung them in the air.

'What are you doing?'

'Getting rid of the evidence, stupid. They might think we had something to do with it.'

'I'm off,' shouted Kevin over the noise. 'There might be another bomb.'

They all ran back the way they had come, through the central hall part where everyone seemed to be running amok and outside into a wild pit of confusion with people everywhere and police in fluorescent jackets. Together they puffed out of the gates and towards the tube.

'Shitting hell, that was lucky,' gasped Kevin.

'What do you mean,' demanded Peter bitterly. 'We lost our chance, thanks to some bloody terrorist.'

'We were lucky not to get killed is what I meant,' said Kevin. 'Didn't you see that man back there? He was covered in blood.'

'I'm surprised we weren't stopped,' said another man from the fathers' group.

'Just as well we weren't,' grinned Kevin.

'Why?' asked Roddy suspiciously, pulling open Kevin's jacket. 'What have you got there?'

It was a small stone statuette head.

'It was just sitting there on a plinth,' said Kevin, shrugging. 'No one noticed in the panic. Don't look like that, Rodders. I'll share the dosh. I know exactly who I can unload this off to.'

'No thanks.'

'No need to act so high and mighty, mate. Have you thought what's going to happen when they find Peter's leaflets? You should have ripped them up – not chucked them on the ground. Now they're going to think you lot are behind this.'

It was true, thought Roddy bitterly when they'd got back and switched on the television. They would think that. At the moment, however, according to the news bulletin, no one had admitted responsibility. Amazingly, the bomb hadn't done as much damage as had initially seemed likely. It had been planted near the Gallery on the House of Commons terrace where a function had been planned but cancelled at the last minute. As a result, there were only a handful of injuries, one serious.

The phone rang and Roddy jumped.

'They've got you already,' teased Kevin with a nasty grin.

'Roderick Pearmain speaking,' he said without his usual confidence.

'Dad?'

'Daniel!'

'Look, Dad, I can't be long because Mum won't like it. But we wanted you to know that we didn't mean to tell Mum what happened after the barbecue. She saw Helena was upset about something and she made us tell her.'

'That's all right. I understand.'

At any other time, he would have been thrilled, but his eyes were still on the television and the plume of smoke rising from the Houses of Parliament.

'I wanted to make sure you were ok, too. You know, after the bomb. You weren't there, were you?'

'Of course not.' Roddy laughed lightly. 'I haven't been to the House for ages. Besides, I told you. I'll take you one day if your mum lets you.'

'I'll ask her. She's said Helena and I can come down next weekend, if you want.'

'She has?'

'We told her we missed you and I think it upset her.'

So he'd done this for nothing! He'd got himself involved with some zany group to see his kids and now his wife was letting him do it anyway.

'Fantastic, Daniel. Fantastic!'

He put the phone down feeling awful, but he'd had to tell that lie about the House. Almost immediately it rang again.

'Roderick,' boomed a voice. 'Saw the terrible news on the telly just now and wanted to make sure you were all right.'

It was his father's friend; the one who had given him the tickets. Roddy managed to reassure him but came off the phone feeling slightly sick. All these people who believed in him . . . What kind of person was he to deceive them like this?

*   *   *

He didn't feel any better the next day. If it hadn't been for the stupid, *stupid* thing he had done, he would have been deliriously happy. Already, he had so much planned for the kids. He'd take them to the new museum which had opened in central Oxford and then they'd go to Browns, which he knew they loved. And they'd go fishing in the lake.

'Tidying up, are you?' asked Sally when she arrived for her usual weekly clean.

He still wanted to be cross with her after her interfering comments the other week but her cheery smile made it difficult. 'My kids are coming on Saturday.'

'So your ex has relented?'

How did she know? That was the trouble with living so close to other people. They all knew your business, just as he couldn't help knowing theirs.

'Yes, well, things have been a bit tricky between me and my wife but hopefully we're working it out.'

'Yeah, right.' Sally undid the lid on the polish. 'That's what I used to say. What are you going to do with your room-mate then, when they come?'

Sally had made it clear that she didn't approve of Kevin. Roddy didn't blame her. No one wanted to clean a room full of fag ends and God knows what else.

'I've told him to clear out for the weekend.'

'Well, I hope you have a good time. Off now, are you?'

'I've got to go into London. The shop I've been doing some work for wants to give me some more commissions.'

'That's great.' She ran her finger down the cupboard. 'Did you make this?'

He nodded.

'It's really nice.'

She said it as though she meant it.

'Actually, there's just one thing before you go.' She looked awkward. 'I think you might have forgotten to leave my money out last time.'

'I put it on the shelf, like we arranged.'

'Yes, well it wasn't there.'

He tried to think back. Kevin hadn't been in that day, otherwise he'd have been the first suspect. Tim had come round for some help with his fishing rod but, apart from that, no one else had been around.

'I'm not trying to get paid twice if that's what you're thinking,' said Sally coldly.

'Of course not. I'll leave two weeks out, although I'm afraid it will have to be a cheque.'

Roddy walked towards the station, feeling uneasy. He didn't like it when things like that happened. There had been a definite unease when he'd said goodbye to Sally. She thought that he thought she'd been trying it on. But if she hadn't been, someone else had.

Amazingly, Kevin did agree to go away for the weekend.

'But only because I've had an offer I can't refuse,' he said, tapping the side of his nose to indicate secrecy. 'And if the little brats sleep in my bed, make sure they don't pee or do something worse. I remember what it was like at that age. At it all the time, I was, when the door was shut.'

Roddy, shuddering, changed the sheets on Kevin's bed. There wasn't much else to be done. Sally had done a good job on the flat.

There was the crunch of tyres on the drive outside and a squeal of brakes. Roddy's heart jumped. Through the window, he could see Annabelle's car – perilously close to Suzette's BMW – and the children getting out of it. Almost instantly the car shot off. Clearly his ex-wife wanted to see him as much as he did her.

'Daniel. Helena!' He clasped them to him, breathing them in, feeling their warm bodies next to his.

'Dad.' Helena was still hugging him. 'It's so good to see you. I'm really sorry about last time.'

'Can we go exploring?' asked Daniel. 'I want to go down to the cellars you told us about.'

'Absolutely,' said Roddy. 'Blast, there's the door. Hang on while I get it.'

The kids came with him.

'Tim.' Roddy was momentarily taken aback. 'How nice to see you. These are my children, Daniel and Helena. You might have met them at the barbecue.'

'Hi,' said Daniel quietly. Helena said nothing.

Tim spoke as though they weren't there. 'I wondered if you wanted to go fishing.'

'I'm sorry but my children are here for the weekend.'

'Ok.' Tim turned to go. Even from the back, Roddy could see he was upset.

'Maybe next week,' he called out.

Tim didn't reply.

'You take him fishing?' said Daniel with an edge in his voice.

'Well, his father doesn't live with him either and he asked if he could come along. You don't mind, do you?'

'It's your life,' said Daniel testily.

'Look, Dan.' He caught him by the sleeve. 'I don't want to spend time with other people's children. I only want my own.' His voice became thick with emotion. 'I can't tell you how much it means to me to have you here. I really can't.'

'He's back,' said Helena. 'It's the door again.'

Roddy threw it open. 'Tim, I'm sorry but . . .'

He stopped. A man in a dark grey suit was holding out a plastic wallet. 'Lord Pearmain? My name is Inspector Grey. Could I have a word?'

Forty-one

**Hello. This is the answerphone of Roddy Pearmain.
I'm afraid I can't take your call at the moment . . .**

'Look,' said Roddy wearily, after ushering the bewildered children into the kitchen and inviting the inspector to sit down. 'I think I know why you're here.'

The inspector, a tall thin man in his late fifties, looked surprised. 'You do, sir?'

Roddy took the seat opposite him; a comfortable armchair that had belonged to one of his great-aunts. 'I was given some guest passes for the House of Lords. And before you ask, the person who gave them to me has absolutely nothing to do with this.'

'Can you give me his name, sir?'

Roddy felt his mouth going dry. Too late, he realised he should never have implicated his father's friend in this. 'I'd rather not, if you don't mind. We belong to a group called Kids Need Dads and our aim is to improve rights for fathers who don't see their children as much as they want to. We planned to state our case and distribute some leaflets. But then the bomb went off.'

He faced the inspector directly. 'The bomb was nothing to do with us.'

The inspector nodded. 'I know that. We are aware of the originators. However, I still have to warn you that you could be in breach of the law for intending to cause a disturbance.'

Roddy began to sweat. 'Tell me, inspector, do you have kids?'

'I do.'

'And how would you feel if your wife wouldn't allow you to see them any more?'

'Sir, that isn't exactly the question.'

'Isn't it?' Roddy moved closer. 'Let me tell you something. Annabelle – that's my ex-wife – wouldn't let me see my kids for over a year. Now, for some inexplicable reason, she has relented and I actually have my children down for the weekend. The same children who are waiting in the kitchen, wondering why a policeman is interviewing their father. Now I grant you, I shouldn't have gone to the House with those leaflets and companions but I was desperate. However, I can assure you that nothing like this will happen again.'

Roddy looked pleadingly at the inspector. There was a silence. He'd been mad to think that a direct appeal would carry any weight with a tall, grey-complexioned inspector who knew nothing of family break-ups and whose wife was probably a granny and baked fairy cakes every Sunday.

The inspector stood up. 'I'm taking a gamble here, you understand. But I'll let you off with an informal caution. However, if anything like this happens again, you won't be treated so lightly.'

Relief flooded through him. 'I'm very grateful to you. Please, let me see you to the door.'

The inspector paused on the step. 'My son doesn't see his kids any more,' he said quietly. 'His ex-partner married again and the kids are more fond of the new chap.'

'I'm so sorry.'

The inspector nodded curtly and Roddy shut the door behind him. Almost instantly, the children came out of the kitchen.

'You didn't really have anything to do with the bomb, did you?' asked Daniel, worried.

How much had they heard?

'Of course not. I'm no terrorist.'

'But you lied to me, Dad. You said you weren't there.' Daniel's eyes were wide with reproach.

'I'm sorry.' Roddy felt a complete prick. 'It's because I was scared. Even adults do the wrong thing sometimes. In fact, especially adults.'

'And were you really going to hold some kind of demonstration?' asked Helena, wide-eyed. 'You know, with those leaflets?'

So they had been listening.

'Because you want to see more of us?'

He nodded, holding Helena close and reaching out for Daniel. 'Look, let's start again, shall we? We've got the whole weekend and we can do some great things together. Actually, we could go down to the cellar. I went there the other day and you'll never guess what I found?'

'What?' said the children together.

Roddy's eyes sparkled; their excitement was infectious. 'Something from when I was a kid. Come on: I'll show you.'

They loved going down the steep, stone steps, heavily worn by goodness knows who in the past, just as he had at their age.

'What's that funny smell?' sniffed Helena.

'It's history, dumbo,' scoffed Daniel.

Roddy couldn't have put it better himself. That wonderful dank, damp air that sang of past ages; of the times when there had been wars and family feuds and love affairs. In fact, all the things that happened now.

'Watch the bottom step, it's broken,' he pointed out.

'Wow,' gasped Daniel, looking around.

'Look.' Roddy opened the trunk. 'No!'

'What is it?' asked Daniel.

Roddy lifted out the photograph album to check it wasn't underneath. 'My coin collection. It's gone. It can't have! I should have taken it upstairs but I thought it would be safe here and I wanted you to see them where I'd left them as a kid.'

'Could anyone else have taken them?' asked Daniel.

Roddy thought of Tim. The kids would be jealous if he admitted Tim was with him. But really, there was no other explanation.

* * *

When they got back, there was a fantastic smell coming from the oven and a note on the kitchen table.

'*Thought this might come in handy. I made too much for my lot. Have a gt weekend. Sally.*'

'This looks amazing, Dad,' said Helena, who was already bringing out Sally's bubbling cheese-topped lasagne with Roddy's worn oven gloves. 'Who's Sally?'

'My cleaning lady. She takes pity on me every now and then when she's not being rude to me.'

Helena wrapped her arms around his waist. 'I'll come and look after you when I'm older, Dad. Mum won't be able to stop me then.'

Tears welled up in his throat, threatening to choke him.

'Thanks, Helena. But I want you to have fun in your own life. Besides, I'm not doing too badly at looking after myself.'

'Aren't you?' said Daniel teasingly. 'In the short time since we've been here, you've nearly been arrested by the police and you couldn't even find something that you left only a few days ago.'

Roddy gave him a mock cuff. 'Watch it, sunshine, or I won't give you any of this delicious food.'

He dug a spoon into the rich cheesy sauce. 'Now, who's hungry? Because I am.'

It was so good having the place to himself without that awful Kevin. The kids were happily curled up on the sofa in front of a video, waiting for him to join them. But there was something else he had to do first which he'd much rather put off.

'Are you suggesting,' asked Louise, her face pink with anger, 'that my son is a thief?'

'No,' he said hastily. They were sitting at the kitchen table where she had reluctantly invited him to sit down after he'd turned up at her door. Now all he wanted to do was get up and run. It had been a mistake. He should have just left it. 'No, not necessarily. But when I took Tim down to the cellar . . .'

'That's another thing.' She looked at him suspiciously. 'You should have asked my permission first.'

He went cold. 'You're not suggesting that . . .'

'I don't know what to think, Lord Pearmain.'

'You've got it all wrong,' he said desperately. 'I wanted to cheer him up. He seemed depressed about . . . the situation. I understand because I've been through it myself, so I thought he'd like to see the places I explored as a child. When I found my coin collection, we were both so excited.'

'And now you think Tim took it,' she said flatly.

'Yes. No. I don't know.' He stared at her pleadingly. 'But you must agree it's odd.'

Something flickered in her face. 'Tim has been acting strangely but I don't think he's a thief.' She covered her face with her hands. 'This is such a mess.'

There was the sound of the front door slamming and children running in. Roddy felt sick. Louise tried to wipe her face with a tissue from her sleeve but it was too late.

'What's wrong, Mum?' demanded Nick.

'Tim, I need to ask you something. Lord Pearmain was telling me about finding his coin collection in the cellar with you the other day.'

Roddy stood up. 'Look, please, can we just forget this?'

'No.' Louise's eyes were blazing. 'If someone has accused my children of something, I need to get to the bottom of it.'

'Accused us of what?' asked Tim, looking scared.

'The coin collection has disappeared,' continued Louise. 'Lord Pearmain wondered if you knew where it had gone.'

'Tim's not a thief,' shouted Nick, putting a protective arm around his brother. 'Get out of our house.'

'What have you got to say, Tim?' insisted Louise.

'Fuck off.' Tim pushed Nick away and ran out of the room. Through the kitchen window, they could see him racing through the grass, followed by the dog.

'I'll get him,' said Nick, eyes flashing angrily. 'Don't you think my mother has got enough to cope with without you causing trouble? Mum has just lost her job, you know. And now we've got this.' He pushed past him and slammed the door behind him.

'I'm sorry,' said Roddy. 'Really sorry.'

Louise's head was in her hands again. Her voice was muffled. But he could just about make out the words.

'Please go. Please go away.'

Forty-two

KEEP OUT OF THIS ROOM!
TRESPASSERS NOT WELCOME!

The noise made Marcie's head pound so that she couldn't think rationally. Not that she'd been able to do that since her sister had arrived.

'Will you turn that music down?' she said, banging on Katy's door which had that ridiculous notice about trespassers on it.

No answer. Damn the summer holidays. If only Katy and Robert were safely back at their expensive boarding school. One of them had turned up the volume. Right! Marcie threw the door open. The kids were lounging on the bed, Robert with his iPod plugged in and Katy doing her nails with *her* expensive nail polish.

'Turn that down,' yelled Marcie. 'Or that residents' association woman will be at me again.'

Reluctantly, Katy swung her legs over the bed and walked over to the music system David had had installed for them. The reduction in volume was minimal.

'I said, turn that down!'

'Please,' corrected Katy, staring coldly at her.

'Please,' said Marcie through gritted teeth.

The girl finally complied.

Thank God. The relief made her cross. 'You can't even call that music,' snapped Marcie.

Katy was frowning at her. 'Weren't you ever young once or did you just miss out that stage?'

'I am young,' said Marcie defensively.

'Oh, yeah, I forgot. Mum says Dad wanted someone young and stupid who wouldn't see what she was letting herself in for.'

'Is that so? Well your mum clearly didn't know what she was letting herself in for either when she got pregnant.'

'What's that meant to mean?'

Marcie knew she should stop right there but the words just came out. 'Well it wasn't as if you were planned, Robert, was it?'

The boy's eyes narrowed. 'You're saying I was a mistake?'

Cold sweat began to trickle down Marcie's back. David would kill her.

'What's a mistake?' asked a voice coolly.

Robert jumped up off the bed. 'Hi, Virginia.'

The kid always did that when her sister turned up. It was almost as though he had a crush on her. Katy too seemed to get on far better with Virginia than with her. It was only because Virginia didn't have to discipline them. So unfair.

'Marcie said Robert was a mistake,' said Katy, tucking her arm into Virginia's. 'Isn't that an awful thing to say?'

Virginia was looking at her, horrified.

'I didn't mean it.'

'I thought I'd do some shopping in London today,' said Virginia jauntily. 'Anyone feel like coming too?'

'Great,' said Katy. Robert was standing with his arms folded, sending darted looks in Marcie's direction. 'I'd like to but I've promised to meet someone.'

'Bet it's Justine,' said Katy.

'Who's Justine?' cooed Virginia, flicking back her hair.

'One of the neighbour's daughters,' said Marcie shortly.

'Yeah, she's gone to live with her father now so she can see Robert whenever she wants.' Katy gave Marcie a nasty look. 'She doesn't have anyone nagging her any more.'

'Bring her too,' suggested Virginia. 'Lunch is on me. Thought we might go to the London branch of the Hard Rock Cafe. Have you heard of it?'

'It's cool,' breathed Robert.

'Want to come too, Marcie?' asked Virginia.

She felt like a child who was only being included because an adult felt sorry for her.

'I'll pass on this one. It will give me time to catch up with my thesis.'

'Robert says that work is a four-lettered word,' said Katy.

Virginia laughed. 'Well, your stepmom always was a nerd but she got great grades. So we'll leave her to it, shall we?'

The house was very quiet when they left. Not the nice quiet she had been expecting but an excluded quiet. Through the window, Marcie watched David's children climbing into the taxi with Virginia – they'd politely refused her offer of a lift down to the station – and sat down at her desk.

She hadn't done anything to her thesis since going away and now it was difficult picking up the threads. All she could see was David's face. Since that awful revelation in Italy, something had gone missing between them. Something which might never come back again.

Virginia was wrong. She shouldn't have told him. And she definitely shouldn't have told Robert he wasn't planned.

There was a knock at the door. Sally? No, it wasn't her day. The kids couldn't have come back or she'd have seen the taxi. Unless it was . . . Automatically, she smoothed her hair back and glanced in the mirror. The Italian sun had gently tinted her complexion.

'Hello,' she said through the caller box.

'Hi. It's me.'

Marcie's skin prickled. She could say she was busy. She could say she was about to go out. Letting him in was dangerous, she knew that. Dangerous and stupid. She'd already gone too far but it was still retrievable.

A flash of the red truck passed through her mind, as it so often did. The truck had made her dirty. People like David with his fancy English upbringing couldn't understand that. But Kevin was different. He was a street dog. She wouldn't have to pretend with him.

'Hi,' she said, opening the door.

His proximity both excited and terrified her. 'Thought I'd call to see how the holiday went.'

She shrugged. 'It was all right.'

He raised his eyebrows. 'Only all right? Why don't you make me a cup of coffee and you can tell me all about it.'

She hadn't done anything she shouldn't have. She kept reassuring herself with that, after he left. They had talked about Italy, that was all. But it had been the kind of talk where he had looked at her in a way that almost made her feel good about herself.

'I bet all the Italian waiters flirted with you.'

'Not really,' she had replied, twisting her hair in embarrassment. 'It was Virginia they were looking at.'

'Well, I saw your sister this afternoon getting into a taxi with your stepkids, but you're far more beautiful.'

She hadn't known how to take the compliment so she'd changed the subject awkwardly. And then he'd asked if he could use the toilet, as he put it. He had brushed her cheek when he'd said goodbye and she could still feel the roughness of his skin, a good hour after he'd left.

He'd left the toilet seat up. Feeling slightly prudish, she put it down and then glanced into the mirror.

Her eye make-up was smudged. Had it been like that before his cheek had brushed hers or afterwards? Stop it! She was married. Happily married. Less so, perhaps, than before that confession she should never have made but still married. Until, of course, David decided to go.

'He might not,' said the voice in her head.

Ah, but she had known he would, ever since the look on his face had changed. It might not happen in the next few weeks or even the next few months. But her rape had changed her for ever in her new husband's eyes. Her marriage was in trouble, just as that clairvoyant had predicted.

Kevin would understand. Rape to him would probably be part of life.

Tearfully, Marcie began to rub her eyes with eye make-up remover pads. Instantly, they began to sting as though on fire.

What? Rubbing her eyes with the towel, she examined the make-up remover pads again. Then she unscrewed the lid on her nail polish remover pads and examined those.

The little shits had swapped them over.

She sat in darkness, waiting for them to come home. Finally, she heard the taxi on the drive and the sound of laughing.

'Marcie,' called out Virginia in surprise as she opened the front door. 'What are you doing in here, in the darkness?'

'Have the lights fused?' asked David.

'What are you doing here?' asked Marcie flatly.

'We met on the train.' He spoke coldly and she knew immediately that Robert had told her what she'd said.

'Sweetie,' cooed Virginia, sweeping across the room and putting an arm around her. 'Your eyes are all puffy. Are you ill?'

'Why don't you ask the kids?' she said dully.

'What have we done now?' asked Katy huffily.

Marcie turned on her. 'You know perfectly well. You swapped my nail polish remover pads with my eye make-up remover pads.'

Robert sniggered.

'Did you?' said David quietly.

'It was only a bit of fun. Like the toothpaste.'

'Shut up, Robert,' hissed Katy.

Marcie ran into the bathroom. Instead of the toothpaste tube in the holder was a tube of Canesten, a cream she'd needed to buy recently for personal reasons.

She sank to the floor, sobbing.

'They were only fooling around,' soothed her sister.

'Virginia's right,' added David. 'But I'll have a word with them. Although I must say . . .' He glanced backwards to check the children couldn't hear '. . . you were really out of line, Marcie, to tell Robert he wasn't planned. Do you know how damaging that can be to a child? Diana would go mental if she found out.'

'Come on, you two.' Virginia patted her on the shoulder. 'Why don't we have a nice glass of wine and we can tell you about our day. London was swell. And Justine was really cute. No wonder Robert's sweet on her. We had a really great time.'

'Hang on,' said David strangely. 'What's this?'

A cold tremor passed through her as her husband distastefully picked up a cigarette butt on the windowsill of the bathrom. 'Has someone been smoking in here?'

Marcie began to shiver. 'If you really want to know, it was me.'

'But you don't smoke.'

She turned away from him. 'Well maybe I do now. Maybe you and your kids have driven me to it. And don't bother saying that it's bad for the baby because at this rate, there's never going to be one. Is there?'

Forty-three

**INVITATION TO THE BRIDGEWATER
RESIDENTS'
MASKED BALL!**

To mark the end of summer, the Residents' Association is
holding a masked ball in the grounds. We plan to have a
wonderful marquee and four-course supper with a
string quartet. Tickets will be £50 each and strictly
limited to residents and friends. Please inform
Lydia Parsons of special dietary needs.

'Cheer up, Mum,' said Nick, walking past her. 'You'll find
another job. How did you get on at the agency today?'

'They didn't have anything suitable,' said Louise dully. They
probably did, of course. But after being sacked, she could hardly
blame the agency for fobbing her off.

'Well maybe they will, next week.'

Louise watched Nick go into the sitting room to turn on the
television. She really shouldn't get so depressed in front of the
children. It wasn't good for them and if she wasn't careful,
they'd all be defecting to Jonathan's.

'Mum,' yelled Tim. 'Quick. The washing machine's flooding.'

Shit. And double shit.

'Quick,' yelled Louise. 'Get a bucket. And some towels. Oh
blast. It's going everywhere.'

It took ages to clear up. And now she'd have to call someone
out to fix it. More expense.

'We could try mending it ourselves,' suggested Tim.

Since that awful man's accusation – how dare he, considering he'd actually kissed her on both cheeks only the other week? – she'd tried to be particularly nice to her youngest. 'What with?'

'Well, it's only a small tear in the hose. Look.'

He might have a point. Louise got out a roll of thick adhesive tape.

'See,' said Tim. 'It's ok. It's holding.'

Louise felt a rush of excitement. It might be a bodged DIY job but Tim was right. It was working. What's more, she had done it herself – or rather with her youngest son.

'You know, you wouldn't have been able to do that when we first moved in,' said Tim solemnly. 'You'd have just got all upset.'

Sometimes she couldn't believe how mature her youngest son was. 'You're right,' she said slowly.

'We're getting there, aren't we?' asked Tim hopefully.

She nodded. 'I think we are.'

Later that night, when the children were asleep, she switched on the computer and began to type. Afterwards, she put on her coat and went outside. It was a crazy idea and it wasn't easy, clambering on the trampoline and scraping her knee. But it was worth it when she started to bounce. It was amazing how high she could go! She could almost see into Mollie's sitting room. Higher. Yes higher! It was a wonderful feeling of exhilaration; of freedom. And for a few moments, she felt really hopeful. She was going to get there. She really was.

The rush of optimism she'd felt on the trampoline had gone by the next day. Louise knew why. Justine's absence hurt as much – if not more – than the pain of her birth. Her daughter's empty chair at the kitchen table screamed at her every meal time.

'Have you heard from your sister?' she asked over breakfast.

'She texted me.'

Louise felt a stab of hurt. 'She doesn't text me.'

Nick gave her a cuddle. 'Give her time, Mum. Robert has asked her to the ball apparently. Can we afford to go too?'

She hadn't the heart to say 'no'. How could they stay away with everything going on outside the house?

'Probably, although I haven't anyone to go with.'

'You could ask Guy to keep you company.'

She flushed. 'I can't.'

'Why not?' Nick persisted.

Because Guy would get the wrong idea. Second-thoughts, she'd just think about it.

'It's absolutely fucking brilliant,' said Mandy. 'I loved that bit about the washing machine and the trampoline. It really shows how far you've come.'

'You won't run it under my name, will you?' asked Louise worriedly.

'Stop panicking. We agreed on the pseudonym. Now, in the next instalment, I want to know more about this singles dating group.'

'It's not a dating group. It's a social group to help people practically as well as emotionally.'

'Fine.' Mandy was sounding bored. 'I need it by the end of the week. Ok? Eight hundred words, like last time.'

The text message came just as she'd walked the dog and was about to go to bed. 'Nick says there's going to be a ball at your place. He's asked me to come. Is that all right with you?'

'Fine,' she texted back. 'But only if you want to.'

His reply came within seconds. 'I do. I also want to buy the tickets. My treat.'

She stared at the phone in her hand for a few more moments before deciding not to text back. Then she went into the boys' room. Tim was asleep but Nick was sitting up in bed reading. At first, she had felt so bad about the boys having to share a room, but they'd assured her that they liked chatting to each other at night. In some ways they were closer now than before.

'You got Guy to ask me to the ball,' she said, sitting on the edge of Nick's bed.

'Yeah, well, I reckoned you wouldn't.'

'Tim accused me of . . . of seeing Guy as more than a friend,' she said slowly.

'He told me. I told him not to be such a prat. Guy's our friend. Tim was stupid to see it any other way.'

Forty-four

Going to a fancy dress party!

Fancy That

has a wide range of costumes
at reasonable prices.
All sizes available.

Mollie tried to divert herself with silly irrelevant things. Like what to wear for the masked ball. Or whether she should buy that lovely frilly crib in town, as a surprise present for Poppy.

But her mind kept coming back to the same problem. She had to have a blood test for Nigel.

'What would Gideon want you to do?' asked Poppy.

They were sitting, as they did so often now in the evenings, in the drawing room, the French windows open very slightly, with the smell of lavender and stocks wafting in from the pots outside. Mollie had been asking herself the very same question. Gideon hadn't appeared or spoken to her for some weeks now and she was beginning to get really worried.

'He'd probably say that if Nigel's ill, I have to do it, don't I?'

'They can't test for his paternity without Gideon,' said Poppy quietly. 'I don't think you've got anything to worry about.'

'I hope not, dear.' Mollie lit a cigarette and then, remembering Poppy was there, stubbed it out again on a pretty china dish that she and Gideon had bought in Morocco several summers ago.

'So when are you having the blood test?'

'Tomorrow.'

Poppy frowned. 'Would you like me to come with you?'

'No thank you, darling. Besides, Nigel's sending a car. I'll be fine. Honestly.'

It was a private clinic. Rather nice, thought Mollie. Tasteful prints on the walls and pretty girls on reception who could have been behind a hotel foyer desk. She sat for about ten minutes in the waiting room on a rather comfortable settee, catching up on a glossy monthly magazine. In fact, she was rather disappointed when called in for her test.

'Would you mind signing this form, Miss de May?' asked the nurse.

Her hand performed its usual majestic sweep.

The nurse watched entranced. 'My mother thinks you're wonderful. I don't suppose that . . .'

'Of course,' said Mollie, who loved giving her signature. 'Do you have something to write on? And what is your mother's name?'

By the time the doctor came in, she'd almost forgotten why she was there.

'For Nigel, you daft stick,' whispered Gideon.

'Gideon!' she said delightedly.

The doctor gave the nurse an odd look. He thinks I'm batty, thought Mollie, amused. 'Sorry.' She flashed her most charming smile. 'I always say my husband's name when I'm nervous. It seems to give me strength.'

'I see. Now this shouldn't hurt. Just a little prick. Some people find it helps to look away.'

Mollie was already doing that but Gideon was conspicuous by his absence. Still, she had heard him and that was the thing. It meant he couldn't be too jealous about the adverts. And besides, even if he was, she had a right to make a comeback. Didn't she?

The results would apparently go to her own doctor within

five days. In the meantime, she had an audition for a stair-lift company. Frankly, she wasn't very keen on that one. But, as her agent said, she should consider all possibilities. In the meantime, one of her old costume designer friends was going to help her find the perfect outfit for the ball. Mollie felt slightly guilty at the excitement this induced in her. She should be more worried about Nigel really. But gut instinct told her that Nigel would be fine. A little tired, maybe. But surely not ill?

'It's lovely,' breathed Poppy.

It was a few days after the blood test and the dear girl had insisted on coming with her to help select an outfit. It was just as well really because Mags, her friend from Wardrobe, had so much crammed into the room at the back of the theatre that it was extremely difficult to make the right choice.

'I've always wanted to play Nell,' she said, alighting on a blue costume. 'But then again, I'm not sure about this particular shade.'

'How about Queen Elizabeth?' suggested Poppy, fondling a magnificent dress in scarlet silk.

'A little on the heavy side, I think, darling. Now do sit down, won't you, or you'll exhaust yourself.'

'Joan of Arc?' suggested Mags.

'Too plain,' said Poppy. 'Mollie needs to shine like the star she is. Goodness, what is this?'

She lifted out a tangerine gold ballgown with a little nipped-in waist. 'That,' breathed Mags, 'was once worn by Elizabeth Taylor. It actually has a little mask to go with it; you did say it was a masked ball, didn't you?'

Both Mollie and Poppy nodded, unable to speak. It really was utterly beautiful.

Eventually Mollie found her voice. 'Could I take this? I'll take great care of it, I really will.'

Mags hesitated. 'It shouldn't really be here, by rights. Normally, when an outfit is worn by someone that famous, it goes into a special archive collection.' She hesitated. 'But seeing as it's you, Mollie, we won't tell anyone.'

Mollie clapped her hands like an excited child. 'Thank you so much. It's lovely. Now what about you, Poppy? What are you going to wear?'

Poppy laughed gaily. 'I've got an Indian sari which is perfect for hiding my bump. And Rupert, bless him, has got me a mask.'

'Then we're sorted,' said Mollie. 'You know, you look a bit pale, darling. I think we'd better get a taxi back.'

Poppy didn't argue. 'I do feel a little tired. If you're sure, although you must let me go halves.'

'Nonsense,' said Gideon deeply.

'Nonsense,' repeated Mollie gratefully. Her husband had put in the odd remark over the last few days and even though she still couldn't see him, it was reassuring. 'The treat is on me.'

'Isn't that Nigel's car?' exclaimed Poppy as the taxi bumped its way up to the house. Mollie, who'd been making a mental note to mention the poor state of the drive to the residents' association, shielded her eyes from the evening sun. 'You're right. Dear me, I wasn't expecting him.'

Nigel stood stiffly in his suit, ready to open her side door. 'Hello, Mother.'

He nodded curtly at Poppy. 'Can we have a quiet word?'

A cold shaft of fear flashed through her as they walked to her flat. 'The blood test?' she asked quietly.

Nigel nodded.

'I'll go to my room,' said Poppy quickly.

'No,' said Nigel firmly. 'Please stay.'

Mollie was dumbstruck. Nigel, of all people, hated outsiders knowing anything about his public life.

'Do sit down,' said her son, as though the drawing room was his and not hers. Silently, she obeyed.

'I presume you didn't read the hospital form very thoroughly,' continued Nigel. 'If you had, you would have seen that you gave permission for the results to be sent to me too.'

'Why?'

Nigel leaned forwards. 'The blood tests would show you weren't really my mother and that I was adopted.'

'What a ridiculous idea!'

'Is it? Even though Gideon wasn't my father?'

Mollie stared at Poppy. 'You told him?'

Poppy looked uncomfortable. 'It's not what you think. For a start, I already knew about Max before. Gideon told me before he died that Nigel wasn't his.'

'But why would my husband tell you that?'

'Oh, for God's sake, Mother, stop being so naïve,' spluttered Nigel.

'Mother, is it?' Mollie suddenly felt very, very angry. 'So the test showed that I was your mother after all?'

Nigel nodded, his eyes watering. 'After Poppy told me about Gideon not being my father, I began to wonder if you were really my mother. After all, you've never been very maternal, have you?'

'That's not true,' began Mollie. 'But Poppy, why did you tell Nigel about Gideon?'

Poppy began twisting her hair, avoiding Mollie's steely gaze. 'I was upset. It was when Gideon was dying. Remember that day I came to visit – about two weeks before he went? I bumped into Nigel on the way out, in the car park, and we started talking. I didn't mean to but it just all came out.'

'You said you had more cause to be upset than me because I wasn't even his son,' said Nigel tautly.

Mollie looked shocked. 'Poppy, that's dreadful.'

The girl buried her head in her hands. 'I know. I know. But I'd just found out . . .'

She stopped.

'Found out what,' asked Mollie, shaking.

'Don't ask,' thundered Gideon in her ear.

'Tell her,' insisted Nigel. 'Tell her what you told me.'

'I'd just found out,' whispered Poppy. 'That I was pregnant.'

'And the baby was mine,' said Gideon sulkily.

'And the baby was Gideon's,' stated Mollie flatly.

Poppy nodded.

'What about the married man who wouldn't leave his wife and two children,' asked Mollie in a cracked voice.

Poppy covered her face with her hands. 'I made him up. I'm so sorry, Mollie. So very, very sorry.'

Forty-five

CHARISMA MAGAZINE

TELLING LIES – KIND OR CRUEL?
THREE WOMEN CONFESS ALL

'A masked ball?' repeated Annabelle doubtfully on the phone.

'Other teenagers are coming.' Roddy tried not to sound desperate. 'It will be fun for them, and besides, it's part of their history.'

'So you keep saying. I must say, your residents' association is a thriving bunch.' She sounded almost amused. 'By the way, have you ever thought of renting that place out to a film company? All my friends are doing it. You just contact one of these location companies that are looking for places to film in and they pay you a fortune. They need all kinds of different locations, even little flats.'

'Bridgewater House isn't a little flat,' he said tersely.

'No, it's a series of little ones, isn't it? But it looks like a big house from the outside. God, I don't know why I'm bothering to help you. Forget it.'

'No. Wait. Sorry, it's just that I didn't expect you to be . . .'

'Nice?' suggested Annabelle.

'Something like that.'

'Daniel and Helena really enjoyed coming down to see you. Maybe I haven't been quite as fair as I should have been.'

Roddy sat down heavily.

'Well, maybe I haven't either.'

'I agree.' She sounded sharper now. 'But people can change and I'm prepared to give you a chance. So the children can come down on condition that you make sure they don't drink, don't smoke and don't do anything else they shouldn't. Oh, and one other thing.'

'Yes?' His spirits were so high that she couldn't say anything now to upset him.

'I'm pregnant, Roddy. I thought you ought to know before the children told you.'

'A film company?'

Lydia sounded far more excited than he had expected. He'd presumed she would have worried about the sort of things people usually worry about when giving their home over to strangers. Damage, arson, pregnancy . . . he just couldn't get that word out of his head. Annabelle was pregnant with another man's child. It didn't matter that he hadn't loved her for years. The fact was that they'd had two children together. It was inconceivable that either could do the same with anyone else.

By the end of the day, Lydia reported back to say everyone, even the American woman, was in favour. So he rang the number Annabelle had given him and explained the background. The location company's scout was definitely interested.

'Can we come down on Friday to have a look?'

'It might be a bit hectic. We're having a masked ball next weekend and the marquees are going up.'

'Unbelievable! We're actually looking for something like that for a documentary on old houses.'

The agent then named a fee that almost knocked him on to the floor.

'Friday would be great,' murmured Roddy. 'See you then.'

Of course, they had to have a meeting about it. That's what happened when you had different people living under one roof. It was such a lovely evening that they held it in the pavilion and Lydia was in her element. It was almost, but not quite, enough to make him forget about Annabelle's pregnancy for a couple of hours.

'I'm not sure I like the idea of being filmed when we are meant to be having a party,' said the stiff husband of the American woman. 'Supposing someone has too much to drink. Do we really want that on film?'

'Planning to be get pissed, are you?' called out Kevin.

'No,' replied the American woman's husband steadily. 'But I can't be a guarantor for everyone else.'

Someone giggled at the back. 'Well,' said Lydia, her pearls riding up and down her crinkly neck, 'I think we should take a vote on it. Who is in favour of a film location company coming down to see if Bridgewater House is suitable for a documentary to be screened on Channel 4?'

A large number of hands went up.

'And those against?'

There were only a couple, including, to Roddy's surprise, Kevin's.

'Then I take it we are in favour of the motion,' said Lydia grandly. 'I suggest we let Lord Pearmain take over from here and do all the liaising with the company. Is everyone happy with that?'

Most people nodded and then began to leave. Louise swept past him, without her children. He'd have liked the opportunity to apologise for the other day but she didn't give him a chance.

'Why didn't you agree?' asked Roddy as Kevin joined him.

He shrugged. 'Don't want my face all over the country. There are certain people who might recognise me.'

'Well you'll either have to stay away or keep your mask on,' said Roddy. 'And frankly, I hope you choose the first option.'

Kevin grinned. 'Nice to know I'm wanted. But don't worry. I'm not planning on being with you for much longer.'

'Good. Where are you going?'

Kevin's eyes flickered briefly to the right, where the American girl was talking earnestly to her stiff husband. 'Let's just say I have my plans.'

'I agree he's a weirdo.' Sally sat cross-legged on the carpet, cupping a steaming mug of coffee. Having mid-morning coffee together had become a habit and Roddy looked forward to it, especially if Kevin was out. Sally was so easy to talk to.

'There's something about him that I just don't trust – and I'm not merely referring to his shifty eyes.'

'Just because you've nearly finished that psychology module of yours, you're getting all introspective,' joked Roddy.

He admired Sally for doing her Open University course and for her determination to teach afterwards.

'What I don't understand,' she continued, ignoring his remark, 'is why you let him stay here.'

He shifted awkwardly. 'He knows stuff about me from the clinic,' he admitted. 'There were a couple of incidents involving certain substances which no one else knows about. And something else since then.'

He was tempted for a minute to tell her about the House of Lords stunt. Although it was over now, Kevin could still discredit him for their intended demonstrations.

'What would you have to lose?'

'Annabelle would go nuts. She could stop Daniel and Helena coming over.'

Sally made a sympathetic face. 'But she's pregnant.'

Roddy winced. 'Yes.'

'So she'll have other things to think about now. Besides, the kids are growing up. It will be more difficult soon for their mother to stop them coming down. Why don't you tell Kevin he's got a month more and then he has to clear out.'

'I think I will.'

She smiled. 'That's the spirit. By the way, what's this I hear about the ball being filmed?'

'It was Annabelle's idea, actually. One of the film people's scouts is coming down later today.' A thought struck him. 'Say, you wouldn't like to come to the ball, would you?'

She had her back to him, rinsing the mugs. 'Thanks, but I couldn't afford it.'

'No, I mean as my guest.'

She turned round, surprised. 'Why? It's really kind of you but you don't have to feel sorry for me.'

'I don't. I just enjoy your company. You make me laugh.'

'Well, thank you, m'lord.' She touched her forehead, half-mockingly. 'Then I'd love to take you up on your kind invitation to the ball.'

'And this all used to belong to your family?' asked the young film scout. He was wearing jeans that were too long; the kind that skirted the ground and picked up dirt along the way.

'Yes,' said Roddy, 'it did.' They were standing by the lake, looking back at the house. It looked even more magnificent than usual.

'Doesn't it hurt to see other people living in it?'

'At first. But there are advantages in having so many different kinds of people living in it. It means you don't get bored.'

Funny. Until he'd said that out loud, he hadn't realised that was how he felt.

'And the ball? How big will it be?'

'About 150 people. It's invitation only and we've got two marquees.'

'Sounds great. We'd love to do it.'

Just then Roddy saw Tim walking towards them with his fishing rod, eyes dead ahead.

'Hi, Tim,' said Roddy. 'Any luck with the fish?'

The kid ignored him.

'Look,' said Roddy quickly, 'do you need anything else? Because if not, I need to dash.'

*   *   *

'Tim,' he panted. 'Wait. Please. About the other day. I didn't mean to accuse you of anything. I just wanted to know what had happened.'

'You think I nicked your stupid coin collection.'

The boy's eyes were blazing.

'No. No. It's just that you were the last person to see it.'

'Just fuck off, can you?'

The boy opened his front door and slammed it behind him.

'That's telling you, isn't it?'

Roddy swung round. Kevin was standing behind him. 'For Christ's sake, you startled me.'

'Sorry. I can't help it if I walk quietly.'

Roddy had his breath back now. Enough to breathe in and look hard at this man who had walked into his life without any invitation. 'I want you to leave, Kevin.'

'And suppose I tell your wife and stepfather about your little habits in the clinic? And your day trip to the House of your forebears?'

'Go ahead. Besides, the police didn't make any charges and as far as the other thing goes, I'm clean now. So I'm going to repeat it one more time. Get out of my house after the ball. Is that clear?'

Forty-six

Bridgewater Gazette

SITS VAC

Experienced copywriter required for
busy advertising department.
Min of five years exp.

★

Mother's help needed for busy family.
Must be able to work evenings and weekends.

★

PA for lively solicitor's office.
Knowledge of Excel essential.

Marcie actually felt quite optimistic after returning from the fancy-dress outfitters. It wasn't just that she was pleased with her costume. She was also four days late.

'You will have your baby but not in the way you expect.'

That was what Caterina had said. She played the tape enough times to know it word-perfect. Well, she hadn't expected to get pregnant this month (they had only done it once) and now maybe she was!

No! Getting out of the car, she trod in a large clump of wet, squelchy dog muck. Wiping her shoe on the grass, taking care not to touch anything with her hands, Marcie marched up to Louise's front door, banging the knocker loudly.

'Hello?'

The woman had been crying; Marcie recognised the signs. Something inside her wavered but then she remembered the baby, the baby that Caterina had said she would have, the baby who could be marked by toxoplasmosis.

'I've just put my foot in the poo that your dog left.'

'Sorry. I thought I'd cleared it all up.' Louise rubbed her eyes and Marcie inwardly flinched in case her hands weren't clean.

'It's simply not acceptable.' Marcie glared at her. 'Didn't you see the notice on the lawn? There's a £100 fine, you know. I'll have to bring it up at the next residents' meeting.'

Louise sighed. 'I understand.'

Marcie looked at her. 'Are you all right?'

Louise laughed hoarsely. 'Well, I've been sacked from my job for trying to write something during my lunch hour. There's nothing suitable in the Jobs column of the local paper. I'm on my own after twenty years of marriage. And my youngest son has been accused of stealing.'

Marcie hesitated. Much as she disliked Louise, something inside her felt sorry for her. 'That doesn't sound great. Well, just do something about your dog, can you?'

She turned round and headed for the safety of her own home. It wasn't fair. She had every right to tell the woman off and yet Louise had made her feel as though she was in the wrong.

As she turned the key in the lock, Marcie heard laughing. Damn. She'd thought Virginia was in London for the day.

'Marcie!' Virginia's face was shining. 'There you are! I've been entertaining your visitor for you!'

'Visitor?'

Marcie's heart did a scared little flip as Kevin jumped up from the sofa to shake her hand. His skin felt warm on hers and he kept it there a little longer than necessary.

'Did you forget you'd asked me round for coffee?' he grinned.

She hadn't asked him. But it would look rude to say so.

'Kevin is a friend of our neighbour, Lord Pearmain,' she

began carefully, knowing that the title would impress her sister. 'I met him when I got locked out and he kindly did something to the locks to let me in.' Then she remembered. 'But don't tell David or he'd go mad. You know what he's like about security.'

'How very clever of you,' said Virginia, directing her clear gaze at Kevin. 'And are you a locksmith?'

He threw back his head and laughed. 'You could say that. Then Marcie and I found we had quite a lot in common, didn't we? Especially our interest in English literature.'

Marcie felt as though she was dreaming. She and Kevin had never discussed English literature in their lives. But again, she found herself smiling and nodding.

'Is that what you majored in?' asked Virginia intently.

Kevin nodded. 'I did a course in major nineteenth-century novelists in a clinic I was in.'

'A clinic?'

Virginia's tone was decidedly edgy.

'I wasn't well for a while. It was how I met Roddy, actually. But now we're fine.' He laughed again; and this time his eyes looked crinkly with amusement. 'Don't worry. It's not catching.'

'And do you and Marcie manage to see each other quite a lot?' Virginia was really suspicious now.

Marcie bristled with indignation. 'No, Virginia. Kevin occasionally comes round for coffee. Would you like one now?'

She made her way to the kitchen, her cheeks burning.

'Not for me, thanks.' He was following her. 'Your sister's already made me one and besides I need to get going.' He lowered his voice, standing close behind her while she put on the kettle. Her skin burnt with the proximity. 'I just came round to see if you were going to the ball.'

Deftly, he moved to one side as Virginia came in.

'Yes, we are going to the ball,' said Marcie clearly. 'And then afterwards, my sister is going to France to see one of our cousins.'

'I am?' Virginia squeaked.

'Yes,' said Marcie, looking straight at her. 'You are.'

Neither of them heard Kevin close the door. Both were too intent on the impact of what had just been said.

'What are you talking about?' demanded Virginia. 'We don't have any cousins in France.'

'Well you're going there, anyway. You wanted to see the Louvre.'

Virginia looked uncertain. 'I thought you might want to come with me.'

'No thanks.'

'What's wrong with you? You haven't been the same since Italy. All jumpy and difficult.'

'Difficult? Me?' Marcie stared at her. 'You're the one who's been difficult. Getting all friendly with the children and making out with my husband . . .'

'Making out with your husband?' Tiny pink spots appeared on Virginia's cheeks. 'I think you'd better explain yourself.'

'You know what I mean. Sitting close to him on the sofa. Always jumping up to help him to more food. And then, making me tell him about . . . about what happened.'

'I just suggested you came clean. You shouldn't have any secrets from a husband. And besides, what about Kevin? Does David know he has the hots for you?'

'Kevin? Of course he doesn't.'

'He can't keep his eyes off you! You must be even more naïve than I thought if you don't realise that.'

'So that's how you see me.' Marcie felt sick. 'Naïve?'

'Yes.' Virginia's eyes were blazing. 'Very naïve. That's how you got into that mess when you were a kid. You don't know how lucky you are now to have found stability.'

'You're just jealous.'

'No I'm not. But admit it, Marcie. You've got a husband who loves you . . .'

'Who used to love me until he knew my past.'

Virginia shrugged. 'Well it's up to you to sort that one out. And as for the kids, if you tried a bit more, you could sweet-talk them round just like I have. Do you think I did that for myself? Why bother if I'm going back? I did it for you, Marcie. To make your life easier.'

'I don't believe you, Virginia,' she said quietly. 'And I meant what I said. After the ball, I want you to go.'

Forty-seven

Last-Minute Travel

Flights to Washington, New York and Denver . . .

One day, Susan had said, she would wake up and feel that things weren't so bad after all. And now, amazingly, she was doing that. For the first time since moving in, she had also slept through the night. And not only that, she had done so without the torch.

Propping herself up on the pillows, Louise looked through the gap in her curtains. The morning sun was glimmering on the lake and a bird – a coot? – was skimming the water. Then she remembered with that sickening, cheating thud that came when you woke up properly and recalled something horrible. Justine was still with Jonathan and was showing no sign of coming back.

What mother could live happily when her teenage daughter had decided, quite clearly, not to be with her?

'Justine's coming to the ball too,' said Nick suddenly over breakfast.

Louise's heart skipped a beat. 'How do you know?

'Because she's going with that boyfriend of hers,' said Tim, his mouth still full of toast. 'The American woman's stepson.'

Louise headed for the phone in the hall. She rang Justine every day but often her daughter's answerphone was on and she frequently failed to return her calls. Today, however, she picked up.

'Justine? It's Mum.'

'Hi.'

Louise's spirits sank again. Justine clearly wasn't pleased to hear from her. 'I just wondered how you were.'

'Ok.'

'Would you like to come over for supper tonight?'

'Can't. I'm busy.'

Louise's hands tightened on the receiver. 'I really miss you, Justine. I'm sorry for our arguments. Please come home.'

'Mum, I've got to go. See you.'

Click. She had gone. Louise stared at the phone as though looking at it might bring Justine back. Slowly she walked back to the sitting room. The boys were sitting next to each other on the floor, watching breakfast television. They loved her. Maybe they would have to be enough.

'It's gripping stuff,' Mandy said. 'A lot of readers are going to identify with this. I can't imagine what it must be like to have a daughter who doesn't want to live with you. Mind you, it could do with some sex. I don't suppose you're seeing anyone, are you?'

'I'm not ready for that yet,' said Louise firmly.

'Maybe we'll have to make something up.'

'You can't do that!'

'Why not? It's anonymous, isn't it?'

'Yes, but even so.'

'Look, Louise. My boss has said he'd like some sex soon. So if you can't come up with the goods, we'll need to talk about it. Ok?'

She should have remembered how unscrupulous some magazines and newspapers could be. In fact, most journalists prided themselves on their accuracy. But others would stop at nothing to sensationalise something.

'Hello, dear.'

Louise hadn't seen Mollie sitting on the bench.

Mollie patted the space next to her. 'Come and sit down.'

'You look cold,' noted Louise. 'Do you want to borrow my cardigan?'

'How thoughtful. Actually, I wouldn't mind. I seem to have been out here for ages, thinking.'

She did look rather troubled. 'Are you all right?' asked Louise gently.

Mollie's knarled hands were gripping her handkerchief. 'I'm not sure, to be honest, dear.' She raised her beautiful eyes. 'Actually, I've just found out something about my husband. I've discovered he wasn't quite the man I thought he had been.'

'It's not a nice feeling,' agreed Louise.

'Of course, dear, you know all about that, don't you?' She patted Louise's knee. 'You'll get over your husband. Didn't I see you with a rather dashing man the other evening; the man who arrived in a sports car?'

Louise flushed. 'He's the family friend I told you about.'

'You liked him,' insisted Mollie. 'I could tell from your body language.' She straightened herself. 'I'm good at that, from all the years of being in the business.'

'I've never told anyone,' said Louise quietly, 'but yes, I do like him.'

'Well, that's wonderful.'

'I still have my doubts.' Louise's voice wobbled. 'But I'm more upset about Justine not being with me.'

'One thing at a time, dear. First that nice young man in the sports car. Sometimes you can't afford *not* to take a risk. As for Justine, take it from me, children will come round eventually. I'm waiting for Nigel to do so right now about something.'

Louise smiled. 'Maybe you're right.' She looked tenderly at the old lady. 'Perhaps we should go in now, it really is getting chilly.'

Mollie took her hand and together they walked past the marquees, which were ready now and waiting, towards the house. A light burned comfortingly in Mollie's window. 'It must be nice for you to have Poppy as company,' commented Louise.

Mollie's mouth tightened. 'Actually, she's not with me any more. She's gone to stay with a friend, Rupert, another actor.'

Something in Mollie's voice made Louise change the subject. 'Are you going to the ball?'

'Absolutely.' Mollie straightened her back. 'Nothing will stop me from being there. I'm looking forward to it.'

The phone rang the following morning, before she'd even walked Hector.

'What the hell do you think you are doing?'

'Jonathan?' She rubbed her eyes sleepily.' What are talking about?'

'Your column in that magazine.'

Louise went cold.

'You've made me look like a complete idiot! Everyone's talking about it; my bloody secretary showed me the article and the whole office is agog.'

She leapt up and ran to the door, barefoot, to where the magazine had been delivered by the newsagent.

'*What it's like to be single again.*'

Louise felt sick. Not only had the magazine run the piece a week earlier. They had also broken their agreement.

They had run it under her real name.

Forty-eight

IS ANYONE INTERESTED IN MAKING UP A BRIDGE FOURSOME?

Please contact Lydia Parsons at number 6 or
Suzette White at number 1. No beginners, please.

Mollie sat in her big old squashy comfortable armchair, next to Gideon's empty one, cradling a heavy glass of Bombay Sapphire. They had bought the glasses twenty years ago after the success of *Lady Windermere's Fan*. It has been a tradition of theirs, to buy something nice after each play, even if it had been a flop. Not, touch wood, that there had been any of those.

Only in her own life.

Mollie took another swig. She wanted to replay that scene with Poppy in her mind; to go over it without allowing herself to make any cuts. To make the girl repeat her words. She could hear them now. As clearly as if she was on stage and Poppy was next to her. What was the female equivalent of a cuckold?

Maybe it was just a stupid naïve old woman.

'Neither of us meant it to have happened,' Poppy had insisted when she had made her recount the whole story. By then, Nigel had walked out, slamming the door behind him, declaring he couldn't take any more and leaving the two of them alone.

'It was last year when I came to see you both. You weren't there and Gideon had just been diagnosed. I didn't know that then but I could see that he wasn't quite himself. I asked him what was wrong.' Poppy's voice faltered. 'So he told me.'

'And then?' Mollie had never heard herself sound so cold, except in character.

Poppy looked away. 'And then, before I knew it, his hands were stroking my hair and . . .'

'Stop.' Mollie leapt to her feet. 'I don't want to know any more. Well, yes, actually I do. Did you tell him later when you were pregnant?'

'Yes. I felt I owed it to him.'

'And what did he say?'

'That was the funny thing. I thought he'd be furious, but he cried like a baby.'

Mollie was incredulous. Gideon never cried.

'Wept and wept. He said it was because he was happy.'

'Happy?' Mollie spat the word out.

'Yes.' Poppy's voice dropped to a whisper. 'Because he thought he couldn't have children. So I said what about Nigel? And he said Nigel wasn't his.'

'So you knew before I told you,' demanded Mollie angrily.

'Well yes, but I couldn't say so, could I?' Poppy looked scared. 'You do see that, don't you?'

Mollie pursed her lips tightly. 'I'm not sure I can see anything at the moment. I certainly, for the life of me, can't see why you invited yourself to come and stay as my lodger. Surely that's the last thing you would have wanted, to have to live with the widow of the man you were pregnant by?'

'No, no.' Poppy reached for her hand but Mollie moved away. 'I was closer to him by being with you. I feel him here all the time when I'm here. Sometimes I think he must be here like a ghost, even though I know that sounds quite mad. And I admire and love you too, Mollie. That's why I asked you to be my birthing partner.'

She stroked her stomach lovingly. 'I wouldn't have chosen to have got pregnant but I have to be honest, Mollie. I wouldn't change things. I have the baby I have always wanted by the most interesting man I knew.'

'Did he have affairs with other people too? asked Mollie sharply.

Poppy looked down at the ground. 'He did have relationships with other women. And I did once hear a rumour about
a man but I'm not sure.' She lifted her head. 'But they didn't
last, Mollie. He told me, afterwards, that no one could ever live
up to you.'

'Then why did he do it?' snapped Mollie.

Poppy shrugged. 'You knew Gideon. He always needed to
be centre stage. Hated it if anyone outshone him. Maybe he
was just trying to prove he wasn't past it.'

'I was a silly old fool,' said Gideon softly into her ear. 'It was
a mistake and I'm sorry. By the way, darling, do put out that
cigarette. It's so bad for you.'

'Fuck off,' said Mollie loudly.

'What did you say?' asked Poppy wide-eyed.

'I said fuck off,' repeated Mollie. 'I want you out of here by
tomorrow. Go and stay with your friend Rupert. But just get out.'

'Hang on, darling,' said Gideon, alarmed. 'Isn't that a bit harsh?'

'I mean it,' said Mollie, rounding on him. 'And you can get
out of here too. Both of you.'

They had, too. Neither had kept in touch. God only knew where
Gideon had gone.

'I was never unfaithful to you,' she said, weeping in her big
old chair. 'That thing with Max didn't count because he forced
me. You've changed everything, you silly bloody fool. A marriage
is meant to be a faithful union of bodies. And you've made a
mockery of that. Damn you, Gideon. Damn you!'

She must have dozed off in her chair for the night because,
when she next knew where she was, she was cold and aware
of noises outside. Stiffly, she eased herself out of the chair and
went to the window. Men were moving around with poles and
canvases. Of course. The ball!

She wouldn't go now.

She didn't feel like doing anything except crawling back to
her big comforting chair and pouring herself another large glass
of Bombay Sapphire for breakfast.

Botheration. The doorbell. Who the hell could it be at this time of the morning.

'Mother?'

Nigel was standing impatiently. 'You took your time to answer.' He sniffed exaggeratedly. 'Have you been drinking?'

She turned her back on him, walking tall back to the chair. 'And what if I have?'

Nigel sat in his father's chair next to her. To her surprise, he took her hand and sat there for a few minutes, not saying anything but rhythmically stroking it. 'I want you to know that I forgive you.'

'*You* forgive me?' Mollie took another swig. 'Bit rich, isn't it?'

'Why?' Nigel raised his eyes. They were bloodshot and she wondered if he too had been drinking or was simply tired. 'You're the one who didn't tell me the truth for years about my father. How do you think I felt when Poppy told me about the baby and then about Max.' He shuddered. 'I can't stand that man. He gives me the creeps.'

'Me too,' said Mollie automatically.

'Then why did you . . .'

'Because he took advantage of me, Nigel. And in those days, it wasn't so easy to get an abortion or I would have done. I had enough gins and hot baths, believe me. Besides, there was something else.'

'Don't tell me there are more surprises.'

'I didn't think your father could have children. Until I got pregnant with you, I had thought maybe it was me that couldn't. We'd been trying for years, Nigel. So when I did get pregnant, part of me was actually thrilled.'

'Really?' Something hopeful flickered in Nigel's eyes and, without meaning to, Mollie reached out and stroked the top of his head. 'When you were born, it was the most amazing day of my life.'

'But I never felt loved as a child.'

She felt a huge wave of guilt pass through her. 'That's because it all began to go wrong. I suspected your father – I mean Gideon

– was suspicious, mainly because you looked nothing like him. And you weren't an easy child. You never slept; you wouldn't suck properly for days; you were a discontented toddler and a very difficult teenager.'

'In other words, you couldn't cope.' Nigel spoke bitterly.

'At the back of my mind, I could never forget that you weren't Gideon's,' said Mollie simply. 'I blamed myself too. I said Max took advantage of me but the truth was that we were on location and I had had too much to drink. I tried to push him away but . . .'

Her voice faltered.

'Please, Mother, I'd rather not know the sordid details.'

He sounded sad rather than angry and Mollie reached down for his hand. To her astonishment, he squeezed it back.

'I told your father the truth just before he died,' continued Mollie. 'He said he had always suspected as much. Now I wonder if he had all those affairs to punish me.'

'Maybe,' said Nigel quietly. 'But I wouldn't in a thousand years have suspected that Poppy's baby was his. Actually, I think she's done us a big favour.' He put his arm around her. 'Maybe we could start all over again. I haven't been very fair on you, either. I felt rejected by you so, mentally, I wouldn't allow myself to be close to you.'

'Nor me to you,' conceded Mollie.

'Do you think it's too late to change?'

'I don't think it's ever too late.'

'Hang on,' said Nigel. 'I remember those words from one of your plays.'

Mollie nodded.

'Having famous parents was the only thing that stopped the other boys at school from beating me up.' Nigel stroked her hair. 'I've always been so proud of you. And those adverts are fantastic. Flora's videoed all of them.'

'Say that again,' demanded Mollie.

'I said Flora . . .'

'No. The bit about you being proud of me.'

'Well, I am.'

'Really?' Mollie's eyes sparkled with tears.

'Of course. Didn't you know that?'

Mollie shook her head, unable to speak for a few moments. When she did, her voice came out thick and blurred. 'There are a lot of things I didn't know.'

'Me too,' said Nigel shakily. 'Me too.'

Forty-nine

**Moving home or need something
collected/delivered?**

CONTACT

STEVEN STEVENS REMOVAL

on the number below.

For some reason, the film company seemed to see him as the interesting one, latching on to the fact that Roddy's family had once owned Bridgewater House.

'I'm not sure that's relevant any more,' Roddy said on the Friday evening when the crew came down to set up and the researcher was asking some prelim questions.

'Well, we'll need to talk about it a bit and also about how you feel about the house being converted. I believe you have a famous resident, Mollie de May? Is she coming?'

'I don't know,' said Roddy, wiping the sweat from his brow. These camera lights were very strong. 'You'll have to ask her.'

Honestly, if it wasn't for his share of the money, he wouldn't be doing this. Besides, another part of him wanted to show the world that he was no longer the irresponsible alcoholic Lord Pearmain whose wife wouldn't allow the children to see him. He was an aristocratic carpenter, now living in his family home.

'I'm so excited about coming down, Daddy,' Helena had screeched down the phone. 'My friends are going to be really jealous.'

Roddy was also looking forward to taking Sally. She made him laugh. And she wasn't in awe of his title or background. Hopefully Annabelle would hear about her too. It amused him to picture her reaction.

The interview went far better than he had imagined. The production team had got him sitting on his sofa, overlooking the lake. The presenter sat opposite. Between them was a rather nice wooden chest which Roddy had made the previous week. It was due to be sold on to the shop but in the meantime, it made a good coffee table and talking point.

'I believe this is one of your pieces,' commented the presenter on camera.

Roddy nodded. They had agreed that the film would give his work a good plug. 'I make chests and restore furniture for private clients and shops,' he said, leaning back against the sofa. 'I enjoy working from home because it means I can also see my children.' He leaned forward. 'As the law stands, it isn't always easy for divorced or separated fathers to see their children if their partners aren't accommodating. I belong to an organisation called Kids Need Dads. We would like to see changes in the law that recognise the importance of a father in a divided family.'

'Cut,' said the presenter. He didn't look very pleased. 'We didn't agree to talk about that one. It's too political.'

'Frankly, if you're going to cut this, I'm not going on with the interview.'

'Excuse me,' said the presenter, getting up.

There was a flurry of conversation behind the cameras. Eventually he returned. 'Very well. We'll keep that bit in but no more. Agreed?'

'Agreed.' Roddy tried not to act cool. Peter had said he would understand if he couldn't slip that bit in. But Roddy had wanted to. All those months without his children had made him realise how awful it was for fathers who were still in that position.

He couldn't wait to see Helena and Daniel tomorrow.

They arrived the following morning. Roddy strode to the entrance – trying not to run – to meet them. Bugger. Annabelle hadn't said *he* was coming too. Bracing himself, Roddy held out his hand.

'Morning, Simon.'

Annabelle's new fiancé winced, as intended, at the strength of Roddy's handshake.

'I must say, this is a nice place you used to have,' said Simon, looking around.

Roddy refused to rise to the bait. 'Actually, it's even better now I don't have to shoulder all the responsibility. Taggert Hall must need a lot of upkeep. And, of course, it's all rather new to you, isn't it?'

Simon's grandfather had been a miner and Taggert Hall, his own place in Wiltshire, had been purchased with one of Simon's banking bonuses.

'I think that's quite enough,' said Annabelle crisply. 'Now, children, have you got your outfits?'

Helena was jumping up and down excitedly. Daniel was mesmerised by the film crew bustling about on the lawn. 'You know, Dad, I've been thinking about applying for a course at the Film Institute after I leave school. Do you think you could fix it so I can talk to the director?'

'No problem,' said Roddy smoothly, enjoying the effect on Simon who was clearly out of his depth. 'By the way, I believe congratulations are in order.'

There. He'd said it.

Annabelle flushed. 'Yes. That's right.'

Helena groaned. 'A baby. Honestly, it's so embarrassing. My friends think it's disgusting at your age.'

Annabelle's face fell and, despite everything, Roddy felt sorry for her.

'Hang on,' said Roddy. 'That's not very nice. Your mother's

still quite young and, anyway, lots of people have babies late nowadays. You'll be able to help out with it. It will probably make your friends envious in the end.'

Helena shrugged. 'Whatever.'

Annabelle shot him a look of thanks which Simon caught. Another point to me, thought Roddy smugly.

'Are you taking someone to the ball, Roddy?' she asked.

'I am indeed.' He looked straight at her. 'My cleaner, actually.'

The look on both Annabelle's and Simon's faces was worth it.

'Sally?' said Daniel. 'Great. She's cool.'

'Really?' remarked Annabelle sharply. 'Whatever turns you on.'

Simon looked at his obviously expensive gold watch. 'Time we were off, darling.'

Annabelle kissed Helena goodbye on the cheek. 'See you later, both of you.' She looked at Roddy. 'And no more swimming in the lake or this really will be the last time they come down.'

He swallowed the reply rising to his mouth and instead held the car door open for her. 'That's a nasty scratch,' he noticed. A sudden thought struck him. 'You didn't happen to bump into a silver BMW on your last visit, did you?'

The red flush spreading over his ex-wife's face was enough to confirm his suspicions. 'Maybe not the last time but I might just have touched it on the visit before that when I was reversing out. Well, honestly, it was so badly parked that it would have been difficult not to.'

'Well it belonged to one of my neighbours and she's not very happy.'

Simon groaned and reached for his cheque book. 'How much do we owe her?'

In the old days, Roddy would have been tempted to have named an astronomically high figure and pocketed the difference. But not now. 'I'll find out and let you know.'

'Quite the good citizen, aren't we?' said Annabelle sarkily. 'I heard you even gave a talk to the locals on Bridgewater House.'

Roddy shrugged. 'Just being neighbourly. We look out for each other here, that's all.'

'You look fantastic!'

Helena did a twirl in her Anne Boleyn costume while Daniel looked very suave in his military uniform.

'You look great too, Dad.' Helena fingered his waistcoat. 'Where did you get it from?'

'They're just bits and pieces I found in some boxes that belonged to your grandfather.' Roddy produced a mask from his pocket. 'This is the only thing I bought. Like it?'

'I wouldn't have recognised you,' gasped Helena.

'That's the whole point of a masked ball, dumbo,' said Daniel. 'It's cool because we can do what we like. Hey, Dad, you did say other teenagers are coming didn't you?'

'I did.'

'What about that weird kid. Tim?'

Roddy could sense the jealousy in his son's voice. 'I'm not sure.'

There was the sound of a key in the lock.

'Please, God, no,' groaned Roddy as Kevin walked in. 'Thought you were away.'

Kevin grinned. He was carrying an expensive-looking bag with 'Fancy That' written on it. 'You don't think I'd miss an event like this, do you? Wild horses wouldn't keep me away. Hello, kids. Been allowed out for the weekend, have you?'

'There's nowhere for you to sleep,' interrupted Roddy. 'I told you. When my kids are down, our arrangement is off.'

'Then I'll just have to kip down on the sofa. Mind if I use the bathroom?'

There was a knock on the door. 'I'll get it,' said Helena. 'Sally. You look lovely!'

Roddy looked – and looked again. She really did look gorgeous. It wasn't just the apple green gown with rosebud trimming round the neck. It was her hair, which she had swept back and up, showing the elegant curve of her neck. She was wearing long drop earrings – he could swear they were diamonds – and in her hand, she held a very pretty delicate mask in the shape of a butterfly.

Helena gave him a little push. 'Tell her she looks lovely.'

'You do,' said Roddy, still stunned.

Sally did a little bob. 'So I scrub up nicely, do I, kind sir?'

'Dad told Mum he was taking the cleaner,' chipped in Daniel. 'But you don't look like one at all.'

There was a deathly hush. Sally had put her mask on and Roddy couldn't see if she was hurt. Stupid. Of course she was.

'I didn't mean . . .' Roddy began.

Sally turned on her heels. 'It doesn't matter.'

She might have a mask on but she couldn't disguise her voice. 'Wait.' Roddy put a hand on her arm. He spoke quietly, aware of the children's presence. 'I was being stupid. Annabelle was putting on the rich wife act and I . . . well, I suppose I was trying to shock her.'

'And he's just found out that Mum's pregnant,' added Helena. 'Don't be cross with him.'

Sally hesitated, her hand on the door handle, and Roddy held his breath. She was perfectly entitled to walk out now.

'It can't be easy for any of you. That's why it's important to have a bit of fun every now and then, isn't it?'

Roddy could hardly believe his luck.

Sally pretended to stamp her foot. She was wearing little black boots under the dress, he noticed. Black boots always had been a big turn-on for him. 'Well, come on, you lot.' She did a mock twirl so the apple-green dress flew up, revealing her shapely calves. 'Are we going to the ball or aren't we?'

The marquee was staggering. Lots of tables dotted with candles. The ceiling of the tent was studded with little lights like stars. Roddy handed Sally a glass of champagne and wondered if she'd slap him if he put his arm around her waist.

'There's something I need to tell you,' she said, taking the glass.

He should have known it. He'd hurt her with that stupid comment to Annabelle about the cleaner.

'Go on.'

'I found something in Kevin's room when I was here last. I wasn't sure whether to tell you or not but I think I ought to.'

'Drugs?'

She took a sip of bubbly. 'No. Some old coins. I mean, they might be his but somehow they didn't seem like the kind of thing a chap like Kevin would have.'

Roddy felt his blood run cold. 'They were mine. I found them in the cellar when I took Tim down there to sort out some wood. I accused him of taking them.'

'Shit.'

'Exactly.'

'Well, you'd better apologise.'

'I will. Is she coming tonight?'

'No idea. I don't "do" for her, as you aristocratic lot might say. She can't afford me.'

This time he did put his arm round her waist. She didn't move away. 'I'm really sorry about that, you know. It was stupid of me.'

'Yes, it was. And hurtful. I used to have a cleaner myself, you know. My husband wasn't posh like you lot but he knew how to make money. Unfortunately, he also knew how to spend it on other women which is why, like you, I've ended up in reduced circumstances.'

Roddy felt hot with embarrassment. 'Is there anything I can do to make up for it?'

'Yes.' She moved away. 'You can dance with me after supper. But first, you can take me to our table so we can eat.' She grinned wickedly. 'A scrubber like me needs feeding up, after all.'

He wanted to slap her bottom lightly and whirl her off her feet. But not yet. Instead, he followed her to their table, feeling happier and more contented than he had for a very long time.

Fifty

Raffle tickets available £5 each. Wonderful prizes,
including a week's villa holiday in Spain.

Everyone else was inside, on their first course. Marcie had told David she needed to go back to the flat to get something but, in fact, she had needed more time alone after that awful argument with Virginia.

Besides, it was so much nicer sitting outside on the bench, watching the marquee lit up against the evening sky. The film crew were still fussing over cables and leads. A couple of women from the ball committee were bustling around outside the tent in voluminous evening dresses, giving orders; looking important. And that bloody dog was sniffing around in the borders when it should be inside.

'Hi. Shouldn't you be in there, having fun with the other toffs?'

She stiffened as Kevin seemed to loom up from nowhere, still in his thin scruffy jeans and t-shirt. Maybe he wasn't going after all.

'Please, leave me alone.'

'You feel it too, don't you?' He wasn't smiling now. His eyes had that animal glint in them; the same glint that the boy in the truck had had all those years ago.

'You're frightening me,' cried Marcie.

'Hey.' His arm came out and stroked hers. 'I don't want to do that.'

'What do you want then?

His arm was still stroking hers, slowly, rhythmically, up and down her bare arms.

'We both know that.'

'It's impossible.' She was really beginning to panic now. 'I'm married.'

'So what? What we've got is real chemistry. It doesn't happen that often, believe me. But when it does, you have to take it.' His hands were moving up towards her throat. 'Just like I need to take you.'

She could hardly breathe. He was squeezing her against the side of the bench so her thigh hurt. Any minute now and someone would notice them.

'I can't,' she gasped.

'Can't you?' Kevin patted his pocket, 'that's a shame. It will mean I have to give your husband the tape then.'

'What tape?'

'The one I found in your bedroom the other day when your sister was entertaining me. I know it was a bit naughty of me but I couldn't resist going in on my way to the bathroom. I didn't know what it was but it looked interesting. And when I played it back at Roddy's place, my hunch was right. So you're going to have a baby but not in the way you might expect. I think your husband might be rather interested in this, don't you.'

'Give me that.' She made as though to snatch it from his hand but he slipped it down the front of his trousers. 'Come and get it,' he taunted. 'But we'll find somewhere quiet first.'

Marcie was shaking with fear.

Kevin's face was almost on hers now. 'I want *you*, not money, although I know a few things about some of the people here that would make them pay up, I can tell you. The other month, I overheard that old actress Mollie whatshername telling someone that her son wasn't her husband's. Just happened to be passing under the window, I was.'

She stood up, pushing him away roughly. 'I've got to go.'

Kevin laughed delightedly. 'So you can fight like a lion, after all. I like that. Tell you what, Cinderella. I'll give you until midnight to come back to me. If you don't, your husband is going to get one hell of a surprise gift.'

Marcie watched Virginia talking animatedly to her husband at the dinner table. But it was too noisy to hear exactly what they were saying.

Marcie began to sweat. Supposing Virginia was telling David about her suspicions concerning Kevin?

'Are you all right, Marcie?'

She jumped at the sound of Sally's voice. In fact, she was surprised she was there at all, bearing in mind the cost of the ticket.

'Fine, thanks,' she mumbled.

Roddy Pearmain, sitting on the other side of Sally, nodded and smiled. So that explained it! He had brought Sally with him; a little surprising considering she was what David's mother called a 'char lady' but she was beginning to learn that the English did a lot of surprising things. At least Kevin was nowhere to be seen.

Marcie glanced at David and Virginia, still in deep conversation. 'You two look as though you're discussing something really important,' she said, leaning forward.

David looked up and smiled, a lovely warm smile that instantly dispelled her fears and reminded her of what had made her fall in love with him in the first place. 'We're discussing Dante's contribution to civilisation. I hadn't realised your sister had studied Italian culture as part of her thesis.'

'There are a lot of things you don't know about my sister,' said Marcie meaningfully.

Virginia looked at her frostily. 'There are probably a lot of things about all of us that we don't know.'

'Very true.' Sally's warm voice cut in. 'Then again, if we did, it would be pretty boring, wouldn't it?'

Marcie shot her a grateful look. 'That's a lovely dress, Sally.'

'Thank you. I found it in that new charity shop in town. It

needed a few things doing to it but it didn't take that long and
I made the mask out of cardboard and Sam's paints. You look
gorgeous too, Marcie.'

She felt a twinge of guilt; all she'd had to do for her costume
was hand over a large cheque. Why couldn't she be talented
like Sally? Why couldn't she be a good wife?

'The dress is all right but it makes her face look old,' said
Katy who was sitting on the other side of her father.

'That's not very nice,' said David. 'Please apologise immediately, Katy. I'm surprised at you.'

Katy scraped back her chair. 'I'm going to the loo. See you
later.'

Marcie took another sip of champagne to hide the tears
welling up into her eyes. Virginia had said nothing during
this interchange. Instead, she was talking again to David who
seemed to be making no attempt to go after his daughter and
reprimand her.

'Kids can be horrid when they want to be,' said Sally consol-
ingly. 'My Sam is a terror.'

'Stepkids can be little sods,' added Roddy thoughtfully. 'I
gave my stepfather hell.'

'By the way,' asked Sally, her voice dropping. 'I've been
meaning to ask you. How are you getting on at the centre?'
Her eyes travelled to Marcie's stomach. 'Any luck yet?'

'No.' Marcie looked away, her cheeks burning.

'You know,' said Sally kindly, 'in my experience, kids come
when you least expect them. Meanwhile, just enjoy yourself.'
She dropped her voice. 'Or at least you will when your busy-
body sister goes home.'

Marcie gasped.

'Sorry. I know I'm being way out of order. But she's pretty
bossy, isn't she?'

Marcie nodded. 'Yes, she is.'

The waitress came to take her first course plate away. She
had barely touched it, even though it was her favourite, smoked
salmon. Pushing back her chair, she stood up rather unsteadily

after those two large glasses. 'I'm going to the bathroom,' she announced.

She needn't have bothered. Virginia and David were still deep in conversation. But it definitely wasn't about Dante. She was pretty certain she heard Virginia say the name Kevin.

Terrified, she wavered behind the back of her chair, clutching the back for support. 'Want me to come with you?' asked Sally.

'No thanks.'

When she got back, David was talking to Sally about extensions. Apparently her husband had been a builder. He gave her a quick non-committal smile which could have meant anything from I-know-what-you've-been-doing to Hi-are-you-all right? Virginia, deep in conversation with Roddy, ignored her.

'Not hungry?' asked David, watching her push the thin slice of beef to the side of her plate.

'No.'

'Are you sure you're all right?' asked David again.

'Maybe she's pregnant,' said Katy sharply. 'I hope not. Granny says it would diffuse the Gilmore-Smith genes to have an American in the family.'

'Katy,' said David sharply. 'That's quite enough. When we've finished, Marcie, would you care for a dance?'

She could almost forget what had happened that evening, pressed against the safety of her husband's epaulette shoulders. He was holding her around the waist with one hand and stroking her back with the other. Virginia was still sitting at the table with Katy who was on her second glass of wine. She'd have liked to have pointed this out to David but it would only cause more rows.

Robert hadn't arrived with Justine yet – she hoped they hadn't taken the opportunity to use her bedroom – and Kevin, thankfully, was still absent.

'I'm sorry about Katy being rude,' he said.

'I won't pretend it didn't hurt.'

'I know.'

He stroked her back again.

'You couldn't have been talking about Dante all that time with Virginia,' she tried to say lightly.

'No, we weren't.'

Her blood froze.

'So what were you talking about?'

'Let's see.' He paused for a second. 'You could have told me about that man.'

Her entire body froze. 'What do you mean?'

He looked down at her quizzically. 'You know exactly what I mean, Marcie. You could have got us into a lot of trouble, allowing him to break into our flat when you locked yourself out before the holiday. You took a serious risk there. I don't like the look of him at all.'

Her mouth was dry with relief. 'Virginia shouldn't have told you.'

He patted her bottom lightly. 'She's worried about you, Marcie. She thinks you're too trusting.'

Why did he constantly have to tell her off as though he was her father?

'Was that all you two were jabbering on about? Me and my faults?'

'Don't talk like that.' David sounded soothing. 'No, it wasn't, actually. Virginia feels she's at a crossroads. She hasn't met the right man yet and she wants to have children. I feel rather sorry for her. She's also worried that she's in our way.'

Marcie sniffed. 'What did you tell her?'

'I said I know the flat is a bit small for a guest but she was welcome to stay at any time. I also suggested she visit my mother in London.' He looked down at her. 'And it would also give us some time alone. I've missed that.'

'But what I told you in Rome. Hasn't it made a difference?'

There was a silence for a few minutes. 'Yes and no,' David said above the music. 'Yes because it's explained why you are as you are. And no because I still love you.'

She felt his body harden against hers. 'Wait for me by the entrance,' he said. 'I won't be a minute.'

Before long, he was back, leading her by the hand across the lawn. He said nothing and, taking her cue from him, she didn't speak either, reluctant to break this unexpected together-time. Behind them, the marquee stood out like a studded round meringue with laughing figures coming in and out. The meal was over now and many of the guests had taken the opportunity to go outside to smoke or do other things.

They reached the pavilion before anyone else. David shut the door behind them and locked it, slipping the key in his pocket.

'Take off your mask,' she whispered.

He shook his head.

The silence made it better. More mysterious. Exciting.

He slid his hand under her dress and moistened her with his fingers, something he didn't normally do.

'Now,' she cried out. And for the first time since they'd first made love, she didn't think of the boy at the wheel of the red truck. David was thrusting now, pushing her against the wall of the pavilion so that her head hurt but she didn't care. His hands were gripping her hair urgently, so hard she was scared he was going to tear it out. Then he was kissing her deeply, passionately, in a way that he hadn't for so very, very long.

And then it came. That amazing detached feeling, as though the lower part of her body had separated from the rest and turned to water. At the same time, he cried out. A thrilling low animal cry that excited her even more, that made her feel she could do anything she liked with him.

And then someone turned the handle of the pavilion door.

Instantly, they sprang apart.

'Can they see us?' asked Marcie scared.

David shook his head.

They waited silently in the semi-darkness until they heard footsteps walking away. David stood up and opened the door. He beckoned for her to come out.

'Why don't you say something?' asked Marcie as they walked towards the marquee. He cleared his throat as though to speak.

'Marcie,' said Mollie, coming up to them. 'It *is* Marcie isn't it? I get so confused with all you lovely young things. Don't you look gorgeous. And your handsome husband too? How is your lovely dog?'

'It's not my dog,' said Marcie tersely. 'It's Louise's.'

'Ah yes, of course it is. How silly of me.'

'David, you have met Mollie de May, haven't you?' asked Marcie, turning to her husband. But all she could see of him was his handsome back in his Cavalier uniform wending his way through the tables.

After she had cleaned herself up in the bathroom, Marcie went back to Virginia, who was on her own, stirring her coffee.

'Don't you want to dance?' asked Marcie quietly.

'Who with?' Virginia laughed hoarsely. 'If I danced with your husband – and I have to say that he did ask me – you'd accuse me of having an affair with him. Your friend Kevin doesn't appear to have turned up at all. And all the other men are otherwise engaged.'

'I'm sorry.'

Marcie sat next to her. 'I haven't done anything wrong, you know, with Kevin. It's not what you think.'

'I know.' Virginia patted her hand and, for a moment, Marcie felt comforted. 'You're not that kind of woman.' She sighed. 'It's just that my own life seems so uncertain, compared with yours.'

'It won't always be like that,' said Marcie. 'One day . . .'

She looked up as David sat down next to her. She held out her hand and he took it.

'Still wearing your mask,' she whispered. 'Very sexy.'

He squeezed her hand. 'Glad you think so.'

Then she froze as an all-too familiar voice spoke.

'Hi, everyone! Sorry I'm late.' He winked at Roddy. 'Had an important appointment.'

'Wow – that's incredible,' breathed Virginia, her eyes fixed on Kevin. 'Absolutely incredible.'

'I wondered if this would happen,' commented Roddy wryly.

'That's what happens when you hire something instead of using your initiative,' added Sally smugly.

Only David and Marcie remained silent. David because he was probably horrified. And Marcie because she was even more so. It wasn't just that Kevin was wearing a Cavalier costume just like her husband. They were wearing identical masks too, probably from the same outfitters. They were also roughly the same build. And as she looked at each of them now, she honestly couldn't tell the difference.

Marcie didn't know how she kept going for the rest of the evening. Kevin had been dancing with all the single women, ranging from the wrinklies like Mollie and Lydia to the younger daughters like Katy.

Had she had sex with him or her husband? He had done different things tonight but then again, that didn't mean it hadn't been David. People changed their techniques; they read books; they tried harder. Oh God. Oh God.

And the clock was getting closer and closer to midnight.

She couldn't take her eyes off Kevin. Right now, he looked pretty engrossed with another girl whom Marcie didn't even recognise. He couldn't have. *She* couldn't have. Could they?

'Smile,' instructed Virginia as she whirled by on the arm of Mollie's son. 'We're being filmed.'

Across the floor, Kevin pointed to his watch, mouthing something at her. Now he was walking slowly and deliberately towards her table. Her watch showed it was midnight. She wanted to run. But there was no escape.

'David,' said Kevin coolly. 'I hate to tear you away from your beautiful wife. But I wonder if we could have a quiet word.' He patted the side of his nose. 'Private like.'

Fifty-one

MENU
*
Wild Scottish salmon on bed of rocket
with cherry tomatoes
*
Beef Wellington with a selection of vegetables
Or
Mushroom stroganoff
*
Eton mess
*
Petits fours and coffee

'Well, maybe it will do him good,' said Guy, holding a large platter of sliced French beans for Louise while she helped herself. 'Reading about how he hurt you might make him finally see what a bastard he's been.'

Louise had never heard Guy swear or heard him criticise Jonathan before. She was also surprised by the anger in his voice. Until now, he'd been careful not to take sides, but tonight he seemed almost pleased about the magazine article.

Perhaps it was being at the ball. They had never been at a social occasion as a couple; it had always been in a foursome with Jonathan and whichever girl Guy happened to be going out with. When he'd first picked her up this evening, she'd been worried that it was going to be awkward. But it hadn't been.

They hadn't stopped talking and not just about the article. It was so easy being with him. So very natural.

'By the way,' said Guy, as they tucked into beef Wellington, 'I haven't told you how lovely you look. That dress is amazing.'

She flushed with pleasure. 'Thank you. It was actually my mother's. I found it when I was packing to leave . . .'

Her voice wavered. For a few seconds, she had a vivid picture of her old house. Her lovely old house with the wisteria and the big garden where her dog could go without anyone making nasty remarks.

Guy put a hand under the table and patted her knee. 'I know it's difficult, Louise. You've been incredibly brave.' He looked around the table. 'But these are nice people here. It must help to have them close to you.'

Louise glanced at Marcie on the table in front. 'Not all of them. That's the American woman who's always moaning about poor old Hector.'

'She looks a bit fed up to me,' commented Guy. 'Maybe she finds it difficult too, in a strange country.'

Louise hadn't considered that.

'But my favourite neighbour is Mollie de May. She's lovely.' She flushed. 'In fact, she's always giving me motherly advice.'

'Mollie de May, the actress?' Guy looked interested.

'Yes. But I can't see her. Funny, she said she was coming. I hope she's all right.'

'Perhaps she's too tired to come. She must be getting on now. I remember my mother telling me about some wonderful film she was in . . .'

Guy chatted on. He was a an excellent storyteller and had been great at telling the children bedtime stories when they were little. He also knew so much about films which she had never seen, and books which she hadn't had time to read, that she felt mentally stimulated in a way she hadn't for a very long time.

It was only when the waitress arrived to clear the second course that she realised Guy's hand was still on her knee.

He took it away just before pudding arrived as though this was the most natural thing to do. And in a way, it was. It had been a friendly, comforting gesture, that was all. Like when they'd been children and he'd held her hand after she got stung by a bee once in his garden.

'This is delicious,' said Guy, digging his spoon into Eton mess with raspberry juice dribbled over it. She laughed.

'What's so funny?'

'You've got juice all over your mouth.'

'Then you can wipe it off for me.' He handed her a napkin. She dabbed at the offending area, feeling rather embarrassed.

'Thank you.' He grinned at her. That's what she loved about Guy. His zest for life, his enthusiasm over something simple like Eton mess, and the easy way he could ask her to do things that any other woman would have misinterpreted, like cleaning his chin.

'You haven't told me what happened next,' he said, in between mouthfuls. 'What did Jonathan do after yelling down the phone at you?'

'That was it.' Louise put down her spoon. The memory of Jonathan's anger took away her appetite. 'He hung up. And I haven't heard from him since.'

'Have the children said something?'

'I don't think they've seen it and I'm pretty sure he won't tell them. He won't want them to read all the gory details. It was pretty bad luck he read it himself. It's not the kind he would normally bother with. Apparently one of the girls in the office saw it and told him.'

'Are you going to get mad with your editor friend?'

She had been thinking about this. 'Well, she won't be in until Monday and yes, I've every right to get cross. But she'll just say it was a mistake by the subs – which it might well be.'

'Couldn't you sue for compensation?'

'Then I'd never get any more work again out of them. And I'm going to need every penny I can get.'

'My offer to lend you money still stands, you know.'

'Thank you. But I think it's best if I don't.'

Neither said anything for a few seconds, although around them the din seemed to be increasing with the clatter of cutlery and raucous laughter. Then they both spoke at once.

'I think I'll go to the Ladies . . .'

'. . . Would you like some fresh air?'

Louise giggled. 'I'd love some. But I'll go to the loo first and then meet you by the entrance. Is that all right?'

'I hadn't realised how beautiful the grounds were,' said Guy as they strolled past the lavender beds towards the lake. 'Do you manage to sit out here?'

'Not really. It's too public. I prefer to sit in my own little garden but it's nice for the boys. They can run around and kick a football, providing Marcie or Lydia don't start moaning.'

'So this is the pavilion!' Guy seemed truly taken aback. 'It's stunning. Can we go in?'

He tried the door. It was locked.

'We'll come back during the day,' promised Louise. 'It's nice inside. We have our yoga classes there.'

'And the lake is where Tim goes fishing with your resident aristocrat?'

'That's right.' Louise tensed up. 'I still can't get over those terrible things he said about Tim and his stupid coin collection.'

Guy patted her arm. 'You know Tim's not a thief and that's what matters.'

They stopped by the side of the water. 'Louise,' said Guy softly. Something in his eyes said, 'Stop me now and I'll never mention it again.'

Something inside her refused to allow her to look away.

'Louise,' he said again but this time it came out like a low groan.

Suddenly, his face was coming down to hers. His lips were moist yet hard at the same time. Her mouth melted into his; it was sweet and loving and innocent and desperate and wanting and so very very right, all at the same time. She didn't want it to stop; not ever. And nor, it seemed, did he.

Eventually, they broke apart.

'I feel as though we've been doing that for ever,' whispered Louise.

'Me too.' This time, his body pressed against hers urgently and she felt a flash of fire. She wanted him. God, she wanted him. Right here on the grass.

'Where can we go?' he said in a low voice.

'Over here.' She led him to an old pony shelter by the lake. His hands felt her breasts; uncertainly at first and then more surely. He unbuttoned the front of her dress.

'Take off your shirt,' she demanded. She'd never demanded anything before of Jonathan; he had never made her want to. His skin fused with hers. His hand crept down to her waist and she suddenly remembered her wrinkly stomach. What would he think? What was she doing?

'No. Not yet.'

'I'm sorry.' He sounded repentant.

'No, don't be. But it's too soon.'

How daft was that? She was in her forties, for pity's sake, not a teenager any more. But it was still too soon. She wanted to savour this bit, taste it. It was as though he had opened a room in her body which she had never known existed.

They lay together, their upper bodies naked, for some time. 'It feels so right,' whispered Guy.

'Doesn't it?' agreed Louise. 'It's incredible.'

He leaned over her and she could see his face clearly in the moonlight. 'I've always wanted you, you know.'

'But I was married.'

He nodded. 'That's why I never said anything.'

'You had all those girlfriends.' She had tried, once, to count them up in her head but had reached the figure of thirty before giving up. And those were only the ones she knew about.

He was stroking her hair now. 'I always used to compare them with you and none of them matched up.'

She was shocked but flattered. At the same time, she needed to know where she was. She was too old for games.

'I can't be one of your conquests that comes to nothing. It wouldn't be worth losing our friendship over.'

'I agree.' He was sitting up, kneeling facing her. 'That's why . . .'

'Mum. *Mum!*'

Louise stiffened at the sound of Tim's voice. Shaking, she quickly did up her dress.

'Stay there,' she hissed, leaping to her feet. Across the lawn, she could see Tim running towards her. She ran to meet him so he wouldn't see Guy. 'I'm here, Tim. What's wrong?'

He was panting, breathless. His hoodie – which she'd asked him not to wear on a formal occasion like this – was ripped and his eyes looked scared.

'Justine wants to talk to you.'

'Is she here?'

'Yes.' He looked worried.

'What else, Tim?'

'Dad's here too. And he wants to talk to you as well.'

Justine was waiting for her by the pavilion. To Louise's surprise and delight, she flung her arms around her and burst into floods of tears. 'Mum!'

She'd been drinking again, realised Louise with a shock. She could smell it on her daughter's breath. Robert was behind her in full evening dress. Justine was sobbing still, her head against Louise's chest. 'I hadn't realised how much pain Dad had put you through. I hadn't realised how much any of us had hurt you. I didn't mean to be difficult. It's just that it was so strange moving out of the house and into this place. And you were always angry with me and snappy. It was only when I read your article – especially the bit about me going to Dad's – that I realised how much you love me.'

'Well, of course I love you.' Louise's ran her lips over the top of her daughter's hair. 'You children are everything to me.'

Justine lifted her tear-stained face. 'I told Dad what a cunt he'd been.'

'Justine! Don't use words like that.'

'Well it's true, isn't it,' said Tim hotly.

'I don't think he's very happy with Gemma. They're always having rows and the other night she asked him why he didn't just go back to you.'

'I'm afraid it's too late for that,' said Louise quietly.

'Is it?'

She swung around. Jonathan was standing there; not in evening dress but in cords and a jumper. The same jumper she had given him last Christmas when she hadn't realised he was having an affair. Gemma was nowhere to be seen.

'Kids, can I have some time with Mum?' asked Jonathan quietly. Reluctantly, they peeled away into the shadows of the marquee.

'Is it too late?' repeated Jonathan, his eyes travelling admiringly down her dress and then up to her face. 'The children are right. I have been a prat.' Suddenly, he looked like a small, frightened child. 'Will you take me back, Louise?'

'What about Gemma?' she heard herself say.

'She's lost the baby.'

Lost the baby? Part of her felt sorrow and part of her felt wickedly vindicated. 'Does that make a difference?'

'Yes.' Jonathan spoke so softly that she could barely hear him. 'Gemma was pregnant before I left you. It made me feel I had to do the right thing . . .'

She laughed hoarsely. 'You mean leave the children you already had?'

'I know,' said Jonathan wearily. 'But I couldn't see anything clearly and I thought you didn't care. As soon as I moved in with her, I realised I'd made a terrible mistake but I felt I'd caused so much disruption that I had to stick it out. But now . . . now there's no obligation for me to stay. Please, Louise, give me a second chance.'

Before she could answer, she felt a shadow across her. It was Guy. A fully dressed Guy. And from his face, he had clearly heard what Jonathan had just said.

'Guy?' said Jonathan. He was clearly shaken. Louise could see the shadow of doubt and then anger cross his face. 'What are you doing here?'

'I asked him,' said Louise quickly.

'As an old friend,' said Guy smoothly.

'Then for God's sake, Guy, ask Louise to think about taking me back.'

There was a long silence. 'That's up to her,' said Guy gruffly.

'I thought you were mad at me after the article,' said Louise shakily to her husband.

'I was. But it also made me realise how badly I'd behaved. Please, Louise, please. Just think about it. For the kids' sake.'

Fifty-two

Please sign here if you would like to order photographs of
the ball. Prices below.

Mollie was glad now that Nigel had made her come to the ball.
She had no idea her son could be such fun. It was as though
their conversation earlier in the week about him being proud
of her had made the scales drop from her eyes. It was such a
relief to have made all those confessions to him.

'Not so fast,' she gasped as her son twirled her round the
dance floor.

'Sorry, Mother. I'm getting carried away.'

Nigel never got carried away with anything. His military
soldier costume seemed to have gone to his head. But as she
watched him dancing now, she wondered if she had ever really
bothered to get to know her son. Somehow it was easier now
Gideon wasn't here to cast his disapproval.

'I'm so glad you asked us,' said Julia, Nigel's wife, after the
dance had finished. 'Flora's having a lovely time. She's found
some other children to dance with. Look.'

Mollie had a lovely warm feeling as she watched Flora
talking earnestly to a tall, lanky boy who, she seemed to recall,
was one of Louise's boys, the one who was always fishing in
the lake. 'So nice to see the young enjoying themselves,' she
said.

'Poppy chose not to come then,' said Nigel tautly.

'Well she wouldn't dare, would she?' said Julia defensively,
putting an arm around Mollie's shoulders. Mollie had never

known her to do that before. Had she got her daughter-in-law wrong too?

'I believe she is staying at Rupert's,' said Mollie, sitting down back at the table. 'But to be honest, I don't really care.'

'The marquee looks amazing,' said Julia, in an all too obvious attempt to change the conversation. 'And everyone's made such an effort to dress up.'

'The local costume company has probably sold out,' agreed Nigel. 'There are an awful lot of Cavaliers and Roundheads who look incredibly similar. Is that your phone ringing, Mother?'

Nigel had insisted on getting her a mobile some time ago, in case she 'suddenly needed help'. At the time, she had seen it as interfering but now, in the light of their new relationship, she could see it was his way of caring.

'Hello, hello? You're absolutely certain that that's what she said? Very well.'

Slipping her phone back into her evening bag, she stared pensively into the distance.

'What's wrong?' asked Nigel.

'That was Rupert. Poppy has gone into labour early. And apparently she's been asking for me. She won't allow Rupert near her. She just wants me.'

'What are you going to do?' asked Julia quietly.

Mollie waited for a suggestion from Gideon but nothing came. 'I'm not sure.'

'But if she's gone into labour early, you might not have much time.'

'I know,' said Mollie thoughtfully, still not moving. 'I know.'

Of course, she had to go. It was just shock that rendered her incapable of making an instant decision. Julia drove her. Nigel said he was sorry and that it was laudable she felt able to go but he'd rather not be anywhere near that woman.

At the hospital, Mollie insisted that Julia returned to the ball and walked briskly up to Maternity reception. It still didn't feel real.

'I'm here to see Poppy Marlowe,' she said grandly. 'I'm her birthing partner.'

The receptionist's eyes travelled down Mollie's body and she suddenly remembered she was wearing her costume. 'Oh, this,' she said casually. 'I've been at a ball. A masked ball. I got an emergency call and didn't have time to change. Elizabeth Taylor actually wore this dress. Beautiful, isn't it? Now please tell me where I can find Poppy.'

The receptionist looked at her again. 'Aren't you that actress who does those vitamin adverts on television?'

Mollie nodded. At any other time she would have lapped up the recognition but now reality was beginning to set in. Poppy was in labour. The child needed her. Of course she was still cross with her. But she couldn't ignore anyone's plea for help at a time like this.

'Please. I may not have much time.' She gave the receptionist Poppy's details and suddenly it all started to happen. A nurse arrived to take her into an empty side room and she was instructed to wait.

'What's happening?' she asked, feeling scared.

'Your daughter is having an emergency caesarean.'

The shock prevented Mollie from correcting the nurse about the daughter bit.

'Why?'

The nurse was helping her into a green gown. 'The baby was showing signs of distress.'

'But she's going to be all right?'

'I'm afraid I can't say. I've been told you can wait outside but you'll need to wear this.' She handed her a mask. 'Your daughter has been given a general anaesthetic so, providing everything's all right with the baby, you can hold it after delivery.'

The nurse spoke as though this kind of thing was perfectly routine.

'Where's Rupert?' demanded Mollie.

'Here.' He spoke weakly from a chair in the corner. 'Sorry,

Mollie. This sort of thing absolutely finishes me off and I'm in no fit state to hold a baby.'

'What happened?' demanded Mollie.

'We were sitting down after dinner and she suddenly announced her waters were breaking. Waters, darling? It was a bloody ocean. All over my lovely new ottoman that I'd spent a fortune re-covering in the most gorgeous Regency pink and cream striped chintz. And all the dear girl did was cry out for you.'

'For me?' That's what he'd said on the phone but Mollie still couldn't understand it. 'But why?'

'Look, darling,' said Rupert taking her hand. 'I know the background. Poppy told me. Don't worry. I won't tell anyone. But what you've got to realise is how much she loves you. Yes, she loved Gideon too but the pair of you went together in her head. Darling Poppy has always been a bit immature. Comes from having parents who were always abroad, if you ask me.'

'So are you going to hold the baby when it's delivered or not?' demanded the nurse who'd clearly been listening to every word.

Mollie took a deep breath. There was no way she was going to allow a newborn to be plonked in a Perspex cot.

'I will.'

It seemed like an interminable wait. Mollie actually found herself saying the Lord's Prayer which she hadn't done for years. Then suddenly the doors opened and a nurse came out, carrying a white bundle.

'You've got a granddaughter!' she said, beaming from ear to ear. 'Look! She's absolutely beautiful!'

'How's Poppy?' Mollie could hardly get the words out.

'Absolutely fine.'

Mollie looked down at the baby. Her face was red and crinkled and wet and her black hair – masses of it – was plastered to her head. 'Is she all right?'

'Absolutely. With a very commendable Apgar score too, considering the scare she gave us. Here, sit down.'

The nurse helped her to a seat. Mollie gazed entranced at the baby who seemed to be looking at her with deep, knowing eyes. She was the spitting image of . . .

'Mother!'

'Nigel! What are you doing here?'

'I had to come. I couldn't leave you to cope on your own.' He stopped as he realised what she was holding and his face tightened.

'Take a look,' she said tenderly. 'Do you see what I see?'

Nigel gulped. 'It looks a bit like Flora did when she was born.'

'It,' corrected Mollie, 'is a girl. Beautiful, isn't she?'

Nigel nodded wordlessly.

'It's not her fault,' began Mollie . . .

'Just as it wasn't mine that Max was my father,' completed Nigel.

Mollie nodded. 'Exactly. Here, hold her.'

Gingerly, Nigel held out his hands. 'I suppose she's my half-sister. What a weird thought.'

'But you don't mind too much?' prompted Mollie.

'I suppose not. I was upset before but now, when I look at it – I mean her – it seems different.'

Gideon coughed and Mollie jumped.

'So I'm forgiven then?'

Had Nigel heard? He didn't seem to have; he was still studying the baby, stroking her cheek with his index finger.

'You'll have to try a bit harder than that,' she whispered.

'I told you, I'm sorry.'

Mollie stood up and walked to the window so Nigel couldn't hear her. 'Where have you been? I'd given up on you. Aren't you going to look at your daughter? She's very like your grand-daughter, you know. Or should I say, half-granddaughter?'

'Stop being facetious. You know perfectly well that I adored Flora, despite Nigel's parentage.'

His voice didn't sound quite right.

'Something's happened, hasn't it?' she asked, suddenly scared.

'Yes.' He spoke urgently. 'Go home, Mollie. Go home. *Now.* Get what you need before it's too late and get out. But be careful, please. Very, very careful.'

Fifty-three

ROLL UP FOR THE TOMBOLA!

Everyone guaranteed a prize!

'Tim!'

Roddy stopped the boy as he crossed him in the marquee doorway. Unlike his own two, who were in fancy dress, Tim was wearing jeans and a hoodie; hands firmly tucked in the pockets. 'I've been looking for you. Have you got a second?'

Tim looked at him coldly. 'No.'

'Please. There's something I need to tell you. And your mum. Is she around?'

He jerked his head back into the tent. 'In there somewhere. 'Scuse me, I'm going home.'

'It's about the coins.' He should really be saying this in front of Louise but he'd find her later. 'Look, I'm really sorry about accusing you but . . .'

'Found them now, have you?'

The boy's face was rigid with dislike. Roddy's chest thumped; what kind of damage had he inflicted on him by suggesting he was a thief? As if the boy didn't have enough to cope with.

'Yes,' he said lamely. 'They were under the . . .'

'I don't give a shit where you found them,' flashed Tim.

'Look, I can understand you're upset. But when this is all over, I wondered if you'd like to come fishing with me and my son.'

Tim gave him a withering look. 'And you think that will make me feel better?'

'Well, yes. No. I don't know.'

'Fuck off, *Mr* Pearmain. A real lord wouldn't act like you have. I don't need your charity or your false accusations. My mum says she wishes she'd never moved here now. In fact, she's going to sell it. We're going back to London. She says people are normal there and don't hate dogs or accuse others of stealing.'

Roddy ran his hands through his hair despairingly. 'Tim, I'm really sorry.'

'Dad, Dad!' Daniel came rushing up to them. 'Come outside. You too.' Daniel tugged at Tim's sleeve but the boy angrily shook him off.

'Come outside. Quick.'

Marcie was running as fast as she could away from the marquee. Running so hard that her chest was thumping and making it difficult to breathe. Her worst fears had been realised. Kevin was going to tell David. In fact, he'd probably told him now. He would have said they'd been meeting secretly and, even though nothing had happened, he would insinuate that it had. And he would have given David the tape.

David despised clairvoyants; he'd always said he thought they were dangerous. Christ, he didn't even approve of horoscopes. Marcie felt sick as she finally sank down on a bench on the far side of the lake, well away from the house or marquee. She could still feel Kevin – or had it been David? – inside her from earlier on. This was a nightmare. An absolute bloody nightmare. Just like the one that had happened all those years ago.

Something soft nuzzled her knees

Leaping up with horror, she saw it was a dog. Not just any dog but that woman Louise's dog.

'Get away,' she said, pushing it off. But it was whimpering, scared and shaking. And it kept pawing her as though it wanted her to stroke it.

'Go home,' she said. 'Go home, will you?'

Clearly it didn't understand. What was the right kind of command to give a dog? She had to do something; it was standing on its hind legs now, trying to put its muddy paws round her waist.

'Sit,' instructed Marcie. '*Sit.*'

To her relief, it obeyed. But then it started whimpering again. Something inside her weakened. It was as upset as she was. Hardly knowing why she was doing it, she put out her hand. 'It's all right,' she whispered.

The dog immediately licked her hand all over and Marcie shuddered. She ought to wash her hand now. God knows what kind of disease she might get. But the dog continued licking and then a strange thing happened. The warmth and the wetness actually felt quite comforting. And the way the dog was looking up at her adoringly was startlingly flattering.

Slowly, very slowly, she reached down and stroked his fur. He lay down with a satisfied grunt at her feet, sitting on her toes. It made her feel warm; it helped her to stop shaking. Her fingers found the collar round his neck and then his name tag. Hector. Of course. She'd heard that woman yell it out enough times in the grounds.

'Hector, I've done something really stupid,' she found herself saying. 'I've been flirting with someone and now he's going to ruin my life with my husband.'

The dog looked up at her. 'It will be all right,' his eyes seemed to say.

'How do you know?' Marcie said out loud. 'Nothing ever goes right for me in life. Nothing.'

Now he was licking her ankles, below her dress. But this time she didn't try to push him away. 'What do you think I should do?' she asked.

The dog stood up, stretched and made a strange noise.

'Where are you going, Hector?' asked Marcie. 'You'd better not just leave. You'll get lost.'

He walked round to the other side of the bench and Marcie

followed. She'd have to take him back to Louise's flat. She'd have to . . . and then she saw it.

'No,' she gasped. 'No, no, no!'

'Just think about it, Louise,' pleaded Jonathan. 'That's all I'm asking.'

Her eyes flashed. 'Let's see. You get Gemma pregnant when you're meant to be happily married to me. You break up our family and we have to leave our house to live in a flat.'

'Well, it's hardly a flat . . .'

'Shut up and listen, will you? I have to find a job when I've been out of the employment market for years and we're so broke that we have macaroni cheese twice a week when you take Gemma to fancy restaurants. You persuade Justine that she'd be better off with you . . .'

'Hang on . . .'

'Let me finish. You're livid at my column which, all right, I suppose you're entitled to be. But now, to cap it all, you want us to get back together just because Gemma has, conveniently for you, lost her baby.'

'That's not fair,' whispered Jonathan, his eyes red. 'And you know it.'

'Really?'

She looked up at him. Against all her better instincts, her heart lurched at his face which was sad, pleading and handsome all at the same time. She knew every line on his face, every mark on his body. They had been through so much together and now he wanted another chance. Could she really put all that hurt behind her? And what about Guy? That kiss had blown her away. If she was going to give her marriage another chance, she could never see him again.

'Shit. Fucking hell.' Jonathan was staring behind her, his eyes open wide with terror.

She swivelled round.

'Oh my God,' she screamed. 'Where's Justine? Where's Tim? Where's Nick?'

★   ★   ★

Mollie left the baby in the care of the nurse, asking her to tell Poppy, when she came round, that she'd had an emergency and would be back shortly. The nurse clearly thought she was bonkers.

'I'm coming with you,' insisted Nigel. 'What's this all about?'

'Ask your father,' she retorted.

Nigel's face was such a picture that a few days ago she would have enjoyed the discomfort written all over it.

'You might as well know,' she said, putting her hand on her son's knee in the back of the taxi, 'your father still speaks to me in my head.'

Nigel looked almost relieved. 'Lots of people think that when someone dies. It's nature's way of helping them through a bereavement.'

'No, dear boy, it's more than that.' She smiled at him. 'He comes to visit me, you know.' She dropped her voice as the taxi driver sped towards the house. 'He's made love to me several times since he died.'

The taxi swerved slightly. Perhaps the driver could hear after all.

'Mother,' began Nigel gently. 'I know how much you miss him but when you talk like this, you really worry me. I really think you should go and see the doctor.'

'Shh, your father's saying something.'

'Find Flora and her mother first to make sure they're safe,' growled Gideon, 'and then get our Oscars. They're irreplaceable.'

'But they're in the drawing room. If someone tries to break in, they'll set the alarm off.'

'Mother,' said Nigel, taking her hand. 'Please, you're frightening me. What's in the drawing room? What are you talking about?'

And then the taxi rounded the corner and headed up the drive.

Mollie's eyes widened with fear. 'Now I see what you mean, darling.'

Nigel's jaw dropped. 'Bloody hell. Bloody, bloody hell.'

All the lights were on at Bridgewater House so it looked like a squat incandescent Christmas tree. Except that they weren't lights.

They were flames, licking and twirling their way up into the late-summer sky.

Fifty-four

THIS IS AN EMERGENCY ANNOUNCEMENT.

Will everyone please leave the marquee immediately
and meet at the main gates. Do not, we repeat not,
try to go back to the house.

Roddy's first thought was the kids. Daniel was with him but where
was Helena? He tried to think straight but the marquee had
suddenly become an enclosed prison with everyone pushing past
him, screaming and shoving, rendering logical thought impossible.

'Hang on to me,' he yelled out to Daniel but even in the
confusion, he could see that Tim had gone. 'We've got to find
Helena,' he yelled. 'And Sally.'

'I'm here,' called out a voice.

Gratefully he grabbed her arm. Sally looked scared. 'Helena
went back to the house to get a pashmina.'

His chest tightened with panic. 'Wait there with Daniel. Don't
let him go near the house.'

'No.' His son's voice was firm. 'I need to find my sister too.'
All three began to run.

'Keep back,' said someone in a fluorescent jump suit. Fuck that.
Leading the way, Roddy dived through a bush and ran towards
the house. There was a scream of sirens. Someone must have called
the fire brigade. Thankfully the fire seemed to be at the other end
of the house so he was still able to open his own front door.

'Helena,' he yelled, running from room to room. 'Helena!'

'Maybe she went with Justine,' gasped Daniel.

Roddy couldn't think straight. Where was Louise's front door? Of course, round the corner.

Near the fire.

He hadn't realised Louise's apartment was on two floors.

'Dad,' screamed Helena from an upstairs window. 'Help!'

Where were the firemen?

Roddy tugged at the wisteria. It was firm, solid, just as it had been when he was a boy. Years ago, he'd been caned by his father for shinnying down it to go fishing at midnight.

'Dad, *Dad*!'

Helena was hysterical. Behind her was the other girl.

He was hauling himself up now, his feet scrabbling for something sturdy to balance on.

Snap.

For a few seconds he floundered. 'Up to the right!' called out Tim's voice from the ground. Helena's hand was almost touching his now.

'Climb on my back,' he instructed.

'But Justine!'

He couldn't take both of them.

'You go first,' said the other older girl. 'But come back. Quickly. Please.'

Helena clambered over the sill and flung her arms round her father's neck.

'We're coming up,' shouted a voice from the ground.

Thank God! Gently, he passed his daughter to the fireman.

'Help me, help me.'

'Now you, sir, down. Quick.'

At the bottom of the ladder, he and the kids clung to each other. From the upstairs window, there was a crashing sound and a crescendo of light.

'Justine,' screamed Louise.

'Back please,' thundered someone.

And there she was. A figure on the shoulder of the fireman coming down the ladder. But unlike Helena, she wasn't moving.

*   *   *

The dog whimpered again. Marcie couldn't leave him, He might get hurt. 'Here, Hector,' she said, shaking. Amazingly, he obeyed. Swiftly, she fastened her silk belt to his collar like a lead.

'Come on,' she said, running towards the house.

'Let me through.' She tried to push against a burly fireman.

'Please, madam, stay back.'

The dog was whining again. 'But that's my home. My husband might be in there.'

She could see it all so clearly. David would have stomped back home, white with anger, after Kevin had told him. But someone was pulling her away.

'Hector!'

Suddenly the dog pulled away in panic. Instinctively, she ran after him down the drive, remembering those warm loving licks Hector had given her; an unconditional love that she hadn't had for so long. Anyway, what was the point of staying now Kevin had told David?

She was getting closer now. If she had run like this when she was fifteen, she might not have been raped.

'Hector!'

The dog was almost at the kerbside now but at the sound of her voice, he stopped. She reached him just in time to lock her fingers round his chain; haul him back from the stream of cars flying past.

Then she stopped. The dog looked up. 'Why don't we just go?' he seemed to say.

Marcie stared at the red truck approaching. The same red truck from all those years ago, coming to get her again. It hooted warningly as she stepped out in front. And then all of a sudden, she could see it was a car after all.

In the dim distance, she could hear David yelling, as though through a fog of cotton wool.

'Marcie, look out!'

And then it went black.

Fifty-five

EMERGENCY PARKING ONLY

Louise bent over her daughter as the fireman put an oxygen mask on her. Please God, let her be all right. Jonathan put a hand on her shoulders. This was their daughter. Whatever happened to them, there was no shaking off that history.

Guy had his arm around Tim and Nick. Miraculously, he'd found them while running to the house.

'Is she going to die?' whimpered Tim.

No one said anything. Robert was by her side, his eyes never leaving his girlfriend.

'She's breathing,' said one of the crew.

Louise burst into tears.

'Shh, it's all right,' said Jonathan soothingly. 'It's all going to be all right.'

Instinctively, Louise looked across at Guy, wishing he could be holding her, not Jonathan. Then Justine started coughing and Louise fell to her knees beside her daughter.

'Mind out, love. The stretcher's here.'

'I'll go with her to the hospital.' Louise spoke urgently. 'Take the boys back to your place.'

'Hector!' said Nick suddenly. 'Has anyone seen Hector?'

How could she have forgotten?

'Don't let them go back into the house, Jonathan!'

'Don't worry,' said Guy firmly. 'I'll find him.'

★   ★   ★

Somehow Mollie managed to get into her house without being stopped.

'The rest of the place is on fire. This could go up any second,' panted Nigel.

'Grab the Oscars,' instructed Gideon.

'For God's sake, Mother, I know these are precious but our lives are more important.'

There was a deafening crash from outside. Mollie felt surprisingly calm. 'I've just got to get one more thing from the bedroom.'

'No,' roared Nigel, pulling her back.

'Second thoughts,' said Gideon quietly. 'I've been a bit selfish, old girl. Forget the Oscars. It's too late now.'

Mollie felt a stab of terror.

'Watch out!' roared Nigel.

She felt herself being pushed towards the window which was cracking in the heat. A shard of glass cut her face and she was vaguely aware of the taste of blood. Then suddenly she felt herself being lifted up through the window. Just as her feet touched the ground, there was a terrible cry. She had never heard her husband sound like that ever before. Not even on film.

'Gideon!' she screamed. 'Are you all right?'

Hector was nowhere to be seen. A few people had spotted him; one had thought the American woman had him.

'Bollocks,' said Tim. 'She hates Hector.'

There was only one place left. As they went down the drive, Guy saw an ambulance and police car parked by the main road.

His heart tightened. 'Please, Tim . . .'

'No.' Tim was already running. 'He's *my* dog.'

Hector looked as though he was fast asleep on the verge, his eyes closed. Slowly, Tim rolled him over and let out an agonising cry.

Hector's stomach was a sticky red gaping cavern.

Wordlessly, Guy gathered Tim to him, holding him tightly, allowing the boy to cry uncontrollably. He also wanted to shield him from the sight beyond. Someone was being lifted on to a stretcher, a man watching silently. The ambulance doors were slammed shut and the vehicle roared off, siren and lights screaming and flashing.

Tim lifted his head. 'Has someone been hurt?' he sobbed, his face swollen with grief.

'I'm afraid so,' said Guy quietly.

Fifty-six

Bridgewater Gazette

FIRE SWEEPS THROUGH HISTORIC COUNTRY HOME. AT LEAST ONE PERSON FEARED DEAD

'Your father's dead, isn't he?' said Mollie dully. She was sitting up in the hospital bed, her face a mosaic of lintel plasters and her right arm in a plaster cast.

'Yes, Mother.' Nigel, sitting by her bed – miraculously, he only had a twisted ankle – patted her arm. 'I know it's been hard for you to take in, even after this time. But yes, he is dead.'

'Don't patronise me, Nigel. I mean he died in the fire. I heard him scream after that crash. No one could have survived that.' She shuddered.

Nigel put his arm around her. 'Mother, I'm afraid I'm going to be brutal. Father didn't die in the fire. He died of cancer at the beginning of the summer.'

'Really? Mollie's bright blue eyes bore into his. 'Then how do you think we got out of that place?'

Nigel hesitated. 'I remember someone lifting me up. One of the firemen.'

'Did you see his face?'

'Not exactly.' Nigel looked worried. 'It was as though someone had come up from behind and lifted me down.'

'And you really think that was a fireman?' asked Mollie softly.

'Well who else could it have been?'

Mollie looked sad and very frail in her floaty pink night-dress. 'Think, Nigel. Think.'

Later, he rang the fire officer in charge that night. 'That's right. We found you on the ground. You must have fallen. Amazing that your injuries weren't any worse. You must have had a guardian angel looking after you, sir.'

When Nigel went back that night to visit, he found – to his annoyance – that Poppy was there, baby strapped to her front, beaming as though they were at a bloody dinner party.

'I've come across from the maternity wing,' she said airily. 'Thank God you're both all right.'

The bundle in front of her made a strange mewing noise. To his horror, Poppy opened some kind of flap in her nightie and the baby started sucking noisily. Mollie laughed delight-edly. 'How clever of you, darling. I never managed to do that with Nigel.'

'Mother,' hissed Nigel. 'Can I have a word with you?'

'Of course,' said Poppy. 'I'll go.'

'No, don't.' Mollie tapped the side of the bed imperiously. 'You're feeding. Stay where you are.'

He tried to speak quietly. 'This woman slept with your husband. She's had his baby. But you're chatting away as though she's an old friend.'

'But she is, darling.' Mollie's beautiful eyes were serious. 'I've been doing a lot of thinking. I loved Gideon but he was a selfish man. But I really saw the light in the fire. He told me to go back, you know, just so I could rescue his precious Oscars.'

'They were just voices in your head,' argued Nigel weakly.

'No,' said Mollie quietly. 'Just as that wasn't a fireman who lifted you and me down. Your father saved us. And do you know why he finally went?' She patted his hand. 'Because Gideon knows I'm safe with you. The new you.'

She paused. 'He'd also forgiven me for killing him.'

'What on earth are you talking about?'

'Oh, Nigel.' She clutched his hand. 'He was in such pain at the end, you know. And the doctor had prescribed these morphine tablets. Well I gave him one or two more than I was meant to. I had to, to try and make him feel better. I didn't mean to kill him . . . but he died a few hours later.'

Nigel drew his mother to him. 'That's not murder. That's being humane. He was going to die anyway. I'd have done the same.'

'Would you?' she murmured thickly into his shoulder.

'Yes.' He stroked the back of her head. 'I would.'

'Bless you, darling. I can't tell you how it's been troubling me.' She glanced at Poppy, who had fallen asleep in the chair while still feeding her baby. 'At least Gideon is still living on through that little bundle. Do you know what Poppy's going to call her?

He gave up now.

'Mollie!' She beamed. 'Now isn't that nice?'

Roddy and the kids had spent the night at Sally's small terraced house in town until Annabelle drove down in the morning.

'I still can't believe it,' she had said, holding Daniel and Helena tightly to her. 'You could all have died.'

'Justine nearly did,' said Helena. 'Dad got me down, you know.'

'What about you?' asked Annabelle, looking directly at him. 'Where will you live?'

'The insurance assessors will be down later on this morning. I'll just find a hotel room or continue staying with Sally.'

Annabelle looked disdainfully round the sitting room. It was tastefully furnished with a beige flecked three-piece suite and pale ash coffee table but it certainly wasn't up to Annabelle's standards.

'Where is she anyway?'

'Working,' said Helena.

'Ah, yes.' Annabelle smiled smugly. 'I'd forgotten she was a cleaner.'

'Just like I am a carpenter.'

'Please, Roddy, this isn't the time to argue. Come on, children. Time to go, I think.'

They both hugged him tightly. 'Love you, Dad,' said Helena.

A flicker of sadness passed over Annabelle's face. He knew exactly how she felt. They could have been a family if he hadn't messed up. But now, it was time to move on.

He was surprisingly pleased when Sally came back from work.

'I need to get back to Bridgewater House to meet the assessors.'

She looked at him seriously. 'You've got to live life for the present, you know. I learned that when my old man buggered off.'

He smiled weakly. 'I know.'

'Great. So you've got time for a cuppa first. A nice mug of peppermint tea to calm you down.'

She waved one of her herbal tea bags in front of him and he wavered. It would be so nice to sit next to her on the sofa and . . .

'The door,' said Sally, exasperated. 'I'll get it.'

'Roddy,' she called out from the hall. She sounded concerned. 'It's the police. They want to talk to you.'

They had found a body. Only in the last hour. They weren't sure who it was. Would Roddy mind going to the mortuary to see if he could identify it?

He'd never been inside a mortuary before. It was a bit like the changing rooms at a gym. Pristine clean with huge locker drawers that opened out with grisly contents.

Roddy already knew who it was. The sneaking suspicion that had dawned on him when the police first told him about the body had grown. It wasn't anyone from the film crew, the police had said. They were all accounted for. So was everyone else, it seemed. Everyone except . . .

. . . Kevin.

Roddy looked silently at the body. Even someone like Kevin

didn't deserve this. Sally's words came back to him as he wiped away the tears. *'You've got to live for the present.'*

And he would now. He really would.

They were waiting for him to say something. 'Yes,' he said quietly. 'I know him.'

Fifty-seven

**Visiting hours strictly 10 am to 11 am
and 5 pm to 7 pm.**

'It was my fault,' said Marcie numbly. It was difficult to talk with the bandages, although they'd said the cuts should heal. Her broken leg, in a plaster cast, didn't feel as though it belonged to her. 'If I hadn't stopped still in the middle of the road, he might have been all right.'

'Why did you stop?' demanded Virginia.

'I saw the truck,' said Marcie numbly. 'The red truck from all those years ago.'

'Shhh,' said David. 'Don't think about that now.'

'Absolutely!' Virginia's forced jollity was infuriating, even in her condition. 'You're lucky to be alive. Not like . . .'

'Virginia,' said David warningly.

Marcie froze. 'Not like who?'

He took her hand. 'We were lucky there weren't more casualties. Justine had to be rescued from a window – poor Robert was beside himself – and so did Roddy Pearmain's daughter.'

'Who died?' repeated Marcie.

Virginia put an arm around her sister. 'She deserves to know, David. I'm afraid it was your friend Kevin. They found him in some bushes, clutching Mollie de May's jewellery box and one of Lord Pearmain's pictures. Someone said it might have been a Picasso. There was a gold watch, too, which Suzette says is hers. Isn't that dreadful?'

After they'd gone, the nurse gave her something to sleep.

But it didn't work at first. Kevin was dead! Part of her was relieved and part of her grieved for the loss of a life. He might have been a common thief but he had cared for her. But had he told David about the tape?

When David came back that evening, she had made up her mind. 'I've got to ask you something,' she said, grateful Virginia hadn't come too.

'I'd rather you just rested.'

'When Kevin wanted to talk to you, before the fire, what did he say?'

David looked evasive. 'We were just chatting.'

People like David and Kevin didn't just chat. 'Did he give you a tape?' she demanded.

He nodded.

Her heart froze.

'Did he tell you what was on it?'

'No. He just told me to listen to it.'

'And did you?'

David shook his head. 'I had it in my pocket but when the fire started, I threw it into the flames.'

'Why?' asked Marcie confused.

'Because,' said David, taking her hand, 'I didn't think it would help if I listened to it. Marcie, darling, I love you. We've both made mistakes. I've thrown you into this new life. And you . . .'

He stopped.

'I've been immature and childish.'

He shook his head. 'No. But I think you could do with some counselling after this to deal with all that stuff that happened as a child. I'd also like to send Virginia back to the States, if you don't mind. Somehow, I don't think she's been doing us any good.'

Marcie felt as though a huge weight had been lifted from her chest. 'That would be great. How soon can you get her a flight?'

David tapped his breast pocket. 'Funny you should mention it but I took the liberty of booking one on the way over . . .'

'Just one more thing,' interrupted Marcie. 'Do you remember us going into the pavilion before the ball?'

'The pavilion?' repeated David.

'Hi, everyone,' said Virginia bursting in. 'Thought I might find you here. Did you know that Mollie de May is in the next ward? I really must pop in and say hello afterwards.'

'We might not have time, I'm afraid,' said David.

'Really?' Virginia's eyes sparkled. 'Where are we going? Somewhere nice? I must say, I can't bear hospitals. Such a shame you're going to be here for a while, Marcie. Now tell me, David, what kind of lovely surprise have you booked for us?'

Fifty-eight

DANGER!
DO NOT ENTER.

Her home, which she had only just finished making into a home, was ruined. Not by the flames but by smoke damage. Louise wandered through the rooms, stunned by the black walls which had been magnolia only a few days earlier. It had been a while before they'd allowed her to go back in. They needed to make sure the structure was safe.

Roddy, whom she'd met on the way in, had explained the rebuilding would start as soon as the insurance people had finished their paperwork.

'I'm sorry about your dog,' he said awkwardly.

His kind remark would have brought tears to her eyes if she hadn't already cried herself dry.

'The children want to scatter his ashes on the lake,' she said flatly. 'Do you think that's all right or will it have to go to a residents' association meeting?'

He smiled wanly. 'I don't think there'll be any of those in the immediate future. I'd say you should just go ahead.'

She nodded. 'Do we know how the fire started yet?'

He rubbed his eyes with exhaustion. 'One theory is that it might have been an overloaded cable from the crew set.' He sighed. 'It makes me feel so responsible. If I hadn't suggested they came in, none of this would have happened.'

'You don't know that,' said Louise. 'It might have been something to do with those electricity repairs we had the other month.'

A flash of relief passed over his face. 'I hadn't thought about that.'

Poor man! Until recently, she had seen him as a rather aloof aristocrat. But now, after his heroic attempts to rescue Justine, she saw him as he really was; another parent on his own, trying to do the best for this children and attempting to make a second stab at life.

'Where will you live in the meantime?' she asked.

'I'm staying with Sally while I'm doing up the gate lodge. Then I'll go there. Lydia and the others are going to a mixture of friends and hotels. Where will you stay?'

She shrugged. 'Jonathan booked us into a hotel for the week but I'm looking for a rented house. He wants to come too.'

Roddy looked surprised.

'I know.' She laughed awkwardly. 'But it didn't work out with his girlfriend and he suggested we tried again.'

'How do you feel about that? He seemed kindly, concerned.

'I'm not sure. This whole thing has taken away all the confidence I was slowly getting back.' Her eyes filled with tears. 'It would be nice to have another adult around and it will be good for the children to have their father there.'

'You might not want to come back,' he had said.

'Oh, I think I will.'

But now, as she wandered through the chaos that the smoke had caused, she wondered if he was right. There was something comforting about being with Jonathan after this horrible fright. Yes, he had behaved appallingly – she still couldn't really believe it – but he was genuinely sorry about Gemma.

Besides, she thought, as she wiped the soot off one of her precious books, she owed it to the children. Even if it meant giving up Guy.

'I understand,' he said, his voice shaking with emotion, when she rang to tell him. 'If there's a chance that you two might get back together, I couldn't live with myself if I thought I had ruined it.'

'And I couldn't live with myself if I thought I had ruined the children's lives.' Her voice was shaking too. 'They need a father.'

'I know,' he said. 'But I'll always love you, Louise. There'll never be anyone else like you.'

I love you too, she wanted to say. I have never ever felt before what I felt with you. Even if I die tomorrow, that kiss has made me complete; has shown me what it's all about. But I can't destroy my family.

That's what she wanted to say. But as she pictured his kind, loving face at the other end of the phone, she found herself completely and utterly unable to speak.

Fifty-nine

Bridgewater Gazette

BRIDGEWATER HOUSE APARTMENTS 'NEARLY READY', RESTORED AFTER SIX MONTHS OF REBUILDING AND INSURANCE COMPLICATIONS

'I'm very proud of you,' said Peregrine, handing him a glass of whisky.

It was clearly a test.

Roddy shook his head. 'No thanks. I'll stick to lime juice.'

'Seriously, Roddy. I am proud of you. Not many men would have had the balls to climb a wall at your age, even if it was to rescue their daughter. I hope they show it.'

'Shh,' said his mother. 'I'm trying to watch.'

They were sitting in the grand drawing room at Redding House, Peregrine's Edwardian place in Sussex. It had nothing compared with Bridgewater House, in Roddy's view.

'Look at that!' giggled Helena. 'Marcie is looking really cheesed off with her sister.'

That was the beauty of film, thought Roddy, amused. They showed you things which you might not have noticed at the time.

'I can't believe it was six months ago,' said Sally softly.

Roddy squeezed her hand. It couldn't be easy for her to come here. Damn it, it wasn't easy for him either. But his mother had made her feel very welcome and even Peregrine had been kind and courteous.

It had been a very long six months. The insurance company had initially stalled because the cause of fire was still under doubt. But in the end, they had stumped up and work had begun. The house was supposed to be completed by the summer but not everyone was moving back. Lydia had decided she couldn't face the house again and had moved permanently to her villa in Spain, where Suzette was a regular visitor. Louise was back with her husband. And no one seemed to know about the American couple. Mollie de May was with her son and apparently was planning on coming back with her tenant – Poppy, wasn't it? – and the baby. Roddy was pleased about that; she added a certain life to the place. Meanwhile, the fire had in a strange way attracted would-be buyers.

'There's Robert snogging Justine,' teased Helena, pointing to the screen. 'She emailed me the other day to say they weren't seeing each other any more. She'll be so embarrassed!'

'Goodness me,' said Roddy's mother, putting on her bifocals. 'What *is* this Justine wearing?'

'Not much, in my opinion,' replied Peregrine gruffly. 'In my day, it wouldn't have been on.'

'Well there's not much on now,' pointed out Roddy's mother. 'Who's that rather short, podgy man over there?'

'Nigel, Mollie's son,' said Sally. 'He's in middle management which is ironic, considering he can't even manage his own middle.'

Peregrine let out an admiring guffaw.

'Shh, dear,' said Roddy's mother. 'This is where it all starts to happen.'

Roddy stood up abruptly and went out. He couldn't look. He didn't know how the others could either. He still had nightmares about hauling himself up the wisteria. Suppose he had dropped his daughter? Suppose the fireman hadn't got there when he had?

'It's all right.'

He felt a hand rest lightly on his shoulder and lent his head back against Sally's warm, supple body. She could do that for him; make him feel all right.

'Maybe you should go back and watch it,' she suggested quietly. 'It could drive out the demons.'

'I'm not sure.'

They both looked up as Peregrine came into the kitchen. Some kitchen, thought Roddy ruefully. It was almost the size of Sally's house which, over the last few months, had become surprisingly familiar and welcoming. Suddenly, he wanted to go back there, back to the cosy comfort of sitting on her three-piece suite in front of the television. To play with Sam and to be normal.

'Mind if I have a word?' boomed Peregrine.

'Not at all,' said Sally. She cast a quick look at Roddy which said, 'You're twice the man he is; stand up to him whatever he's going to come out with.'

Roddy leaned against the Aga. Its warmth had always given him strength, even as a gawky teenager when he'd first visited Peregrine's place.

Peregrine pulled up a large oak kitchen chair. 'I meant what I said back there, Roderick. I am proud of you. Not just for your heroic actions but for the way you've turned over a new leaf. You've kicked the drinking and you're doing quite well at earning your own living. And that's why I've reached the decision I have.'

Roddy knew what was coming. 'So you're going to stop giving me my apartment rent-free?'

Peregrine nodded and Roddy felt a stab of panic. His stepfather was right, he was doing quite well at earning his own living. But it wouldn't be enough to pay the rent to Peregrine. And he knew the bastard, he'd definitely charge the going rate.

'You're right,' Peregrine repeated. 'I'm not giving you the apartment rent-free any more because I'm giving you the apartment outright.'

'You're what?' Roddy couldn't believe his ears.

Peregrine chuckled. 'Thought you'd be surprised, my boy.' He stood up and patted him on the shoulder. 'Well, Bridgewater House should have been yours by right and I suppose I do feel a bit guilty about it. But let bygones be bygones. Use it as a chance to start again once the place is ready to move back into. But just don't go back to your bad old habits, will you?'

'Roddy,' sang out Sally from the television room. 'What on earth's this?'

Still reeling from Peregrine's surprise, he sat down next to her.

'Play it again, dear, will you?' commanded his mother.

Sally complied. As the credits rolled, a shadowy figure flitted across the top right corner of the screen. It wore the characteristic Roundhead helmet but there was something odd about it, something grainy and almost transparent.

'It's just one of the fancy dress revellers,' said Peregrine dismissively.

'But you can see though him,' said Sally, leaning forward.

'Maybe there's something wrong with the film,' added Roddy's mother smoothly. 'What do you think, dear?'

Bewildered, Roddy rewound again to take a better look. Astounding! It looked for all the world like someone he hadn't seen for many years. Someone who, over the passage of time, had become a figment of his boyish imagination. But this – this suggested otherwise.

'Henry?' he said out loud. *'Henry?'*

Sixty

VIEWING CHOICE

Don't miss tonight's fascinating documentary:
'Old House; Nouveau Owners'. Channel 4. 8 pm.

Marcie didn't want to watch the documentary. But she didn't have any choice. Just as she didn't have any choice when David had suggested – insisted, virtually – they live with his mother when she came out of hospital.

'It makes sense,' he had said. 'Knightsbridge is very central. Frankly, I've had enough of commuting and it will be easier for you to get to the British Library. Besides, you still need looking after – especially now – and I'd be happier going to work knowing that my mother is with you.'

In the old days, Marcie would have disagreed. But the stuffing had been knocked out of her, as the English said. She hadn't heard a word from Virginia since David had bought her a single ticket home and, although she was relieved on the whole, a small part of her fretted over the loss of the sister whom she'd thought she could trust.

Getting pregnant had also diluted her will to argue back. She hadn't actually been surprised when the test had proved positive. It was part of life's conspiracy against her. For months she had made love with her husband, trying to conceive without any luck. And now she had done it, after having sex once with someone who might or might not be David. No wonder she couldn't feel excited.

Not a day went past when she did not agonise over who was
the father. It still didn't seem possible that Kevin was dead.
She still expected him to knock on the door and lounge against
the wall with that oddly attractive lopsided smile.

Since that night when she'd asked him about the tape, she
and David had never discussed Kevin. He had never accused
her of doing anything wrong and she did everything she could
to avoid discussing a subject that might lead to him. She hadn't
even wanted to go back to the flat after the fire. Marcie had
allowed David to sort all that out. Most of their possessions
had been ruined anyway but, thankfully, she had already sent
a back-up of her thesis to her tutor.

After the baby was born, said David, they'd find their own
place, probably nearby. She went along with that; just as she
went along with everything now. After what she had done, she
owed it to her husband to be a meek, compliant wife.

Which was why they were watching the documentary about
the ball in her mother-in-law's drawing room.

'My goodness, Robert's getting a bit carried away there, isn't
he?' sniffed David's mother disapprovingly as the camera zoomed
in to her grandson. 'Isn't he a bit young for that sort of thing?'

'He's seventeen, Mother,' said David coolly. 'They grow up
fast nowadays.'

David's mother leaned forward. 'There's Mollie de May!
Hasn't she worn well? She was amazing in that wonderful film
with Olivier. *So* nice to see her on television in those adverts
now. It shows there's hope for all of us.'

'I don't remember seeing her at the ball,' said David.

'She left early,' said Marcie, trying to make herself more
comfortable on the sofa. 'That young girl who was staying with
her went into labour and Mollie went to be with her.'

'How very neighbourly,' said David's mother. 'Oh, my goodness, isn't that you two?'

Marcie could hardly breathe as the backshot of a couple,
walking hand in hand towards the pavilion, came into view. It
was definitely her all right but as for the masked man next to

her . . . She leaned forward. Kevin had been roughly the same height as David. He even seemed to walk in the same way, swinging his arms slightly.

Marcie's heart threatened to stop as the couple approached the door of the pavilion and the camera zoomed closer.

'Why were you going in there?' asked David's mother tightly.

Marcie forced herself to look at her husband. He was impassively facing straight ahead, staring at the screen and not her.

No one said anything.

Then the camera got even closer.

'Extraordinary,' said Marcie's mother-in-law, 'that it can show such detail. I can even see your signet ring.'

Marcie looked at the screen and then at David's right hand. It had been his father's and his father's before him.

David was smiling at her now, in a conspiratorial manner.

'I didn't know they were following us. Did you, darling?'

Marcie could barely shake her head.

'I still don't understand,' said his mother. 'Were you meeting friends there? What were you doing in there?'

'For God's sake, Mother.' David laughed awkwardly. 'What do you think?'

Sixty-one

CHARISMA MAGAZINE

SURROGATE GRANNIES – THE NEW TREND

Mollie was in Nigel's sitting room, Flora at her feet. Poppy was in a comfortable armchair with baby Mollie on her lap, fast asleep. Nigel and his wife were perched on the opposite sofa.

The documentary was almost ending.

'Well!' said Poppy. 'There are going to be some rather embarrassed faces after this. I must say, I didn't think the American woman was the kind to go in for nookey in the pavilion. Or that strait-laced husband of hers either.'

'I saw someone else kissing a man too,' piped up Flora, 'and I don't think it was her husband. They were in the . . .'

'I don't think we want to know, dear,' said her mother. 'Are you comfortable there, Poppy?'

'Yes, thank you. It's lovely here. So much nicer than my horrid rented flat. It's really kind of you to invite us round.'

'Well, you're family,' said Mollie firmly. 'Besides, it won't be long until my own flat is ready and then we can move back together.'

She didn't look at Nigel as she said this. Although they had a good relationship now, this was the one sticking point. He didn't know how she could welcome the woman who had had an affair with her husband. Mollie saw it differently. Poppy was clearly repentant and besides she adored her 'granddaughter by proxy'. It was like being given a new life all over again, especially as the advertising people had renewed her contract.

'I didn't like the fire bit,' said Flora.

'They didn't show much.' Mollie automatically reached down and massaged her ankle, which still ached every now and then.

'I agree with Flora,' said Nigel. 'In fact, I think it was in pretty poor taste, especially as that thief died.'

'His name was Kevin,' said Mollie, rather too sharply. 'And he might just have been rescuing my jewellery box.'

'Oh, come on, Mother. What about the painting he had that belonged to Roddy Pearmain?'

'Look,' said Flora excitedly. 'They're showing what it was like after the fire, when everyone had gone home. Doesn't it look spooky?'

And it did. The fire had finally been put out and the grounds were only dimly lit by the film crew. There was a shot of the marquee which looked, thought Mollie, like the *Marie Celeste* with the fruit and cheese and dirty plates abandoned on the table.

And then the cameras focused back on the house.

'What was that?' demanded Flora.

Mollie's skin began to crawl. She had seen it too.

'Play it back,' demanded Flora.

'Wait until it's finished, darling,' said her mother.

'No.' Flora had jumped up and was heading for the television. She pressed a button and then sat close to the screen, her nose almost pressed to it.

'Move to one side so we can all see it,' said Nigel firmly.

They watched as one. A dark shape seemed to loom up at the top right of the screen. It seemed to be wearing a round hat and it was grainy, almost translucent, although, as Nigel said later, there might have been something wrong with the film. It appeared to do a mock bow at the camera and then disappeared. It happened so quickly that it was difficult to make out more.

'That looked like Grandad,' said Flora quietly.

'Nonsense,' said Nigel.

'I know you miss him, darling,' said Julia. 'Come here for a cuddle.'

'Cameras can play funny tricks,' said Poppy guardedly.

Only Mollie said nothing. But she knew this was Gideon's way of saying goodbye. His way of saying sorry. His way of giving her his blessing for this new life without him.

'Goodbye, darling,' she whispered. 'See you one day.'

Sixty-two

Let by

RENTAL ESTATES

Louise sat on a different sofa from Jonathan. They had been doing that more and more recently. At first, when she'd moved into the rented house – thankfully, paid for by the insurance – she had felt comforted by his presence after the trauma of the fire. He visited so often that it seemed to make sense when he suggested moving back in.

A year ago, she would have been ecstatic but now it seemed so weird. Jonathan was trying; she'd give him that. In fact, he had been pathetically grateful that she had let him return and couldn't do enough to make her happy.

They would buy their own home, he had promised, as soon as the full insurance settlement came through. They would go somewhere different. Make a fresh start.

But it hadn't proved that easy. Justine seemed pleased to have both her parents back together again but both boys had been decidedly cool with their father. 'He was a prick, Mum,' Tim had said simply. 'How can you expect things to be the same again?'

It was hard, too, living in a rented house that wasn't their own. Every wall was magnolia and there were bare floorboards downstairs which she had covered with rugs but which still emitted a cold, unfriendly air.

As for the sex . . . Louise inwardly shuddered. Once a week

or so, she would force herself to go through the motions but it seemed horribly shallow and false.

'I can't believe I ever fancied him,' squirmed Justine as the cameras showed her with Robert.

Jonathan put his arm around his daughter protectively. 'He was all right but you're far too young for a serious boyfriend.'

'I'm not!'

'Well I think you are. And another thing, your mother's told me about the drinking. You've got to be careful, you know.'

Justine squirmed. 'I am.'

'You ought to go straight-edged,' cut in Nick. 'Some of my friends at school are doing it. It means giving up alcohol, drugs and pre-marital sex.'

Louise tensed. Even the word 'sex' in front of her husband made her feel awkward. Thankfully, the cameras changed back to the dance floor. No! Silently, she gasped with dismay. She hadn't been aware they were being filmed at the time. There she was, Guy's hands round her waist, laughing. The sight of his face after all these months completely threw her. They had spoken briefly on the phone a couple of times but neither had suggested meeting up.

Now it was as if he was there, right there with her in the sitting room. Her heart ached with longing.

She didn't dare look at Jonathan.

'You were clearly having a nice time,' he said coldly.

'Piss off, Dad,' snapped Tim. 'You were the one who buggered off. Why shouldn't Mum have enjoyed herself?'

'Tim,' said Louise, 'you mustn't be rude to Dad like that.'

Jonathan's lips tightened. 'I'm used to it. You're not tough enough on them, Louise.'

'It's not her fault.'

'Please,' said Louise wearily, 'can we just watch this?'

Anything for a distraction. Over the last months, the arguments had got worse. 'Can't you just forget about it?' he would say when she tried to talk about Gemma. She was pretty certain he wasn't seeing her now, partly because Jonathan would shudder when she mentioned her name, referring to her as 'that woman', as though the affair had been solely her fault. It made her despise him even more for not taking his share of the responsibility.

Louise hadn't continued with the column, of course, but a publisher had approached her with the idea for a book on how to cope after divorce. She was halfway through it now and there was already talk of a national newspaper serialising it. At some point, she'd have to tell Jonathan about it.

Strangely, she missed the company of her old neighbours, especially Mollie de May. Roddy had been good at keeping in touch and telling her what the others were doing. He'd seemed sorry when she'd told him they probably wouldn't come back. No doubt he felt guilty about making those dreadful accusations.

'Have you seen Guy recently?' asked Jonathan, cutting into her thoughts. His tone was light but it didn't fool her. He was suspicious now after that shot. Considering what he had done to her, it was a damn cheek.

'No, I haven't.

Her eyes returned reluctantly to the screen. To her embarrassment, the cameras were still focused on them. We had something, Louise thought suddenly. And I threw it away. She looked at the children sitting around her. Would they have coped if she had followed her instincts? Nick would be going to university soon, Justine would follow soon after. And Tim didn't talk much to his father anyway.

She got up abruptly and went out to the tiny narrow galley kitchen. Tim followed her. Still haunted by the documentary and all the emotions it had aroused, she struggled for something normal to say.

'How was school today, Tim?'

She hadn't really had a chance to ask him earlier.

'Ok.'

'And was history interesting?'

'Yeah.'

'What did you do?'

'Nothing. We didn't have history today.'

'But you said it was interesting.'

'It was. Because we didn't have it. The teacher was sick again. Mum?'

She felt his arms creep around her waist. He was getting taller. Like her, he'd done a lot of growing up that year. 'Mum, are you happy with Dad?'

She closed her eyes.

'Of course.'

'You're not, are you?' Tim had always been perceptive as well as insistent.

'Not always,' she conceded.

'That programme. Those pictures of you with Guy.' Tim's voice was quivering. 'You like him, don't you?'

She nodded silently.

'I don't mind. You know. I don't mind if you want to marry him instead of Dad.'

She couldn't help laughing. Children saw things so simplistically.'

'I don't know about marrying him,' she began.

'But you do like him, don't you?'

She nodded.

'Then tell him.' Tim's earnest face stared up at hers. 'If you don't, he won't ever know.'

She couldn't, of course. How could she? Hi, Guy. I've made a terrible mistake. You were the love of my life and I messed up by going back to my husband out of duty, even though there's nothing left between us any more.

Maybe, instead of writing this survival guide, she should turn to fiction. Stuff like that only happened in novels.

Louise pressed the Save button on her computer and stood up, stretching. It was the day after the documentary. The children were at school and Jonathan, thank God, was at work. She felt hideously guilty at her relief when he left in the morning.

But it had been her choice and she had to stick to it. Maybe when Tim had gone to university, she would leave then.

There was a knock at the door. She must remember to tell the agency that the bell had stopped working. That would be Mollie. Louise had been spurred by the programme to ask her round for coffee.

Louise glanced in the hall mirror as she went towards the front door. She should have taken more care with her make-up this morning. Her mascara was smudged slightly below one eye but there wasn't time now for any last-minute repairs. It was always like that when she was writing. She didn't know how the minutes flew by.

'Hi, Mollie . . .' she began. Then she stopped. A pulse throbbed in her throat as their eyes locked.

'Tim texted me,' said Guy simply.

She tried to talk but the words wouldn't come out.

'He told me what you'd told him,' he continued. His eyes were still locked on hers, fast, secure.

'Guy,' she managed to say. 'Guy, I . . .'

As she spoke, his mouth came down on hers. It was like being swept up, all over again, as it had been before. But this time it felt even more right, if that was possible.

'I love you, Louise,' he whispered.

'I love you too,' she whispered back, burying her head in his neck, hungrily gulping in his smell.

Then she stopped. She had to say it. 'I can't live with you yet. It's too soon.'

'You don't mean you're going to stay with him?'

'No.' Until she spoke, Louise hadn't decided. But now she knew exactly what she had to do. 'I'm going back to Bridgewater House. The apartment is virtually ready.'

He began to smile again. 'And I can visit you there?'

She tilted her face up to his, feeling a wonderful surge of relief, warmth and happiness washing through her body. 'I've got a better idea. Why don't you keep my spare key?'

VISITORS' PARKING BAY

Please park with consideration for others. Spaces limited.

The Bridgewater Residents' Association